PASSAGE WEST

PASSAGE WEST

D0034733

ALSO BY RISHI REDDI

Karma and Other Stories

PASSAGE WEST

A Novel

RISHI REDDI

ecco

An Imprint of HarperCollins*Publishers*

HarperCollins books may be purchased for educational, business, or sales promotional use. For information, please e-mail the Special Markets Department at SPsales@harpercollins.com.

FIRST EDITION

Library of Congress Cataloging-in-Publication Data

Names: Reddi, Rishi, author.
Title: Passage west : a novel / Rishi Reddi.
Description: First edition. | New York : Ecco, [2020] | Summary: "A sweeping, vibrant first novel following a family of Indian sharecroppers at the onset of World War I, revealing an unknown part of California history"—Provided by publisher.
Identifiers: LCCN 2019050704 (print) | LCCN 2019050705 (ebook) | ISBN 9780060898793 (hardcover) | ISBN 9780060898809 (trade paperback) ISBN 9780062198587 (ebook)
Subjects: LCSH: Domestic fiction. | GSAFD: Historical fiction.
Classification: LCC PS3618.E4265 P37 2020 (print) | LCC PS3618.E4265 (ebook) | DDC 813/.6—dc23
LC record available at https://lccn.loc.gov/2019050704
LC ebook record available at https://lccn.loc.gov/2019050705

ISBN 978-0-06-089879-3

20 21 22 23 24 LSC 10 9 8 7 6 5 4 3 2 1

To Nikku,
for whom all this might have mattered,
and
to Maya, and Jay, and Anji,
for whom perhaps it someday will.

It is now no more that toleration is spoken of as if it was by the indulgence of one class of people that another enjoyed the exercise of their inherent natural rights. For happily the Government of the United States, which gives to bigotry no sanction, to persecution no assistance, requires only that they who live under its protection should demean themselves as good citizens in giving it on all occasions their effectual support.

—George Washington, letter to the Hebrew Congregation in Newport, Rhode Island, 1790

A New Problem for Uncle Sam

PRINTED IN *SAN FRANCISCO CALL* NEWSPAPER
AUGUST 13, 1910

CAST OF CHARACTERS

Ram Singh—native of Shahpur village, Jullundur District, Punjab, living in Chenab Canal Colony, Lyallpur; arrives in Fredonia in 1914 at age twenty-one

Padma—Ram's wife, native of Jullundur District, Punjab, living in Chenab Canal Colony, Lyallpur

Santosh—Ram's young son, living with Padma in Punjab

Ishwar Lal—Ram's first cousin, living in Chenab Canal Colony, Lyallpur, Punjab

Karak Singh Gill—native of Tarkpur village, Ludhiana District, Punjab; former British Indian Army soldier; arrives in Fredonia in 1913 at age thirty

Jivan Singh Gill—native of Tarkpur village, Ludhiana District, Punjab; former British Indian Army soldier; arrives in Imperial Valley in 1905 at age forty-three

Amarjeet Singh Gill—Jivan's nephew, native of Tarkpur village, Ludhiana District, Punjab; arrives in Imperial Valley in 1910 at age fourteen

Kishen Kaur—Jivan's wife, native of Ludhiana District, Punjab; arrives in Imperial Valley in 1910 at age thirty-eight

Leela Kaur—Jivan and Kishen's daughter, native of Fredonia, born 1911

Rosa María Fernandez Delgado—native of Saucillo, Chihuahua, Mexico; field worker; arrives in Imperial Valley in 1914 at age sixteen

Esperanza Fernandez Delgado de Felix—Rosa's older sister, native of Saucillo, Chihuahua, Mexico; seamstress; arrives in Fredonia in 1910 at age twenty-seven

Alejandro Felix Moreno—Esperanza's husband, native of Saucillo, Chihuahua, Mexico; foreman; arrives in Fredonia in 1910 at age thirty-five

Adela Rey Vasquez—first cousin of Rosa and Esperanza, native of Saucillo, Chihuahua, Mexico; arrives in Fredonia in 1918 at age thirty

Haruo (Harry) Moriyama—Amarjeet's high school friend and neighbor, native of Fredonia

Tomoya (Tom) Moriyama—Haruo's father, native of Satsuma, Kagoshima Prefecture, Japan

Hatsu Moriyama—Haruo's mother, native of Satsuma, Kagoshima Prefecture, Japan

Masa and Yuki—Haruo's sisters, natives of Satsuma, Kagoshima Prefecture, Japan

Clive Edgar—native of Kansas; land agent for hire; arrives in Imperial Valley in 1910 at age twenty-one

Stephen Eggenberger—Singhs' absentee landlord, native of Lucerne, Switzerland; living in Los Angeles

Harnam Singh, Gugar Singh, Hukam Singh, Inder Singh—Sikh natives of Punjab, farmers in Imperial Valley

Malik Khan, Sikander Khan, Ahmed Khan—Muslim natives of Punjab, farmers in Imperial Valley

Sheriff Frank Fielding—native of Arizona; Imperial County sheriff

Deputy Elijah Hollins—native of Alabama; Imperial County sheriff's deputy

Maurice Roubillard—native of Louisiana; cotton sharecropper of portion of Eggenberger's land

Jake Smiley—native of Pittsburgh; owner of the cotton gin, cotton broker

Clarence Simms—Fredonia lawyer, well known for criminal defense

Jonathan Hitchcock—native of Atlanta, Georgia; wealthy vice president of Consolidated Fruit Co.

Pala Singh—Ram's family friend; leader of Hindustani work gang in lumber mill in Hambelton, Washington

Jodh Singh—Ram's fellow worker at the lumber mill in Hambelton

PART ONE

Know for certain
nothing endures.

One cherishes the shade
of the most regal tree, and

when it ages and dies
mourns what is lost.

All that is visible
passes away;

only the ignorant, unseeing,
cling to it.

—from the Sukhmani, *Guru Granth Sahib*

1

APRIL 1974

YESTERDAY IN THE HOSPITAL, WHEN HE WAS STILL ALIVE, KARAK SINGH
Gill had sat up in the bed and, with trembling fingers, placed the
key to his apartment in Ram Singh's hand. Ram protested; he did
not want it. Karak thrust it toward him. "Keep the box," he insisted,
"of things only you and I know about."

There was the occasional beep of the heart monitor, the bounce
of light on the telemetry screen, the tang of urine and Dettol together; it could have been a hospital in Jullundur, but it was the
Los Angeles sun that glared through the window. Occasionally a
loudspeaker in the hall was heard calling for a doctor. But mostly, in
Karak's small room, it was the chants of the sacred paath that were
heard, Ram rising to flip the cassette tape every forty-five minutes.
When the evening nurse entered, a tear glistened in her eye. She was
very young. As she took Karak's temperature she was too cheerful,
speaking loudly, smiling too broadly, and that was how Ram knew
Karak had only a few hours left.

Ram asked if the sound of the prayer was too great, and Karak shook his head. They both knew—how could it be otherwise—that Ram had won. Karak had faded first. They both knew—this too was inevitable—that Ram found some satisfaction in this, but it did not matter. Women had loved Karak; he had always been dashing. Now that his fine eyes had melted into the hollows of his skull, Ram knew that he, Ram, had had the better life. He felt a twinge of regret.

His fingers closed around the key and he slipped it into his pocket. It was not easy to forget, it would never be forgotten, what had happened only fifty years ago. The mind does not know time. What had happened was ever present between them, made itself known in every meeting, every conversation, every occurrence, as when Karak allowed a breath to escape him, neglected to draw another, and Ram stood, solemn and empty, in acceptance of this fact.

KARAK'S APARTMENT WAS MORE GLUM than Ram remembered. Ram had taken him to the hospital only ten days before, but it was clear that Karak had not cared for his home since long before that. Cobwebs hung low at corners. Paint peeled from the far wall. A smell hovered near the refrigerator. Dust motes whipped through sunlight when Ram swept back the curtains.

The box was where Karak had told him it would be, tucked behind stale clothes in the bedroom closet, two feet by three feet of cardboard. Ram had possessed it once before, decades ago, when Karak had been at San Quentin. *Crap,* Karak had called it. The American slang sounded strange in his Punjabi accent. But Karak never let such things bother him. The box had been lighter then. Now Ram sat on Karak's worn chair in his dim living room, sifting through the private documents, spreading them out on the dented coffee table and faded sofa, a pile for each period of his life. Karak said—Ram heard him clearly—that he spent too much time on neatness and organization, on planning, when what was needed was real work. In his mind, Ram answered him—he had not wanted the box, but now that he had accepted it, he had to be sure that he had everything. When Karak's children entered tomorrow or the day after, surely they would not be as forgiving as Ram. Perhaps they would forbid Ram from coming again. They would not understand the squalor, the evidence of despair. Karak's voice seemed to accept the explanation.

Ram did not like the emptiness. He was old, but he did not like the smell of age. Before him Karak's life lay spread out on paper: the official discharge from the British Indian Army, the San Quentin release form, the AARP documentation. The strange coincidence of Karak's chosen birthday, the same month and day as the killing, appearing again and again.

The date was a falsehood. When had anyone from their part of the world known the date they were born? Or if they did know, who had translated that date from a Punjabi calendar to the Julian one? The men from 1913 had been born "in the middle of the rains" or "during first harvest after the earth shook." One didn't state that to the immigration officers on Angel Island or in Seattle. Birthdates had been made up, had been approximated, so they could gain entrance into the country.

He rubbed his eyes, weary. Last night he had called Karak's daughter with the news. In response, she informed him there would be a Catholic wake and funeral and burial, all things that Karak had not wanted but now—being dead—was powerless to stop. She felt she was doing her father a service. He had committed a mortal sin and, as far as she knew, had not repented. It was a short conversation. "A cremation at the gurdwara might be better," Ram had said, lightly, but he had not argued with the daughter. Why should he? If the situation had been reversed, if it were *his* body lying in the mortuary, Karak would not have argued for Ram, even if Ram had cared about such a thing. Which he did not.

It was bright outside, high noon in Los Angeles. The Santa Ana winds blew in from the east, late in the season, lifting particles of gritty desert soil and sweeping them to the sea. Ram pulled aside a curtain and stared. In the parking lot, a young couple walked a stroller to the neighboring building. The sun gleamed off the cars, shone stark against whitewashed walls. The woman was pushing, her skirt swept against shapely legs. When the man bent to lift the front wheels to the curb, the baby grabbed his hair. Suddenly, Karak's apartment was unbearable. Ram reached for the kitchen telephone and called his son to pick him up. He threw the dead man's papers back into the cardboard box. Karak's voice was silent. Ram hoisted the container to his waist—it was heavier than he had imagined—and carried it outside to wait.

DAVE CAME FOR HIM in the station wagon with all three grandchildren. On the way home, they stopped at the grocery store. Ram walked behind his son as Dave pushed the cart through the produce section; the boys squabbled in the front while little Anika, Ram's favorite, tagged along with Ram. Ahead of them, he saw his eldest grandson reaching up to the refrigerated shelves, touching three or four zucchini. He was chewing gum, one hand in his pocket. He tossed a zucchini into the cart, even though his father had wanted a cucumber. The boy, Ram realized, did not know the difference.

Ram grunted. Even at thirteen, it was clear, to Ram at least, the boy would be a failure. A lifetime spent tilling the soil, swaddling cantaloupe, shipping lettuce at just the right time, cajoling three harvests from a field of cotton—only to have his descendant come to this.

Several nights ago at the dinner table, chewing a mouthful of spinach, the boy had claimed it was stupid to farm, boring to be a farmer. Ram had not reacted. He had sold his last acre in the Imperial Valley a decade ago to move to Dave's home in Los Angeles. He felt he had chopped off an arm and left it behind. The boy could not know that. Ram had not grown spinach but he had grown lettuce, peas and asparagus and carrots, thousands of bales of cotton; he had rotated through so many seasons of alfalfa. Ram had glared at his grandson. That had been the end of it, but the words still stung.

Now Ram inspected the zucchini and returned it to the cart, saying nothing. He wanted to leave, wander to a corner of the store without the others, but when he turned to go, a Chicano man stood before him, blocking the narrow passage between the shopping cart and the avocados.

"¿Perdón, señor, sabe usted dónde están los chiles?" the man asked softly. Ram's stomach clenched.

"Why would I be knowing where the chilies are?" Ram snapped. "You saw my brown skin, so automatically I must be speaking Spanish too? And eating chilies? Chilies?" The man shrank back, and Ram stepped toward him, but he felt his son's grip on his arm.

"What's the matter with you, Pop?" Dave hissed. "Pretending you don't speak Spanish." A blond couple near the bananas had turned to look at them.

Ram snatched his arm away. "What a rude fellow," he said, his voice quivering, his manner too dignified. He scowled at Dave. "You will find me at the checkout," he announced, and walked slowly past the couple.

"What's the matter with Bapu-ji?" little Anika asked her father.

"He seems to have forgotten who he was married to," Dave said, then caught himself. His mother, even when alive, had never needed defending. "He is upset about Grandpa Karak," he added. Dave looked up to see the blond couple, inspecting apples now, farther away. At a cocktail party tonight, or at dinner, they would tell their friends about the scene between the loco foreigners at the grocery store. The thought came to him suddenly and he knew he had arrived at the truth: It was an old shame his father had felt. A visitor from the past.

GRACE TORRES, KARAK'S ONLY DAUGHTER, telephoned the house that night, asking for Ram. "I have been making arrangements for the funeral," she announced. "I have a favor to ask." Ram had known her as Grace Singh, long ago when she and her brothers were toddlers, but that changed after her mother had remarried.

"What favor?" Ram said. His voice was calm and sounded like gravel.

Ram had been present when Grace had visited Karak in the hospital. She had seemed an interloper, anxiously watching one old man taking care of another. Even now, Ram felt *he* should make these arrangements, not she. But hadn't he done enough for Karak over sixty years? He did not want to do more.

Besides, Grace had fulfilled her duty, convincing her older brother to make the copayment to the hospital, visiting when Karak had asked to see his children's faces just once more before he died. Neither of her brothers had come with her. Now she would give her father a proper Catholic burial with a mass, even though nobody, most of all Karak, could want it.

"What favor?" Ram said again, because she had not responded.

"I would like you to give the eulogy," she said.

Ram snorted. "Why?"

"People at the senior center have been calling since he passed. They want to come to the funeral. They want to speak. I can't bear the thought of any of them . . . the falseness of it. You were the only one who knew him . . . before."

Ram sighed. "Catholics don't allow eulogies," he said.

She was silent. Ram felt he had scored something against her. He was an outsider, but an insider too. Had he not also been married to a Catholic? Had he not known Grace's mother for years? They were not so distant after all.

"It would be at the vigil, Mr. Singh. The night before the mass." There was pleading in her voice; both of them heard it.

"I will let you know tomorrow," he said.

"The wake is tomorrow night," Grace said.

"I will call you tomorrow," he said again.

"Thank you." Her voice was small.

KARAK'S BOX SAT IN THE CORNER of Ram's bedroom. It cast a shadow on the far wall and another on the floor, which Ram could not explain by the position of his reading lamp. A gray-beige line on the carpet. A man, a whole man, is more than a sum of his deeds. Was he being unfair to Karak Singh?

Ram reached for the box and scooted it beside the armchair, delved to the bottom, where he had not reached this morning. Karak's papers stared up at him, aged and yellow and brittle. There, he saw it—an envelope addressed to Karak in the Imperial Valley, with Ram's return address of Hambelton, Washington—a letter that Ram himself had written more than six decades ago, his own script beckoning to him through the years.

He blinked. He could not imagine that Karak Singh would keep a letter of his. Karak had not been a sentimental man; this was yet another difference between them. Ram had saved many letters, some from Karak in the early days, many from his mother, even a few from his uncle. And from Padma, of course, before and after 1918. The letters told the story of his life. So many men he knew from those days did not know how to write; the country—the world—thought they did not have stories to tell.

Ram picked up the envelope. The paper was thicker than he expected, stiff and dark at the edges. For a moment, he thought he remembered writing it, sitting cross-legged in the corner where he stored his blanket in the cursed house in Hambelton. His fingers shook as he eased the letter out. The paper trembled on his palm.

Dear Bhai Karak Singh-ji, he read, *Sat Sri Akal.* He slapped the letter down on his lap. His twenty-one-year-old hand had written this Gurmukhi script—had he once addressed Karak in that formal way, with that much respect? Had he followed Sikh custom so closely, when he was not himself Sikh?

Ram rose and went to his closet, reaching up to the top shelf, feeling under the kurtas that he had worn while visiting Punjab twenty-five years earlier. He found the stack of manila envelopes that contained his old letters, sifted through them until he found what he wanted. He settled back into the chair with his letters and Karak's own, allowing them to rest for a moment on his lap. He was at the end of things now; he could not resist the return to the beginning. Not when he was the only one who remained. Not when all the others—Jivan, Amarjeet, Kishen, even little Leela—had died years before. He sat until he could no longer bear the loneliness. His letter to Karak was sixty-one years old. Slowly, he picked it up and began to read.

2

Ram Singh
13 K Street
Hambelton, Washington

Mr. Karak Singh Gill
In the care of <u>Jivan Singh Gill</u>
Rural Route 9
Fredonia, Imperial Valley, California

25 November 1913

Dear Bhai Karak Singh-ji,
   Sat Sri Akal.
   May this letter reach you and find you in good health after six
months on this shore. You see, I lost the paper on which you had
written your cousin's information when I left you at the depot.
Somehow in the confusion of my disembarking at Hambelton,
seeing the new people, and feeling deprived of the safety of your
company—I was almost struck by a carriage in the bazaar—your

slip of paper must have flown from my pocket and landed on the doorstep of some puzzled shopkeeper. Bhai-ji, it is only by memory that I have written your cousin's postal address on the envelope, and that too using English letters. You know they are not familiar to me. I pray that you located his home without any obstacles and that you are comfortably settled in California State. If you hold this paper in your hands, it is by the Guru's grace.

After leaving you at the train station I walked more than twenty furlongs to find the home of my village-mate, Pala Singh. I wandered from the main street of the colony to a dirt path. I was soon lost. I returned to the depot and asked the ticket seller, "How to find K Street?" For hours I had practiced the pronunciation of the English words just as you taught me, but still this fellow—so pale, so very pale!—looked at me with a question on his face. He said, "K Street?" and I felt fear straight to my backbone, thinking I had left the train at the wrong stop. He studied my face, my clothing, my shoes. He asked, "You are from British India, or China, or Japan?" From your tutoring, I knew enough to understand him. I told him I was from Hindustan. Suddenly, giving me a big smile, he said, "Ah, Hindu Alley . . . Hindu Alley is what you mean—" and he gave me directions for turning right at the power generator, crossing the railroad tracks, and going straight. He asked me, gesturing with his hands, why I don't wear the dastar on my head. I was taken aback by his question.

Must I tell him—this first man that I meet in this strange country—that my father was Sikh but that he is no more, that I was raised by my Hindu mother and her brother . . . must I tell a stranger these things? Would he know the meaning, anyway? For they call us all Hindu, Karak-ji, whether we are Hindu, Sikh, or Mussulman. I do not take offense, for we are all sons of Hindustan. What is the use of feeling insulted when our motherland is so distant? We are as familiar to each other as brothers are, and we should stay united against these local people. From what I have seen, they have little affection, their skin is too white, their women are too forward, their clothes are too fitted, their food is like a punishment. How I will survive here for two years, I do not know. But the children—they are so beautiful! Like fairies! How can that be?

This place that I have arrived in is not at all like busy Seattle with its markets. What my humble Shahpur village is to worldly Delhi, that is this place as compared to Seattle. Still, I am comfortable here due to the influence of Pala Singh. Like you, he speaks English because of his British army service and so he is leader of our work gang; sometimes he is even asked to enter the company offices to speak about some labor matter. The bosses trust him.

Through Pala Singh my uncle will know of all the work I do for the good of our family. I must earn enough so that Chacha-ji can buy the acres he wants in our ancestral Shahpur. It is his great dream to leave the canal colony and return to our home, to shift the entire family back, before he grows too old. Now I am contributing American dollars to the family earnings. Mother tells me that they are depending only on me. You know I am a fatherless man who was raised on my uncle's generosity. How much my standing in the family will be improved if I can send enough money to buy that land! That is my wish now. This is the lot of a man such as myself, bhai, I must always work for my good name! I am joking, but in every joke there is a kernel of truth. I have heard you say the same.

There are 120 of us now, living in ten houses on K Street, about four furlongs from the lumber mill. I am operating the machines to cut and chop the wood as it is brought in from the forest. The work is hard. But I am making $2.00 a day and am satisfied. The locals do not like us. There are so many strange people here from other lands, and their faces are not natural: men from Japan, or the children of the African slaves, and so many workers from China. I am suspicious of all these people. Still, it does not matter much. We keep to ourselves, and they keep to themselves, and in this way harmony is maintained.

Here our people cook and live together, so I do not miss home that much. A few days ago a meeting was held for all our countrymen, and leaders came from San Francisco City to give speeches on the topic of India's status under British rule. You know I do not believe strongly about such things, bhai-ji, but I felt so so happy to be with that many of our people. They asked for money because a newspaper has been started under the name of Ghadar and printed in Urdu and Gurmukhi and distributed everywhere here in the U.S., so you see, we need not feel homesick at all.

At the meeting I met Asif Khan, who says he knows your younger brother and fought alongside him for the English king in Shanghai. Every Sunday at the mill we have a wrestling match. The top winner to date has been Bishan Singh Grewal, from Ganeshpur near your own village. He is not tall but he is very strong, and his skin is so fair I think he cannot be a farmer. Do you know him?

Bhai-ji, I thank God every day that I have the good fortune to know you. Even when I am an old man, lying on my deathbed, I will remember our three weeks together in Sri Guru Singh Sabha in Hong Kong. I am sending you a check for the amount of the medication that you bought for cousin Ishwar. Forgive my delay in getting the money to give you. He has recovered fully and instead of coming onward to America, he has gone back to Punjab. My uncle has stated that there is no doubt you saved him. When Ishwar returned, my uncle gave a celebration in your honor, Karak-ji. You will always be welcome there at my home.

*Just this morning, I received a telegram from home saying
that my wife has given birth to a boy. While you and I were
together in Hong Kong and on board the ship, I did not know
the happy news that I was to be a father. It seems my son is a
large and healthy boy. He has not yet been given a name, and
being a devout Hindu, my uncle will insist on waiting the
proper amout of time before holding the naming ceremony.*

*Did I tell you the name of my wife, bhai-ji? It is Padma. I
neglected to tell you during all that time we were together. Now
I have such a strange feeling, both happiness and homesickness
together, and everything seems half-half, broken and split inside.
Think of this letter as if I am putting a sweet in your mouth as
we do at home, telling you of good news.*

*Bhai-ji, when I feel discouraged here, I remember the night
we walked to the border of the cantonment in Hong Kong,
near your old army posting. We dared to drink with the British
officers—served by those local women, do you remember?—and
how the Englishmen laughed at your jokes.*

*From the hand of your brother,
Ram Singh*

25 December 1913

Ram, my brother,

*Many thanks for the money, but you did not need to return
it. I am much relieved to hear that Ishwar has recovered. It
is better that he returned home. We both know that life is not
always easy here. I am happy to learn that you are settled in
a good place. But it is a shame that you did not go to the real
Hindu Alley in Astoria, near you, in Oregon. Have you heard
what they say of that place? Mutton and chicken cooked every
day, all the whiskey you desire, the North Country girls who
come for love? I wish to go myself and enjoy life there for a*

while—but perhaps your lumber town is similar and you are too shy and respectable to tell me the truth.

Ram, do not be such a naive boy. You are married and have family obligations—you must become more worldly in your outlook. You feel suspicious of all those people in Hambelton, but they are just as you are, making a living here and sending money home. They are no different.

Pay some attention to what I am suggesting now, instead of that past nonsense. You are making $2.00 per day. That is fine, if you want to labor for another man, but it is a pittance compared to what I will earn here. I have cultivated forty acres with my father's cousin-brother, Jivan Singh, growing cantaloupe. If it brings the expected price, calculating the hours I have spent over these months, my share will come to $5.00 per day. Compare that to your circumstances. Do you understand my meaning? Think of your new son and how you will heighten his status. Think how much you will lift Padma's position in your home—with your uncle, with your cousins—as the wife of such a provider! Think of the benefit for your mother!

Perhaps you are wondering—what is a cantaloupe? It is our kharbooj, only a little smaller—our simple kharbooj! Anglos are mad for this fruit. Our shipments go as far east as Boston and Philadelphia. The soil is rich and we have a system of canal irrigation, like your own Lyallpur. You won't suffer the humiliation of a work gang and an American boss. Ram, you come from a farming family, so you understand the importance of independence and honor and cultivating your own land. It is something I am only now learning. I think often of the laughs we enjoyed together, not only during the nights in Hong Kong, but that bloody long journey on the ship itself. Your company made those endless weeks seem like days. The other passengers were too serious, but I felt that you could take a joke. Come and join me and remain positive in your outlook. I can teach you one or two things about life's realities. Think about it.

In chardi kala,
Karak Singh

22 April 1914

Ram,

Why have you not responded to my letter? Did you receive it? How is your health? It is odd to neglect an invitation such as the one I extended. Perhaps you thought I was falsely boasting about prospects here? You should know the profit from our crop was larger than I thought possible. The Philadelphia market was very high and Jivan Singh and I made more money than you lumberjacks can imagine. Now will you come?

Your brother,
Karak

26 May 1914

Ram,

Do you remember me or not? I am the man who saved your cousin from certain death and still you have given no answer to my request to join me—what should I think of that? Does our friendship mean nothing to you? Do you still wear the kara I gave you or have you forgotten me? After all I have done, isn't it your duty to meet at least once after our arrival on this shore? If you will not come to farm, then come for a visit. In early August it is too hot to work and I'll have a few days of leisure.

—Karak

TELEGRAM

originating: Portland Depot, Oregon, July 6, 1914

destination: Fredonia, California

RE LETTER 26 MAY ARRIVING 9 JULY A.M. TRAIN FROM LOS ANGELES

RAM

3

JULY 1914

THE TRAIN DEPOT IN FREDONIA WAS ERECTED ON SILTY CLAY, WITH A floor of coarse wood and walls of canvas, flapping against the desert's dust-wind. It was an appropriate location. Farther east and the tracks would lay in shifting sand; farther north would have been a misuse of fertile loam. The wood and canvas had arrived by an eight-mule team and wagon in January seven years prior; the loam and the dust-wind had come eons before that, when the ocean had receded and the sea creatures had died, leaving only bones and chalk, salt and silt.

The ticket agent glared at Ram, his stare as harsh as the dust-wind itself, so Ram turned back to the platform with his blanket and carpetbag and stood in the shadow near the belching train. The man had no reason to stare; all of Ram's wounds were hidden under his long pants and a work shirt buttoned at the wrists. The pain in his side softened when Ram was standing. Gazing west from the platform, he saw storefronts with awnings lining the dirt road: HAN-SON'S IMPLEMENTS. EDGAR BROS GENERAL STORE. CHARLIE'S HORSE

AND MULE RENTAL. Farther along stood a brick building with arched promenades. To the east sat a string of shacks, and beyond them sky and air and earth stretched away in every direction. A mound of sand rose in the near distance covered with gray-green brush; odd trees stood upon it, tall and waiting, tentacles reaching to the clouds. To the south, a jagged line marked the edge of mountains on the horizon.

A cluster of men strolled toward him, too slowly, and too pale, but Ram searched their faces anyway. Behind them, dark clouds sailed in the distance. The dust-wind played with a nest of brambles near his feet. Still, Karak Singh did not appear.

The horizon seemed to shift, falling away on his left; he gripped the fence rail to regain his balance. A horse whinnied from the road. He heard the jangle of spurs. The sun, the ache in his side, the blood-scent that rose from his bandaged arm, all of this unmoored him. He smelled coal ash mixed with manure and dust and heat and something else he could not recognize. A fragment of the wooden fence pricked his wrist, stinging him, and the earth righted herself.

He was not well, he knew that, even though Pala had wrapped the wounds so capably, stopping the flow of blood with a torn piece of his own clean shirt. Three days traveling down the Pacific coast and he had slept so much, but he still did not feel rested. He had not wasted money in the dining car. When the train stopped, he had struggled into the depots and found only almonds and toast for sale and washed them down with milk. The heat had alarmed him. The car had been a prison; the small windows, mounted high, had allowed only a whisper of a breeze. In Portland, they had taken on a hundred new passengers and the cars had been overcrowded, grown men sitting shoulder to shoulder, knee to knee, backs forced upright. He had struggled to walk through several cars before he found one in which he could rest. He didn't mind the sound of the whistle and the ash coming off the engine. Other passengers stared at him. But he could lie on the bench while the train groaned and shuddered and rocked underneath him. He used his folded blanket as a pillow, covering his face with a bandana to block the light. With his back jammed against the hard bench, half-conscious, he heard the sounds of the attack again: The smashing of glass. The snap of axe against wood. The sounds woke him in daylight, just as they had that night; he could not escape the fear. He imagined his mother coming to soothe him. As a boy, when he had startled awake while napping on his charpai, she would whisper that dreams dreamed under the moon came true, those dreamed under the sun did not.

After two days, the pain in Ram's chest had begun to lessen. After four, he'd begun to use both arms.

With each stop, the train had moved farther away from the lumber mill and he had felt safer, looking forward to this moment of seeing Karak Singh again. But now that he had arrived to stand in the dry heat on this wooden platform, reeking of sweat and soot and the third-class car, blinking as the dust plagued his eyes, now that he had trusted Karak Singh and his invitation so completely, he wondered if he should not have come.

The Imperial Valley was not like Seattle, or even Hambelton. Here, the sky and the gray-green earth felt familiar, like the desert surrounding Lyallpur. A sign announcing CITY OF FREDONIA, AMERICA'S DREAM hung crookedly from a rusted chain and piece of wire. Only five other passengers had disembarked from the train and they had stared at him too: a Chinese man and an elderly Negro had emerged from the car next to his, and three Anglos had come off a front car, wearing suits and carrying briefcases. He had seen them board in Los Angeles. Now, they seemed out of place, but he could see they were coming home. The men walked past the depot to the road, where a motor car had raised a cloud of dust and stood sputtering, its honk calling playfully. A woman—the first he had seen here—and her driver were inside. One of the Anglo men stepped up toward it, leather shoes gleaming, pocket watch smartly jangling on his vest. The woman smiled widely. The driver opened the door.

Had Karak Singh forgotten him? Was he punishing him for not accepting his invitation sooner? Had he not received the telegram Ram had sent from Portland? Ram had stood so long that his calf had begun to throb again. He found a wooden crate abandoned near the track, turned it over to sit. Two men, wearing wide-brimmed hats, sat on a bench under the awning of the general store, watching him silently. He thought of the $5.50 he had in his billfold. What would he do if Karak did not show up? One of the men said something to the other, and Ram thought—the way he tilted his head, the way his companion responded—that the comment was about him.

Ram sensed them at the edge of his vision: three men with dastars regally wrapped about their heads, as if they were soldiers, as if they were farmers; he knew they were both. He felt a relief akin to love.

The earth swayed again. His vision blurred. Ram could not help himself. Despite the flash of pain, he picked up his bag and blanket and raced to meet them.

KARAK SINGH EMBRACED HIM, slapped him affectionately on the back, sending a dart of pain along Ram's side. The men laughed for no reason. "You are so anxious to see me?" Karak said in Punjabi. "Did you think I would not come?" Karak grinned broadly at him. Both knew that Karak had intended to keep Ram waiting. Both knew what the other knew: that Ram had minded this, had felt fear. Ram felt the humiliation sweep through him, then he pushed the feeling away. Karak put his hands on Ram's shoulders and turned him toward his companions, presenting him to the older man. "Ram Singh," he said, "originally from Shahpur village in Jullundur; now his family is settled at Chenab Canal Colony near Lyallpur. Father is Sikh. Expert in irrigation farming. They helped the British clear the jungle there."

"The British cleared it before we arrived, bhai-ji," Ram said modestly, smiling, then looked up to see the older man's face: hazel eyes, a still gaze, the indigo cloth of his dastar cast against a dusty sky. His beard was flecked with gray, twisted and neatly tucked. For a fleeting moment, Ram felt ashamed of his clipped hair, his Hindu childhood. Karak had written about Jivan Singh: Almost every Punjabi in the Valley deferred to him. He had found them work, loaned mules and implements, given seed for free. Ram did not know that the man would be so dignified, taller than most other men in this desert settlement, whether Anglo or Hindustani or something else.

Ram put his palms together and whispered, "Sat Sri Akal, bhai-ji." After all, his father had been Sikh, and he was among his own people, no matter how they prayed. Jivan Singh grasped both Ram's hands in his own. "So happy you have come. Karak has told us much about you. You are like family to us; we are from branches of the same tree." His Punjabi was familiar; only a word or two different from the language of Ram's Jullundur home. Ram felt a surge of longing. He looked away out of respect, stared at the torn leather at the tip of his boot. It was an old phrase, used by old people. Only a year ago Ram would have smiled at it, but now, after the train journey, after the pain in his side, after Hambelton, the words made his throat constrict with emotion.

"My brother's son, Amarjeet Singh." Jivan indicated the younger man, wearing a white shirt and dungarees, dark eyes and fair skin set against a cream dastar. Karak had written about him too. Amarjeet's father had sent him to live with Jivan Singh when he was fourteen. Karak had known him as a small boy, had taught him how to wrestle. Although he had completed high school in Fredonia, he seemed a boy still, barely meeting Ram's gaze, broad shoulders awkwardly hunched. He reached for Ram's bag and blanket and Ram allowed him to take them. That was when the ground shifted again, and Ram felt his legs give way as the earth loomed up to meet him.

HE WOKE ON A COT inside a darkened shack, gazing at a roof of split cedar shakes, sunlight glimmering through cracks. For a moment, in his weakness, he thought Padma lay beside him, and he felt whole. Then the canvas shades swayed and yielded to the wind and he realized where he was. In a corner stood a table with a few bottles, beakers, trays, and a microscope. Near it, Amarjeet sat in a wooden chair, reading a newspaper. Their eyes met. Amarjeet slapped the paper on his lap and called, "Doc Paulson! Doc Paulson!" his voice exploding inside Ram's head. The boy spoke like an American. "He's awake! He's awaaaake!"

"Stop!" Ram said in Punjabi, more crossly than he meant. Amarjeet stared at him. Ram tried to smile. His cheeks felt stiff. So did his arm where Pala Singh had wrapped it in Hambelton. When he looked, he saw that it had been freshly bandaged. The wound on his shin was bandaged too, with dark blood seeping through. He was shirtless. They had examined him, he was sure of it, unclothed him and noted all his injuries while he was unconscious. They would know everything. They would sense that he was a coward.

A curtain drew back and Karak entered the room, followed by Jivan Singh and an Anglo, whose presence filled the space, although he was shorter than Jivan. In the darkness, Ram could barely see them. Amarjeet raised a shade and sunlight flooded the room. "Ah, our patient is awake," the Anglo said, too full of cheer. He wore spectacles; their fragility set against his coarse features.

"This is Doc Paulson," Karak said.

"Why am I here?" Ram whispered in Punjabi.

Karak told him that they'd carried him down the street to the doctor's clinic, that the doctor had cleaned his wounds and stitched the cuts in his arm and chest. They saw the gash on his shin, but could do nothing about that. He had been resting for hours in Amarjeet's company while Karak and Jivan finished some business in town.

Ram saw the doctor glance back and forth as they spoke, tolerant of their Punjabi, seemingly unaffected.

Karak did not ask the question—how did these injuries happen— and Ram did not answer it. He saw Jivan observing him silently.

"How many days since you were hurt?" the doctor asked.

Karak translated, but Ram understood the question well enough.

"Pain is less," Ram whispered, wrapping his tongue around the English words. There were questions he did not want to answer, for which he could feel only shame. Jivan Singh and the doctor exchanged a glance.

"It's the local anesthetic," the doctor said. "It will wear off. It may hurt more in coming days."

Karak translated this too.

Doc Paulson stepped forward. "May I ask how you came to be injured?" Later, when Ram knew the Valley more, he would learn the man was a friend of the sheriff's, helping him keep the peace, warning him if visitors had seen trouble, as if it were his duty to know and report.

Ram closed his eyes, shook his head in the slightest motion.

"He doesn't understand me," Doc Paulson said.

"Do you want to tell?" Jivan Singh said to Ram in Punjabi.

Ram felt a surge of gratitude. He looked down, inspected the cloth of his bedsheet. "I was struck by a carriage in Los Angeles, before I boarded the train." He felt Karak's intake of breath. Ram gazed at Jivan Singh.

"Shall I tell him that?" Jivan asked. Ram nodded yes. Jivan Singh translated Ram's answer into English. Ram had feared missing his train, Jivan added, so did not wait to see a doctor in the city.

Doc Paulson nodded, but he looked at Ram for a moment too long.

"We brought a lunch for him, Doc," Jivan said quickly.

The doctor allowed that Ram could eat it there before they left, and they should take their time, because it was still too hot to hurry.

"Thank you," Jivan said. They shook hands. Jivan smiled at him, and the doctor smiled back.

"What will be the cost for this?" Ram asked Karak after the Anglo left, but Jivan interjected, "I've known the doctor for eight years. He's grazed his cattle on our field." Ram was surprised by the generosity. He had been surprised by the handshake too.

The Punjabis propped Ram up with pillows. Amarjeet brought out a brass tiffin, its handle inscribed with the letters BOMBAY BRASS AND IRON WORKS, and unlatched its clasp. Inside were chole, paneer, lime pickle, and roti. The aroma of cumin and cilantro made Ram's stomach clench. "My wife is a good cook," Jivan said. "Even her simple meals are delicious." Ram tore the roti and ate in large bites, gulping water, while the others stood by his bed.

But the question lingered.

"How did this happen to you, bhai?" Karak asked.

"Did no one help after the carriage hit?" Amarjeet asked, looking at Karak.

Karak smiled a ghost of a smile, exchanged a glance with Jivan.

The boy was too old to be this naive, Ram thought. "It happened, brother," Ram said. "What more can be said?"

They did not ask again. Ram took that as a sign of respect between men. He felt a burden lifting. He had been a coward, but his injuries had not been trivial; he had needed a doctor's help. There was vindication in that.

THE LAND THAT JIVAN SINGH FARMED was nine miles away, forty-five minutes on horseback, less than two hours with a wagon and rested team of mules. Dusk came quickly. The air grew cool and the breeze more insistent. The Imperial Valley was empty, made of only chalk and space, so different from the lumber mill and Hambelton's dark, lush woods, with their sharp tang of wet soil. Sitting up in the hay in the wagon's bed, Ram felt unable to focus his mind. He dreaded the openness, the vast darkness that fell upon them from all sides. Night announced itself in the strange chirping that came from the sand, in a creature's distant howl.

"There are jackals?" Ram asked.

"Coyotes," Amarjeet said. After the meal, he had grown less shy. While Jivan and Karak shared the driver's seat in front, he sat across from Ram, leaning back in the wagon bed, talking, asking Ram questions that Ram did not always answer.

Looking up at the dark sky, Amarjeet pointed to the darker outline of Mount Signal looming from Mexican soil. He knew the Valley almost as well as Ram knew Shahpur. He named the farmers who had homesteaded the land they passed. He told Ram of a great flood that had overtaken the desert towns several years before, of how men had held back the river, how Jivan Singh—his chacha-ji, he said proudly—had been one of them. He spoke as if his uncle were not present. "Chacha-ji cannot homestead any territory because he is an alien, but he says it does not matter."

Ram had propped himself up at the angle at which the pain was tolerable. The wagon's sturdy frame, the musk of the mules, the strength of their backs, their muffled footsteps on the sandy loam, all these comforted him, and slowly, he allowed himself to forget desperation. The desert was unknowable, but in this tiny wagon the four of them formed something familiar—he did not know how to name it. The dust-wind had grown gentle. The half-moon sailed white and brilliant beside them. Padma was under this same moon. She perhaps had looked up that same night, showing it to their son, teaching him the word "chanda." He wondered whether the boy had begun to speak. Despite Amarjeet's tales, he drifted in and out of a pleasant sleep.

At a random swath of land, in a break between fields of waist-high alfalfa, the wagon turned west and stopped in front of a small building—a house that faded into the darkness. A figure stood in the doorway, holding a lantern. The light shone in a circle around her, showing off her Punjabi dress, the delicate chunni lying about her neck and shoulders. Jivan put down the reins and clambered down from the wagon. "She is my wife, Kishen Kaur," Jivan said, without looking at her. "At home, it would not be proper to introduce you. But here, it would be improper if I did not."

The woman drew the chunni around her hair and lowered her eyes. Ram felt a surge of warmth. He had not seen a woman from his part of the earth for so long. Kishen Kaur offered him lime juice with sugar and he drank until satisfied.

"It was a long ride, Kishen-ji." Jivan's voice was soft. "Some food would be appreciated."

A small girl ran from the back, tottered past the woman, and made a circle around Amarjeet. "Veer-ji! Veer-ji!" she cried. Amarjeet picked her up and swung her against the dark sky. She screamed with delight.

"Come, Leela, say hello to Ram Uncle," Jivan said.

Ram edged into the circle of light. But the girl turned her head away and held close to Amarjeet, refusing to look again. The adults laughed. They were filled with a sense of goodwill and health. Ram had not realized what he had been traveling toward: a family that lived in the desert, a home.

4

KARAK AND RAM AND AMARJEET SLEPT ON COTS IN THE BREEZY COMFORT of the outdoors, fifteen yards south of the wooden battenboard structure that was Jivan and Kishen's home. Their cots sat on sandy loam that belonged to a man born in Switzerland, living now in Los Angeles. Karak thought himself a practical man, a hardworking man who wanted only to grow rich, but he cared about land.

To own land was honorable, to farm it even more so. At night before sleeping he would gaze out at the fields that stretched to the desert and the outline of the Chocolate Mountains beyond. Karak knew that before the land had belonged to the man from Switzerland, before it belonged even to the United States government or the Republic of California or the United Mexican States or the king of Spain, it had been home to the Quechan and the Kumeyaay, to the Ivilyuqaletem and the Xawił kwńchawaay, and they knew the land the way a lover knows a beloved's body, like one possessed, like one who owns, but even more so.

The injustice of their loss did not bother Karak much. He knew about the loss of land firsthand; during his boyhood in Ludhiana his father had surrendered his last five acres to Hindu moneylenders. By coincidence, the day before they were exiled from that soil, Karak had fed green corn to the ox, without a thought as to whether the animal would bloat. His father had been distressed, rageful. He had tied Karak to the post where the goat was kept and thrashed him with a stick. He thrashed him as if the lost land had been his fault.

Only later did Karak learn that the moneylenders had called in the loan. When Karak's family left the following morning, with their belongings piled on their bullock cart, the back of his shirt was still red with blood. He watched his father sitting on the driver's stoop, his hands on the reins, his face expressionless. Then his father turned back, taking one last look. The land had once been owned by Karak's great-grandfather. But no, injustice did not bother him too much. Injustice was the way of the world; what mattered was what one could accomplish between its cracks and fissures; happiness could still be found, money could still be made, comfort could still be enjoyed.

His father was guilty of other beatings, other omissions. When Karak came to the Imperial Valley, he knew that Jivan knew about them; they shared the same great-grandfather, after all, and word spread easily in a village, and between villages too—between brothers and cousins and their wives.

The army had saved Karak. The British-imposed hierarchy, its predictability, its gestures toward fair play and justice, the military's defined world all had been safer than his home. One of his younger brothers had joined the army too, another had died during the famine; the older had stayed in the village and cared for their mother after their father had jumped into River Sutlej. Karak spent years in Hong Kong, wearing the uniform of the British without wasting his allegiance on them, seeing the world, learning its ways, enjoying himself. He spent years working in Manila.

When he left the Philippines, Karak still had not married. No duties tugged at him. He arrived in California released from his father's cruelty, from the military's grasp, fingering $124 in his pocket, and he thought himself a new man. He did not need America, Americans, to tell him he was free. The land his father had lost was available here, all around him. He did not know how to farm with irrigation in the desert; he had forgotten how to farm with the rains in the Ludhiana countryside, but that did not matter. In everything, chardi kala, fearlessness, optimism.

On the morning after Ram's arrival, in the crisp and fragile dawn, lying on his cot near Ram's, Karak wondered how to present the matter to him. His plans pressed in until he could think of nothing else, not the latest return on the cantaloupe, not the letter from his older brother, telling of the failure of the wheat crop. He rose and saw that the boy was still asleep. Ram was an innocent; Karak did not know how he had been hurt, and he felt the boy could be easily bullied. Yet Karak enjoyed his company. He enjoyed how much the boy enjoyed him.

Now Ram was curled up on his side on the cot, like a child. Karak nudged him, not gently, on his thigh.

"Let him be," Jivan said. He had been standing near the porch, and his tone was sharp. Karak had not seen him. Karak held up his hand in acceptance.

Amarjeet brought food that Kishen had prepared, but Ram did not wake. His breathing was shallow and he slept without moving. The sun's first ray gained the mountain ridge. The heat bore down on them. No breeze swept across the miles of flat land. The men moved Ram's cot into the front room of the house, closed the screen door so he was near the open air but in shade. They refilled the fan with kerosene and covered its blades with wet cloth. Kishen picked up Leela and instructed her to stay away.

Late in the morning, Sheriff Frank Fielding trotted his bay gelding up the roadway and greeted Jivan near the house. Karak was making a repair to the chicken coop and came out to join them.

"Heard about your visitor," he heard the sheriff say. Jivan glanced at Karak. The sheriff dismounted, held his horse's reins. He was a tall man with a large belly, solid. But he moved with grace.

They took him to see Ram, and he peered through the front door screen. Ram's face was turned toward them, unlined and peaceful; his eyes were closed. His left hand clasped the folded blanket that lay under his head.

"He won't make trouble, Sheriff," Jivan said. "He's calm boy. Honest boy."

"How do you know?"

"My cousin," Jivan said. "A village-mate. I've known him for much time—many years. Also, his father and grandfather I knew. Good family."

Their eyes met. "Aren't you his cousin too?" the sheriff asked, turning to Karak.

"Our family is big," Karak said. Karak liked the sheriff. He was a fair man. He knew Jivan liked him too.

Jivan offered him some water, pouring it from the olla that hung near Ram's cot. The sheriff drank. "I'm putting him in your care— Jivan, Karak. He's your responsibility."

"Don't worry," Karak said. "Nothing to worry."

5

JULY 1914

RAM WOKE IN THE EARLY MORNING OF THE THIRD DAY. IN THE GRAY LIGHT before dawn, he could almost see everything: he was sitting on a cot placed in a small room with a table, a few wooden chairs, lamps, and a cabinet. A phonograph stood in the corner. A curtain hung at the threshold to another room, where, he assumed, Jivan and Kishen and Leela slept. He stood up and stepped through another doorway to a large porch surrounded by a screen. Beyond the mesh, he saw something slither through the sand. Jivan's house was small, only two rooms and the porch. Already he wished he were outside.

Past the sand and the slithering creature, a brittle field lay fallow and waiting. He could see another structure on the far side, a larger home than Jivan's, a string of small trees along a roadway. He was glad to find his boots near the cot and he slipped them on.

In the dimness, he checked for his things. His blanket had been laid on top of the cot. His bag was tucked away near the phonograph. He looked inside. He found the photo of Padma, the amulet his grandmother had given him, his billfold with $5.50. He dug further.

The packet of letters was there too. He had memorized almost everything that Padma had written to him; but still, if he had lost the letters themselves, he would have mourned. Her skin had touched each one. Her own fingers had held the pen. Only a week after he left, she had written with her own hand, *My esteemed husband—my world, today I realized the good news that you will be a father. Now you must hurry home before your son is named on his first birthday. No one else can be allowed to whisper his name in his ear.* He had received that letter, and its news, two long months after she wrote it.

Ram held his head in his hands. He could not focus his mind. He had a mosaic of memories of the last three days; there had been no time or order, no day or evening. Every few hours he had stumbled to the outhouse. Sometimes he had woken to the sound of Leela's squeals outside, or the braying of a mule, or his mother's voice, but he could not resist the tyranny of sleep. Once Amarjeet touched his shoulder to ask if he wanted to eat, but he did not know whether it was lunch or supper. Once Padma sat with him, the jewel in her nose gleaming against dark skin, liquid eyes filled with worry. Her chunni was draped around her nakedness; she held a baby to her breast. Once he woke in the darkness and saw Karak leaning over him, staring, speaking words Ram barely heard, head and shoulders silhouetted by a nearby lamp. A coyote had howled. What had Karak wanted? The truth about his injuries? The events of the past year?

Ram had been aware of a vague idea: he would ask Karak to lend him money for passage home. But something blocked Ram from telling Karak everything. How would he borrow money from Karak when he could not reveal his recent shame, why he wanted to return? It was a problem he would solve after he healed; it had been easier to sleep.

Ram stepped outside through the porch door. The dawn was coming. The air was hot and dry. He walked toward the moon and saw a small pond, the ditch that fed it, a fence on which hung large clay urns. Jivan's house was modest, made of wooden boards. In the corner between the porch's screen door and the house wall sat a small stove, a sturdy bench, a stack of crates. A green-yellow field of alfalfa reached to a pink sky, a distant mountain. Ram closed his eyes. The morning air refreshed him. He walked for a while in the fields, stepping on the bare dirt between the rows. How familiar it felt, these lines of young plants, the desert dust, the crusty earth underfoot. How different from the forests of Hambelton in the north.

When he turned back toward Jivan Singh's home, Ram could see the household awakening. While he had been walking the fields, Karak had woken and bathed in the pond. He was standing near the house, looking in a mirror propped on a window ledge, wrapping a green dastar. As Ram approached, he turned and waved. Kishen bent over the stove near the porch. Jivan sat on a rock a few paces from the house, facing the sun's glow. Karak had written to him that Jivan was a religious man, rising every day at 4:00 A.M. to bathe and say prayers. The rock on which he sat was unusually large, rounded in one section with a smaller mound in the other, and a skyward protrusion in the shape of the ear of a hare. Ram looked about. There was only dust and sand. The stone was the only one of its kind. Later he would learn it was called the jackrabbit rock.

"Oye!" Karak hailed him. "You are healthy again!" Ram had forgotten how pleasing his features were, the long, straight nose, the full lips. During the three weeks that they had lived together in the Hong Kong gurdwara, waiting for the SS *Minnesota* to ferry them to Seattle, he had noted how everyone—young and old, male and female—reacted to Karak. The Hindustanees considered him dark but handsome. In the public houses, the barmaids would often glance his way. Standing at full height, broad shouldered, he was not easily approachable, but friendly enough that they would want to approach. Sometimes he would disappear for an hour or so. Ram would stay in the drinking hall with the other lodgers from the gurdwara, drinking whiskey, waiting for him.

Ram bathed in the pond and put on fresh clothes. The Earth

had turned fully toward the sun by then. His mind felt cleansed and light. He and Karak moved his cot back outside, near the others, and sat down to breakfast at the porch table. Amarjeet joined them, glancing shyly at Ram. His gregariousness from the wagon ride was gone. Leela was outside, collecting pebbles from the dirt, inspecting them, rubbing them with her finger and forming a careful pile just beyond the porch screen. "Good morning, little Leela," Karak sang to her.

"Good. Chacha-ji," she responded, nodding as if she agreed. She eyed Ram suspiciously. When Ram looked at her, she looked away; when Ram ignored her, she scrutinized him again.

"Don't be afraid of Ram Chacha," Karak said. "He only eats children taller than four feet, and you are not yet big enough."

The girl looked again at Ram, then at Karak. "He won't," she said. "You won't let him."

Ram smiled.

"Leela!" Kishen Kaur said sharply.

Karak made a face at the girl that her mother couldn't see.

Kishen scooped breakfast onto the men's plates: eggs mixed with peppers and onion, rotis dripping with ghee. She nodded slightly at Ram, her chunni draped over her hair. She still had the energy of youth, luminous eyes and gleaming hair with only a few strands of gray. She was perhaps ten years younger than her husband. Ram was sure Jivan did not allow her to work in the fields; her hands had no calluses and her skin was unweathered. Her slender fingers spun the rotis on the pan until they bubbled and rose and she hurried them, soft and warm, onto the plates. She walked from porch to stove, picked up the child, listened to the men talk, straightened the chunni when it fell from her braid. She was quiet, less animated than his Padma, but she was free and sure in a way that disturbed Ram.

For a few moments, the men ate in silence. Amarjeet scooped

the eggs with a fork with the manners of an American. The thought gripped Ram: the boy was strange.

"Bhabhi-ji, Jivan Singh is still saying prayers?" Karak asked. His manner was respectful, but Ram could tell—Jivan Singh's wife did not matter much in Karak's estimation of the world.

"He woke late today," Kishen said, without looking at him.

"The egg is good, eh, Ram?" Karak asked.

"Perfect," Ram said. But an egg was not a complicated item to prepare. Why pay such attention?

"Bhabhi-ji must be trying to impress our visitor." Karak grinned again, looking at Ram, inviting him to join in his casual teasing, just as he had on the steamship. In that way, he would form a circle about them, separate from the others.

Kishen turned away, dignified.

Perhaps she was too free, Ram thought, or perhaps she did not like Karak. He pitied her. How could she be happy in this place, far from everything and everyone she knew, with no other Punjabi women with whom to pass the time?

HE DID NOT SEE Jivan and Amarjeet again until the late afternoon, when he spotted them standing at the far corner of a field, bent over their shovels. The rays of a dying sun reached across the crusted soil. Gold shimmered off the angles of their clothing, their bronzed hands and necks, off the surfaces of their tools. Jivan greeted him as he approached. "You have recovered," he said, smiling.

"I can help you," Ram offered, reaching for a shovel that was lodged in the dirt. He had spent most of the day resting. Karak had gone to meet a banker in town. Ram had helped Kishen bring buckets of water from the pond to a washtub. He had moved slowly and it had not been too painful.

"You have planted?" Ram asked.

"No. Only allowed the water in to make the weeds grow, so we can remove them later."

They were lifting silt from the bottom of the ditch to the side, so that the water could flow freely. He had done that chore himself, routinely and often, at his uncle's farm. But when he bent to lift the weight of the dirt, the pain flared in his chest.

"Why are you working with your wounds?" Jivan said, taking the shovel from him. He plucked a kerchief from his pocket and wiped his forehead. "It is a constant fight with the silt, and we never win. It is like a punishment." He turned to his nephew. "We have done enough for one day. What do you say, Jeetu?"

"These were to be resting days, Chacha-ji," the boy said. "We are working too hard."

Ram would not have spoken to his own uncle in that way. He had been too timid, and his uncle too cross. But Jivan did not seem to mind. He gathered up the shovels that lay on the bank.

"Bhai-ji, look," Amarjeet said to Ram, his tone respectful now. The sudden change made Ram uneasy; he glanced at Jivan. From the pocket of his dungarees, Amarjeet brought out an object. "I found it just this morning." He held up a stone the size of his thumb, embedded with tiny lines splayed like a fan. "See here." He pointed. "A fish's bones. It lived when everything here was under the ocean." He spoke as if he were responsible for it. He gave it to Ram. The stone lay smooth and cool in Ram's hand. "Very old. Ancient," Amarjeet said. In his face was an expression close to hope.

Ram rubbed his finger over the surface, impressed. Amarjeet still had the cheeks of a boy, plump and new, eyes outlined by needlessly thick lashes. "We are not far in age, Amarjeet. It is true I am married, but if agreeable to your uncle, call me Ram."

A shade of pink rose from Amarjeet's neck to his cheeks. He glanced at Jivan. His uncle nodded curtly.

Ram held out the stone.

"You can keep it," Amarjeet said. "From time to time we find them here."

THAT NIGHT, the men sat outdoors under an arc of stars that pressed down on them, imposing and fearsome and unbounded, the flat land stretching to an unreachable distance. They were contemplative and content, laughter lifting from their circle into desert space, velvet sky. From inside the home, Jivan's phonograph was playing: a soprano voice serenaded them in Hindi. They were surrounded by a dim halo of lamplight. Karak opened a fresh bottle of whiskey that he had bought in Mexicali. They drank a toast to Ram's recovery, then to his arrival.

"It is good you have come," Jivan said.

Embarrassed, Ram mumbled a question about Jivan's life before he had moved to the Valley, and Jivan told him he had been a risaldar-major in the British Indian cavalry. He had performed well, been awarded medals, given the honor of leading his mounted unit down London streets for the queen's Diamond Jubilee. "When we passed her, riding in our formation—you see—I am sure that she looked directly at me. I saw her turn her head," Jivan said. There, from other men who had served all over the world, he had first heard of Canada, of Oregon, of California. "I knew that I wanted to come after my posting was finished. Afterwards I fought for the queen in Shandong Province. In 1902 I went home to Punjab, then came to Oregon and laid rail. When the Colorado River flooded, I came to the Valley to find work and met Mr. Eggenberger. That is his house there, although he lives in Los Angeles now." Jivan indicated the larger house on the other side of the field. "Few years later, 1910, I brought Kishen Kaur and Amarjeet. Leela was born the next year."

"At first I didn't want to come with him," Amarjeet said. "But it was a good decision my father took." His uncle nodded at him.

"A good decision," the boy repeated, and Ram wondered if that was what he truly thought.

Ram felt daunted. How easily Jivan Singh spoke of faraway places, the peoples of the world, navigating the Earth. Ram had not known that, like Karak, this man had traveled the planet on British ships. Ram's dead father had fought for the British too—a true soldier, and a religious man, a Khalsa Sikh. Ram had not known him at all.

"You have done much, bhai-ji," Ram said to Jivan, and felt Karak's gaze on him. Perhaps he envied Jivan's attention. Or perhaps Karak was amused.

Jivan waved away Ram's comment. "What else can we do? We must live."

Karak refilled their glasses.

"A few years ago, it was not easy to be in Oregon or Washington," Jivan said. "How did you feel there now?"

The vague allusion to the lumber mill chilled Ram, made his heart beat faster. He pushed away his sense of alarm and forced himself to speak. "The locals do not like us. Among our people, there is a great feeling against the British. The Ghadar Party—have you heard of it?" As soon as he said it, Ram regretted the words. He did not know what Jivan would think.

But Jivan did not seem bothered. "The British are not fair to us, but how would Indians govern if suddenly the British are overthrown? And if war comes now in Europe and we fight well for the English king, he will give us self-rule and dominion status—like Australia, like Canada."

"We are not white men, bhai-ji," Karak said. "We will not get dominion status."

"See how they treat the *Komagata Maru* in Vancouver Harbor," Amarjeet said, looking at Ram, as if Ram had not heard of the ship. "It is full of Indians—British citizens. Isn't it our right to travel from any part of the empire to another? Those passengers started on British soil in Hong Kong and are going to British Canada, but they won't let them land."

"Of course they will be allowed to land," Jivan said.

"Chacha-ji, that is not how the Canadians think," Amarjeet said.

"Perhaps not. But it is the law."

What did the law have to do with it? Ram thought. The attackers in Hambelton had not cared about the law. Karak's eyes met his.

"People are not concerned with the law," Karak said, as if reading Ram's thoughts.

"Hambelton—that town where you are working—is not far from Vancouver," Jivan said. "They must talk about it there."

"We heard that all passengers passed medical inspection when the doctors boarded the ship in Vancouver Harbor," Ram said.

"So you know all about it?" Amarjeet said.

"For days we heard. It seems the Vancouver waterfront was lined with the local Hindustanees, immigration officers, Anglo politicians, and the whites who do not want the *Komagata Maru* to land. It had become like a circus."

"Ghadar Party says that if the Hindustanees are not allowed off the ship and into Canada, we should all go back to India with guns and fight the British for refusing to support us," Amarjeet said.

"Ghadar was saying that even from the first meeting in Astoria," Ram said.

"You were there, Ram-ji?" Amarjeet asked, eyes wide.

"It is not that I believe wholeheartedly in them." Ram glanced at Jivan. "But I was there. All the Hindustanees in the area attended. Not only Astoria and Portland, even Hambelton and Bellingham too, even from Vancouver. I met Har Dayal, the leader then. He was arrested in April. I met RamChandra too, the current leader," Ram spoke slowly. He felt Amarjeet's admiration riding in a wave toward him. Suddenly Amarjeet jumped up from his seat and ran inside the house.

"Scoundrels," Jivan said. "At least the leader of the people on *Komagata Maru,* Gurdit Singh, is somewhat an honorable man."

"Do you think Har Dayal is a scoundrel, bhai-ji?" Ram asked.

"Why else would he escape to Berlin?"

Amarjeet returned, holding open a newspaper, reading aloud, shouting the words as he walked: "'Desh Pain Dhakke, Bahar Mile Dhoi Naa. Sada Pardessian Da Des Koi Naa! Humiliated at home with no solace abroad. For us foreigners there is no refuge anywhere!'" His face flushed with excitement. "See here, Ram—" Amarjeet said.

"I have seen it," Ram interrupted. "I know the paper—"

WANTED: ENTHUSIASTIC AND HEROIC SOLDIERS FOR ORGANIZING GHADAR IN HINDUSTAN

REMUNERATION: Death
REWARD: Martyrdom
PENSION: Freedom
FIELD OF WORK: Hindustan
Freedom fighters should make their appearance at the
U.S. Ghadar Headquarters in San Francisco, CA.

"Ghadar means revolution, Jeetu," Jivan said to his nephew. "There will be no revolution anytime soon." He waved his hand dismissively. "Amarjeet wants to join them," he explained to Ram.

"They are heroes, Chacha-ji," Amarjeet said.

Karak chuckled lightly.

"They are *not* heroes," Jivan said. "They are foolish. They will have no followers in India itself."

Karak sucked his teeth, unperturbed, smiling. "We must stop speaking ill of the British! Our Ram is from the Canal Colonies. Who dug the river canals there for the village farmers? The British did."

Ram shifted uncomfortably in his chair. The discussion had

grown too heavy. A few moments before, they had been telling riddles. Jivan Singh had asked, "What is a black shawl embroidered with gold?" and Ram had answered, "the night sky." He had been enjoying himself. What did the Ghadar have to do with his life, his Padma, his new son? "Ghadar is very extreme," Ram said.

Jivan glanced at him with appreciation. "Even Ram-ji agrees, Amarjeet," Jivan said. "If I let you join them, your father would cross the ocean and put a sword to my neck. I have a responsibility to him." Then he added, "And to you."

The boy knit his eyebrows. "What do *you* say, Chacha-ji?" Amarjeet asked Karak softly.

"I say I want to grow very, very, very rich, not to play at politics."

"Please!" Amarjeet said.

Karak sighed. "My real feeling is that we should no longer be loyal to the British Raj. We must lay the axe at the root of the British tree, not the branches."

"You were a soldier once," Jivan said. "You served them too."

"I was only a halfhearted soldier, bhai-ji," Karak said.

Ram could not decipher the expression that flashed across Jivan's face. Jivan stood suddenly, moved to the bottle of whiskey. "Why don't *you* go with the Ghadar then?" he said lightly.

"Because your nephew doesn't care one damn about farming, bhai-ji!" Karak said. "I must stay and take care of him as if he were my wife."

Jivan snorted. The tension gave way. Amarjeet, looking surprised, joined in the laughter too. "Between the three of you," Jivan said, "at least Ram has some sense!"

13 July 1914

Padma-ji, my life,
     I write to you from a place far south of Hambelton, in a
farming colony called Fredonia in California State, in a desert

*valley named Imperial. I have come here to visit a friend. It
is not that I have grown lazy—no, please do not think so, my
dear—it is only that I need a short rest. Be assured, 10 days back
I sent Uncle $30 and he telegraphed that he received it and he is
happy. Perhaps he has told you that himself?*

*I have come to stay for a short time with Karak Singh. I
wrote to you about him before—the man whom I met in the
gurdwara in Hong Kong. For three weeks we stayed there
together, waiting for the ship to carry us to Seattle, then we were
together for six weeks more as we journeyed across the sea. We
became great friends, although you will laugh to know that I do
not always trust him.*

*Karak Singh is from Ludhiana District, from a farming
family that somehow lost their lands. When the family was
desperate, he joined with the British Indian Army and served in
Shanghai, then in Hong Kong. For a few years he worked as a
security guard in Manila. I do not know what sort of family he
is from, but he has been generous to me. He has joined up here
in a farming venture with his cousin-brother, an older man of
50 or so, Jivan Singh, who seems very honorable, and to whom
I've taken a great liking. Jivan Singh is here with his wife and
very young daughter and also his nephew. Altogether, they are
good people. Can you believe that there are other Punjabis in
the Valley, Padma, perhaps 200 or so, and that among them
is a woman? It is true what they say—wherever the earth can
sustain life, the potato and the Sikh will reach there sooner or
later. Please give a kiss to my son. Every day, every moment, I
think of you both.*

Thera,
Ram

The next morning Karak showed Ram around the farm. The large
field bordering Jivan Singh's home would be planted in a few weeks

with cantaloupe, and there were smaller fields of strawberries, date trees and a grapefruit orchard. Farther away were acres of alfalfa and barley. One hundred and sixty acres that bordered the other side of Jivan Singh's home were sharecropped by a Japanese family, the Moriyamas. When Karak and Ram stood on the roadway near the entry to Jivan's fields, they could see the Moriyamas' house, three-quarters of a mile away.

The home that stood across the cantaloupe field from Jivan's house belonged to the owner of the entire property, Stephen Eggenberger, a Swiss immigrant who had married the daughter of a wealthy family based in Los Angeles. Eggenberger lived in Los Angeles permanently now, Karak said.

To Ram, the home seemed a luxury: clay brick that would keep the heat outside and leave the inside cool, so different from the wooden boards that formed Jivan's home, the metal screens framing his porch. Through the window in the door Ram could see several rooms, well swept and clean.

"Why doesn't he live here?" Ram asked.

"His wife suffers from an ailment and cannot tolerate the heat." Karak explained more: Eggenberger had helped Jivan settle here when he came in 1905. Jivan had come to find work fighting the flood, but after the waters receded, he had wanted to stay. Eggenberger hired him to help on the farm. When Jivan wanted to grow a field of melons, Eggenberger offered him a crop share and some seed to get started. "They are generous people, bhai. Once Eggenberger's wife nursed Jivan Singh through an injury. He will not forget that."

Ram did not know what to say. The thought of an Anglo woman nursing a Punjabi man back to health seemed impossible. Now he realized: that was why the shrubs were watered, why the doors and windows remained shuttered against scorpions, snakes, and desert creatures, why Kishen swept there every week.

"We use Stephen's silo and his barn," Karak said. "Jivan Singh built the packing shed and ramada. Jivan Singh pays Eggenberger some part of the crops. His land agent, Clive Edgar, reviews the books every month and takes payment. Twice a year Eggenberger visits the land office, pays his taxes and water rights, and stays a night in his home."

Ram was quiet. He was thinking of how the bosses at the lumber mill spoke to the members of the work gangs, calling them ragheads, towelheads.

"You did not expect this," Karak said. "That we have so much independence."

"No." He heard his voice crack with emotion.

Karak walked to the house and knocked on the door. "Not like our huts back home, is it?" Ram could see how much he admired it, running his hands along the edge of the doorway. "If I had a place like this, and so much land, I would not have gone back to Los Angeles where my in-laws could dictate to me," he said, laughing.

So now Ram knew: Karak was jealous. Jealous of a white man living in America, as if he had the right to something this white man had.

Karak went on: Jivan knew other farmers, shippers, bankers, the district official for the water company, many zanjeros by name—everyone needed to plant and harvest a crop and make a profit. People trusted him. He purchased seed, hired the pickers and the packers. He kept the books. "I think he should share more of these responsibilities with me, but he doesn't want to give up the power," Karak said.

Ram did not respond. Karak was jealous of Jivan too. Suddenly he did not want to hear more. "How did he manage to bring Kishen Kaur?"

"Things were not so strict in 1910," Karak said. "If she is unhappy, I don't know. She never complains. Leela was born here."

He was not the same man Ram had known on the steamship. He was more serious, more jealous. In the past year, the desert wind had etched lines around his lips and on his forehead. A tanned border on his neck and wrists was prominent; his teeth flashed whiter than before. His letters had told of large crops of cantaloupe and melons, another of barley, two fields made level after the grazing cattle had been moved off. Seeing the farm, comparing it with what Ram knew from his uncle's lands, Ram had no reason to think he was lying. But Karak did not appear relaxed. Ram knew he was mulling something; when their eyes met, Karak knew that Ram saw this too.

"Eggenberger has more land, bhai," Karak said. "A half section just two miles from here. He gave one hundred and sixty acres to a man named Roubillard. The other one hundred and sixty acres are free. For cotton—perfect." Karak raised his eyebrows, accentuated the word with his hand.

Ram nodded, nothing more.

"I have not yet seen it," Karak said. He was looking carefully at him. "Would you like to come with me?"

"Now?" Ram gave a little laugh.

"Now. Why not?"

"The sun is high," Ram said, and the wound in his side felt raw today, but he did not want to reveal that to Karak.

"It's still morning. We'll go and return before noon. In the wagon, it won't feel so hot."

Ram wanted to please Karak, and Karak was eager, and they both knew Ram was flattered that Karak wanted to show him something. They hitched the mules to the wagon and shared the driver's seat. The sun beat through the fabric of their shirts and stung their backs. Ram, still recovering from his injuries, felt light-headed. He grasped the side of the wagon but said nothing.

They passed fields of lush green separated by sand and smoke tree and creosote. Karak egged the mules into an irrigation canal. The wagon dipped and rattled forward and up. Water splashed from the wheels and the bellies of the mules, sloshed at the soles of his boots. Ram closed his eyes against the motion and swallowed hard, willing his stomach to remain calm. They turned south and stopped under the mottled shade of a mesquite tree. Every bump of the wagon had vibrated through Ram's wounded chest. When he stepped onto the sand, his leg buckled and he grabbed the side of the wagon. Slowly, he followed Karak.

They stood at the corner of an alfalfa field that lay in neat strips of vibrant green and chocolate brown. On one side lay the road they had just traveled, on the other, sand and scrub stretched, uninterrupted, to the west. Gazing out at the horizon, the endless sky, the white slivers of cloud above Mount Signal, Ram forgot about his unsettled stomach. He had seen this moment before, felt this heat before, smelled the sandy loam and dust-wind since he was a child. For a moment, the sky spun above him, but it was not only dizziness that he felt. If he looked past Karak's dastar, past this sparse cluster of trees, he would see his uncle's farm near the edge of the lower Chenab Canal. Water running from Himalayan snow and Shivalik rains, thundering, tremendous, toward the Indus River and the Arabian Sea. At the southeast corner of his uncle's land stood this same mesquite tree that sheltered tired travelers. The village women would send them water in tin cups, rotis and chole served on leaves. On the far side, in blessed privacy, stood the hut where he and Padma spent their nights. A gust of wind lifted sand into Ram's eyes. His vision skewed; he saw a single point of light surrounded by darkness.

"THIS IS WHERE IT STARTS—the boundary," Karak said, pointing to a small flag set in the dirt. He had not seemed to notice Ram's frailness. "That land belongs to Eggenberger but was just leased to Roubillard, who came out from Louisiana. Eggenberger tells me that Roubillard wants to try cotton too."

Karak was disturbed by something; Ram could sense that. Karak pointed to figures in the distance, a team of mules pulling an implement, a cluster of men around them. "The water delivery ditch is being dug there. This land will be in great demand very soon." Karak shaded the sun from his eyes. "The most important thing is land, bhai," he said. "There is no other way to have wealth or to be settled. In Ludhiana, my father had good land. Very good land."

"Then why did you leave Punjab?" Ram had known the man for almost a year and a half, and he did not know the answer to this question.

"The rains failed for two years in a row, but still the British government was taxing us. My father took a mortgage, but it did not go well. We lost everything. Only choice for me was joining the army." Karak spoke lightly, as if that did not matter. "But this land can make us rich, Ram. The ditch will come right here, you see, right on the border. The soil has tested to be good for cotton. We must only level the land and plant it."

Ram knew it was more complicated than that. "Karak-ji? You have seen this land before?" Karak looked at him. They both realized that Ram had caught him in a lie.

"I wanted you to come and see." Karak held up his hand. "With an open mind." In response to Ram's silence he said, "It's true. I came here for a short time about one month back." He avoided meeting Ram's eye.

Ram felt a small bubble of anger, then it burst and fizzled away. He allowed himself to feel flattered. After all, Karak had only wanted to show him something.

Karak pointed to a small structure a quarter mile away. "That's the shack that Eggenberger built to prove the homestead to the government. So much land is still open, but we are foreigners. We cannot do the same."

"Eggenberger isn't a foreigner?" Ram asked.

"He is from Switzerland, bhai. That is different."

Ram looked at him.

"Oye!" Karak sucked his teeth to show he did not really mind. "That is the law. In Punjab, we keep the city families away from the farming districts. It is the same, isn't it? One can understand, of course. And what does it matter? We can farm and make a profit and grow rich. What do you say, Ram?"

Ram did not understand what he was asking. His heart began to thump inside his chest. "Bhai-ji?" he said.

"Come and work with me. We will grow cotton. Everyone says there will be war in Europe soon. The cotton market will be high. We Punjabis know how to grow it. You will have too much, Ram! Too much money to send to your uncle, you will have to spend some here just for entertainment! At home, everyone will be celebrating your name and honoring you."

Ram felt a constriction in his chest. His wound began to burn. He had not earned much in the fifteen months he had been in Hambelton. And he dreaded going back. But to farm again, to earn enough money for his uncle to purchase land, how many harvests would that take? How long until he saw Padma and his son? "I want to go home in two years, bhai," he said. "That is my only wish."

"Yes, yes, you go home in two years." Karak nodded. "Well, make it three," he said. "We will take a three-year lease from Eggenberger." Karak picked up a stone and threw it a distance, fast and hard. It bounced in the dirt near the shack. "You wanted to return in two years when you arrived. It has already been more than a year."

Ram felt like a boy. He could not disagree.

"Make a good profit here and go home. Two years, three years, whatever you wish. The arrangement would be the same as Jivan's— Eggenberger gets one-third profit. We will work the land together, rent mules when we need, hire the people to cultivate and harvest. I will take half of the crop. The rest is yours."

"You take half the crop?" Ram was not sure that he heard correctly.

"I am putting the seed—"

"Half?" He did not want to farm again, but still, the word stung.

"I pay for the rental of mules and equipment—that is fair. You would get the remainder, bhai," he said, turning toward Ram. "I said it already, didn't I? Far more than two dollars a day?"

Ram's cheeks grew hot. He stared at the outline of the far hills, trying to swallow the anger. Half? He had come to Karak seeking refuge, wanting to confide what had happened in Hambelton. He had hoped the man would lend him money for passage home. Even without knowing all this, Karak had betrayed him.

"You have experienced a huge shock," Karak whispered, his eyes traveling to Ram's chest. Ram felt the gash burn again, as if Karak's gaze had caused it. "Don't take any hasty decisions now. And you are young. You may not realize the opportunity I am giving."

Ram snorted; he could not help it. "I will think about it," he said, and would not allow himself to say more, because his anger would be fully revealed.

"Of course you must look at the matter yourself. You must not trust me only because I am ten years senior to you."

They mounted the wagon and Karak turned the mules toward Jivan's home. But something dark and almost tangible had moved between the two men. Karak was talkative at first, pointing out more landmarks than he had previously, more enthusiastic than before; then he grew silent and they traveled the last minutes without speaking. Ram remembered a moment on the SS *Minnesota* when Karak had mocked a shipmate—a chappal maker from the Deccan—for not knowing that western women wore corsets. *What, brother, do you think they are shaped that way naturally?* Karak had spoken in Urdu so that everyone could understand. The fellow was known to be dim. The Hindustanees sitting in the steerage communal room had laughed loudly; the man himself had joined in. The joke had lasted for many days. It had helped to pass the time.

6

H E HAD PROMISED PADMA HE WOULD COME BACK. WHAT IF HE FARMED for two years, or three, and had three bad harvests; what money could he send home? Would he be required to stay longer? That was his worry.

They had argued on the last night that they had spent together, during the peace of day's end, when the hut's cool walls released their mud scent and he stretched his bare legs on the charpai. This time of day, this small space, was their haven from the searching eyes of his family. Padma stood with her back to him, lighting the oil wick before the small collection of deities, the flame reflecting off their metal frames. Goddess Durga fixed him with the sacred gaze, questioning, and he felt a spasm of anxiety, a shadow of conscience. But then it passed.

"It is not right that Chacha-ji is sending you away." Her head was bent, her hand was by her cheek, and he wondered if she was smoothing away a tear. "My mind is disturbed about it." Her voice was always beautiful to him, dark and deep, almost like a man's.

He did not answer for a moment. She had never been so bold before. She spoke as if she believed that he did not want to go. He had said months ago—when Chacha-ji had decided to send him and

Ishwar together, when twenty acres east of the canal were mortgaged to buy their passage—that he did not want to leave, but he suspected that she always knew the truth. It had been a dishonest game between them: Ram acting as if he wanted to stay, Padma silently berating his uncle for sending him.

He wanted to go, he did not want to go; both were true. She still stood with her back to him, although the flame was lit. He could see her shape through the kurta: the square shoulders, the small waist. He suddenly remembered their wedding night, when she had laughed with him as they sat by the waterwheel. His longing felt like a blade in his belly, a wound.

"I will come back," he said. He was standing now, because the statement required it.

"Will you?" she said. He was surprised by her bitterness.

"Ishwar and I will come back. We will make enough money to buy more land in Shahpur. Nothing can replace the village where our ancestors lived. Isn't it true, Padma?"

"By your going, we can move back there in two years or three. If you stayed, maybe it would take five years, or six, even seven. What does it matter? I would rather have you stay here in the canal colony with me than return to the village sooner."

This was true. Lyallpur was not like the districts to the east, where famine raged on and off. The British would not let Lyallpur fail, not when they had invested so much in the canals, not when the gins were always busy there, and the cotton was being carted out by wagon and boat. The family did not really need him to go, did they?

He had not dared question his uncle. With money Ram made in the U.S. they all would move back to Shahpur quickly. His uncle would give the land in the canal colony to Ram's eldest cousin. The rest of the family would be settled back in Jullundur. Years later, when he was more American, he would wonder why he did not consider his own life in this calculation.

"I will bring great prestige on the family if we can settle back in our old village as wealthy people."

"I did not marry you for the prestige."

"Ishwar is going. Who will look after him?" It had been flattering that Chacha-ji had held him equal to his own son, when Ram was only his sister's child. Ishwar too had been surprised that they were traveling together.

"Ishwar is not a boy."

"He is younger than me."

"Only by a season or two." He waited for more, but she did not say the most obvious thing: Ishwar was not married. He would not leave anyone behind.

His heart beat loudly inside his ears but he stayed quiet. If he said more, they would have to reveal what they both already knew: that some part of Ram wanted the adventure, desired to see that distant place. He would earn his uncle's praise. His mother would no longer be reviled as a widow who had raised her son off a brother's charity. Ram would pay off that childhood debt and return as a man, equal to his cousins. For Padma and himself, there would always be later. He would be back.

He did not recognize the emotion he felt until he left the hut, walking under the violet sky by the canal waters. He was angry with her.

Ram went to the temple, although he had already visited that morning, although the pujari had already put the Goddess to sleep and had retired himself. Then he walked a furlong more and entered the gurdwara. The langar was closed, the oven extinguished and the seating area deserted. The holy book had already been put away for the night.

His father had been a member of the Khalsa, but Ram had been raised a Hindu. Years before, his father's older brother had come to fetch him to his father's village. That man had come too late, when Ram had already become a boy who loved his home. Perhaps the delay had been intentional; his father had three brothers, and already the lands that *their* father would apportion between them would be too small; none of the three tiny allotments could sustain a whole family. If Ram had gone to live with them, he would have had a right to that land. It would have been divided into four. But Ram refused to go. Whenever Ram came to the gurdwara he felt a spasm in his consciousness, a vast space—the absence of the father he never knew.

He returned home after several hours, walking silently past the waterwheel where the women came every morning, past the shed where the oxen were kept. He did not want to disturb anyone. He did not want them to know that he had been out. When he entered the hut, he knew that Padma was still awake, although she lay on her side facing away from him. Her hip curved invitingly. He put his hand on her thigh. They made love without taking off their clothes, and then again, slowly, through tears that they both shed. Years later, when he thought of that night, he would tell himself that the tears had come only because of his innocence; he had been very young. Long after the rooster had crowed and members of the household made their way to the field for their morning ablutions, long after the moon disappeared behind the grove of trees, Ram and Padma were still asleep.

They woke to bright sunlight streaming across their dirt floor. No one had disturbed them. Ram was grateful for this kindness. He and Ishwar would soon leave to catch the train to Lyallpur, then another that would take them to Calcutta.

Padma went to the kitchen to help with the day's meals, and they did not speak again. His cousins' children stayed with him as he arranged his travel bag. They squatted on the ground and made lines in the dirt with their sticks and asked questions, chattering: What will you bring us, Ram Chacha? Will you bring a wagon that runs without horses? Will you bring a glass bubble containing the sun?

Inside his travel case were the snacks and sweets the women had made, the western clothes—three shirts, two pairs of pants—that the tailor had sewn. His mother and aunt had each pawned some gold bangles; this money he folded carefully and wrapped in a cotton handkerchief that he kept in his shirt pocket. In the kitchen, his mother drew him aside, pulling close the curtains in the entry. Just for one moment, the other women could not enter. She was holding a small bowl of yogurt that she had sprinkled with sugar. She fed him herself, wishing him a sweet journey, an easy journey. She muttered a prayer under her breath, asking for the Lord's protection.

He and Ishwar went together to receive Ishwar's father's blessings. Chanda Lal waited for them in the house, sitting on his favorite cushion in the front room. Some of the women—Ram's aunt, his grandmother, the wives of his cousins—watched as Ram and Ishwar each touched their forehead to the older man's feet, and he rose and placed his hands on their shoulders. He spoke to them as if he loved them equally well, his son and his nephew.

When Ram and Ishwar emerged, the afternoon brightness hurt Ram's eyes. Three hundred villagers gathered around; he had known many of them as a child. Ishwar climbed on the bullock cart. Ram mounted the step and paused to find Padma in the crowd. She stood apart from the others; only Ram's mother was near her, at her elbow. Her veil hung about her cheeks, partially hiding her face, and he could not read her expression. He turned away to climb onto the bullock cart.

The oxen began to move and the village children ran beside them, shouting, their bare feet kicking up dust. Ishwar looked at Ram and grinned broadly. That grin was like a knife in Ram's heart. Ishwar had spent the previous evening bragging to childhood friends about the train journey, the ocean voyage, the money he would make in the west. He was the youngest son, unfettered, setting off to embark on a life. He could be abroad and not be cracked in half. Their lives were completely different. It would be years before Ram understood that.

WHEN RAM AWOKE THE NEXT MORNING, the sun was already low in the sky. He had drunk too much; he could smell the whiskey on his skin and feel it in his head. The other cots were empty. There was no sign of Karak or Amarjeet. Ram felt unsettled.

He rose and splashed water on his face. Across the field, he could see Jivan Singh in the animal shed. Ram smelled the comforting scent of horses as he approached.

"Bhai-ji?" Ram said softly.

"Sit, sit." Jivan was toying with a harness, pulling the leather straight while it was hooked to a nail on the wall.

Ram perched on the edge of the stool that stood nearby. He felt odd sitting while Jivan stood and worked. "I haven't seen Karak Singh," Ram said.

"He left early to speak with the banker in town."

"He is unhappy with me," Ram said lightly, wanting to say it but not wanting it to be important.

"Is he?" Jivan glanced at him. "I am trying to fix this harness," he said. "I may have to take it to town."

Ram did not answer. The man intimidated Ram, even though he did not dictate terms.

"How do you like our valley?" Jivan asked. "Heat is just like home?"

Ram agreed politely. "May I help you?" he asked, but Jivan waved him away. Ram found a twig on the ground, traced it in the dirt in front of him.

"So you decided not to stay and join with Karak?"

Ram was startled that Jivan knew. "That is what he told you?"

"He told me that you had not yet decided. I took that to mean that you had said no." He smiled, but was distracted by the harness, the leather, the ruler that he was using to measure.

Ram smiled too. "Not yet. But I will."

"It is hard work. Right now, cotton is still experimental here. But together you could bring in a large crop next season."

"You are flattering me," Ram said, then, clearing his throat, unsure of his boldness, he asked, "Bhai-ji? Why don't you join?"

"I know nothing about cotton. In Ludhiana, we do not grow it. But for you—it is different. You come from a canal colony. You know cotton. You know the desert. You know how to flood a field correctly."

Ram heard his own intake of breath. "Karak does not know about farming in a canal district?" Ram said.

"Not at all. We use well water." Jivan snorted. "We pray for rain." He still was not looking at Ram. "In my first season, I did not irrigate correctly. The front ten acres had too much water and the back ten too little. I did not level the field properly. Twice I burned the soil, because I watered when the plant was not high enough to keep the moisture under the desert sun. What does Karak know of irrigation? He joined the army at sixteen years old. It's true that I have been teaching him. But your knowledge of cotton, your knowledge of irrigation"—Jivan's eyes finally met his—"is very valuable."

"I have a wife," Ram said.

"I was in the same situation as you. But see what I accomplished here," he said, without pride. "Kishen Kaur came to join me. That was good."

Ram felt a wave of perspiration. So many things possible and impossible at the same time. He had not expected this. "I have a home, bhai-ji. I want to go back."

HE HAD KNOWN PADMA since they were children. Not only when their families had shifted to the colony near the River Chenab after the British enticed them to move, but before that, in Jullundur District, where his uncle had five small patches of land near River Sutlej. His uncle and her father had served in the army together. They had been friends. At Vaisakhi and Diwali, when their villages would go to the riverbank to celebrate, the families would set up camp next to each other. Their mothers and the other women, the children from both families, sat together in that throng of people, while the men settled themselves apart. That was his earliest memory of Padma. She was a baby when he was a child. In the confusion and noise of the festival, he would fetch things to help her mother: fruit for the baby, or her sling, or rice mixed with buttermilk. He would make faces to stop her from crying. The boys were free to go from the women's camp to the men's circle. But Ram preferred his mother. Not that he didn't play kabaddi at the edge of the water, or take part in the wrestling matches, or run in the footraces with Ishwar and his other cousins. He did those things too.

One year it was different. When Padma was five she grew ill, and for a week burned with fever, so high that her mother thought she would die. They called the doctor from the town, twenty miles away, but he could do nothing. Her parents went every day to the temple to pray. Padma recovered from the fever, but after that, her right leg began to grow weak; for a while she could not even stand. But she was a determined child. She forced herself to rise, stand, hobble along, although the muscles of the leg could barely support her. She began to walk with a limp. It was weeks later that the full scope of the tragedy became apparent: the leg would not return to its former strength; she would always walk that way.

Her father was a literate man, a follower of Ajit Singh. For the months that Padma lay weak and alert on her charpai, he taught her how to read and write. In her village, only three other girls and one woman had that knowledge. It came to her easily. Later, she wrote poetry, stories to entertain the younger children.

During the festivals by the river, Ram would watch as she sat with the other girls. At first, she needed a crutch to walk. Later, she refused it; she refused even the slender cane her mother and aunts told her to use, forcing it upon her. She walked with only a limp, a peculiar rhythm to her gait, and in this way, she could join in with all the children.

Other men had not wanted her. Although one's eye was drawn to her form when she stood with a group of girls, although her face was round like the moon, her eyes as dark as a raven's wings, her one defect led the villagers to believe there might be others: that she might not bear children. That she would bring misfortune upon her household. It was understandable that she would be given to Ram, and that Ram would accept her. Who else could he hope for when he had no father, when he had been raised on his uncle's generosity in his mother's village?

His mother did not like the match. His uncle was happy to have this bond with his friend, even though he would not have formed it through one of his own sons. At the Vaisakhi festival after the marriage had been settled, when the families gathered by the riverside, Ram could not meet Padma's gaze. He had things he wanted to say to her, but now he found himself incapable.

It was not until their wedding night, when they sat together near the silent Persian wheel, that he had said, "Does it not disturb you that I have no father? That I do not know the people of my paternal village?"

She looked puzzled. Then she hugged her knees close and spoke without looking at him. "When I was eight, at Diwali, I was playing marbles with Ishwar. Don't you remember? When I won, Ishwar wanted to take the marbles from me. He was so angry. He called me 'saali,' and I began to cry. I went by myself to the tent and sat there and read quietly. He grabbed my book from me, like this." She grabbed his hand and pulled, hard. The touch of her skin excited him. "But when you came, you took it from him. You scolded him and gave the book back to me." She looked at him now. "Don't you remember?" she asked again.

"No," he said, although he remembered it very well. It frightened him, the thought that she had remembered this small kindness for so long.

"That is why I do not care that you have no father." She leaned forward and kissed him. He had been relieved. It was their first kiss.

For years afterward, he regretted that he had not confessed to remembering the fight with Ishwar and the stolen book. But he had not known what he felt about his marriage. Not because of Padma's limp, but because his childhood was unfinished. Too many questions were left unanswered.

HE DID NOT WANT to accept Karak's offer. He did not even want to speak of it again. But that night after dinner, after the drinking, after Amarjeet fell asleep on his cot, when just he and Karak lay awake in the darkness, he could not help himself. "You have not made a fair allotment in your offer, Karak," he said. It was his pride talking. He had never before called Karak by only his first name.

For a long time there was no answer, and Ram thought he had fallen asleep. Then he heard Karak clear his throat. "What would be fair?"

"One-third to Eggenberger, one-third to you, one-third to me."

"That is very bold of you."

Ram was quiet.

"Has your status in life changed, bhai?" Karak said softly, with a chuckle.

Ram swallowed. "No, but neither has my knowledge of how to grow cotton in the desert, when to water and when not, how to have three harvests from one planting."

He hoped he had not gone too far. Karak lay on his back, saying nothing. If he had known Karak well then, Ram would have realized that the man was seething, his mind racing through all the things that he had done for Ram over the past year and a half, the money lent for Ishwar's medicine, the camaraderie on the ship, the iron kara gifted at the moment they parted, the hospitality at Jivan's home. He would have known that Karak had not understood Ram at all; that Karak's only concern was to not show weakness, or what others might think to be weakness.

Ram felt his anger mount. "I will be going tomorrow. Back to

Hambelton. I have been away for more than a week. They want me back."

He heard Karak's cot squeak as he shifted position. Unexpectedly, Ram felt his heart sink. He was freshly humiliated. Now he realized what he did not know before: he had hoped that Karak Singh would beg him to stay.

7

WHEN RAM WOKE, THE SKY WAS BRIGHT AND IT WAS ALREADY WARM. Karak's cot was empty. The night had brought strange dreams; he had walked—run—in woods like those surrounding Hambelton. An unfamiliar presence had wielded a hatchet. He had woken several times in a sweat, then felt clammy and cold in the summer night. Ram could still taste his terror on his tongue.

With relief, he saw Jivan Singh at the edge of the field, inspecting a portion of land with another man. Ram quickly washed and walked across the field to join them. He was hungry, but it was important, urgent, that he speak with Jivan. Now that his mind was made up, he needed to act.

As he approached, Jivan and the stranger turned toward him. He was an Anglo; despite the wide-brimmed hat, his cheeks were pink from the heat and sun. His hair was of that impossibly light shade, as if all natural color had been drained from it. Jivan said, in English, "Meet Clive Edgar, Mr. Eggenberger's land agent." He turned to Clive. "Ram is my cousin."

"You have more cousins than any man I know, Jivan," the man said loudly, laughing at his own words, holding out his hand.

Ram shook it, but addressed Jivan quickly, his heart beating inexplicably fast. He tried to keep his voice steady. "Bhai-ji, I hope you will excuse me," he said in Punjabi. "I am leaving suddenly. I must return to Hambelton."

If Jivan was surprised, he did not show it. "Something has happened?"

Ram felt caught between protecting Karak's dignity and telling the truth. He did not want to let Jivan know that Karak and he could not agree; that might seem petty. "I cannot keep—neglecting my duties. I have heard from people in Hambelton—my friend Pala Singh, who has been a great help to me—I must return." The explanation sounded false, even to himself. The words hung in the air between them.

Jivan glanced at the blond man. Clive had busied himself with inspecting the soil, not seeming to mind the conversation in Punjabi.

"Has Karak done something?" Jivan asked gently. Ram was surprised at Jivan's meaning. What did Jivan know of Karak that he did not?

"No, bhai-ji," Ram stuttered, shaking his head. He wondered where Karak was.

Jivan peered at him. "Clive and I have been assessing the salt content in the soil. It is a problem here. Do you have it in Lyallpur?"

"Bhai-ji," Ram said, breathing deeply, shifting his weight from one leg to another.

"Okay. Let it be." Jivan nodded, closing his eyes. "Don't let him dominate you, Ram."

Ram stood humbly, his arms in front of him, his left hand holding the right wrist, staring at the ground, unseeing. He was not saying goodbye to Jivan. He was requesting permission to leave.

Jivan must have realized this too. "If you are taking a good decision, then I should not put obstacles in your way. At least let me accompany you to the depot. I will be finished with my work in just two hours."

"Bhai-ji, do not trouble yourself. The train leaves very soon. I will ask Amarjeet."

Jivan looked pained. Ram did not yet know the pride Jivan felt in helping new settlers to the Valley. He had given the Khan brothers their first season's seed, lent them his Fresno scraper and mule. He had helped Harnam Singh raise his tent house and referred him to the loan officer at the Imperial Bank. Gugar Singh had stayed at the Eggenberger farm for three months before finding work in Holtville. Now Jivan put his hand on Ram's shoulder. "You can return at any time," he finally said. "What did I say when you first came? We are branches of the same tree."

Their eyes met, but Ram looked away. An emptiness swept over him, an intensity of emotion he did not know he possessed. He put his palms together. "Sat Sri Akal, bhai-ji."

He was rude to leave so abruptly. He was sorry that he would not see Jivan Singh again. He hoped the man would not think less of him.

AT THE HOUSE, Kishen was serving Amarjeet breakfast. Awkwardly, after he finished the meal, Ram told them he was leaving. "I have to go quickly," he said, "they need me back." He looked from one to the other. Leela sat on the floor, talking to her doll, but even she was silent at Ram's words.

"Amarjeet, will you send me off at the train?" he asked.

"What about Karak Chacha?"

"I told him last night. I cannot find him today."

He could feel the weight of Kishen Kaur's gaze. "Thank you, bhabhi-ji," he said quickly, palms together, not sure what was expected of his manners. "Please excuse my haste." She made a slight gesture of acknowledgment. "Goodbye, Leela," he said, bending down to the girl. She tolerated his hand tousling her hair, and smiled, as sweet as a sparrow.

DURING THE RIDE IN THE WAGON he told Amarjeet the same lie that he had told Jivan: that he had heard from his friend Pala and been called back to the mill. The lie sounded more believable this time. Even so, when Amarjeet asked innocently, "Did a telegram come?" he mumbled a response and commented instead on the strength of the wind.

Now he had begun to regret his decision, but the path toward his departure had been laid. He had lied to protect Karak. What else could he do?

Within a mile of town, images from his dreams of the previous night returned to him. Lamplight piercing the darkness. Jodh Singh crumpled on a bench. The snap of an axe splintering wood. Laughter. The sound wounded his ears.

Amarjeet was mouthing words he could not hear. Ram pressed his eyes shut and shook the images out of his brain. The day before he had felt like a coward for staying so long in Fredonia, and now he felt like a fool for returning to Hambelton.

"Ram-ji?" Amarjeet said. "Ram-ji?"

"Yes—"

"I said, it is funny Karak Chacha is not around and—"

"Yes. *Yes.*"

At the depot Amarjeet jumped from the wagon to tie the mules, but Ram insisted he leave. The more Ram insisted, the more Amarjeet objected, until at last Ram shouted, "Amarjeet—go!"

Confusion appeared on Amarjeet's face. He reluctantly climbed back on the wagon, gathered up the reins, and nudged the mules forward. He looked back, waving at Ram, until Ram could no longer tolerate it and took up his bag and blanket and crossed to the platform. He asked the clerk for a one-way ticket north, third class, and barely registered the clerk's response, the counting of his money, the giving of change. He did not understand why Amarjeet had grown so attached to him in such a short time.

The train arrived with the screech of metal against metal. The passenger cars were almost empty. He boarded, put his things on the seat beside him, and looked out the window. The car was searing hot. The train belched and groaned as the engine built up steam. The sound vibrated in his belly, his wounded chest.

In the safety of the train, for a moment, he felt calm. Karak had invited him to the Valley as his guest, had offered work and a partnership. No one in his uncle's household would have thought him worthy of such honor. He felt another flicker of regret. But Karak was *not* honoring him. How long had he been plotting? Since the moment Ram had shown off his knowledge on the steamship? The constant talk of his younger age, his lack of worldly knowledge . . . Forcing Ram to accept a lower profit . . . Was Ram not a man? Was he not worth more than that?

He remembered suddenly the long nights near the River Chenab, waiting by the canal for the water to flood his uncle's land. He would stand on the bank, awake but tired, carrying a spade, ready to use it against anyone who would try to divert the water before his uncle's allotment was full. That is what he would be doing here, again. Working hard to make another man rich. Karak was wrong; it would be years until he earned enough money to go home.

From the corner of his eye he saw movement on the platform, the glimpse of a scarlet dastar, then the hand at his window knocking hard. Karak was speaking to him, but the sound was muffled by the train's rumble, by the glass between them. Karak's face smiled at him—a crooked smile, a quick tilt of the head inviting him to come back out, as if nothing had happened. At first, Ram felt a flash of satisfaction. He breathed in a molecule of hope. Karak had come back for him. But the grin was false; the man was false.

He shook his head slightly, then looked at his hands in his lap, his palms that still bore the cuts from the attack. The train belched loudly. The wisps of steam swept past the window. The train shuddered. He would be gone soon. Karak's knuckles hit the window again, harder. He heard the man's voice inside his head. *You take things too seriously—such a naive boy.* Ram turned to look. Karak was

yelling. Ram did not know if he heard faint words or read his lips—
"Oye, come out! What are you doing in there?" A vein appeared on
the side of Karak's temple. He wasn't smiling now. Ram swallowed.
The train swayed, the beginning of the long passage north. The whistle blew like an alarm, blocking out all other sounds. Karak was still
mouthing words. Ram clenched his jaw.

He saw Karak run to the ticket stand, talk briefly to the man,
scribble on paper with a pen. The train nudged forward. Karak strode
in long steps to the platform. The paper appeared in the window,
slapped against the glass. *1/3, 1/3, 1/3.*

Ram stood and gathered his blanket, his bag. Wheels clicked
against metal track. He grasped the back of a bench to keep his
balance. At the door, the dust-wind caught his cheek. Wooden floor-
boards flashed past his foot. He jumped easily, landing at the western
edge of the platform.

20 July 1914

Meri Pyari,

I am writing after taking a big decision. I will stay in the Imperial Valley and farm cotton, which the Americans value as we do. It is a place much like our land in the colony outside Lyallpur. It is a desert that, through canal irrigation, has been made into fertile soil. Just as in our Canal Colonies, there is everything that a village could need: market, general store, school, banks, hospital with doctor, courthouse, inns. All of this has been built in just ten years.

But because it is America, the colony is even more advanced than ours. Here, they have even an electric generator. Think on it, Padma—our old villages in Punjab have existed for fourteen to fifteen generations, perhaps even since Time's beginning, and we do not have electricity, but this Fredonia colony does. Government, or maybe an industrialist, built the generator along with the settlement itself. Yesterday I was in the town as the sun was setting, and I saw the gleam of electric current shining through so many windows at once. The current is so different from the light of kerosene lamps that it seems a ghost has visited each home and place of work, lighting up the interior with its glow. And it does not cause one's eyes do not burn; one's breathing is clear . . . Like a fairy land . . . Padma-ji, can you imagine?

I must tell you that I hesitate about my decision. To make my uncertainty worse, last night I had a dream that I was living in a village that was not familiar to me, but it was also very familiar, as if the bricks of its buildings were made of the substance of my bones, as if its fields and roads were made of my

muscles and sinews. Then came a movement in the ground, as if
this village were not stable, as if its foundation were not built on
the earth, as if what I stood upon would move and shift. I woke
up and, despite the threat of snakes and scorpions, walked in
bare feet to the canal from where the water enters the cantaloupe
field. My heart was beating too fast. I stood there for a while in
the darkness—long enough that the moon changed its position
in the sky. Only then could I return and lie down on my cot. I
thought of you and imagined our son and it calmed me.

The day I took my decision, I had my supper as usual in Jivan
Singh's home. He congratulated me, but I said that I could not
accept unless Kishen Kaur, his wife, also extended an invitation.
Jivan Singh gave me a funny look, but then he called her to
come to the table and give her opinion on whether I should stay.
At first she would not, but Jivan pressed her and she answered
yes. The others cheered like boys playing kabaddi. I hope I did
not embarrass her. Sometimes our people here, after staying
away from Punjab for so long, have strange customs.

How is our son, Padma? Watch over him, take care of my
mother. I count the weeks until I return.

Your devoted husband,
Ram Singh

15 November 1914

My esteemed husband,
You flatter me by writing of your choice to stay in this
Imperial Valley. I know that whatever decision you take will be
only the best one. Why do you need bother with telling me? Yet
I am happy to hear of it. That you are staying with a family of
our people. That you will have something of a home. Last month
when Father went to the district headquarters, I asked him to
find information on this Imperial Valley. He came back saying

it was a new place, a good place. Of course I know you will
find success in farming, for that comes naturally to us and is our
honorable lot in life.

   Husband, you will be glad to know this. We have finished with
our son's naming ceremony. Uncle has chosen a name: Santosh.
What do you think of it, my husband? I am so anxious to know
your thoughts and feelings. I believe that Mother-in-Law may
have believed it to be proper for her grandson to have such a happy
name. When Uncle whispered it into his ear, in front of the sacred
fire with everyone watching, our son laughed. I would not lie to
you. It was a small affair, but still, I was proud. What mother is
not proud at her son's first birthday? Yet, you were missing. You,
who are the only person who should be present most of all, even
more than me—a son's father.

   Yesterday I was remembering the circumstances of his birth.
You did not know this, husband, but when he was born there
was so much blood, and I had a great wound, and the midwife
did not believe that it would heal properly. Of course our son's
spirit is so large there must be something to mark his arrival! The
midwife summoned four villagers to carry me in a palanquin
to the hospital. It is only four miles distant, as you remember, so
it was not too strenuous. At the time I did not think this at all
important, dear husband, but I am writing it now in case you
should hear of it later from others, and wonder that I did not
tell you. My health is good and all that happened before is of no
consequence and there is never any cause for you to worry about
me here. I would not lie to you.

   You have told me that you have been sending money to
Uncle. This makes me happy, but not at all for my sake. I care
only that it puts you in a good light, that your reputation is good
and strong.

                              Theri—,
                              Padma

PART TWO

East Indians are the least desirable race of immigrants to have in the community. They are industrious, but not adaptable, and require a great deal of supervision in order that the work may be properly done.

—*Immigrants in Industries,* United States Immigration Commission report, 1910

Why do we feel low and humiliated?

—Ghadar protest song

8

SEPTEMBER 1914

IN THE VALLEY, BEFORE AND AFTER THE GREAT FLOOD, EVERYONE HAD come from somewhere else. This is what Jivan told Ram when he asked. Five thousand people lived there, about seven hundred in the town of Fredonia itself. Over the past weeks, since Ram had decided to stay, Jivan thought he asked too many questions, like a boy, like a naive lad, even though he was married. Jivan listed the places they had come from, the people who came: Germans, Chinese, Greeks, Filipinos, Swiss, Portuguese, Japanese, Italians, Irish, the Africans who had been slaves, moving west from Dixie because freedom had not yet arrived. The Texans and Kansans and New Yorkers. Of course, the Mexicans, who had once owned it, and the natives too, who knew the land best of all.

Jivan and Ram were in the wagon, going to town to pick up a seeder that had been repaired. Ram had insisted on driving. "But how did they know there would be work for them?" Ram asked. "Why would they come when the river had destroyed so much?"

"They came to help hold the river back. It was the reason they came. The entire country knew the dam had broken and the land was flooded. The Imperial Land Company did not know what to do. The Valley towns were new, some of them did not have even a post office. Most everything was built only with wood and canvas. Some families lived in tents. Shacks served as bank, hospital, jailhouse. They were swept away. Gone just like this." He flicked his hand. "The water took them. Every day, I saw a wagon being carried off, sometimes horses and cows—one time, a man. So many fields completely flooded. Roads and paths gone."

"Seeing it now, bhai-ji, it seems impossible," Ram said.

"Everybody living here labored to hold the river back, rich and poor, women and even children. We used shovels to keep piling dirt on top of dirt to make levees. But still more workers came to build jetties and new embankments. Government paid them, fed them, made places for them to sleep."

"Who would come for such a job?" Ram said.

Jivan was struck by the boy's innocence. Had he never known real hardship? He was clicking to the mules now, urging them ahead, unaware of the insult he had given.

"I would," Jivan said.

The boy glanced at him, brushed his hair away from his dark eyes. "Forgive me, bhai-ji."

Yes, the boy was naive, but Jivan liked his deference.

"So many different people living together?" Ram continued, more cautiously, it seemed. "By their own choice?"

"Why not? For two days without sleep I bailed water to protect the power generator, side by side with the sheriff. We hauled sacks filled with gravel to make barricades. We kept the water back. I was so exhausted. From that time on he has been a friend to me. He introduced me to Stephen Eggenberger, and Stephen gave me a place to live and eat and work."

HE HAD COME TO ESCAPE. That is what Jivan told Ram when he asked. They were once again clearing the silt in the irrigation canal, heaving the mixed weight of soil and water.

"Escape from what?" the boy asked.

"Escape the death of my son," Jivan said, surprising himself with his honesty. "He would have been your age."

The boy was quiet. He and Jivan both knew he did not know what to say. Jivan let the silence linger.

"So bhabhi-ji came then too?" Ram finally said.

"No. After he died, I did not want Kishen Kaur with me." Jivan thrust the shovel into the brown ooze. He felt perspiration trickle through his hair, seep to the cotton edge of his dastar. "But I knew my duty. And I did not want to be tempted here. I did not want to look at other women. In 1910, I went back to fetch her. My brother sent Amarjeet with me then."

"You *wanted* to live here, bhai-ji, to settle here? You stayed on purpose among strangers?"

"Stephen gave me land to sharecrop. He introduced me to men who operated the banks, who knew the laws, who controlled the water in the canals." Jivan stared into the soil, the wet grains of sand in the dryness of the desert. "I did not know such people in Ludhiana. Why should I not stay?" he said. But he knew the boy came from a better family than his, and might not understand.

"THERE IS A PLACE FOR US HERE." That is what Jivan told the boy when he asked again. They sat in a circle of dim lamplight on the porch, breathing in the sting of kerosene. The desert night pressed against the screen. Ram, who had been reading the Ghadar paper, had just flung it aside.

"They need us," Jivan said. "Nothing here is settled yet. Fredonia is only seven years old. Brawley and Calexico are only slightly older.

They need us to cultivate the soil, to build the towns. In Mexicali, Chandler hired three hundred Chinese to dig the canal from the river. Everyone says he did not want white workers."

Something in the Ghadar paper had agitated the boy. Jivan unfolded it and spread it out on the table. He pointed to a string of Punjabi letters, then felt a familiar surge of shame. "I read too slowly," he said, not meeting the boy's gaze. "It is difficult for me—" Understanding flashed across the boy's face. He leaned over the paper quickly—more quickly than Amarjeet ever had—and began to read out loud. Jivan felt a tinge of relief.

HINDUSTANI WORKERS ATTACKED AND EXPELLED. ONE MAN DEAD. NO PROTECTION PROVIDED. There was a photo of a mill worker. Jivan saw Ram swallow; his face turned pale.

"What is it?" Jivan asked, but the boy ignored him.

"'In Hambelton, Washington, on the night of July fifth, men attacked the homes of five hundred Hindustani work—'" Ram's voice quivered. There was the slightest intake of breath. "'Police were approached for help. Our countrymen were locked up in the city hall basement and told it was for their own protection—'"

Ram stopped reading, but his eyes did not leave the paper. The night closed in on them. The hum of cicadas swelled, then receded.

"Ram?"

Ram shook his head. "Bhai-ji," he said quickly, then read more. "'One countryman had a broken leg, another a—'" Ram took out his handkerchief and wiped his forehead. "'We at Ghadar say—Is this not the country that promises freedom? Are we not entitled to life, liberty, the pursuit of happiness? Are we not men?'" Ram sat staring at the paper, silent.

In Jivan's mind, the events came together like the parts of a machine, precise and metal cold. Suddenly, he knew. "You were there, son," he said.

The boy turned his dark eyes toward Jivan, but they were without feeling. Years ago, while commanding a regiment in the North China Plain, Jivan had seen that same emptiness on his cavalrymen's faces.

"No," Ram said.

Jivan blinked.

The boy glanced at him. "I was there, bhai-ji," he said, looking away, but he need not have. Jivan understood the boy's lie, his silence about his wounds. He understood all of it.

"You are not at fault." Jivan clasped Ram's shoulder. "Remember that," he said. Ram walked off quickly, leaving him alone in the circle of lamplight.

WAR HAD BROKEN OUT in Europe. For a short while, a very short while, Britain was not involved, then she too entered, bringing along her dominions, colonies, and protectorates—a quarter of the world's population, cultivating a quarter of the world's land. In early September, Jivan received a letter from San Francisco from a man he had never met but whose name he knew. That Sunday afternoon he went to Fredonia Park, where Malik Khan sat under a ramada, speaking of his village to thirty others lounging on benches and blankets on the ground, enjoying the shade. He was relaying news of a couple who had eloped, only to be captured a day later by men sent from the village panchayat. It was the time of week when the local Anglos left the park to the Hindu farmers. Jivan stepped through the gate and the men stopped talking. The youngest, a fourteen-year-old from Hoshiarpur, stood up.

Jivan Singh addressed them without taking a seat. "Pandit Ram-Chandra Bharadwaj of the Ghadar Party is coming from San Francisco," he announced. The men listened intently. RamChandra was now the president of the party, and worthy of respect. "He has written to me with a request to hold a meeting. Next Sunday, please come to my home. He will give a talk."

The men looked at each other. "Bhai-ji, if I may," Malik Khan spoke up, "we thought your beliefs did not mix with the Ghadars'?"

Jivan paused. He had not realized his views were so well known.

"There is no harm in hearing what a man has to say," Jivan said. He wanted to believe this was true. The leader of the Ghadar Party had approached him. He could not say no.

"What time shall we come, bhai-ji?" Harnam Singh asked.

"Afternoon, one o'clock is fine. Tell the others," he said, knowing they would all come.

He did not tell them what else RamChandra had written in the letter—*Bhai, I do not know your feelings on all matters, but your help to our countrymen has not been exceeded by another on this Pacific shore*—or how proud Jivan was when Ram read to him these words.

PANDIT RAMCHANDRA BHARADWAJ WAS a dignified man, with a thick mustache and oiled hair, disembarking from the first-class section of the Sunday-morning express along with the white businessmen, arriving in the desert heat dressed in a vest with jacket and tie. The man spoke with the accent of the Punjabi officers in the British Indian Army, or the civil servants who worked as engineers and accountants in district offices. Meeting him, Jivan was conscious of his own dungarees, his rough hands, of the shaky wagon in which they rattled home, the dust that covered them by arrival. Jivan addressed him as pandit-ji even though Jivan was his elder. RamChandra asked for a moment to refresh himself. With relief, Jivan showed him the bedroom in the Eggenberger house, which Kishen had swept clean the day before.

RamChandra emerged an hour later in a crisp and starched red cotton kurta and white churidar. He had fastened the collar on this simple dress with gold buttons and chain. Jivan had doubts about the man's expected lecture, had hopes that he would not talk about revolution, but approved of this transformation; suddenly, Pandit RamChandra had become familiar.

The Indian men of the Imperial Valley arrived by early afternoon in a stream of wagons, on horseback, on buckboards, even in a gleaming Model T, the dust rising on the path to the Eggenberger farm. Under Jivan's direction, Amarjeet told them to leave the vehicles in a fallow field in the back, where the gathering remained hidden from the road. The men arrived red-faced, with glistening skin, sweat-dampened shirts carrying the scent of physical exertion. Heat was trapped inside dastars and beards.

Amarjeet watered their horses while the guests stepped over crusted dirt, gathered under a large tent with open sides. They settled themselves on the rented wooden chairs that stood in long rows facing east. Behind them were tables with vessels of food, some of which Kishen and Ram had cooked, others that had been brought by the men themselves: bowls of lentils, fried vegetables, chicken curry, and goat korma.

More than two hundred men had come from the surrounding towns, and Jivan Singh knew them all. He had lent them farming implements, recommended them for loans, found them work. He had been their sardar and protector in an unfamiliar land. They greeted Kishen with humility, with palms pressed together, addressing her as chachi-ji, bringing her dishes to the tables and pouring water for other guests, things they would not have done in Punjab. It was not often that they gathered like this: all the countrymen living in older Calexico and younger Niland and all the fields and towns that lay in between.

They would not quiet down. Not even after their plates were emptied of food. Not even when Karak laughed with a small group in the back—"Make your tongues quiet or I'll cut them out and dump you in the pond." Only after RamChandra emerged from the Eggenberger house and appeared under the tent did the men, realizing him to be a stranger, sensing his importance, grow still.

Jivan introduced him. "Today Pandit RamChandra Bharadwaj

has chosen to speak at this humble home." Jivan faltered; he did not know what the man would speak about. "May some of his light shine on us."

RamChandra took his place in front of the gathering. Jivan felt a flash of disappointment; he was without a warrior's build, and perhaps unmanly. But when he opened his mouth to speak, when the attention of all was upon him, something great, something beyond the air of the Imperial Valley settled upon them.

"How many of you men are missing your families?" he asked, in the lilt of educated Punjabi, the language of a man who had read many books, who had spoken with political leaders, who had published newspapers read by the elite. "This man"—he indicated Jivan—"is also your family. For each of you, he has done some supreme good, just as your father would do. But tell me, are you not sick with the absence of your children and wives, who can never join you?"

Jivan stood to the side and watched as the men shifted their bodies. RamChandra had struck upon the quiet truth that bound them together. Perhaps his talk would not be about revolution after all.

"The American government will not allow them to come, yet *other* men, from *other* countries, bring *their* families. The Irish, the Germans, the Swiss—any European is accompanied by his bride. Or they tell their sweethearts, before they leave for this shore, 'Wait for me. I will send for you.' Even the Mexican, the African, the man from Japan may bring a wife.

"Just like these others, we Hindustanees have come to America for betterment." His eyes scanned the gathering, as if he spoke to each man about his particular concerns. "But after arrival, we become the target of race prejudice. We are not invited into restaurants, or theater halls, or homes. The locals give us trouble in the streets and knock our dastars to the ground. They publish newspaper articles against us."

The men were quiet. Every one had experienced the truth of RamChandra's words.

"What is the difference between us and them? As men, there is no difference. Thomas Jefferson, the great American patriot, the third president, wrote these words in English, but I will say them in Punjabi: All men are created equal. We have certain inalienable rights. In the course of human events, it sometimes becomes necessary for one people to dissolve the bonds which connect them to another.

"These noble words describe a nation made of people with similar ideals. They have nothing to do with being of the same blood, or coming from the same soil. If that were the criteria, then only the native tribes should be here now.

"We are not treated as equals in America. We are not treated as men. I ask you, my brothers—why? We have all heard about Hambelton; our men were ripped from their bunkhouses and beaten with sticks and bats." Jivan craned his neck and searched for Ram among the crowd. He was seated in a corner near Kishen. His face had grown pale.

RamChandra went on. "They were pulled from their workstations at the mills. The police knew of this but instead of doing their work, they locked up our innocent countrymen in the city hall jail and said it was for their own protection! The next day they took them to the depot and told them to board a train and leave the town."

A murmur went through the crowd. Jivan turned to the audience. No one had known that the police had escorted the Indians to the depot. Jivan felt a flush of foreboding. The gathering could not—should not—be pricked and prodded into rage on the soil of his farm.

But RamChandra did not seem bothered by the heightened feeling. His face was glistening. From out of the pocket of his kurta he plucked an embroidered handkerchief and dabbed his forehead. "When we at Ghadar heard of this, I made an appeal to the British consulate in San Francisco. After all, we are all British citizens, are we not? I demanded their help in bringing the rioters to justice. Do you know what they did?"

The audience looked toward him eagerly.

"Nothing."

Once again, a murmur spread among the men.

"If we were white men from their country, or even white Canadians, or white Australians, how much they would have helped us!"

Jivan's jaw clenched.

"That is when I knew the British were not, and could never be, our rightful government!"

Some of the men nodded. RamChandra wiped his brow again and spoke more slowly. "Then, a second insult. The *Komagata Maru*." He whispered the words.

"Who among you has not heard about this ship? The steamer carried 376 of our countrymen, including two women, along with several children, across the Pacific Ocean to Vancouver. But when the ship reached the Canadian shore, the passengers were not permitted to dock. Already they had spent thirty-nine days at sea, but they were made to stay on board the ship in the harbor, and they were not provided enough food and water. Brothers! They were healthy when they arrived at the harbor! The immigration officials did not find any illness on board! But by the time they were forced to depart, they were sick and weak. In that condition, they are now journeying for weeks on the open ocean back to Calcutta. The Canadian government gave them food only after they submitted and agreed to turn back! Is it not cruel! Is it not unjust!

"I ask you—how many of you have on board that ship a cousin, a village-mate, a brother?"

As Jivan looked, four people raised their hands. Then he, slowly, raised his own. He had grown up in the same village as one of the men who had been listed on the ship's manifest. The man was older than him by only a few seasons. Their families had known each other for generations; for years their mothers had chattered and yelled to each other from their huts, sometimes as friends, sometimes as enemies.

RamChandra continued: "Canada is a dominion of the British Empire. When an Indian journeys to Canada, he is a British subject traveling from British soil to British soil. But our people were not allowed to land. And the British consulate did not help us. Would a ship of white passengers have been treated the same way? Is this anything other than race prejudice of the white man against the brown man?"

Jivan was suddenly alarmed. To speak so openly of race prejudice—and on Stephen Eggenberger's land—that felt like betrayal. What if Clive suddenly arrived and saw this gathering of Hindustanees and learned their purpose? What if he informed Stephen? The landlord had always been kind to him—but still. What if the sheriff came to know? Jivan breathed deeply to settle himself.

"The false peacefulness of the British Empire has made us impotent. The British tell us that being a citizen of their realm gives us greater freedom than we would have as mere Indians, but at every turn, they fail to represent us."

Jivan stood, placed his hands on his waist, and approached RamChandra. Perhaps if he stepped close to the man, RamChandra would understand his discomfort and end his talk.

"In their British army, we serve as a subjugated race, helping them to subjugate other races. We serve as a colonized people, helping them control other colonies! We fight their wars, we build their railroads and bridges and farm their empire. We do the work the slave used to do! We replaced the African slaves when the slave trade was ended! Even now, we are fighting their war in Europe, which is of no concern to us. This is the global color line, my brothers! That everywhere around the world, the red man, the yellow man, the brown man, the black man . . . will be subjugated by the white man. This is the global color line!"

"Zulum!" someone yelled in the audience. "A crime! Zulum!" All the men began to talk at once, shouting, yelling.

It was a harangue, Jivan realized. He should have foreseen it. How could he end it now without embarrassing himself before these men?

"You all know—these Americans are full of hypocrisy. For the white man stole this continent from the red man who existed here before him, depriving him of every right. You will say, every day the white man subjugates the black man as if he were not human at all. You will say, the white man attacks us and robs our possessions even though we do good work at a too-low wage, a wage no white man would take, building the railroads for their travel, providing the lumber for their cities. Yet we cannot bring our wives and children with us, so that we may lead good and moral family lives! You say, America is not so different from Britain. They speak of equality for all people but they will not act to bring it about. Here is the truth, my comrades: the equality cult of these western democracies has rung hollow! Hollow!

"I am young and am not filled with your life knowledge. But I know that the ideal of equality itself cannot ring hollow. We Indians must have an equal nation. We must have a separate country. We must govern ourselves and stop our humiliation under British rule! Jai Hind! My brothers! Jai Hind!"

"Jai Hind!" A few men took up the cry. RamChandra paused. He dabbed his forehead with the handkerchief. The men quieted down.

"Pandit-ji," Jivan said. But the man seemed not to have heard him.

"Now Britain is at war in Europe," RamChandra continued. "She is distracted and weakened. We Hindustanees must return to Hindustan and take up arms against the oppressor!"

Fear clutched at Jivan. It had been years since he had fought in the British Indian Army, but he could not easily forget the pledge he had made. From across the tent, he saw Karak, Ram, Amarjeet, Kishen even, looking at him.

"That is why I ask now," RamChandra continued, "who will join me in this fight to free India? Who will go back to our mother-land and take up guns and rifles, link our arms—Sikh, Hindu, and Mussulman—and free our country? Who will rise up against the global color line and show the white man that they do not lead us, we lead ourselves! Who shall put muscle behind our salute, 'Vande Mataram'? I ask you now—who will join us and fight? Become a hero, perhaps a martyr?"

The audience was shouting now, "Vande Mataram! Vande Mataram!"

"Pandit-ji—" Jivan said, courteous.

"The time is now, my brothers!"

"Pandit-ji!" Jivan said again, loudly, in the voice of command. "Stop this! I cannot allow it!" But he could barely be heard.

RamChandra held up his fist. His eyes grew wide with emotion. "Ferenghi maro!"

"Kill the foreigner! Ferenghi maro!"

Others took up the cry.

With two long strides Jivan placed himself between RamChandra and his audience. Some of the men began to take up the chant. "It is enough," Jivan shouted, his voice booming. "It is enough! Let us finish now." He turned to the men, indicated the tables. "Come. Take some more food," he commanded.

RamChandra's eyes darted from Jivan to the audience. "If I have given offense with my words, I beg your pardon," he said. He wiped his forehead again. He held his arms out wide, ignoring Jivan, shouting once more. "If any would join our just cause—stand! Stand now!"

There was a heated silence. A gust lifted sand from the scrub and swept it under the tent, stinging the men's eyes. Jivan's heartbeat echoed in the stillness. Then, slowly, in the back, Atta Singh stood up. Jivan felt faint. Ali Khan rose too. And Pakker Dillon. By the end, thirty men had stood.

"IT HAS GONE WELL for Ghadar today," Karak said that evening. Some of the guests had not left until after sundown. The Singhs and RamChandra sat in the dark, drinking Karak's whiskey. "So many new recruits. And money too."

"We raised almost three thousand dollars," RamChandra said.

He was no longer in front of an audience, and Jivan felt the man diminished, false, a viper in his own home. In the corner, sitting outside the circle of lamplight, his nephew watched and listened. He had been quiet ever since RamChandra had finished his lecture.

"Pandit-ji," Ram said quietly.

"Brother." RamChandra turned his full attention on Ram. His eyes were kind.

"I had two friends in Hambelton. Pala Singh, Shahpur village—"

"Pala Singh with hazel eyes?"

"Yes."

Jivan and Karak exchanged a glance. Jivan had not told Karak about Ram's fleeing the riot, but now he saw that Karak knew.

"He has joined the cause and sailed for Burma with some comrades," RamChandra said. "He will join up with others in Japan."

"He is in Burma?" Ram asked. To Jivan, he appeared relieved.

"Pala Singh is a very brave man."

"And Shahpur Jodh Singh?" Ram asked, more boldly now.

RamChandra's face darkened. "You know him?"

"Yes."

"He could not join," RamChandra said. "He was greatly injured—"

"How?" Ram asked, too quickly.

"His arm. He has gone to the gurdwara in Stockton to recover. Maybe he'll stay there permanently, if the granthi can find work for him. He cannot use his arm again."

Ram was quiet.

"You know those men well?" RamChandra asked.

"We worked together at the lumber mill. Please—tell Jodh Singh on my behalf that I wish him well."

"Pandit-ji." Amarjeet's voice came from the darkness. "If someone wants to join, what should we do first?"

"What?" Jivan turned to his nephew, but the boy refused to meet his eye.

"I want to join Ghadar," Amarjeet said to RamChandra.

RamChandra's glance darted between nephew and uncle.

"I do not give you permission," Jivan said. His voice sounded like gravel.

Amarjeet shrank, his eyes wide with humiliation.

"His father might be quite pleased that he went in service of his people," RamChandra said. "For the cause of our freedom."

"What do you know of his father, pandit-ji?" Jivan felt the weight of RamChandra's gaze. "Over the past ten years I have tried to form a settlement of our people here, with homes, maybe families. You are needlessly sending these men to their deaths. Freedom will not be bought in the manner you think," he said, sharply.

"Needless deaths?" RamChandra raised his eyebrows. "How shall we gain our freedom then? By remaining loyal servants of the British army?"

"India is not yet ready to throw off the British. By fighting in the European war, we can prove ourselves worthy of self-rule within the empire."

"Dominion status! Like Canada? Like Australia? White settler countries?"

"Like South Africa!" Jivan countered.

"I did not know you felt this way, bhai-ji," RamChandra said.

Jivan refused to be belittled. "You did not ask. I did not tell you." The air was still.

"It's growing late," Karak murmured. "Time for rest," he said, rising.

THE ARGUMENT STILL BURDENED JIVAN at breakfast the next morning. The household had risen early. Kishen Kaur had made a large and delicious breakfast in honor of their guest, and all of them ate together quietly. Jivan wished he had been more politic the evening before; now he wanted to rid himself of the man. "Pandit-ji," he said, "it is no trouble for me to take you to the depot."

RamChandra blinked. He took another bite and chewed slowly, as if he did not know how to respond. "Yes, that will be quite good," he finally said. That was how Jivan knew that he had not planned to leave that morning at all.

"Ram, come with us," Jivan said. It was not a request. He could feel Amarjeet's glare, but he was determined that he would not ask the boy.

Jivan need not have worried. RamChandra was a sophisticated man. He did not approach Amarjeet again. On the ride into town, he filled the time with questions about how the Valley towns had been formed, how Jivan had come to settle on the farm. He asked Ram about the development of the Canal Colonies in western Punjab.

At the depot, the men waited on the platform in the farthest corner. Few locals could see them. "Khair nal jao," Jivan said, determined to maintain propriety. RamChandra nodded. The man expressed no gratitude and Jivan felt his resentment rise.

In the wagon on the way home, Jivan's mood sat heavy upon both Ram and himself. "Tell me," Jivan finally said. "Did you give him any money?" RamChandra had walked among the men himself, holding a wooden collection box. In the throng, Jivan could not see who had donated.

"No, bhai-ji."

"Why not?" He did not meet Ram's eye.

"I send all my money home. My uncle is in need of all of it."

The answer mollified him, but at the farm, he asked Karak too.

"I gave," Karak said.

"How much?"

"Forty dollars."

Silence. Forty dollars could have bought a new buggy or a harness for the mules, which was sorely needed. Jivan was shocked. Even more, it bothered him that Karak did not defer to him by hiding the truth.

"You are angry about Amarjeet," Karak said. "But a boy wants adventure. I was no different. Perhaps you were not either."

"What do you know of me, Karak?" Jivan said, feeling betrayed.

EVERY EVENING Amarjeet read to the family a stream of news stories happening in other places: from the *Los Angeles Times,* or the *Fredonia News,* or the *Ghadar*—filling the darkness with his clear English, or with Punjabi, translating between them for Kishen and Ram— tales of a world gone mad. Jivan could feel the boy's resentment. He read without looking at him, as if every word were an accusation against his uncle.

By September's end he read to them of the French and British fighting the Germans at the River Aisne, trenches that stretched for miles. The thousands of dead.

He read about Britain's army recruiters desperately traveling to the same Punjabi villages that they had visited in June. They assured the villagers that dastars could be worn in service and promised regular wages. They reminded the Punjabis to show their loyalty to Government, of how much the British had done for them.

He read that the *Komagata Maru* had been diverted from Calcutta's port and forced to anchor off the town of Budge Budge. British officers searched passengers and ship for copies of the Ghadar newspaper, for arms, for other seditious items, but found none. They demanded the Indians board a train to Punjab, but most refused. Passengers tried to deliver the ship's holy book to the local gurdwara. Officers forced them back with guns. Passengers tried to chant the sacred rehras while seated near the dock. Police beat them with lathis. Passengers tried to escape the beating, escape the gunshots, escape the bloodshed. Many succeeded but some failed. Bystanders died too, Indian and English. By twilight, twenty-six bodies lay at odd angles on the dock and shoreline, their blood mixing with waters that would run, eventually, into the sacred Ganga.

In the desert darkness, Amarjeet identified those who were killed. "Ishar Singh. Arjan Singh. Ratan Singh . . ." He read slowly, shaping his tongue around all twenty names, allowing each their dignity. Last, he mentioned Mastan Singh, from their own village.

When he heard the final name, Jivan leaned forward in his chair. The ground beneath him seemed to rumble and move. He stood, placed his whiskey glass on the table, and escaped the circle of lamplight, leaving the others to wonder after him.

Jivan woke early in a moonless morning. The household was still asleep. His mind went to the scene from the previous night. Mastan Singh had shared his boyhood with Jivan, had been his older brother's playmate, had saved Jivan when he had fallen into a well at the age of six. Jivan was tempted to say that the dead man was in the wrong. Hadn't the British built the railways, dug the irrigation canals, gifted land, brought civility? He was tempted to proclaim that Government should eradicate the disloyal wherever they found them, for the supreme cause of political stability. But he could not. He opened the safe that stood in his bedroom and gathered his cavalry medals.

They were firm, solid in his palm. He had been awarded the first in Shandong Province for taking an injury to his leg while saving a comrade. He earned the second for discovering guerrillas who lay in wait by the roadside. The third and fourth were for taking charge of his unit in Shanghai when the commanding Risaldar had been struck down.

Jivan tucked the medals into the front pocket of his dungarees and saddled the mare. In his mind, he heard RamChandra's nasal voice. He rode north toward the Chocolate Mountains, headed northwest at Niland, and arrived at the Salton Sea by late morning. In his gut, he felt the truth of Ghadar's global color line. Anglos had not arrived first to the Imperial Valley. The Kumeyaay had been here thousands of years before, but still, they did not matter. He thought of his commanding officers, little things they had said, a telling expression on a familiar face. He'd thought they had respected him, but now he was not sure. He knew he was an uneducated man; he knew math enough to live but he did not know letters well. Perhaps that explained it. When he reached the edge of the water, the sun was high.

Jivan held the medals and felt himself transported. Not to Shandong Province, but to the creature he was before—before the graying California farmer, before the cavalry officer, before the young bridegroom, before the newly enlisted lad—to the scrappy boy on a dirt path, fetching water for his mother's cooking.

He shuddered. He dismounted and stood by the briny water. He breathed in and filled his lungs. The sky was large, overpowering. Who belongs in what place on this earth? The British did not belong in India; the thought came to him clearly. Perhaps he did not belong in the Imperial Valley either. Years ago, he had witnessed the river filling the basin to form this inland sea, so large that a man could stand on the edge and see a liquid horizon, imagine a tide. Tears filled his eyes, but he did not know for whom, or for what. He felt light. He felt correct. One by one, he grasped the medals, rubbed the inscriptions with his thumb, and flung each into the water.

9

OCTOBER 1914

RAM SAT WITH THE OTHER MEN NEAR THE BACK PORCH. THE DAY'S WORK was finished, but light lingered in the sky. Leela ran behind the house to her father. "Pita-ji! Pita-ji!" she shouted. "Man has come!" Her voice seemed worried.

"Which man, Leela?" Jivan asked.

"Agent man."

"Ah," Jivan nodded. He had been carving a doll for her third birthday, and now he put the wood block aside and rose immediately to greet the visitor. Karak retrieved a glass. Amarjeet fetched another chair. But when Jivan returned with the guest, Ram saw that it was only Clive Edgar, Eggenberger's land man, whom he had met the morning he had almost left Fredonia.

"John," the agent said, nodding at Jivan, extending his hand.

"We were expecting you, Clive, my friend," Karak said, standing, holding an empty glass in his right hand and a bottle in his left.

"'Bout to drink it up?" Clive said. He was even larger than Ram remembered, grinning aggressively, cheeks and neck splotched with sunburned pink.

"I'll get the books," said Jivan, heading inside.

Clive nodded at Amarjeet. "Amjee," he said, hesitating with the name. No one bothered to correct him. Clive's enormous hand grasped Karak's. He did not glance at Ram. "Thought you might be laying off for a while, Karak, after your performance last week." Ram knew Karak would sometimes see Clive in Mexicali, where he visited the bars and Chinatown south of the boundary. He sometimes asked Ram to come with him, but Ram would always say no.

"That was five nights past," Karak said, smiling, drawing himself up, his chest expanding. "Here is a new night."

Ram wondered what had happened then. What was this relationship Karak had with the Anglo?

Clive chuckled, removing his hat as the light grew faint. "A man can always expect a good time with you boys."

Jivan walked back with the ledger. With only his eyes, Karak indicated to Clive that the evening was not to be spoken about. Jivan opened the book to the correct page and laid it on the table. Karak poured whiskey into Clive's glass. Clive opened his satchel, found his own ledger, copied numbers from the book that Jivan had laid out. "These look really good, John." He whistled in admiration. "You boys did good."

"Season was good," Jivan said. "Everywhere cantaloupe numbers up in Valley."

"But yours are better than the others."

"Could be," Jivan said lightly. His lips peeled back into a smile, reluctantly given.

"But now you goin' into cotton?"

"Not me," Jivan said. "Them." He lifted his chin toward Ram and Karak.

Clive's eyes met Ram's for the first time. Ram quickly turned to

Karak; he had been understanding most of the English conversation but hesitated to speak.

"Why you going into cotton, Karak? It's loco."

"Why not?" Karak said.

"Nobody knows how it'll do. Why not just stick with canta-loupe, squash, tomatoes, peas? Cantaloupe's bringing in a haul."

"Cantaloupe will be having a glut again," Karak said. "I feel that. With the war in Europe, cotton market will be high."

Clive leaned back in his chair. "I'd just stick with something that's bringing a profit."

"For two years, Wilsie Ranch making money only with cotton. Why not me? Jake Smiley at the gin is quoting ten cents a pound."

"Don't matter to me, Karak. Mr. E says that between what you and Tom Moriyama brought in this year, he's the richest man in the Valley without doing a lick of work himself."

Karak's eyes flashed. "Is it so?" His lips curled into a smile, gener-ous, vindictive. He leaned forward to refill Clive's glass. Ram won-dered if Clive knew that Karak was offended.

"But not Roubillard?" Karak asked.

"Not Roubillard." Ram had heard about this man from Louisi-ana, who was leasing a third portion of Eggenberger land, bordering the fields on which he and Karak would grow their cotton.

Karak gulped his whiskey. "How is digging on the Highline?" he said.

"Land Office says they won't finish that section of the canal for two more springs, at the earliest."

"Still that long," Karak said.

Through the night air, against the chirping crickets, they heard the jingle of bridles. Amarjeet rose and peered around to the front. "It's Harry and Mr. Moriyama," he announced, smiling. The boy liked company, Ram thought.

Two figures appeared around the corner of the house. Ram's gut clenched. He had never talked to the Japanese lumberjacks in

Hambelton. He had not liked the humming efficiency of their work gangs, their arrogant aloofness, how they deferred to the Anglos while ignoring the other workers.

The boy grinned at Amarjeet. The father approached Clive first, extending his hand.

Clive rose to shake it. "Howdy, Tom," Clive said.

"Haruo say Mr. Clive come from town." Tomoya's eyes went to the boy, who had already seated himself near Amarjeet. "Good to say hello to you all." He grinned. "I hope to see you do this." He indicated the bottle sitting on the table. The men laughed.

Jivan rose and offered Tomoya his seat.

"Meet my countryman, Ram," Jivan said.

Tomoya extended his hand, and Ram hurried to offer his own; he could not disappoint Jivan. The father shook Ram's hand with the smallest of bows. His broad face was weather-beaten, sun-lined, but he carried himself like a younger man. Ram did not like the touch of his skin, but for Jivan's sake, he tried to hide his feelings. Perhaps Tomoya sensed them anyway, because he did not look at Ram again.

Karak handed the Japanese man a full glass. Tomoya took a sip.

"We are talking the Highline Canal," Jivan said. "How many years do you say?"

"At least three," said Tomoya.

Karak shook his head.

"Not enough people working," Tomoya insisted.

"With only Indians and Mexican labor, we'll be lucky if we get it in three," Clive said. "Mañana this, mañana that. Not like you boys. You bring it in, I'll say that much." Clive took a sip. "You too, Tom."

Ram saw Jivan take in a breath, glance at Karak. But Karak seemed unperturbed.

"How is your mother, Clive?" Karak asked.

"Pretty good, thanks for asking." A smile spread over his face. Ram saw that he was a young man. He hadn't realized this before, not with the height, the ringing voice, the roughness. "I guess you boys should know—I'm getting married." The smile spread into a broad grin.

"Hey, hey!" Karak said, clapping him on the back.

"Congratulations," Tomoya said.

"Becoming a responsible member." Jivan raised his glass.

Ram felt a pressing need to say something—"You must give us some sweet." He put the English words together slowly.

Clive looked at him.

"That custom is not followed here," Jivan said lightly, in Punjabi. "They don't share sweet foods when giving good news."

"No, no, that is a Punjabi custom," Karak said in English, grinning. "Us Hindus—you know, Clive." He turned to Ram. "Here in America, we drink to the bride." He poured more whiskey, ignoring Ram's refusal, and the men raised their glasses again. "Wish you many good years together!" Karak said. The men drank.

"Good whiskey, Karak," Tomoya said.

"Last week I brought it from Mexicali."

"We wish Clive more good fortune," Tomoya said. The others laughed. Karak poured another round.

"Who is the lucky lady?" Karak asked.

"Jim Riley's youngest girl. We're getting hitched in January. Don't know what she sees in me."

"Respectable too! One of the first families!" Karak slapped him on the back.

"Look," Clive said. "The whole family loves me. Her father gave me this."

He reached into his satchel and pulled out a .45 Colt revolver and laid it on the table. Lamplight gleamed off the mother-of-pearl inlaid in the grip.

Karak whistled. "You are knowing how to shoot it?" he joked, picking up the gun.

Clive chuckled. "See here?" He pointed to the muzzle, where the initials appeared, finely engraved—C.S.E.

"You fool them, Clive!" Karak said. "How you convince that good girl from a good family to marry you? And convince her father too?"

"More important—how you hide your other women?" Tomoya asked.

"What about all those bastards of yours?" Karak said. "You hiding all those from her too?"

Clive laughed, slapping his knee. The whiskey had colored his cheeks. Amarjeet and the Japanese boy laughed too, mouths open, shoulders bouncing.

Tomoya asked his son a question in Japanese. "Charm," the boy responded in English. "The word is 'charm.'"

"Ah!" Tomoya said. "Mr. Clive have charm we don't know. You see!"

"Drink to that!" Karak said. "All Clive's charms that we don't know."

Kishen emerged from the house, her chunni draped around her face, holding a bowl of popped corn and another filled with biscuits. Clive rose, tipping his hat. Years in the future, when he was gone, Ram would remember his earnestness, this respect paid to Jivan's wife when he could have ignored her.

"Ma'am," Clive said, but his knee hit the table and it toppled, spilling the bottle and his half-full glass. Whiskey splashed on his pants, Ram's arm, Karak's foot. A liquor-fueled cry went up from the group and Kishen jumped. Ram stood quickly and righted the table.

"Oh, such charms, Clive!"

"So good with ladies!"

"Yah, yah," said Tomoya. "Mrs. Singh, you come just right time!"

Kishen's face was half-hidden inside her chunni, but Ram could see her smiling as she retreated to the house.

They sat again and ate the biscuits and popped corn.

"Sorry about your whiskey, Karak," Clive said.

"Don't worry, old man," Karak said. "More is there." He spoke gently, but Ram could see he enjoyed Clive's bumbling.

Tomoya stood, called to his son in Japanese—it was time to go home. Clive rose too. He mounted his mare first, and the Japanese and Hindustanees watched him set off at a trot, raising their hands silently.

"He will get marry," Tomoya said after a while. He exchanged a knowing glance with Jivan. Ram had not realized the extent of their friendship.

Tomoya nodded, once, and Jivan returned the gesture. He put his palms together—then the men clasped hands.

Father and son mounted their horses. Ram felt peace descend. All was simpler with just his countrymen present. They sat at the table that Kishen set on the porch, eating rotis while the night surrounded them.

Moments later, they heard hurried hoofbeats on the dirt path and Clive reappeared. He slipped off the saddle. "I left my satchel," he said, his face flushed. "And my ledger. I forgot to put in the totals." Amarjeet gave him the book. Clive made hurried notations and slapped it shut. His horse started, ears up.

"See you boys," Clive slurred, tucking the ledger and satchel into his saddlebag. "Thanks for a good time." He turned the mare and trotted off.

He was past the turn when Jivan said in a low voice, "The boy is a fool."

"He drinks too much," Karak said. "But he doesn't interfere. That is the important thing."

"Eggenberger is satisfied," Jivan said. "*That* is the important thing."

"The important thing," Karak countered, "is Ram should learn Americans do not give sweets to announce a wedding."

"I have learned it," said Ram.

10

THE LAND THAT KARAK AND RAM LEASED FROM EGGENBERGER HAD BEEN planted in alfalfa, then left fallow for long enough that it would once again need leveling; the ditches would need to be redefined. First they plowed, then they borrowed Jivan Singh's team of mules, drove them out to their new cotton fields, and hitched them up to the Fresno scraper. Ram told Karak how much they should slope the soil, how to subdivide the tract to irrigate efficiently; he insisted on digging a pond to receive water from the delivery ditch before it was dispersed to the fields. He argued that 160 acres half-cultivated was less desirable than 40 acres closely cultivated. Karak deferred to him but he questioned why certain things needed to be done. Ram was surprised at how little Karak knew. Ram had steadied a leveler behind a mule since he was a child.

One morning Jivan and Amarjeet came with them, driving a second team, attaching another scraper borrowed from Tomoya. Karak was grateful, but Ram felt unsettled: now he owed something to the man from Japan. He did not like that feeling.

When the work was finished, the land lay neat, raw and pungent, sloping away from the canal headgate where the zanjero would meet them regularly to dispense water. Jivan Singh returned the borrowed leveler to Tomoya. Ram never acknowledged the loan; that way he did not have to feel indebted. Through the winter chill, he and Karak plowed and disked. When the threat of frost was past, they were ready to plant. Then the early March winds grew strong and warm. Wildflowers dotted the scrub and desert prairie, and the earth was crusted with alkaline. Soon it was time for Jivan and Karak to harvest their cantaloupe. Of course, Ram would help. He had become part of them now.

This season, they were lucky to find help easily. The men were building crates in the packing shed when pickers arrived one evening, nine men and two women kicking up dust along Rural Route 9, wearing sombreros, leading two burros weighed down by burlap sacks. One of the men carried an accordion, another a guitar; two teenage boys leaned against the weight of bags slung on their shoulders. There was an older man too, of unknowable age, with wrinkled skin but a strong back.

Both Jivan and Karak rose when they saw them.

"They are here already?" Karak said.

"I told them to come after two days. Not now," Jivan said.

"Buenos días," one of them called in a cheerful voice. Jivan and Karak ducked out of the packing shed to meet him, a rough man scarred on his right cheek. The others waited under a tree by the field. The burros stamped at the flies. Karak and Jivan spoke with the man in rapid Spanish. Ram felt a surge of his own ineffectiveness. He stacked the finished crates with Amarjeet. "They are angry at the harvesters for coming early," Amarjeet said, translating for him.

"The crop will not be ready for a few days," Ram said.

"But they want to harvest tomorrow and then leave for another job. Chacha-ji does not like that foreman, that man with the scar,

Carlos Guerrero. He beat one of his boys last year, then argued about payment."

"We'll find others."

"There are never enough workers, Ram-ji," Amarjeet said.

Outside, the argument went on, Karak's voice rising and Jivan's remaining calmer, but still insistent. There was a break in the stream of words. The Mexican man glanced back at his workers and spat nonchalantly, as if relishing the upper hand. Jivan and Karak returned to the packing shed.

"These people want to come a week early and be paid for doing nothing," Karak said.

"Not a week. A few days. Better to be early to market than to be late and caught in the glut," Jivan said.

"I would have found the workers if you had just allowed me!" Karak slapped off his work gloves.

Ram looked for Amarjeet's reaction, but the boy had returned to stacking crates. The crop was one-third Karak's, two-thirds Jivan's; Jivan was the older man and would make the decision.

"What will you say now?" Karak asked Jivan.

"I will accept."

Karak turned and strode out toward the house, his footsteps shaking the shed.

Jivan's face showed no expression. He returned to the foreman, pointing to a patch of clear land bordering the field.

"What are they saying?" Ram asked Amarjeet.

"Chacha-ji is asking why he brought only nine men, when he had asked for eleven. He said that only eight seemed capable and one is too aged. The older woman only cooks for them but the younger one wants to pick too."

The girl stood at the edge of the group, wearing a large brimmed hat that shaded her face, her skirt shifting in the breeze. She glanced at them and looked away, round-faced and stoic. She was pretty, Ram thought. More plump than his Padma, yet not delicate. She was fair-skinned like an Anglo. He could see her youth: the smoothness in the cheek, the clear eyes. She pursed her lips as the men talked about her, her eyes fixed on the ground. The other woman spoke to her but she did not respond. The old man stood near her protectively.

Ram agreed with Jivan; perhaps he was too old to work in the heat. Another man joined Jivan's conversation with Carlos Guerroro. The talk bounced quickly back and forth.

"It will be too hot for the girl," Ram said. He would not have allowed Padma to work in this way.

"They told her," Amarjeet said. "But she wants to work anyway."

By evening the workers had erected tents and unpacked their belongings. Sitting near the settling pond, sifting lentils for Kishen, Ram watched them: three tents for the men, one for the women. Karak explained the contents of the fifth: a statuette of the blue-robed Virgin of Guadalupe, a wooden cross, pictures of Villa and Hidalgo. In a clear space outside they placed a small stove.

The Hindus went to bed early. Lying on his cot, before sleep came, Ram could hear the sound of the accordion from the workers' camp. He closed his eyes and listened. The notes rose in the night air and were distorted by the wind. He heard laughter, the clipped sounds of Spanish. A guitar strummed and for a brief moment the camp seemed cheery, as if before a celebration, and then everything lay quiet. On his uncle's farm, it would have been the same: workers sleeping near the fields, plants waiting for harvest, the rest before the coming hard work.

The Mexicans gathered near the jackrabbit rock before the sun rose, before Jivan called them. Kishen had given them eggs from the coop and the women had cooked them quickly on their stove, boiled coffee and poured it into tin cups in the morning dark. It was cold now but they were dressed for the midday sun: loose pants, long sleeves, gloves, and wide-brimmed hats. The women's faded skirts fluttered in the predawn gray. The sun broke over the horizon. Immediately, the air warmed. Emerald rows alternated with lines of

sandy loam that converged in the distance. The workers spread out
to the first rows of plants, seated themselves on the measured space
between them. Leaves huddled near the ground and shifted in the
tepid breeze. Ram pulled on a pair of gloves that he had found in a
corner of the packing shed. The musky smell of the fruit filled his
nostrils and satiated him.

"Those will not be strong enough," Karak said.

"No matter," Ram said. He did not think that harvesting cantaloupe would be as difficult as picking cotton or cutting and bunch-
ing wheat.

Dastars and sombreros dotted the field; Hindustanees and Mexicans bent low and removed the brush covering each fruit. Jivan had
told Ram that it was a technique that Tomoya had perfected; it has-
tened the ripening process, prevented the sun from burning the cantaloupe's skin. He had shared the technique with Jivan only after
Amarjeet and Haruo had become friends.

The workers walked the rows with sacks slung behind them,
bending low, twisting and pulling the melons. The east side of the
field was not yet ripe and fruit was left on the vine. Other fruit was
not at full slip but Karak told the pickers to break it off anyway, it
was still ripe enough to pass inspection. Ram felt bad for Jivan and
Karak; any fruit that could not be easily twisted off was not at its
sweetest. Would the agricultural inspectors comment on this? He
did not know. When a bag was filled, the picker walked to the waiting crates and pulled the drawstring at the bottom, gently emptying
the fruit.

Later, the March sun beat down on them, slowing their movements, scalding bare skin. Bandanas were tied to shield eyes from
perspiration. Sweat poured down temples, necks, backs of thighs.
Kishen arrived with jugs of water laced with lemon juice and sugar.
Leela followed her mother, stared wide-eyed at the workers, handing
out cups. *Gracias, gracias chiquita.*

Ram's gloves tattered and finally tore. He threw them aside.

Twist and pull. Twist and pull. Sometimes, pull and cut. The cantaloupe skin grew painful to touch; the fine hairs rubbed his palms
raw. Still he clasped the roundness, the sandpaper skin and pulled toward him. He kept his eye on the fair-skinned girl. She was fast and
worked hard, carrying more fruit in her sack than the teenage boys.
He knew where she stood, when she drank water, when she emptied
her sack, but their eyes never met. Her skirt rustled around her legs.
Her hand swept the hair from her face. All of this disturbed him. He
forced himself to think of Padma.

At noon, they stopped to rest. The workers knelt at the pond and
splashed water on their faces. They sat under the ramada or inside
their tents with the flaps thrown open to the breeze.

They did not resume work until three thirty, long after the sun
had begun its descent. Even so, one of the teenage boys approached
Jivan when the foreman could not see, holding his head. "Me voy
a desmayar, señor." Jivan noted the wan face, how the boy swayed
unsteadily on his feet. He told him to rest for a while. He would still
pay him the wage. At nightfall, the workers prayed inside the Virgin's
tent. The accordion and guitar remained silent and the lamps were
snuffed out soon afterward.

High above them, cool air from the Pacific lay atop the warm
wind rising from the Superstition Hills. Thunder rumbled. Lightning jittered through the clouds, flashing a shadow of Mount Signal
on the soil of Baja, but no rain reached the Valley's soil or the Colorado's waters.

In the dark of early morning, a tent collapsed in a warm gust.
The Mexican men righted and pinned it again, but they did not return to sleep. They ate breakfast quickly and joined the Punjabis in
the field. The wind blew in their hair like a blessing. But when the
sun broke the horizon, they felt the burning finger of its first ray.

Before lunch one of the workers leaned over a vine, convulsed,
vomited, stumbled, then collapsed in the eastern field. Ram dropped
his sack and ran to him. Amarjeet reached him at the same time.

He is too old to work, Ram thought when he realized who he was. Grabbing the man's ankles and armpits, they carried him to the shade of the packing shed. Other workers ran to see. From a distant corner of the field, crouched over a vine, Karak yelled, "What is happening?"

They laid the old man on the shed's wooden floor and Ram slipped a folded sack under his head. One of the workers came to kneel by the old man. With shaking fingers, he unbuttoned the man's shirt. "Ángel, Ángel . . . soy yo, Alejandro. Le habla Alejandro."

"Amarjeet, get us more water," Jivan directed in Punjabi. The workers formed a circle around Alejandro and Ángel. The fair-skinned girl knelt beside them.

"You do not watch your people!" Jivan said to the foreman. "Has he been ill?"

"He has a mouth to speak! I told him this morning that he is an old man. That it would be too hard for him to work today," the foreman said.

A few moments later, Karak appeared in the doorway.

The old man made a small noise, a short intake of breath. His shirt was open now, revealing deep creases carved by years in the sun. His body told the stories that he would not tell himself, that the others did not know: an ancient scar on a forearm from a rattlesnake's bite, a line chiseled on the belly by a Villista's blade. Alejandro took off his own bandana, wet it, and wiped Ángel's face and chest. The skin was dry, red. His chest heaved.

"Is he your kin?" Jivan asked Alejandro in Spanish.

"He is a friend. Ángel Cruz. He told us of this job with you."

The foreman, Carlos Guerroro, stood to the side, gripping his sombrero in his hands, his face stoic.

"It is not right," the girl said, crossing herself. Her eyes were tear-filled, luminous. Carlos was watching her intensely. He did not care about Ángel Cruz, Ram thought, but he cared about the girl.

"It is not right," agreed Jivan. "Where is his family?"

"His nephew lives in the barrio," Alejandro said. He gave Jivan the man's name.

Alejandro's wet rag did not revive Ángel Cruz. Jivan felt the skin on his forehead, on his neck and hand. "Karak, go and get the doctor," he ordered in Punjabi.

Karak was standing beyond the circle of people. "Let us wait and see," he answered. "Perhaps he will awaken."

"If Karak does not go, I will," Ram said. Karak glared at him. But Ram had touched the man's skin, had seen the anguish on his face when he collapsed.

Jivan hesitated. "The doctor knows Karak," he finally said.

Ram's face flushed. Didn't the doctor know Ram too? He stared at the girl, kneeling now near the fallen man, wiping his forehead. She had taken off her sombrero and the bandana covering her mouth; she fingered a string of wooden beads in her hands. Her lips quivered as she whispered the prayers, her eyes luminous. Her hand brushed the crucifix that hung at her neck.

Ram looked away and saw that Karak was staring at her too.

Amarjeet appeared with the saddled mare. "Ride to the barrio and tell his nephew too," Jivan commanded. Ram could see Karak clench his jaw, angry but compliant. He mounted quickly and rode off at a gallop.

They covered Ángel Cruz in wet bedsheets. They brought the kerosene-powered fan from Jivan's bedroom. The doctor came quickly, but when he saw Ángel Cruz unconscious, lying under soaked sheets, he told them he could do nothing more for the man than what had already been done.

Later, the nephew arrived and entered the shed, tightly clutching his hat. Alejandro and the fair-skinned girl rose to meet him. Ram noted the lad's ragged clothing, his desperate eyes. When he saw Ángel Cruz lying on the floor of the shed, his eyes widened in alarm. He crossed himself quickly. He spoke quietly to Jivan in Spanish, looking at his feet, at the wall, anywhere but Jivan's face. Ram could not understand his Spanish.

"No," Jivan said, his palm held up, shaking his head.

The boy said something in response, but Jivan walked away. To Ram, his manner seemed brusque, impatient.

Ram and Alejandro shifted Ángel Cruz onto a blanket, then lifted him onto the bed of Jivan's wagon. The man's breathing was light. He did not awaken. The nephew said nothing more.

Later Ram asked Amarjeet what had happened.

"The nephew wanted to pay Jivan for the doctor, but he had no money, and said that he would bring it later. But Chacha-ji refused payment at all."

Ram's eyes met Amarjeet's. Jivan Singh was a good man.

His mind went back to Karak, riding off on the horse, with that pretty Mexican girl watching. How beautiful he had looked in that moment, Ram thought: the sinews in his arms as he gripped the reins, his roughness with the horse's mouth, the scarlet of his turban. He had played the hero without shame, when he had not even wanted to go.

11

MARCH 1915

THEY TOOK THE HARVEST INTO TOWN WITHOUT KNOWING WHAT HAD happened to Ángel Cruz. Each man drove one of the four wagons, weighed down with crates and melons. Clive met them near the railroad depot and climbed onto the driver's seat next to Jivan. They stood in line behind a string of other wagons leading from the inspection booth. They were under contract with Consolidated Fruit Co., and the company's refrigerated boxcars stood waiting to take the early-season cantaloupe to market in Los Angeles.

Clive would speak for him; that was what Jivan always preferred. He pulled up to a booth staffed by a tall man with a full head of gray hair.

"Howdy, Will," Clive said.

The inspector glanced up, not too friendly. "Howdy, Clive." He signaled for random crates to be brought off. Amarjeet took off the ones he indicated, handed them to Ram and Karak. The inspector rolled up his sleeves and picked through the fruit. Clive stood near him, Jivan was at Clive's elbow. Karak and Ram sat in the shade on the platform where the cars loaded up. Consolidated shippers' men waited there for Jivan's load. They wanted to make the evening train to L.A., which left in two hours, or Jivan's cantaloupe would have to wait until morning.

"Too many greens in these two," the inspector said, signaling the last of Jivan's four wagons. "You boys need to sort those again."

Karak opened his mouth to speak, but Jivan silenced him with his eyes. Clive stepped forward. "Aw, come on, Will. They don't look that bad."

"Commission'll have my hide if I let a bad one through. It's the new law. You know that."

"Check this one again," Clive said. "This one's just fine. Just fine."

The inspector looked at him. A glance of impatience.

"Come on," Clive said, laughing. "Check it."

The inspector climbed on the platform again. Jivan wanted to tell him, *The workers could not wait two more days,* but he said nothing. The inspector nosed around the melons. "I'll let this one go. Only just. If you weren't here"—he looked at Clive—"I'd pull it."

Amarjeet led the third wagon through. Consolidated's men waited on the platform, chewing tobacco, busy not looking at him. One of them spat onto the rail. "Bring 'em up! Bring 'em up!"

"But this one ain't going," the inspector said, indicating the fourth wagon.

"Willy," Clive said, jovial.

The inspector glared at him. "Our wives are sisters, but that don't mean nothin' here."

Clive's face shrank.

"Pull it over," the inspector commanded Amarjeet. He did. Behind them, a hundred yards down the line, two other farmers had been pulled over too. Amarjeet told Jivan he recognized them from his old high school. Anglo families who lived even farther outside town. Jivan shrugged.

"You got to educate your sharecroppers on the right time to harvest," the inspector said, "or be runnin' afoul of the standardization laws."

"I do what I can, Will," Clive said. He hitched up his pants. "I know about 'em new laws. I ain't the best farmer around, but I know when to bring in a crop." He drifted off toward Consolidated's men, talking with them as cantaloupe from Jivan's first three wagons were loaded.

The Punjabis sorted through the fruit from the fourth wagon and tossed out the green melons, leaving them loose and wasted in a pile on the side of the road. Cantaloupe broke open, oozing pink. Flies buzzed around them. The next wagon in line had passed them and pulled up at the inspection station. The farmers stood in the shade, staring at the Singhs as they worked. Consolidated's manager walked by, slowing as he passed the Punjabis. "Out of the ground too early, Singh," he said. Jivan felt the words like a kick in the belly.

Clive approached them when the culling was nearly complete. "I got a close enough count to know how much we're sending out," he said. "I'll be getting along now." He looked down the line at the other farmers. Jivan followed his gaze. Consolidated's agent was sharing a laugh with a farmer a few wagons away.

The Punjabis returned the wagon to the line and trundled up to the inspection shack again. Clive walked toward the shops on Main Street. The inspector opened the crates again. Jivan wished Clive had not left, but he would not have asked him to stay.

"What game you boys playing? There's still too many green. Re-sort these again." His manner was harsh now; Clive was gone.

Jivan was quiet. Karak said, "They are good." Jivan's eyes flashed at him.

"I'll tell you when they're good," the inspector said.

The Punjabis pulled over again. They threw out more fruit.

When the Consolidated agent walked past again, Karak asked, "How many minutes to the train?"

"You missed it already. Last load been hauled." The men could hear the engine building up steam. It rose in a cloud, gray against the desert sand. The Singhs' fruit would have to stand in an iced car overnight, waiting for the morning train.

When they coaxed the mules back into the line, the inspector let them through. "They're on the green side," he said, "but they can go."

The Punjabis watched as the cantaloupe was hauled onto the waiting refrigerator car, number 417.

"Don't worry, Singh," Consolidated's agent said as he wrote Jivan a receipt. "We're nice and early in the season. Can't see nothing bringing the price down—not unless there's another glut." Jivan kept his face expressionless. He had lost a fifth of the crop by the side of the road.

THE MORNING TRAIN CARRIED four carloads of cantaloupe to the market in Los Angeles. Jivan knew his finances would be determined at the exchange in the ag pit, by men in a large room smelling of sweat and adrenaline. They negotiated fortunes and failures by a show of fingers, by gestures of hands. A raised index and middle finger meant his family would have meat five days a week for the season. Two arms held skyward meant that he could buy the seeder from Hanson's Implements. Two thumbs down, and they would skimp on the cumin and turmeric that Kishen purchased in Brawley. They had to trust Consolidated to take their cantaloupes to market safely. They had to trust the sales agent too.

Other carloads would converge on the stock exchange, from the San Joaquin fields and the Central Valley and Palo Verde. That week, it was too many. The men in the ag pit showed thumbs down, thumbs down, thumbs down. Sweat trickled down backs inside starched shirts, beaded on foreheads wiped by silk handkerchiefs. A certain trader representing Consolidated Fruit, representing other shippers too, made a single phone call to the vice president of the company.

Afterward, that vice president of Consolidated Fruit called an operations officer of Southern Pacific. When the engine pulling car number 417 steamed into the depot the stationmaster checked his roster. Carloads 417 and 420 were disconnected and left on a siding in the afternoon heat. They were picked up thirty-six hours later by another engine. By then, the soft flesh of the fruit had turned to water. All of this, Jivan did not know.

In the newspaper, Amarjeet showed Jivan the list of violators of the standardization laws. Jivan Singh's name was included. FEE IMPOSED FOR EARLY HARVEST AND SHIPPING, the headline said. But he could not find the names of the Hamiltons and the Proutys, who had also been sorting green fruit that day.

A letter arrived from Consolidated Fruit three days later. Payment was being made for three of the carloads, but one carload, number 417, had contained only overripe melons when it arrived. Sale at the exchange had not been possible and no money for that carload would be forthcoming. *Mr. John Singh,* the letter said, *should take note that fruit should be shipped at the appropriate time.*

On the porch in the late afternoon, the men listened as Karak read the letter to them twice. His face was dark with sarcasm. "Our melons were overripe when they arrived, but they were too green when they were shipped. How can it be?" He did not have to explain the calculations to the others. The fourth carload—417, the lost one—contained the whole of the Singhs' profit.

"We will go to court," Karak said.

"What is the use?" Jivan said. "Who will side with us?"

"You will just accept this, bhai-ji?"

Jivan knew what Karak hinted at. "They treat all the farmers like this. Not just us," Jivan said. "It happens to everyone."

That evening Jivan found an envelope of cash on the bureau where the ledgers were kept. It contained the wages Jivan had paid Ram for his work during the harvest. Jivan approached him late at night, when he was lying on his cot. "What is this?" he asked. His

voice was soft, but he could not hide his disgust. He thought the boy
had better judgment, more pride.

"You insult me," Jivan said, leaving the envelope on the cot beside him.

SHERIFF FIELDING ARRIVED on horseback the following week, in the
midmorning. Kishen saw him first, through the window, then drew
her face back quickly. Karak, Ram, and Jivan gathered around the
sheriff on the porch, anxious about the reason for his visit.

"Ángel Cruz is dead," the sheriff said.

"Who?" Karak asked.

"The Mexican you hired for the cantaloupe harvest." He looked
around at the men. They were too stunned to speak.

"You understand, Jivan, it's my duty to inquire."

"Of course," Jivan said, looking away.

"We don't usually do this just for migrants, but after the coro-
ner's notice, I have to file something. I know you all run a good
operation here. I know you look out for people working your land. It
was a hot spell of days. Poor bastard shoulda known better."

"He needed to work," Jivan said. "Like all of us. He needed the
money."

"Have a seat, Sheriff," Karak said.

The sheriff sat. "Shoulda known when to stop."

"The foreman contracts with Consolidated Fruit," Karak said.
"Nobody allowed to stop."

"This didn't come from me—but I can't say you're wrong," the
sheriff said. The Punjabis were surprised at his sympathy, but they
did not show it.

"We had a bad time with Consolidated last week," Karak said.

"No need to bother the sheriff—" Jivan said.

"They knock a carload over," Karak kept on. "A quarter of our
crop."

Jivan shifted his weight.

"You wouldn't be the first, I don't reckon," the sheriff said. "Still, it hurts. I know you boys work hard. You don't make no trouble for me. I 'ppreciate that about you. You don't shout about unfairness and make a ruckus neither."

"We know our place," Jivan said, looking at Karak, at Ram.

"You know your place," he repeated, with a chuckle. "Goes a long way in keeping law and order. Like I said, I 'ppreciate that." He was holding his hat casually, amiably, dangling it between his legs.

Silence.

"How'd the melon do, anyway?" the sheriff asked. "If they knocked over a quarter of your crop, sounds like you boys got caught up in that glut."

Karak snorted. "We did," he said. He kicked the dirt with his foot. "That's what happened."

12

RAM KNEW COTTON WAS NOT LIKE CANTALOUPE. IT DID NOT HAVE TO be shipped off at a certain time, at a certain temperature. It was not delicate. If market prices were low, a farmer could hold until prices went up; hard work, labor, aching muscles, and scorched afternoons need not dissolve in a puddle of rotted produce by the roadside.

Karak and Ram's land was perfect for cotton. The papers reported the big ranches—Timken, McPherrin, the C. M. ranch across the border—were growing cotton despite the falling price, banking on the future needs of Europe's war that, through its colonies, had become the world's war.

At Fredonia Park on Sunday afternoons, sitting in the shade of planted trees, lying on benches with hats covering their faces, twenty-five or thirty Hindus discussed the blockade of the European ports. Cotton was needed to manufacture the wings of warplanes, to stitch uniforms. But how could its price rise if it could not reach the markets in Europe?

"We have decided to plant anyway," one of the Khan brothers said.

"Another ten test acres," Gugar Singh said. "Just last like year. No harm."

"Foolish," Harnam Singh insisted.

In the wagon going home, Ram thought of his promise to Padma. He had given her his word that he would return soon. But the sacrifice of his absence must prove worthwhile. Something tugged inside him. Longing for her? Ambition? Many men who had left behind their wives did not need justification, but he did.

"We are still planting cotton," he said to Karak. "All one hundred sixty acres to cotton." His voice—the tone, the confidence—did not sound familiar to himself. Karak looked at him with surprise, as if he thought so too.

"Of course," Karak said. "Who said we are not?"

JIVAN TOOK THEM to the Fredonia Bank to meet the young vice president, Jasper Davis, a nephew of the mayor, and nephew of a local magistrate judge too. Jivan knew him through Stephen Eggenberger and his early days in the Valley. Karak and Ram filled out forms, shook hands with him, and left with money for seed, a newly invented seeder, another team of mules.

Next morning, Karak woke Ram before he wanted to be woken. "It's time, Ram, the time has come!" Ram found the mules already harnessed to the wagon in the morning dark.

At the field, Karak jumped down and hitched up the seeder. "The crop will not grow any faster if you plant quickly," Ram said, irritated.

Karak turned to look at him. "It will, Ram." He grinned. Ram did not know if he was joking. They planted in long rows, the furrows stretching to meet at an invisible point in the distance. Ram took pride in their neatness. The first time they irrigated, they stood together near the supply ditch as the zanjero opened the headgate. The water swept in. The scent of the soil as it dampened made Ram's mouth water. Near them, a scorpion sidled under a rock. Farther away, a gopher scrambled into his hole. Karak put his arm around Ram's shoulders. "It is done, bhai," he said.

"There is still more to do, Karak Singh," Ram said jovially.

The plants grew. Ram wrote to Padma about the acres under his care, how he had shaken hands with the vice president of the bank. When the green shoots broke through the loam, he showed Karak how to use the cultivator. He boasted to Padma of teaching Karak to clear the weeds so the roots would go deep. White flowers appeared and disappeared. Ram wrote to Padma of learning to speak English, and even Spanish too. The bolls came forth, plump and beautiful, and burst open, revealing the fresh white substance underneath. He told Karak they should pick early; if they let the cotton sit for too long, they would not get a third harvest off the plants.

When Ram held the first fibers in his hand, he felt he held a part of himself, but it was not the cotton of his boyhood. That cotton had come into being through the people who had lived before him for thousands of years on Punjabi soil; they had selected what seeds to plant, they had played with pollen and stamen and pistil to make what had not existed before. That cotton was the offspring of that soil and the people who lived on it, bound together.

The cotton he held now was new, like the settlements of the Imperial Valley itself. It had come from the experimental station in Arizona. It bore the name of people who were of this land—the Pima who worked for the American government to create it. It was new like the American people, built upon the backs of the original dwellers.

When the cotton plants were waist high, the banker Jasper Davis came to look at the field. Ram could not understand their quick English talk to know if Karak had given him credit for his work. He was surprised that it mattered to him.

But the banker looked pleased. Ram understood his words "fine-looking field," which he said while nodding at both Karak and Ram. Next to them, Roubillard's cotton, on land also leased from Eggenberger, stood short and gray and dry. No one stated the comparison. Jasper Davis walked the length of a row dressed in a three-piece suit and polished shoes. He had arrived in a cream Packard, smart and gleaming even though it had been driven on the dusty road. For the first time, for a fleeting moment, Ram felt that he wanted to know English well enough to understand the man. As if he were going to stay and become a part of the land. The Anglo's visit, his smile, his goodwill defined the crop as a success. Ram and Karak stood together and watched him drive off. Ram realized then: The cotton field had changed them. He and Karak were equals.

They hired pickers and cleared the plants in a week, piling the cotton in three wagons. Ram thought of his Padma, his mother, his uncle. "You did good," Clive said, as the loaded wagons stood at the edge of the field. "If those workers picked as clean as it looks like they did, we'll get a great price."

EARLY THE NEXT MORNING, the men set off in a caravan of three wagons to Jake Smiley's gin. Karak took the driver's seat on the lead wagon. They felt buoyant, happy. Jivan, unexpectedly, slapped the rump of the last mule as they left and gave a yell, like a boy.

The air had not yet begun to grow warm. The mules trudged along the dirt road that lay southwest from the ranch. It was a distance of thirteen miles, the gin strategically placed near the railway that would haul the cotton to Los Angeles. On the way, Ram could see other cotton fields in their various stages of harvesting. There were other camps, with tired pickers working the fields.

Ram knew all the other farms now, fields running off the same road that led to the Eggenberger farm: The Kinsey farm, which had the advantage of five able-bodied sons. The Myers Ranch, the Gergen Dairy, the two-thousand-acre spread owned by Hutchins Ranch. He could see the clear line in the fields where the plants stood unpicked and where the task had been completed.

At the gin, they pulled up in a short line behind two farmers—others who had tried to beat the heat and rush. The Khan brothers had told them to come as early as they could. The previous year, the Khans had grown ten experimental acres of cotton and ginned them at Smiley's. He'd quote you a price on shipment and sale. He couldn't guarantee it, but it would be close. There were two gins in the Valley now; even so, the lines were long and grew longer through the day.

It was so early that two boys were still watering down the dirt road to the gin. Smiley came out and walked the line to see who was waiting. When he saw Jivan, he gave a curt nod. "Howdy, Jake," Jivan responded. "Your boys have grown tall."

"I didn't know you were getting into cotton," Smiley said.

"It is belonging to my cousins. First crop. This is Karak Singh, Ram Singh."

Jake Smiley's eyes wandered over the wagons, packed full. "Looks clean and good. How many acres?"

"One hundred and sixty," Karak said.

Smiley raised his eyebrows. "Taking a chance with the first, aren't they?"

"They knew how to do," Jivan said, glancing at Ram. "Good farmers. Very good," Jivan added. Ram could understand so much English now.

Smiley went back to his shed and the first wagon in line moved up to the gin. The others shuffled up behind it. Ram sat on a chair in the shade of the shed. Amarjeet lay on a bench nearby. An hour later, while they were still waiting, another string of wagons filed down the path. They pulled up behind the Singhs'. Ram saw that the man in the lead wagon was irate, the skin on his forehead knotted together. His eyes lingered on Jivan and Karak, who were talking under a ramada, fifty feet away. Jivan was adjusting his dastar, rewrapping it in the half privacy of the ramada.

The man jumped down from his seat and strode toward the gin.

From his place near the shed, Ram could hear the man call, "Hey, Jake, come on out here. I'd like a word."

"Be with you soon," the ginner called out. "I'll come by."

"Sooner rather than later."

Amarjeet sat up as the man passed on his way back to his wagon. "That's Roubillard," he whispered to Ram. "He's no good."

A solitary wagon pulled up with a load and joined the line. Then, after ten minutes, eight more arrived, bearing signs from the Hutchins Ranch. Ram began to grow restless. Amarjeet fetched water and poured it on their mules' flanks. They had been waiting for more than two hours, and there was still a wagon ahead of them.

Smiley emerged from the shack and walked past, ignoring them now. Ram saw him talking to Roubillard, glancing at Jivan and Karak under the ramada. As if they sensed something was wrong, Jivan and Karak approached them. Ram went too.

Roubillard was chewing tobacco. His tongue worked it around and tucked it into a corner of his mouth. "I'm in a hurry." He turned his head to the side and spat. The dark spot landed a foot away from Jivan's shoe. "I'm sure you and your boys wouldn't mind stepping aside."

Jake Smiley's face showed no emotion.

Jivan opened his mouth to speak, but Karak thrust himself in front of Roubillard, looking down into his face. "You not the only man in a hurry, Roubillard."

"Move your wagons over, I need to get through," Roubillard said, without stepping back, so that he and Karak stood only inches apart.

Smiley stuttered. "Maurice—"

Roubillard turned to him. "You go against me, Jake, I swear I'll head straight to Jim Hubbard's operation and I'll take half that lot with me." With a jerk of his head, he indicated the line behind him. "I already talked to them. They know what's at stake here. They all want through right now."

Jake Smiley's eyes followed the long line of cotton-filled wagons.

Ram could see that he was a mild man. His jaw clenched when his eyes met Maurice Roubillard's, but he didn't argue.

"You men please step aside," Smiley said, without looking at Jivan. "We'll get you as soon as this lot is through."

"Jake," Jivan said. Their eyes met, and something unspoken passed between them. Later Jivan would tell Ram that during the flood, they had worked together to move Eggenberger's cattle away from the speeding water. That was how they had met.

"Take the mules to the side, Amarjeet," Jivan said.

"What is this, bhai-ji?" Karak said in Punjabi.

"Let it be—" Jivan said.

"What?" Karak spat again, as if he could not comprehend.

"Listen to what I say. I have a reason," Jivan said.

Karak grimaced in disgust.

Smiley returned to his shed. Amarjeet sprang to the driver's seat of their first wagon and directed it to the side. Ram followed with the second. Roubillard moved his wagon to the ginning shed. Smiley's son directed Roubillard to pull up closer. When Roubillard jumped down from the wagon, he slapped him on the back and chuckled. "That's more like it, my boy!" Smiley's son did not respond.

Jivan looked out at the line, at the eight Hutchins Ranch wagons that followed. Ram knew what he was thinking. If Smiley did not allow them in after Roubillard's load, the humiliation would be too great. He turned to Ram, avoiding Karak's gaze. "Let's return home," he said.

The Singhs' wagons were moving up the dirt path when Smiley's younger boy called out, "Mr. Singh!" He raced past Ram's wagon to reach Jivan's. Ram could see Karak scowl at him. "Mr. Singh. Pop told me to tell you to come tomorrow. Come early." He looked two or three years younger than Amarjeet. A sweaty patch of hair clung to his forehead. He squinted against the sun, hesitating. "He told me to tell you he couldn't help it."

They drove back three hours in the waning sunlight, and the

mules were tired. At the farm, at dinner, Jivan told everyone at the table to sleep early.

"We will rise at one A.M. Amarjeet, hitch up all three wagons by then."

"Why so early?" Amarjeet asked.

"Because that is my wish."

Later, when they lay down on their cots to sleep, Ram asked Karak, "How did you come to know Roubillard?"

"It doesn't matter," Karak said. "I know the bloody bastard, that is enough."

RAM WOKE AT ONE O'CLOCK to the sound of Amarjeet hitching up the mules. Jivan walked past his cot fully dressed, holding a lamp. Ram sat up quickly. "Bhai-ji, I will be ready in a minute." This work was for his own crop, but he could see that Jivan cared about it as much as he.

Ram could feel the wind blowing up dust in darkness. In the animal shed, the mare whinnied. Karak climbed on the driver's seat of the lead wagon, his dastar sloppily tied and his beard tucked too loosely. Ram drove his wagon behind it. His body ached from the previous day, carting the cotton twenty-six miles, baking in the sun, the final humiliation at the end. They had accomplished nothing for all that effort. Two nights before he had written to Padma about picking the cotton, but he knew he would not tell her about the gin. Something about Roubillard's chuckling at Smiley's son left him without feeling. It reminded him of Hambelton. He was grateful that Amarjeet climbed into the seat next to him.

Kishen handed him a tiffin. It was warm and comforting in his palm. They did not speak. The wagon began to trundle forward. Ram opened his tiffin and ate the roti that he found there. Silently, he blessed her.

How different this trip was from the one yesterday, when they had set off in high spirits at dawn. They passed the same farms, silver and luminescent by the light of the three-quarters moon. At the Roubillard place, Karak spit on the side of the road. What good would it do? Ram thought.

The moon was still bright when they pulled off the dirt road to the gin. Karak brought his wagon right up to the shed, so that the mules' noses touched the door.

"What do we do now, bhai-ji?" Ram asked, calling out to Jivan.

"We wait."

Jivan's mule snorted and brayed. In moments, they heard dogs barking, and soon after, Smiley came out, holding a lamp in one hand and a rifle in the other.

"Who's there?"

"Singhs from Eggenberger farm," Jivan called down from his seat on the wagon. "You told us, 'Come early.'"

Smiley held the lamp up higher so he could see Jivan's face.

"Tell me," Jivan said, "is it early enough?"

"John Singh," Smiley said. He lowered the lamp. "What d'ya men want?" They must have seemed menacing; there was a tremor in his voice.

"We have three loads to gin. Same as yesterday," Karak said.

Smiley's eyes swept their faces. "Bring 'em forward. I'll wake my boys." The night was lifting. The sky grew pink. On the way to the house, he turned back. "What happened yesterday afternoon—y'all should know, that ain't how I meant it to happen. Always happy to have your business."

Karak nodded, serious.

"I don't like that jackass," Smiley said. In the dim light of the lantern, they could see him swallow. He shrugged. "He don't really know what he's doing. Brought me the dirtiest cotton I've seen. When the pump pulled it out of the wagon yesterday there were two clods sittin' right there as big as your head. Said his pickers did it on purpose and his weighting man winked at them." He huffed, smiled a half smile, adjusted his cap. He was apologizing without apologizing. "I had to cut him seven dollars a bale. He's blamin' me now."

The information was like an offering, but the Singhs were silent, even Jivan. Smiley turned to fetch his sons.

13

TELEGRAM

originating: Fredonia Depot, California, August 30, 1915
destination: Lower Chenab Colony, Lyallpur
ESTEEMED UNCLE COTTON BROUGHT GREAT PROFIT. $2300
COMING TO YOU. PLEASE CONFIRM RECEIPT. HOPE YOU
PURCHASE ACRES IN OUR SHAHPUR AS YOU DESIRE. IF HERE MY
DUTY IS FULFILLED I WILL RETURN HAPPY.
RAM

The cotton brought so much more money than Ram had expected, he allowed himself to keep fifty dollars before he wired the remainder home. The day he sent the telegram, he walked around the town as if he had grown into someone else—a man with influence and power, who would never again fail, who would never again feel sad.

To celebrate their success, Karak brought Ram to a casino across the border called El Owl. Karak had often asked Ram to come with him to Mexicali before, but Ram had refused, and Karak would go alone. Now Ram did not want to disappoint him, not when Karak had been the cause of so much of Ram's good fortune. On the ride to the border on the buckboard, Karak told him about Avenida Porfirio Díaz, the main street that could be seen across the muddy canal that formed the line between two nations and two cities: Calexico and Mexicali, names created by a clever man who thought the mix of letters showed how the monies, the interests, the people of the two towns would be interlocking, inseparable. He was right, Karak said. The border, the line, the boundary between people and countries, did not matter too much.

They left the mare and buckboard and checked in at the immigration shack. They crossed the wooden bridge into Mexico. It was the first time Ram had been there. It was dusk; the sun was a red disk floating on distant clouds.

A Chinese man strolled toward them. A cluster of Negroes were farther down the street. They passed an opium den before reaching El Owl, which was perched between El Buck Horn Fat's Place and El Climax Cantina. Ram was not morally opposed to such places, as Jivan was. He had accompanied Karak on his adventures in Hong Kong. In Hambelton, he had visited the back alley with his companions. His objection was not about morality—although if he had asked himself for the truth, he would admit that he did not know how to behave in such places; he was never at ease. He thought he worried about more pragmatic things. He could not waste money at the bar. He did not like the smoke of the opium dens. Regarding women, he could satisfy himself in private; he would not risk acquiring syphilis in the cribs.

El Owl had wealthy and well-known clientele, Karak explained to Ram: the mayor's son, heads of Imperial Valley businesses, members of the Chamber of Commerce. Sometimes these gentlemen even brought their lady friends to go slumming south of the line. El Owl had the finest food, the best whiskey, the greatest number of gaming tables. The mujeres públicas had their own bedrooms there; a man never had to leave the building. He said this without shame, which fascinated and disgusted Ram at the same time. Karak had visited several times in the last two years; he was familiar with the place but the employees did not know him, with the exception of the lady whom he favored. Ram hoped he did not have to meet her. They approached the building just as it grew dark. Lamps shone through two windows in the front. Three or four Anglo men milled about the entrance. As Ram and Karak moved to the door, one of these men situated himself at the threshold.

"Whites only," the man said, his eyes scanning Karak's dastar and beard.

Ram looked in the window and saw about fifty Anglo men sitting around gaming tables. In the far corner, two men who appeared to be Japanese leaned into a conversation; the others did not seem to mind them. Ram wondered if he would have been stopped had he arrived alone. He wore no dastar for this man to stare at.

"No sign is here," Karak said calmly, but Ram could feel his anger surge.

"Don't need a sign."

"Many times I have come here," Karak said.

"I don't think so," the man said. He spat on the sidewalk.

"Aw, let 'em in, Pete," another man said, striding up. He was smoking a cigar. Its moving tip made streaks in the dark air. Ram could not place him.

"Rules is rules," the man said. There was liquor on his breath.

The cigar man chuckled. "You got Tom Moriyama in there!"

"That's different."

"Lighten up, Petey." The cigar man chuckled again, good-naturedly. "I'll vouch for these boys. They're good farmers and never cause no trouble."

The other man seemed confused.

"On my word," the cigar man said.

The other man stepped out of the doorway and the light spilled onto their faces. Karak nodded at the cigar man—a quick, smart movement. Only then did Ram see the knowing eyes, the belly. Through a smoky haze, the man tipped his hat. "Sheriff," Karak said.

"Karak," the sheriff responded, grinning.

Karak traded his money for tokens, ordered a whiskey, and sat at a table where they were dealing panguingue. Ram ordered a mezcal at the bar and watched. There were three Anglos at Karak's table, and when he sat they acknowledged him with a glance. In the far corner, Tomoya Moriyama raised his hand in greeting. Karak began to have a very good night; in seven hands, he won four. After the third win, his eyes searched for Ram, who answered him with raised eyebrows. Yes, he had been watching. Yes, he was doing well. Ram had been keeping track; he had followed the strategy in each hand. When Clive Edgar lumbered in and sat down beside Karak, he was sipping his third whiskey and sitting before stacks of neatly ordered tokens. "Makin' good jack," Clive said, and Karak nodded curtly, not acknowledging the wins. Ram knew he would not want to offend the other players. But a moment later, Karak grinned at Clive, easily, comfortably. Ram understood now—Karak and Clive were friends. He thought that odd.

"Clive Edgar," the land agent said, extending his hand and greeting the other three men at the table. They shook with him, stating their names.

"Haven't seen you men before, have I?" Clive said.

"Passing through from Arizona, originally from Kansas. Me and my nephew here," said one of the men. The other man was from Date City, newly founded in the Valley, way north. Clive was dealt in. They played a hand. Another man arrived, sitting down in the chair that stood empty next to Clive's. Ram's and Karak's eyes met.

"Hello, Maurice," Clive said.

"Hello, Clive. Didn't know they were letting the riffraff in here," the new man said. Ram recognized the voice. It was Roubillard, the cotton farmer who had forced them out of line at the gin, who farmed the third portion of Eggenberger's land.

For a moment Clive looked confused, as if he didn't know what Roubillard meant. Then he snorted and tuned back to his cards.

"Ain't you gonna do something about this?" Roubillard said to the dealer.

"Pete let him in." The dealer shrugged. "He stays."

Karak clenched his jaw.

"Have it your way." Roubillard lit a cigarette and took a drag.

Karak looked at Ram. The stare told Ram everything. Karak would not leave now, even if he wanted to.

"That his friend?" Roubillard tipped his head toward Ram. When the dealer ignored him, Roubillard directed his gaze at Clive. "Raghead nigger got a friend who ain't a raghead."

"You been drinking, Maurice," Clive said, as if to explain everything.

"Are you playing this round, sir?" the dealer asked.

"Sure am."

The game continued. Karak won. The dealer swept the chips toward him. Clive was leaning forward now, just staring at the table in front of him.

"Hey, Clive, you know the stuff these ragheads eat?" Roubillard was talking too loudly.

Clive finally looked up. Karak caught his eye, and something passed between them. An expression Ram couldn't decipher. "What d'ya mean?" Clive said good-naturedly.

"They love that slop we give our pigs. What d'ya call it? Butter something—butter water? Butter milk? That's it, buttermilk!" He sprayed the table with his saliva. All the men smelled the liquor. He slapped the table and laughed. "We throw it in the slop for our hogs, but they like to drink it for breakfast. Hank at the woodshop told me that." He leaned back in his chair. "Same stuff, two different uses." He laughed again.

"He is a jackass," Ram said in Punjabi, hoping to hold Karak back. "Keep your temper."

Roubillard nudged Clive. Clive snorted again. "Let it go, Maurice." His gaze returned to the table.

"Why you feeling so bad, Roubillard?" Karak said. His voice came from deep in his throat. "Maybe you feeling that we are farming better than you?"

Ram bit the inside of his cheek. Why could the man not keep from taunting?

"Maybe you bring dirty cotton to Jake Smiley last week?"

Roubillard's eyes narrowed.

"Maybe your cotton so dirty he gave you less payment than he gave to us next day?"

Clive lifted his head to look at Karak. Roubillard scanned the table. He took a drag on his cigarette. "You think you can come in here and do what you want, boy?" His voice softened. He leaned forward almost imperceptibly. "Ya better know your place. Ya hear me? Boy, it'll be better for ya if ya know your place." With one quick movement, he flicked the cigarette butt at Karak. Karak caught it against his shirt—a movement without thought—then snapped his hand away in pain. The cigarette fell to the floor. He stamped it out with his boot.

The dealer signaled a bystander. Two men stepped toward Roubillard and stood on either side of his chair. "You'll have to leave now, sir," one of them said. Roubillard looked up at them.

He started a lazy, drunken laugh. "If that don' beat all—they takin' me outta here 'stead of you." He shoved his chair back and stood up, tottering. "Come on, Clive. They don't want good Valley residents like you 'n' me in here. Place is turnin' into a shithole! El Owl! Rather have these ragheads."

Roubillard backed away; at the neighboring table he stumbled over a chair. A man bent to help him up. In that moment, Clive leaned forward and murmured, holding his palms out. "Sorry, Karak." His expression made clear he felt he had no choice. Why would Clive believe that? What pull did Roubillard have on him?

"I'll see you next time." Clive rose quickly and followed Roubillard out. Karak's face flushed and his lips pursed. A vein appeared at his temple. Ram knew he was furious. But later, in the buckboard on the way home, Karak denied that it bothered him.

November 15, 1915

My dear nephew,

You are like a son to me. That is known to all. Every day I pray to the Creator Parmatma for your good health. In your telegram, you stated you would like to come back. I think that is an excellent idea. Here all is well, very fine.

Perhaps you have learned that I have found a match for your dear little cousin, none other than the eldest son of Gopal Singh, the sardar of the neighboring district. This is a great boon for us. What a fortunate alliance this will be, one that will benefit all of us long into the future, even after you return home. The boy is so desirable that they have asked us for a large dowry. No doubt they know that you are in foreign lands and can provide one. So I ask you, before you come back, please do the needful and send money for the wedding. Because the cotton is bringing so much, I trust that this is not too difficult—another six or twelve months, just one more planting. We must make the wedding a grand affair, as is suitable for Gopal Singh's family, and we must not be seen to come up short. It is an important matter. Our standing in the community is at stake. All will know that it was made possible by you.

Your son is growing beautifully. You will be quite pleased when you see him, and your wife is a blessing on the household.

Your uncle,
Chanda Lal

14

NOVEMBER 1915

H E WAS REQUIRED TO STAY FOR ANOTHER SEASON, TO MAKE THE MONEY for his cousin's dowry that would allow the marriage to go forward. Of course, Ram would do that. That was his duty. But.

It was not that he disliked Karak; he had no reason for that. It was that he did not like him enough.

Some days his longing for home sat inside him like an infestation, eating away at heart and brain. On those days, he could not tolerate seeing Karak pore over the accounting ledgers, planning coldly for the next season. Ram would not say out loud that he hoped he would not still be in the Valley then. That he longed to be back in his hut with Padma, that he yearned to meet his son. He felt he was neither here nor there. Nonexistent.

When Jivan and Karak argued, this feeling only grew worse. Home loomed beyond his reach as the place of peace, the Valley as a place of division. He knew this was too simple to be true.

Jivan and Karak's melon crop was late that winter. So by February, they had joined the other Valley farmers desperately seeking workers, prowling past the labor office looking for the usual line of sun-weathered men. But no one was there. Lettuce had come up in the northern part of the Valley. The shipping companies sent their laborers out to their corporate land first, as they always had, ignoring contracts with the family farmers. Ram heard about it in town, he saw it himself: some small-farm lettuce wilted in the field, some cantaloupe turned soft, and a half year's work was wasted.

Jivan was known among the migrants to pay well, and once a foreman came to offer the services of his crew, two families who brought eight children between them, standing on the dirt path to the Eggenberger farm. Karak and Ram had just arrived from town, where they had been looking for workers too. When Jivan saw the children, he asked, "You are bringing them to work?"

"They are better for you, señor," the foreman said.

"It is against the law," Jivan said. But Ram knew that he had refused children working in his fields even before the new laws were passed.

"They are cheaper."

"No," Jivan said.

"We can pick fast, señor."

"No."

Karak had been listening. "Bhai-ji, what are you thinking?" he said. The ride into town had been too hot, and unsuccessful, and Ram knew Karak's frustration was mounting.

But Jivan would not be swayed. "What will you do when the sheriff comes and sees the children working here?"

The workers had begun to walk away. "The sheriff will not come!" Karak screamed.

"No," Jivan said again.

"Can you see this?" Karak yelled at Ram as he turned away. "What is happening here? The entire crop shall be lost!"

Later, in private, Ram said to him, "You do not understand his concern, because you do not have children."

"And you do?"

He did not know whether in that instant Karak had forgotten, or whether he had meant to be cruel. "I do, Karak Singh," Ram said. The words seemed to clog his throat, prevent him from breathing. Was he a father or not? He was surprised at his reaction.

"At home, children work, always," Karak said. "What is this principle? It's understandable if it's one's own principle and one's own money. What is the selfishness of one man keeping up with principles while another is to lose his profit?"

Ram had to leave him. Karak did not speak to the others that afternoon, and went out by himself without explanation. At the dinner hour, a man appeared at the farm and approached while the Punjabis sat on the porch. He had a broad face that Ram had seen before.

"Do you know me?" the man asked Jivan in Spanish. He was clean-shaven. He spoke politely.

"You are familiar," Jivan said.

"I came with some others to pick cantaloupe last March. My name is Alejandro," the man said. "I have my own people now. I see that your cantaloupe is ready. I remember, you paid us so well."

Neither mentioned Ángel Cruz's death; it did not seem proper.

"How many of you?" Jivan asked.

"Eight. We can finish your work in three days."

"We have more in the back."

"Sí." The Mexican man nodded.

"My cousin's cotton crop is a few miles away. Can you help afterwards with that?"

"Sí," he said again.

"Come tomorrow. We will start in the early morning."

The man left, smiling.

Jivan turned to Ram and Amarjeet and Kishen, sitting quietly at the table. "We are saved," he announced.

THEY CAME THE SAME WAY they had before, six men and two women
on foot, with a mule carrying their burlap sacks. The fair-skinned
girl was there too. On the morning before they began work, Ram
saw her standing in the field with the others, against the backdrop of
the dawn. But she was not talking to them, even though she stood
in their midst, huddled against the morning chill; she was looking
at something behind the packing shed. She glanced again and again
in that direction. It was only when Ram stepped outside that he saw
what it was: Karak, loading crates onto the wagon, his bright green
dastar tied neat and smart, his shirtsleeves rolled up tight past his
elbows, already perspiring in the early morning.

Ram told himself he did not care. She was a strange creature, this
fair-skinned woman—human but foreign, still.

The days were glorious and sunny with a chill in the air by sunset. The third day, following their break for lunch, the Mexican girl
approached them. They were sitting in the breezeway finishing their
meal and she held up the olla from their camp. The vessel had fallen
from its rope and the water had spilled—the last they had filtered
from the settling pond. The men would awaken soon from their rest,
and there would be no water for them. Would the jefes kindly have
any that the workers could drink? She had addressed herself to Jivan,
but it was Karak who rose and said, in Spanish, that he would help.

He brought three extra ollas that Kishen always hung in the back,
one at a time, walking slowly. They talked while he carried them,
his arms embracing the vessel, leaning toward her, from the Hindu
farmhouse to the Mexican camp, back and forth. Months later, the
Mexican girl and the Hindus would laugh together about this.

15

MARCH 1916

THIS IS WHAT THE ANGLOS AND THE HINDUS AND THE OTHERS THOUGHT they knew about the Mexicans in the Valley: they were dirty, lazy, primitive; they were of mañana persuasion. They treated their women like chattel. They did not know how to negotiate an agreement regarding land and property. How could their country know anything but chaos and war between brutal strongmen, even though they called it by the noble name of revolution?

And yet things happened. The Mexican government made money from an international water deal, the country held elections, and despite everything the Americans in the Valley said, the Anglo farms could not run without them.

When the Mexicans came and started work, Karak felt the fair-skinned girl admiring him, and it was irresistible. She was called Rosa. He liked the name. Every night, after the work was done, he sat with her near the jackrabbit rock, eating dates and talking while one or two of the men played a guitar or an accordion at the camp, the breeze carrying the music toward them. Whenever Alejandro saw them together, he would approach, and Karak could see that Rosa was less lively when he was near. Alejandro would glance at Rosa and speak pointedly about the harvest, turning his body toward the fields, and Rosa would wander away.

Karak was not discouraged. His muscles ached from hauling the crates on and off the wagon, driving the wagon through the dust and wind to the shippers in town. Still, he sought the girl out, again and again.

The family did not seem to care. Kishen ignored him as she watered her vegetable garden. Jivan would be in the house, Amarjeet might be lying on his cot. Leela did not bother them. It was only Ram who found a reason to stay nearby. It bothered him that Ram would hover.

On that first day that Karak had fetched water for Rosa, Ram had been hovering even then. After the jugs had been delivered, Karak asked to know her name. He asked the question in the way he would ask a grown man, with respect, certainly not as one talks to a teenage girl: "What is your *good* name?" he had said.

She was about to walk away, but his question made her pause; he noticed the slight hesitation of her foot, the turning of her head.

"Rosa."

He saw her delight, the surprise that he had asked. Karak said, loud enough so Ram could hear, "You are too pretty to be working in the fields." He had spoken in English first, just so *Ram* could understand, even if *she* didn't. Ram had glared at him.

On the day the harvest was finished, Karak approached Jivan while he doled out dollar bills to Alejandro, and the foreman counted them and put them in his saddlebag. After Jivan left, Karak told Alejandro that he wanted to speak with him. Alejandro was astride the burro as if it were a warhorse, looking down at Karak from a height. But Karak had his hand on the bridle.

"Alejandro, does Rosa live with you?"

"Sí, señor. She is my wife's sister." Already, Alejandro seemed to know what he would ask him.

"Her father?"

"He died some time ago."

Karak did not know what to say. He did not know if this was how it was done in the west. But he could not think of any other way to act that would be considered respectful of the girl. It never occurred to him to approach her directly.

"Nothing good can come of mixing two different people, señor," Alejandro said slowly. Karak saw a flicker of anger in his eyes.

"If her father were alive, would he agree with you?"

The man had no answer. Karak felt he had won. Alejandro's cheek twitched. "I will think on it."

SEVERAL WEEKS AFTER THE HARVEST, Karak was repairing the fence next to the animal shed when Amarjeet approached.

"Bhai-ji, a woman has come to see you."

Irrationally, Karak thought, *Could it be Rosa?* He had been thinking of her all this time. Then he reconsidered—why would she come? But he could not help it. As he turned the corner of the house, his heart began to beat faster.

But the woman waiting for him was a decade older, small, and she was stern as he approached, as if she were assessing him.

"Señor Singh. I am Esperanza," she said in Spanish. "You know my younger sister, Rosa María?"

"Sí." He could see Rosa in her features, in her nose, in the curve of her mouth.

"My husband told me—you were asking about her. You would like to spend time with her."

In the roadway, he could see Alejandro sitting on a buckboard, hitched to a mule.

"Sí." He supposed that was what he was asking for. "Sí, señora."

"Please come to our home and visit us."

He did not expect this. Perhaps his surprise showed on his face.

"Por favor. No tenga pena."

"Muy amable."

"Come tomorrow," she said.

KARAK WORE HIS BEST SHIRT AND TROUSERS and a clean dastar of royal blue, which he tied with great care. This show of courting a girl and her family was new to him. Different from the marriage that would have been settled for him at home. Different also from visiting his favorite girl at the brothel in Manila. That was long ago, when he was an innocent, only twenty, but he realized now that he had had feelings for her. He had tried to win her favor with gifts and charm, always arriving freshly bathed, and she always let him believe that he had won her heart. He had wanted no more than that, of course. Even now, thirteen years later, he wondered about her. He would never know the truth.

He decided he would ride the mare; that would appear most dashing. Ram approached as he was saddling her.

"Where are you going?" he asked.

Karak hesitated, knowing the answer would bring judgment. "To the home of that girl. The one who worked here during the harvest."

"Rosa." The heavy way he pronounced the syllables conveyed everything: derision, jealousy, Ram's feeling toward anyone with whom he did not share a culture. "I wonder what type of bean they will serve you—black or brown."

The question was meant to be petty, as if they did not have enough money to serve meat.

"I will tell you when I get back," he said simply, before hurrying away. He would not indulge Ram's pettiness.

THE BARRIO LAY EAST OF THE RAILROAD TRACKS, a cluster of wooden shacks at the edge of the colored part of town. Chickens and barefoot children ran freely on the dusty paths. Each year the cluster grew larger. Some homes were hovels. Rosa's family's was larger than most.

Alejandro answered the door, nodding at Karak, and Esperanza stood behind her husband, holding a baby on her hip. "Mi mujer," Alejandro said, as if he had forgotten that she had met Karak already, when she invited him. Esperanza seemed unsure of herself but smiled immediately. Would he ever get used to the openness of these western women, who freely met one's eye? In Punjab it would have been different; he could have been comfortably passive, allowing an intermediary to do the difficult talking. Immediately he wondered if he should have brought Jivan. Why did he not think of it earlier? He hesitated, standing on the threshold. Jivan was sure to be offended.

"Pásale—come in, señor," Esperanza said, smiling. He sat on the wooden chair that she offered him.

In the room was a dining table, an iron bed, a simple couch, a sewing machine, a child-size mannequin draped with a white dress. A door led to a back room. Next to it, a table held a cluster of saints. It was not a home of wealth, but the curtains were cheerful. The tablecloth was clean. Everywhere were signs of care.

Rosa appeared in a light blue printed frock. He had not seen her look quite so womanly before, and he felt the hair on his arms and neck rise. He was not in love with her—no, he was not an innocent lad. But what he felt was not only desire. It was something in between, that a man could recapture in finding a woman who admired him—something that was close to love. When Karak looked at her, she looked at her hands. Esperanza offered Karak a lemonade. Alejandro, sitting at the front of the table, asked about the value of the crop, but he was the laborer, Karak was the farmer, they did not have much to say to each other. Karak would not reveal such information anyway.

Karak asked about the mannequin. Esperanza told him she sewed baptism and confirmation dresses. She glanced at Alejandro before admitting that women from the barrio sought her out as soon as the babies were born. Sometimes even before.

So that explained the couch and extra bedroom, Karak thought. Alejandro could not have afforded such things only through planting and harvesting the Valley's crops.

Esperanza served him tamales filled with chicken, sitting atop a mound of rice, steaming hot and delicious. Karak remembered Ram's question and felt a small victory. Now the conversation began to loosen. He found Spanish words he had not used in a long time. "How do you make the tamales?" he asked Esperanza. He did not mind asking a womanly question of a woman. Esperanza asked how he had learned Spanish and he told her that for five years he had lived in the Philippines after his service with the British, working as a night watchman at a bank. Local businesses paid good salaries to personnel who used to work for the British.

Karak knew he was the boss, even here. He could feel that in Alejandro's guarded speech. He could see already that Esperanza approved of him. When she mentioned her sewing, Karak asked to see a sample, and she drew back her chair to fetch some. "Esperanza—" her husband said sharply. She glanced at Alejandro and sat back down. Rosa's eyes darted back and forth between them all.

"Señor Singh," Alejandro said, "what is your intention in coming here?"

"I would like your permission to take Rosa out from time to time," Karak said. He did not know all their customs, but he felt this statement to be true. He wanted to spend time with Rosa.

"For what purpose? You think that because we Mexicans work for you that we don't protect the honor of our women?"

Karak saw Esperanza look away. Perhaps she had not wanted her husband's words to emerge with such venom.

"My intention is honorable—to see if we should be married."

Wasn't that what he wanted? Wasn't that why he should have brought Jivan?

He glanced at Rosa. She had fixed her gaze out the small window to the side of the table, but at his statement, her eyes widened.

Karak was encouraged. "If she might have me," he added. In that moment, he was sure she would.

He saw Esperanza nod at Alejandro, and Alejandro said gruffly, "There is no similarity of culture, of language, of religion. You think that because we do not own many things, do not have lots of money, we don't treasure these?"

"We live in America now, Alejandro. The old things do not matter so much. We must think of our survival. Enjoy life while we can. Make a good living and have a family. There is no more than this." He wished he did not have to speak. Why had he risked his dignity and position in this way? He berated himself again: Why hadn't he brought Jivan with him?

"We Mexicans value our culture. Our women."

"I would value Rosa too, if she were to become mine."

Esperanza glanced at her husband, and Karak caught the glance. She wanted the match badly. What would Alejandro do now?

"You go ahead and take her out, Señor Singh." He was making a show of appearing magnanimous. "I will allow it this one time, and we will see."

They agreed there could be a picnic on the following Sunday. Karak was satisfied.

HE CAME TO FETCH HER in the buckboard, having packed up the food himself after Kishen cooked it, and they went to the only park east of the tracks, situated between the Negro settlement and Japantown. When he realized that too many people would be watching them—a turbaned Hindu consorting with a Mexicana—he turned out of town and went along the dirt path that led to the new plank road. He wished he had a machine, one of those new models that were being snapped up more quickly than Ford could make them. That would impress Rosa; he was sure of that.

Where there was still shrub, before the sand started, he pulled up the mare and together they spread out their blanket under a mesquite tree on the side of a delivery canal. Arrowweed framed the water. A pleasant breeze shifted the fabric of her dress, the hair of the horse's mane. He was wearing his finest pants and crossed his legs on the blanket. She hitched her skirt to her calves to sit down. Dainty shoes were fitted on her feet. As they spread out the food, his hand brushed the bare skin of her forearm. He felt a thrill of ice in the heat. In the distance, the sleeping Mount Signal straddled Mexico and the United States.

She was not shy with him.

"Why are you courting me?" she asked as they began to eat. His fluency in Spanish came and went. At this question, he stammered, then felt a moment of lightness and laughed when she did. Then he was bothered by that laugh. Was she making fun of him? Did she not think him manly? He had brought roti and beans; he had asked Kishen to make something as close to Mexican food as she could, in an effort to show they could be familiar. But she was taunting him, giggling. "I am a Mexican girl, and you are a Hindu."

He corrected her, telling her he was Sikh, not Hindu. That was why he wore the dastar. That was why he wore the iron bangle.

"Why do they call you Hindu?" she asked.

"I do not know." Then he laughed again, though he was disheartened by her question. "We are from Hindustan. So to them we are Hindu. Maybe." He looked at her. "We call ourselves Hindustani."

She did not seem to understand all the nuance. "So I am a Mexican girl, and you are a Sikh."

"Don't we live in America, where such things can happen? Where we are equal?"

"Does equal mean that we mix like this?" she said.

SHE CHALLENGED HIM, but not in a way he couldn't surmount. And he didn't feel he had impressed her. He did not want to take her to the cinema, even if they would be allowed in, on the west side. He did not want her to see how the people in town looked at him with his dastar. He felt he could not go to the Mexican Hall; he did not know their customs and dances. What did cinemas and dance halls have to do with life on a farm? This is what puzzled him always about western women. They wanted to be courted, but what did courting have to do with real life?

But she cared about her family, more than she cared about herself. That felt familiar, not like the Anglos, who struck him as cold, distant. She was religious. That felt familiar too. At her suggestion, with Alejandro's permission, he went with her to worship the next Sunday. Mass was held under a large ramada erected at the edge of the barrio. They sat in back, on a crate that had once held watermelon, out of view of the others. They could barely hear the padre as he spoke from the pulpit. When others knelt on a board placed on the dirt, Karak remained seated. When Rosa went for communion, Karak did not rise. Esperanza and Alejandro had sat in front and Esperanza turned around and caught her sister's eye. Esperanza smiled—they could see her pleasure that they were there, together. Karak and Rosa left first, so that people would not see them and gossip, but they came back afterward and Rosa showed him all the saints displayed in a wooden cabinet that stood in the front, under the shelter of the ramada. She explained who they were. She was eager for him to know and Karak listened patiently, recalling the figures that he had seen in the churches in the Philippines, on the sides of the roads, and in the buggies. Rosa explained that three older women took care of them when the padre was not here during the week. To Karak, they did not seem too different from the Hindu deities he knew. Even to a Sikh, there was comfort in that.

Later that afternoon, they drove the buckboard into El Centro. The commercial district was near empty and few people noticed them together, and they walked through the streets, Rosa holding a parasol against the sun. They were in the elite part of town where the Hotel Barbara Worth stood, but even the sheriff's deputies seemed to be home with their families after church. Karak and Rosa were not bothered; there were no teenage boys to follow them, no wealthy ladies to stare. He saw Rosa's eyes widen and her exclamation when they stood in front of the jewelry store; she had a taste for gold and diamonds. This too reminded him of home. In the window of the piano store, they saw instruments for sale: guitars, accordions, and a trumpet were propped up in a separate display in the corner of the window. She told him that her mother used to sing beautifully and worked at a hotel restaurant in El Paso, entertaining guests with live music. That was long after her father died, after they crossed the border, ten years ago. Her grandmother had lived with them. But by the time Rosa was fifteen, both her grandmother and mother had died too. Esperanza had wed and decided to move west to Fredonia because Alejandro had told her there was opportunity in the Imperial Valley. Rosa, of course, came with them.

Rosa and Karak went as far as the furniture store, where the wealthy Anglos shopped, much farther than they would have wandered on any working day. Through the window, they saw the Persian rugs hanging in the back, a mock room displayed with a home telephone hanging on the wall, a showroom for faucets and sinks. A very few houses, the expensive ones close to town, had running water in them.

"So many beautiful things!" Rosa said.

"I can buy them all for you."

She was still looking through the window when she said, dreamily, distractedly, "We will have such beautiful children." That was when Karak knew. Just a moment later her face flushed and she giggled, her eyes darting about as if she did not know exactly where she was. She turned away; surely she had not meant the thought to be articulated.

"You feel so sure about me?" he asked, but he was talking to her back. Her hat sat at an innocent angle.

"Yes."

"Why?"

"Because of the harvest, last spring. I saw how you acted when Señor Cruz fell in the field. You have a good heart, a strong heart. You jumped on the horse and went immediately to fetch the doctor, like a son."

Goodwill swept through him, as it had long ago, when he had loaned Ram money in Hong Kong to buy medicine for his cousin. He had not wanted to ride for the doctor for Ángel Cruz that day. But as he gazed at Rosa's delicate back and shoulders, he thought he could be who she thought he was.

That night Karak approached Jivan alone near the settling pond. Jivan was turned away from him, facing the water with his head bent in prayer, whispering the sing-song of Rehras Sahib. Karak had to pay the man the proper respect. He had already failed by not asking him to come to the barrio, but he would try to fix his mistake now. He waited until the prayer was finished, then spoke. "Bhai-ji, as you are the head of our family here, I request your permission to marry."

Jivan raised his head but did not turn around. If he was surprised, he did not show it. "You do not need my permission, Karak. You are a grown man."

So he had been right that Jivan had minded.

"If you do not grant me your blessing, then to whom can I go?"

"Is it the Mexican girl Rosa?"

"Yes."

"How is the family?"

"They keep a tidy house. They are clean. They are respected by their neighbors. She is an innocent, bhai-ji. And they are not hesitating despite our differences."

Jivan turned to face him. "But why are you not hesitating? You are not Catholic. Your children will be raised by a Mexican. They will be strangers to you. They will not speak Punjabi."

He had not thought that Jivan would resist him. He had thought only of the wound to Jivan's pride in not asking for his permission. "I cannot spare time to go home and fetch a wife," Karak said. But it was more than that; he would not have gone if he could. Something about Rosa made him feel free, unburdened by his past.

Jivan frowned. "Yes, I had the luxury to travel to Punjab. It is true." He turned abruptly and walked back toward the house, leaving Karak there, standing alone by the pond. The water shone like blood under the sunset. He turned and followed Jivan.

"I did not mean to offend, bhai-ji."

Jivan did not look at him. They walked together across the crusted earth. "I give you my permission, Karak," he finally said, without enthusiasm.

Karak hesitated. "Thank you, bhai-ji."

"I went to fetch Kishen in 1910 and bring her back. There was no risk then. I could go without the British government forcing me to stay in India. And the Americans allowed me to reenter without any restriction." He was explaining something to Karak that he did not need to explain. "It was a different time."

"Even if I could, I will not return to Punjab, bhai-ji," Karak said. "I have no one there except my mother. I will leave to my brothers the few acres I have. Better that I marry and settle here. They will be happy too. They cannot survive without the money I send."

Jivan stared at him. "You have my blessing, Karak. Go and do the needful."

Karak would have married Rosa anyway, regardless of what Jivan said. But he felt a weight lift from his shoulders that he had not known he was carrying.

FOR TWO WEEKS, Ram kept his distance from him. After Karak had returned from the first dinner at Rosa's home, Ram did not ask about it. "They served chicken," Karak had said, as they cleaned out the packing shed the following day.

"What?"

"They served chicken." He glared at Ram. He picked up the toolbox and headed for the house, leaving Ram staring after him. He would not stand for the arrogance of a man who already had a wife and son to deny that to another.

That evening, when Karak was bathing in the ditch, Ram came for his bath too. "I mean only that you will lose yourself if you marry her. You know what they say at home, about the mixing of people. Your ancestors will curse you, and your descendants will too. She is outside of our society."

"Perhaps you have forgotten, Ram. I am not Hindu."

"I am reminding you of the dignity of the dastar you wear."

"I know about dignity. We do not believe as you do." He saw Ram flinch. After all, Ram had never known his father, a Sikh man who was said to have died a hero in battle. He knew the words would hurt.

They avoided each other after that. They spoke only when others were near, during breakfast or dinner, and only about matters regarding the fields.

THE FOLLOWING SUNDAY, Jivan accompanied Karak to the barrio. Several children called out to Karak as he arrived. He had some sweets in his pocket, and he gave these out to two or three of them, who scampered away, laughing. The previous two Sundays, men and women had noticed his passing through: a Hindu man with a dastar in the Mexican barrio. But today, with Jivan, Karak drew even greater attention. A few of the Mexicans had worked on Jivan's farm. He stood a foot taller than most of the residents. Men stood on the thresholds

of their homes to stare. Karak could sense their antagonism. He had
been seen leaving with Rosa. He was a threat. Later, Rosa would tell
him that some men in the barrio had questioned Alejandro about
allowing Karak to court her. The women had gossiped about them
as they scrubbed their washboards. Now he saw only that a small
group of men stared at him as he passed, and he, in response, carried
himself with greater boldness.

Alejandro's door opened before they knocked. Karak felt a moment of panic. Should he have asked Rosa to marry him before this
visit? What would a Mexican suitor have done?

"Señor Singh," Alejandro said, looking up at Jivan, allowing
them inside the house. "What brings you here?"

Karak did not want him to grow tense. He said, quickly, "I have
come to ask for Rosa's hand in marriage."

A cry rang out from the other room, and Esperanza appeared,
her hands clasped together. "¡Gloria a Dios!"

Alejandro looked from Karak to Jivan. Karak explained, "In our
country, it is proper for the head of the family to be involved."

Alejandro and Esperanza went into the back room, leaving him
and Jivan alone. Karak saw Jivan cast his eyes around the home: the
table where he had eaten dinner three weeks ago, the saints clustered
near the doorway to the bedroom. Karak wondered where Rosa was.
Alejandro emerged with his hands on his hips, but his face showed
his ambivalence. He addressed himself to Karak. "Sí, señor," he said,
with too much formality. "Tiene mi bendición."

Heat swept through Karak's body. The future stretched out before him, a settled place, secure and hard-won and different from the
past. Rosa emerged from the back room, looking at him brightly. She
had been there all the time. He felt light-headed. He had not known
himself to still be capable of elation.

16

JUNE 1916

ON THE MORNING OF HIS WEDDING, KARAK DREAMED OF MANILA. HE WAS strolling through the Intramuros near the entrance of the grand cathedral, as he used to. His father was with him. His father did not say or do anything; they walked together side by side; although at that time in Karak's life, his father was already dead. They stopped on a bridge spanning the Pasig River and gazed upstream. Karak was wearing his old uniform as a security guard at the bank.

It was not untrue to say he despised his father. He did not know why, on this day of all days, his father would appear to him. He did not know why, after all these years, the city should haunt him. While there, he heard about the Bengalis who had passed through a hundred years before, enslaved, to new shores in Acapulco. He learned these stories from the sailors drinking in the saloons. Manila had always had that Spanish tie with Mexico. Perhaps that was why he thought of it. Now he would have that tie too.

He woke at dawn. Lying on his back in the dim light, he thought of Rosa, sleeping in the small house in the barrio. Tonight she would

be next to him. He surprised himself. It had been a long time since
he had experienced a slow building of desire. There had been Teresa,
the woman he knew in Manila who worked in the brothel. He had
been a soldier; he had been with his share of women, but it was Teresa who stood out in his mind against the fog of years. Now it would
be Rosa.

She was pretty, yes. But he knew some men would think her
face too round, or her arms a bit too plump. No, it was something
else—something else that made his thirty-three years feel more like
her eighteen. A future lay before him, and he liked it. He could be
wealthy; he could be respected. He could surpass who he had been:
the second son of a man who had failed in every way there was to fail.
He, Karak Singh, would *not* fail. He would do everything he could
to not fail. He would make a name for himself, make his wife grateful, become a success, put humiliation behind him.

It was still dark outside, and no one else was awake. Even the
rooster was not stirring in the yard. He poured water from the olla
and splashed it on his face. Rosa was unspoiled by the world. She
would defer to him. When they had been riding together on the
buckboard the previous week, she had leaned into him so that their
shoulders had touched, so that her breast had brushed his arm. "It is
so hot here," she had said, as if it were unfamiliar to her, although she
had always lived in the desert heat and cold. She had shyly, charm-
ingly, over the past few days, made fun of his accent in Spanish; he
could not roll his *r*'s properly, she said. Or, he spoke too slowly.

When they had reached the barrio, he got off the buckboard
first, then took her hand to help her down. He had seen the Anglos
doing this. He thought it sophisticated, a way of showing authority by *not* showing authority, of showing manhood by *not* showing
manhood. She put a dainty shoe on the step. He slipped on the mud
beside the wheel, and caught himself before he fell. He had been
embarrassed, laughing. "You have a beautiful sunrise," she had said
quietly, in English. He was puzzled by this. It was not until he had

left, egging the mare into a trot, that he realized that in Spanish, the word for "smile" sounded like the English word "sunrise." *Sonrisa.* Rosa had been trying to impress him.

Now, in the lonely desert morning, he thought about his future and his past and the man that he had been in Manila and Hong Kong, when he'd worked for the white man in a country far from his home. He thought of the boy that he had been and about his father, who had also worn the British uniform. Even then, the British officers who commanded Indian troops would wear a dastar, in supposed solidarity. But were they not merely manipulating the Indians into compliance? Wasn't it all a sham? He thought about Roubillard and the buttermilk. He pushed that thought away; the humiliation of the buttermilk threatened everything. He reminded himself: He knew the vice president of the bank. He was friendly with the sheriff. The buttermilk need not ruin him.

"Is your country so hot as this?" Rosa had asked that day in the wagon, when her breast had brushed against his arm. "Is it not unbearable with that great turban and your beard?"

Karak could have been angry, but he was not. "The turban gives dignity, Rosita," he said. "It is a mark of honor and courage. I have worn it since I was a small boy." Other men—Jivan—would have said the uncut hair was a divine gift.

He could tell that she did not understand. He found himself wanting to please her. Here was a new beginning for him, and he wanted to meet it as a new man.

His mother was in India and would not need to know. His father, if he had been alive, would not have approved. But even his father had been a man of practicality. It would have been his youngest brother, who had died during the famine, who would have chastised him. But that brother had not been shamed for drinking buttermilk or harassed on the street. The thought caught him, the innocence of his brother's chastisement. He shoved it aside and felt the painful luxury of ignoring a dead boy's opinion.

He saddled up Jivan's mare. He would not be gone long; on horseback, the trip was less than an hour. As he was about to leave, Kishen came to the porch. He told her in a soft voice that he would be back soon. He kicked the horse into a trot before she could ask any questions.

The sun had risen by the time he arrived at Rosa's home. Esperanza answered the door, puzzled. "It is him!" she exclaimed.

Rosa was standing behind her, wide-eyed and startled. "Why do you come?" she asked.

Esperanza interjected—"It is not right, but now I must go, Rosa. Otherwise there will be no flowers left in the market. We will have none for your bouquet." She glanced at them both. "Alejandro will not be happy with me that I leave you two, but what can I do?"

Rosa nodded her head, but she looked away.

When Esperanza had gone, Rosa asked again, "Why do you come?"

"To ask a favor." His hand went slowly to his dastar and unwound it. Underneath he undid the patka and his hair, dark and heavy, fell to his waist.

He felt vulnerable, naked before her. The ends of his hair had been with him for as long as he had been alive, thirty-three years of his life upon this earth, had traveled with him across the continents, as much a part of him as his organs and limbs. He folded the patka and dastar neatly and put them inside his leather pouch.

"I need a haircut and a shave," he said, the way the Americans said it. "Can you help me?"

Her surprise flashed across her face.

"I did not take this decision lightly," he added. "I have given it much thought."

She nodded slightly. She walked into the other room and Karak heard the sound of items being moved, a clattering of possessions. On the table near the doorway stood Esperanza's saints. He did not know them all, only the largest: the Virgin of Guadalupe. The early sun shone in at an angle and cast a shadow across her blue robe.

When Rosa came back, she held a pair of scissors and a straight razor. He sat on a wooden stool near the stove. She poured water from a kettle into a small basin, placed it on a table beside him. "I used to shave my father," she said. "I was the only one in the household he trusted." She asked Karak to strip to his undershirt, and he complied.

His face was level with her waist, at the place her blouse was cinched into her skirt. She was facing him as she drew a part in his hair. Her forehead glistened with moisture. Her arms glowed gold in the sunlight. He could smell the tang of her. She must have been outside before he arrived, perhaps caring for the chickens. She stood behind him now, her hands on his hair, loosening the tangles with a comb. He could feel the teeth sweeping across his scalp.

"Why do you bother with the knots?" he asked, impatiently.

"To keep it neat after it is cut."

Her fingers caressed his forehead, his ears. More water trickled into the basin. She pulled together all his hair at the base of his neck. He heard the scrape of the scissors' blades as they worked. He thought he would not care as the hair fell away, but he did.

When he saw himself in the handheld mirror, he did not know who he was. He felt light-headed. He would never again wear a dastar. The countrymen he met would no longer think he was part of the Khalsa. All this, Rosa had no way of knowing, and she never would. She silently showed him the long black locks, wrapping them around her fist. A part of himself. It was nothing, wasn't it, only hair? He had never thought of himself as a religious man, but now it was evident to him: this was more than hair, and it was more than religion. He had had a choice. Other men would have chosen differently.

"It is thick, no?" she asked, smiling. She twisted the strands, rolling them into a knot. "It is like a snake!"

"It is like a snake," he agreed, and laughed; he must not show that it hurt him.

When this first cut was over, she hummed a tune that he recognized from the fields, soft and low. She tipped his head back to inspect the part, and he felt her breasts against the crown of his head, the sound of her voice vibrating against his scalp. He closed his eyes. The scissors clipped around his ears, around the crown.

Then she stood before him and took up the shaving brush.

She put soap on the beard, spread it with gentle strokes. She dipped the razor in the water. "Don't worry," she said. "You must trust me." She raised her eyebrows for a moment, to tease him. Then their eyes met, and she was serious.

The soap was cold against his skin, but when he felt the blade scrape his cheek he suddenly knew its danger. Small, even strokes. She could cut him on a whim and draw blood. It was in her power. He drew in a breath to calm himself. A small muscle under her collarbone flexed and moved. She breathed softly, intent on her work, concentrating on this spot on his face, the tender area under the jawline, her gaze fixed on him but not meeting his eye. He stared at her intently.

When she was finished, she tipped his chin up toward her. "You are very handsome," she said. He reached up and grasped her shoulders, pulling her toward him, with strength, kissing her full on the mouth. She had violated him, hadn't she? Played with him as he sat, helpless? She kissed back, hard. If he hadn't heard Esperanza return outside, her shoes scraping the gravel, he would have traced his hand up the back of her thigh, and, he knew—she would have been completely willing.

KARAK RODE BACK TO THE FARM and from a distance, he saw Leela hold her arm up and point, and run back into the house, perhaps yelling.

By the time he had arrived, others had come out too: Ram, Kishen, Amarjeet. Now he felt a sudden sadness, a knowledge that what had been done could not be undone, even if he had wished. He did not wish, he told himself. If they blamed this on the girl, he thought, he would not be able to contain himself; it was so much more than the girl. He dismounted without a word.

Jivan was the last to appear. When their eyes met, Karak said only, "Bhai-ji." Jivan turned and walked to the packing shed. Karak could feel the weight of Ram's gaze, cold and judging, as he followed Jivan inside. When Karak entered, he realized Jivan was dressed for the wedding but he was bent over the work table, hammering to assemble a crate.

"She did not ask me to do it," Karak said.

"No," Jivan said. "She would not. She is too mild." He looked Karak in the eye, as if to say *I know it was a decision only you took.* So that Karak could not be absolved through Rosa.

"There are many pressures, bhai-ji."

"Yes."

"I ask your pardon."

Jivan did not say anything. He looked down again at his work, but something in his manner suggested forgiveness, so much so that Karak stepped forward and said, "When we are before the judge, I will need two witnesses. Will you agree?"

Jivan closed his eyes and nodded.

"There is a position of honor in carrying the ring before I give it to Rosa. Will you do so?"

"Find someone better suited to that task," Jivan said.

Karak knew what he meant: find someone to whom that honor would mean something. It was the correct response; he would feel foolish if another Hindustani man were helping him follow a western custom. Even so, for a fleeting moment, he considered asking Ram. But Ram was jealous of him; he was sure of it. How could he trust someone like that? Karak knew who he would ask instead.

THE JUSTICE OF THE PEACE sat on a raised dais, wearing a black robe despite the heat. Sternness was expressed in the lines around his mouth and between his brows, in the straightness of his back. He scanned the entire party: Jivan's and Amarjeet's dastars, Rosa's white dress and tiara, Clive's presence as the only Anglo. He did not smile. "This is in anticipation of a wedding. . . . Is that correct?" he said to Clive.

"It is, sir," Karak said, stepping forward.

"May I see the license, please?"

Karak handed the clerk an envelope. Karak's eyes followed as the clerk handed it to the judge, who slowly put on his spectacles and scrutinized the paper. Perspiration beaded on the judge's forehead, wet the stray hairs that lingered on his balding head.

"Says here you're a native of India. Subject of Britain."

"I belong to Punjab Province."

"But your fiancée is from Mexico."

"Her family is here and in El Paso and Algo—"

"She was born in Mexico," the judge interrupted.

"Sí, señor," Alejandro said.

The judge glanced at him.

"Sister's husband, señor. Her guardian."

"But she has reached adulthood? She has no need of a guardian?"

Jivan explained to Alejandro in Spanish. The judge watched them keenly. "Sí, señor," Alejandro said, when he understood. "She has eighteen years," he said in English.

"A member of the Indian race and a British subject wants to marry a woman of Mexican race and citizenship under the laws of California? I see here that a week ago the clerk identified you as being of the 'brown' race, Mr. Singh."

Karak glared at him. The judge did not seem to notice.

"And she is listed as being 'white.'" The judge took off his spectacles, clasped his hands on the desktop, stared at Rosa. "Can she understand me? Perhaps she doesn't speak English." He looked around the other faces.

"I explain her," Alejandro said.

"I understand good," Rosa said.

"Mr. Singh, are you aware of miscegenation laws?"

"Sir?" Karak said, closing his eyes and opening them slowly.

"In California, people of different races cannot marry. I'd be breaking the law if I conducted this ceremony. I don't know what the city clerk was thinking when he issued this document. He'll get a reprimand from me." He folded up the license, handed it to his clerk. "Give that back to him."

Karak took the envelope, unseeing, numb. He would have struck the judge if he could, if the judge did not have his clerk seated in front of him, if they were not separated by a thick wall of wood.

"I don't need a clerk's license to tell me what my eyes can clearly see. You have brown skin. This young lady here has white skin. Although she's a Mexican girl, she is still Caucasian."

Clive was hearing this, Karak thought. Clive was witness to this humiliation, fingering the ring in his pocket. Ram, Jivan—all who had judged him—they were hearing it too. He remembered a British officer who had befriended him while he had served in Hong Kong. *Funny thing about you Indians. You're Caucasian, but you're black. No one ever expects to see a black Caucasian.* Rosa, Esperanza, and Alejandro, who was his hired man . . . they were seeing this too.

The room was still. In the far corner, the bailiff dropped something, a coin, a button. The noise echoed off the stone floor. Karak forced his voice through the stillness. "I too am Caucasian." He could not allow himself to repeat the word "sir."

"I think not, Singh."

"You tell me that in America, I cannot marry who I choose to marry?"

"Take your friends and go, before I have to call on the bailiff to help me."

Karak's heart pounded in his ears.

The judge rose to leave.

Karak stood. He could not turn to face all those who had come with him. He was still standing there after the justice of the peace had left, after the bailiff was showing the others out.

"Karak . . ." Jivan said. Karak felt the older man's hand on his shoulder.

He rubbed his face absent-mindedly, his fingers searching for the beard that was no longer there. His strength left him. He followed Jivan out of the room. A wooden bench stood outside in the hallway. It was a large bench. They had been sitting there, waiting for the justice, only a few moments before. The image taunted him. He bent and heaved and picked it up, threw it with full force. It landed with a thud, slid only a few feet. Even his rage was ineffective. Karak froze, staring at the bench, its small broken foot, the splintered wood, the mark on the floor.

The bailiff ran back into the hallway. "Hey! What's that you're doing? What?" He grabbed Karak from behind, but Karak lowered his shoulder to slip out of his grasp, shoving him sideways, against the wall. The bailiff reached for the gun in his holster.

"Arre' bhai!" Ram said, inserting himself into the space between the two men.

Karak felt his arms pinned against him. He did not have the strength to resist.

The bailiff drew his weapon, held it poised to the side. His path to Karak was blocked by Ram's body. Karak realized that it was Jivan who had grasped him from behind.

"What's happening here?" the bailiff asked, addressing only Clive, who stood farthest away from him. Cries echoed in the hallway. Kishen held Leela's face to her waist. Amarjeet stepped in front of them.

"Nothin', officer," Clive said. He's a little upset is all. It's been a rough mornin' for him. You can understand." Clive was smiling, too deferential.

"Can't say I do. I oughta bring him in for this—"

"He'll pay for it. The bench. Whatever the cost," Clive said.

The bailiff glared at Karak. Karak could not control his breathing. He could not control his heart.

"I oughta throw you out on your ass right now," the bailiff said.

"You have my word. Here—" Clive extended his hand; he was holding a trade card. "Send the bill to this address. It won't be a problem."

The bailiff took the card. He put his gun back in the holster. He sneered at Karak. "Get this bench straightened," he said to Clive. "And get these people out—whatever business you have with them."

"Yes, officer." Clive turned to Amarjeet. "Will ya help me git the bench up?" he said, though the boy had already done so. "I got it all under control." He nodded at the bailiff. "You can see that."

IN THE SUNLIGHT OUTSIDE, it was a different world. Karak saw the tears welling in Rosa's eyes, and he was reminded she was only eighteen. The tears irritated him, enraged him. He thought he could never love her now, he could never show her affection. Not after she had heard how that justice of the peace had spoken to him. Not after she had seen the bailiff lay a hand on him.

Jivan fixed him with his gaze. "Calm yourself, Karak," he whispered. "This is not the way to behave." He was standing so close Karak could feel his breath on his face.

Clive clapped Karak on the back. Karak could not stand his touch. "Well? What do we do now?" he said, as if they were at a picnic that had been rained out.

"Karak has a license to be married. He should be married," Jivan said.

They were looking at Karak, all of them: Ram and Amarjeet, Rosa and her family, standing in the bright sun, squinting at him. Suddenly, he could not stay there. Especially, he could not tolerate

Rosa, innocent and regal in her white dress, full of expectation. He turned and walked away. To his relief, Jivan followed him. "Karak—" he said.

"You lead, bhai-ji," Karak said in Punjabi. "I will do as you say."

"Let us go to El Centro. The justice of the peace there is more open-minded."

"How do you know?"

"Last month he married a Chinaman and a Mexican girl. So I heard."

Karak rubbed his face. The beard was not there; how long would that continue to surprise him? "I have become a strange peculiarity," he said. "Something other people talk about."

Jivan's eyes were full of compassion. "Don't mind it," he said.

THE JUSTICE OF THE PEACE IN EL CENTRO, perusing the marriage license in his chamber, did not care that Karak had brown skin and Rosa's was two shades lighter, or that the groom's party was a group of ragheads, that the bride's family seemed inconsequential. He was a worldly man in comparison to some; the Imperial Valley was not the only part of the west that he knew. He had been a lawman in Sonoma County. He had been on his own since he was sixteen. His father had dug for gold in '49 before he grew peaches in the San Joaquin valley. After his mother died, a Chinaman had cooked for the family. A Negro had helped feed the livestock on the farm, and because there had been no other families for miles, these men had also been his playmates, had fed him supper and once rescued him from drowning in the levee. A man was a man was a man, as far as the justice of the peace was concerned. For that matter, a woman was a woman. Who a man wanted to marry, who a man wanted to have raise his children, why, that was no concern of his at all. And it was even less of a concern to those city folks with big educations who measured a Negro's skull and jawline, measured a Chinaman's limbs and waist, kept their scientific records of Oriental body types in their bound notebooks on their mahogany desks in the fancy schools out east. Had those fancy people ever lived at all? That was why the justice of the peace had come to the Imperial Valley; it was situated at the edge of things. It had not yet become society. Everyone here had come from somewhere else.

Now he watched as the families gathered before him. It was an odd bunch. Mexicans, Hindus, an American, a quiet woman in Oriental dress. And they seemed joyless: The bride and groom had already wilted in the heat; the others would not meet his gaze. The families did not speak to each other. He wondered if the bride was already pregnant, how much the families had objected to the union. While he was perusing the license, the groom asked, "You will perform the marriage?"

What an odd question, he thought. "'Course," he answered, peering over the top of his spectacles. "I'm the justice of the peace, ain't I?"

Now the group, unusual as it was, seemed to relax. The bride's sister fussed with the bride's tiara and veil. The older turbaned man said something in a foreign language that made the younger one laugh. After signing the papers, the American guffawed and clapped the groom on the back. The matron of honor draped a string of beads around the shoulders of the couple as they stood, side by side. The bride smiled at her. The groom seemed in a daze, unbothered by anything—not when the young girl in pigtails cried, insisting on standing next to him, not when the American dropped something before the vows had been exchanged, which made a clatter against the wooden floor, and the groom picked it up and the justice realized it was the wedding ring. The American was the best man. The groom placed the ring on the bride's finger. He kissed the bride's forehead, embracing her. The Hindus, all of them, looked away.

"Congratulations. Best wishes." The justice of the peace shook the groom's hand, nodded at the bride. Now they seemed happy, the justice thought. No, he corrected himself. They seemed relieved. That was the only way to describe it.

JIVAN HELD A WEDDING RECEPTION for Karak and Rosa at the Eggenberger farm, a party under several tents on the field that stretched between the two houses. Mariachis played, guitars and trumpets drifting over the hum of conversation. Jivan welcomed several groups of Valley residents at the head of the line, greeting all the Punjabi men who gathered on Sundays at Fredonia Park, other countrymen from as far north as Date City, as far south as Mexicali; he clasped their shoulders and held them close. Karak and Rosa stood farther back, receiving their good wishes.

A group of Anglo business associates had come without their wives; this was a business dinner, after all. They huddled together, holding glasses of iced tea and lemonade. Jivan Singh provided them with significant income and they would not stay away. But it was more than that; they liked him too. They would talk about this party at their own dinner tables tomorrow: a wedding reception for a Hindu and a Mexican with Japanese guests. Tomoya Moriyama mingled with the Anglos easily. His wife, Hatsu, helped Kishen fry the rotis that Ram rolled out. As the sun was setting, the food was laid out on a long table near the kitchen. Esperanza and her friends had brought plates of tamales, fried nopales, chilaquiles, mole with chicken. On another table sat dishes of biryani, paneer, chole, chicken with gravy. Guests lined up to eat. Amarjeet and Harry Moriyama hefted jugs of water and lemonade.

As the sound of the guitar rose above the crowd, Karak felt a great sense of satisfaction. He was a married man now. The momentousness of what he had done finally settled on him. He had taken Rosa to Los Angeles the day after they said their vows before the justice of the peace. He had enjoyed her delight in their time away:

their meals, the cinema, strolling about Chinatown and beyond. She had not been shy with him in their marriage bed, and he was relieved and happy. What would he have done with a woman who was too modest with her dress removed? She looked radiant now, clothed in her youth, her not-knowing, in a white dress that he had bought her. They had found it hanging in the window of a strange shop that sold goods from both China and France.

She was unsure of herself; that was part of her radiance. He saw her searching the faces of the Punjabi men. From a distance, they were assessing her too; sometimes their eyes traveled too boldly. He knew she did not like it. Neither did he.

"Do not worry too much about them," he said.

She smiled at him. "No pos, sí," she said, "claro que no."

On the train returning from Los Angeles, she had told him she was nervous about moving into the Eggenberger house. Two weeks before, Karak had signed a lease with the Swiss man to rent his home. Jivan would still farm the land around it. Karak could not believe his good fortune. Now he and Rosa would live in a well-built, private home, separate from the others. He would begin a new life.

When they had arrived at Jivan's home, stepping over the threshold, Kishen Kaur had held a glass of water and circled it three times around Rosa's head. It was the gesture of welcome usually given by a new mother-in-law. That is not who Kishen was to Rosa, but that oddity touched Karak even more. He had always thought Kishen Kaur did not like him. Jivan and he had glanced at each other, as if they recognized it was both the wrong and the right thing to do.

As the Punjabis approached, Karak introduced them. "He is from my village," or "He served in the army with my brother in Hong Kong." Rosa smiled shyly, but she looked full into the men's faces. Out of awkwardness, or manners, or discomfort with her westernness, they would not look into hers. Karak could smell their jealousy and desperation as if it were a predatory thing. Some had wives in Punjab; others were not established enough to marry. He felt everywhere the thrill of unbroken ground, of the new venture. He sensed the undercurrent of their disapproval too. Ram had ignored him since their return and he did not approach them now. Karak pretended he did not cure.

The guests had all arrived, and now the mood of the party shifted. Karak and Rosa approached Jivan as he spoke to the group of Anglos. Clive pumped Karak's hand, bending forward as if he would kiss Rosa on the cheek, but then stopped himself. "Got yourself a pretty one, Karak!"

"Why did you not bring your wife?" Karak asked.

"Her mother took ill. She needed her there."

Perhaps there was another reason, but Karak decided he would overlook it. In their circle stood the manager of Varney General Store, who had sold Jivan so many implements, and the Swiss brothers who exchanged buttermilk for grazing rights on Eggenberger land. A loan officer from Fredonia Bank said, "You've got a nice spread here, Jivan." Another, looking around, added, "I didn't know it was *this* nice." Jasper Davis, the bank vice president, had brought his wife, Daisy, and his baby daughter too. Karak noted this with amazement. He felt a wave of goodwill toward the man.

Daisy Davis mixed freely with all, speaking Spanish with the Mexican women, daring to laugh with their men. Later, she approached Karak and Rosa while they stood with Kishen and Amarjeet. Daisy handed the baby to Kishen, and Kishen held her, smiling and cooing, warning Daisy against the evil eye while Amarjeet translated. Daisy encouraged Karak to hold the baby as well; this too amazed him.

"Mrs. Davis, this baby is so sweet," Karak said, "I hope *I* don't end up giving her the evil eye!" They laughed, and Rosa's eyes met his, heavy with meaning.

Twelve or fifteen families from the barrio had arrived together, and stood clustered near the drinks table. The men were quiet and did not talk much. They called Jivan "señor" and stayed close to Alejandro. They approached Karak only in a group. He remembered how the men in the barrio looked at him when he called on Rosa: the unbroken stares, the resentment. "¡Felicidades!" they said now, those same men—not meeting his eye, making sure Alejandro saw their skepticism, "Many good years to you." They spoke with hardness, with clenched jaws. Without the Hindus, there would not have been an occasion for Mexicans and Anglos to gather together; the space between the two communities was too wide. In a rush, Karak felt something else that satisfied him. He had stolen one of their women, and they begrudged him that. He made them feel small.

But the women laughed and spoke more comfortably. They sought out Rosa and greeted Karak when she introduced them. They looked up at him, smiling, the hems of their full skirts brushing against his pants, their shawls draped flirtatiously around their shoulders. He knew they thought he was appealing, handsome, even if they might not have approved of the match.

In the jumble of people, a man approached Karak. He was slightly built and balding, and he stepped forward with an earnest expression and shook Karak's hand. It took Karak a moment to recognize Stephen Eggenberger.

"I hope that in that house, you will be happy," Eggenberger said. Karak was surprised at his sincerity. He could not know how the Swiss man felt about the home. How it had been the center of the happy early days of his marriage, before his wife's illness forced him back to Los Angeles. Karak had met him only twice before.

"The house is like a gift to us," Karak said, meaning it. He did not speak of the pride, akin to triumph, that he felt in taking it over. He did not say how good it would feel to sleep inside a structure, instead of exposed to the raw dust of the desert. "We will keep it well," he added, as if they were equals.

"A house is better maintained when someone is living in it," Eggenberger said. "My wife and I were happy there."

When he translated for Rosa, she lowered her eyes. "Gracias, se-ñor," she said, giving a short curtsy, not quite graceful.

Jivan joined them, then Karak and Rosa wandered to the tables of food. From the edge of the gathering, Karak looked out at the crowd and felt a deep contentment. He had not ever thought he would be capable of this.

The mariachis played and the sound of the strings and the flute swept over the crowd. The trumpet swelled above the tent and the sand and touched the pale disk of the moon. The Anglos were staying much later than Karak had expected, speaking among themselves easily, laughing with Jivan.

Ignoring Karak, the guitarist approached Rosa and asked the name of her favorite song, and she told him "El centauro de oro." They laughed together over the selection, and Karak felt a flash of jealousy; he had not even known that Rosa supported Pancho Villa. When they finished playing, the guitarist called on his comrades to play music for dancing, but the Mexicans would not dance. The guitarist tried to cajole them and the vihuela player called out to Karak and Rosa too. She looked up at Karak, but he did not respond.

From the sidelines, in a group, the Anglo men gathered their belongings. Some had tried a bit of food, some had not eaten at all, but they said goodbye to Jivan, congratulated Karak once more, strolled past the house, and climbed into their automobiles and surreys and buckboards. As the last of them left the main tent, the guitarist turned his body to see them go. Jasper and Daisy stayed. So did Clive. A cool breeze blew in from the mountains, carrying no dust. The Hindustanees and Mexicans relaxed.

The mariachis began to play more loudly. Harnam Singh brought out bottles of whiskey he had hidden in his satchel, smuggled up from Mexicali. More lemonade was mixed, liquor poured surreptitiously into the lemonade glasses. Bellies were full now, guests were satisfied, and whiskey flowed silver-gold. Two Mexican couples got up to dance. A group got up to join them, young and old, children.

Karak pulled Rosa out to the dance floor. The trumpet blared louder. The women smiled, and the men tapped their feet, catcalling, clapping in time, faces glowing with perspiration. For a few moments, Karak felt their resentment disappear. Rosa's face flushed with pleasure; her eyes grew wide, and she tipped her head back and laughed, leaning into him. He was not an expert dancer, but he could pretend he was. As he danced and held Rosa's waist and spun his wife under the tent, the calls grew louder. He was conscious of Ram's even stare, of Jivan's hesitant smile. He saw Clive observing him intensely, as if to record the moment in his mind. That was odd, he thought. With a flourish the band stopped playing, putting down their instruments to rest for a few moments.

From inside Jivan's house, Amarjeet brought out Jivan's phonograph and Ram cranked it. They played five Punjabi love songs that the men knew from village life, and the men sang along, slurring their words. Sikander Khan brought out three more records, and when those were finished too, Harnam Singh brought out his dholki, hung the drum around his neck, and joined with another song on the phonograph, picking up the rhythm, making it loud and vibrant. The Punjabi men danced in a circle, arms raised. "Va!" the cry went out, "Va!" on the beat. The whiskey was the red in their cheeks, the brightness of their eyes.

Karak watched Rosa. He could sense her simultaneous attraction and revulsion to their loudness, their masculinity—he saw her and Esperanza exchange a glance. Perhaps the men alarmed her. Perhaps Esperanza was uncomfortable too.

In the jumble of bodies, Inder Singh approached Rosa, sweating, wearing a scarlet dastar, shoving something into her hand. Karak sprang to her side. "Arre' bhai! What are you doing?!" He took the money from her hand. "This is not Punjab!" he shouted at the other man, his voice louder than the music. "Why follow those customs here?" He slapped the bills against the man's chest. Some of them floated to the ground. Karak and Inder's faces were close, and Karak smiled, but he felt an affront he could not name—a hesitation for Rosa. Inder Singh backed away. His expression said, *Let it go,* and the moment passed. Around them, the dancing went on, as if the others did not recognize Karak's intensity of feeling. Later, Rosa would tell Karak about her alarm and he would ridicule it—gently—even though, in that moment of possessiveness, he had felt it too.

The Punjabi men were still dancing when another group of Mexicans arrived, only men, whom Karak did not know. The mariachis had already conceded defeat to the phonograph, and were putting away their instruments when a man yelled out in Spanish, "Where is Karak Singh?" Something in his voice made the party quiet down.

Karak and Rosa were standing near the food tables. The new man, surrounded by five or six others, was at the edge of the tent, and twenty people stood between them. Karak did not recognize him, but Rosa said, "It is Carlos."

"Carlos?"

"Our foreman when Ángel Cruz died. He despises Alejandro now—for swaying people against him. No one will work for him now."

As she spoke, Karak remembered more: How Carlos had looked at Rosa then, a young woman on his crew. How he spoke to her differently than he spoke to the others.

Before Karak could respond, he heard Jivan Singh's voice, loud in the darkness, coming from the middle of the crowd. "What do you want, Carlos Guerrero? You are drunk! Why have you come here?"

"We have come to make things right! You have ruined my reputation. Your partner has run off with one of our women. I've come to set the matter straight."

"You and your drunk friends think you can do that?" Jivan said.

Karak could feel Rosa's hand around his arm. She stood in the middle of the tent, in her white dress, and could not seem to move.

"There's nothing to concern you here," Alejandro said, stepping to the front.

"Why does he not show himself?" Carlos asked. "Is he a coward?"

Karak shook free of Rosa's hold and joined Alejandro. "I am here," he declared. "Get off our land." In the lamplight, he could see Carlos's round, grim face. Behind him, a man swayed, unsteady on his feet. But Carlos's other companions seemed alert and malicious.

"Get out, Carlos," Alejandro hissed. "Go home to your wife."

The man's eyes traveled from Karak's hair, to his face, to his shoulders, assessing him. Karak's anger steadily rose.

"I don't need to take care of my wife, Alejandro," Carlos said, his eyes never leaving Karak. "She's married to a mexicano, as she should be. But your sister-in-law must learn some things." He reached into his back pocket. Moonlight flashed on a blade. He seemed to hold both in his fist—the knife, the moonlight. Two of Carlos's friends withdrew knives of their own. People gasped. Karak, unthinking, lunged toward Carlos. A blast shattered the air, the vibration echoing in Karak's chest. He realized, dimly, it was a gunshot. It came from the direction of the house.

Jivan pushed his way to the front of the crowd, pointing the pistol at Carlos and his men. "Get out. Take your pandilla with you. Don't come here again." He aimed the gun at Carlos's chest.

Carlos grimaced and backed away, stumbling, tripping on a chair behind him. His buttocks hit the ground without a sound in the soft sand. He waved to signal to his men, but there was no need to; they had already run off into the dark. He sprang up and ran after them.

KARAK HAD SAVED THE HAIR that Rosa had cut. It lay in the knot in which she had tied it, tucked in a wooden box that he had purchased at the general store. He stored it in the cabinet where Mrs. Eggenberger must have kept her china. He thought that he would be able to keep the hair in his new home, that it would not be present in his mind. But it weighed on him in a way he could not name. Perhaps as a betrayal, or regret. Perhaps as realization that he had harmed himself, but that if he were presented with the decision again, he would make the same choice.

Every day now he shaved and observed himself in the mirror that lay near the basin that Rosa kept in the kitchen. His mind wandered from the mirror, to the room in Esperanza's home where the hair was cut, to Mrs. Eggenberger's china cabinet. No, it would not do. In the early mornings when Rosa would awaken and find him there, shaving, she would smile in a way that was both shy and flirtatious. She would never imagine that he was thinking about the coil of hair, the wooden box, the cabinet.

A week after the wedding reception, Karak rented a motorcar, and he drove Rosa to the barrio. She would spend a leisurely Sunday with Esperanza. He did not stay. He drove for hours on the new Plank Road, crossing the sand dunes, heading east to the Colorado River. The wooden box sat on the seat next to him. It was late June; even at sunset the heat was strong and stifling, but the river still flowed with the strength of the spring rains draining from the Rocky Mountains.

Sacred things must not be thrown away, his mother had said long ago, to a different boy who had borne his name and whom he no longer was. *But they may be placed in water, and the water must be flowing, and the flowing water must merge with the sea.*

He parked off the roadway near Winterhaven. The sky was filled with birds that were not of the desert, that flew from the green lagoons of the Colorado River Delta, where life teemed on the boundary of sea and land. He had been there before, when he had first arrived in the Valley. He picked his way through the shrub and grass and kneeled by the water. He opened the box.

The hair lay in a neat coil, gleaming black. Quickly, before he could think, he topped the box and released the coil into the river. His gut clenched. The hair unwound and swirled and floated off, downstream.

17

AUGUST 1916

FOR A MONTH, RAM STAYED AWAY FROM THE EGGENBERGER HOUSE AND its newly curtained windows, its swept porch, its painted trim. He could not name his feelings. Karak had not acted properly in marrying outside his community, but it was more than that. Was Ram jealous of him? Ram already had a wife and child. What, then?

He and Karak still needed to work as partners, to review accounts together so that Ram could plan how many harvests it would take to earn the dowry for his cousin. When Karak did not emerge from the Eggenberger home at the agreed-upon time one morning, Ram climbed up the porch steps and knocked on the door.

There was no answer. Because Karak would enter Jivan's home without knocking, Ram found himself doing the same, stepping into the parlor, peeking into the bedroom, assessing the furniture, the kitchen.

A rug lay under the new couch. There was a piano, which Ram had heard Rosa play in the evenings; lamps, tables, an armchair wrapped in a dust cover. He had seen so many deliveries to the home in the previous days, wagons drawn by draft horses. Ram could not deny it; he felt a great wave of jealousy.

Suddenly, he heard a sound near the front, and he rushed toward the door. He startled Rosa, who jumped and gave a yelp, dropping the basket she was carrying. It was full of onions she had picked from the garden she now shared with Kishen.

"Perdón, señora," he said, bending to pick them up, ashamed at being caught.

He hesitated. He formed the Spanish words in his mind. "I look for Karak Singh. He said he would be here."

Rosa drew herself up. She answered in English, "He has gone to town."

The English surprised him, then he understood the pride behind it. Padma would have done the same. "My excuses. I will come back later." Karak should not have married her, but, really, what had *she* done wrong? The answer presented itself to him in a flash. She had had the arrogance to accept him, he thought to himself. How had this couple deserved that much freedom? Still, he backed away from her politely, half bowing, regretting his actions.

She hesitated, then her expression grew soft. "You must stay," she said in Spanish. "He will come soon for his lunch. We can eat together."

"I will return later."

"Please—you must stay and eat."

He was reminded of Padma's first days in his uncle's household, soon after they married. She had also been desperate as a new wife, trying to make a place for herself. Ram took off his hat, squeezing it without meaning to. Why should he be stern with Rosa?

"Fine, I will stay, señora," he said in Spanish.

"Good—" She clapped her hands together.

"If you let me help you. I do help Kishen Kaur—"

"Oh no!"

"I am a good cook. I made so many meals for my work gang."

She smiled at him. "Among Mexicans, men do not cook if a woman is near."

He did not push further. He sat in the front room and she took the basket of onions to the back. He could hear her at the stove, stepping in and out of the back door, clattering the pans. Ram sat for a long time, feeling it would be rude to leave, but Karak did not return.

He got up and joined her in back, where she stood at the stove. She smiled, embarrassed. "Do you like it?" she said.

He looked at her with a question.

"We ordered it from the Sears catalog," she said. He realized that she meant the stove. It was royal blue in color, made of gleaming steel. He had seen it delivered by wagon a week before.

She was flustered now and her face had flushed, but she did not stop working. She was adding water to cornmeal and kneading it with her hands. She was strong and worked quickly. Ram pulled up a wooden stool and sat and watched.

"In India, we do just the same. Our rotis."

"Sí—Karak has told me. So many things, señor. They are the same. He has taught me to make roti, chicken curry."

He thought she was nervous in his presence. Her hand hit an empty tin and it clattered across the table. He could have told her to call him Ram, but he did not want to. Still, he handed her a pan without her asking for it. He struck a match for the stove when it was time. She began to make the tortillas. "But Karak says they do not taste the same," she said. She cared about pleasing her husband, and suddenly Ram's jealousy clarified itself. It was not for her—it was for Karak's having her, having someone.

"I have made arroz con leche for today. It is not a holiday, but it is his favorite."

She dipped a spoon into the bowl and handed it to him. The familiar rich taste filled his mouth.

"This is Punjabi only! Pukka Punjabi."

She smiled broadly, relaxed. She had beautiful eyes. "That is what he said too." Yes, she was pretty, but he didn't feel anything for her, he thought with relief.

Karak arrived just then, calling to her as he stepped inside the door. They both looked up as he entered.

"Ram?" Karak's eyes darted between them: Rosa working at the stove, Ram seated near her. But Ram had realized that he did not desire her, and he did not feel guilty.

"I came looking for you," Ram said in Punjabi.

"You have found me," Karak said.

"He is eating with us," Rosa said in Spanish. She was too cheerful, as if to excuse Karak's discovery.

"Good," Karak said. He put down the satchel he was carrying, slinging it over the chaise. "Good," he repeated. He forced a smile.

They ate at the small table outside, set in the porch's shade. It was the first time Ram had been with them alone. Rosa spoke of finding him in the house, and Ram could sense Karak's mood lifting. Her openness and obvious pleasure, her smile, her description of how Ram sat with her as she made the tortillas—Ram found himself joking along. She felt so familiar.

Karak laughed with them, his dark eyes half-closed, his body stretched back, legs crossed at the ankles, arm draped around the back of Rosa's chair. Ram sensed a great space opening inside Karak, the air of freedom, satisfaction, ease. Perhaps even kindness. Karak glanced at him, as if to say—*I told you, see, I made a fine choice for my wife*. It was an intimate gesture—that glance—full of knowing. Perhaps the two men were closer than Karak and his wife would ever be.

10 August 1916

My dear,

 Karak Singh has taken a local girl for his wife. She is a Mexican, her family crossed the border some time ago—like those families that live in Patiala who were born in Kabul. She was under the guardianship of her sister's husband, who arranged the match. They are living now in the Eggenberger house, separately from the rest of us, but only a furlong away.

 He sleeps indoors often now, like a respectable householder, even when the night is warm. He no longer comes for breakfast every morning to Kishen's table.

 It is strange that he is comfortable with marrying an outsider. In so many ways he and I are different! But I can admit to you, my wife, that I am jealous of their happiness. When I see them together, I am reminded only of me and you. This letter-writing is strange, isn't it? I can admit things that I would not if you were standing in front of me. We had too little time together after our wedding. I do not know how you feel about these things, perhaps good women feel differently, but I miss the scent and the feeling of you, and think about these more often than I would admit to anyone. Perhaps they are bad thoughts, but I have them. I cannot think that it is bad for a man to miss his wife. Why should it be that Cousin Ishwar has been allowed to remain home, while I was sent away, when I have a wife and child? The thought makes me sick, day after day, and I am filled with resentment and growing venom. I have given three years of my life without seeing you. It is true that Uncle raised me in his household, but I cannot say that I was like one of his own sons. That would be a lie—all his sons are there while I am here. Am I thinking too much like a westerner? It seems that he looked after me only for his own self-interest. Sometimes I rent myself out to the farms nearby so that I can send even more money to him.

Enough of this bitterness. Here, I have become something that I was not before: a person with knowledge. I am not yet rich, but I have done well with several harvests. Others sometimes approach me for advice. Perhaps that is the only reason that I can look back with this clarity, free of my childhood loyalties. I send kisses to Santosh. My thoughts are with you.

Your husband,

Ram

30 August 1916

My dear saintly uncle, may God keep you in good health.

Greetings to you! With your blessings, I am hale and hearty in all respects. The cotton has grown well, and with God's grace we have harvested a second crop of the plants and sold it for high prices. The war in Europe is creating a great demand. My esteemed partner, Karak Singh, has married and established a good home with these earnings. I hope that with the amount of Rs.3,500 (three thousand five hundred) that I send today, dear little cousin's wedding will be the grand affair that we desire.

If you have no objection, and it is in line with your own thinking, I will make some plans for my return, to see for the first time my son's face. Is it possible? I pray for your well-being always. Please reply soon. Greetings to all.

Your humble nephew,

Ram

21 November 1916

My good nephew,

I trust that this letter will find you in good health and spirits. You know that I seldom engage in letter-writing. But you have been such a boon to this household that I thought it wise to inform you of this in my own words. After all, you are like a son to me.

Here at your home, everything was well until last week. Your cousin had a beautiful wedding. Everyone was happy and singing your praises. The money you have sent these years has accomplished so much. Ishwar and I went to the village and inspected and purchased 32 acres of land of the best soil. It is very near to our ancestral plots, and only 4 furlongs from the district headquarters. You have made me proud, and you have made your mother proud.

But recently, there has been misfortune in our household. Early morning on Saturday last week, the barn caught on fire and burned down. We were lucky that Ishwar rose very early for some purpose that day and roused all of us and we moved all the animals. But the barn will have to be rebuilt. Also, we need to build another home on our new lands, for Ishwar and his soon-to-be wife, so that they may bring those lands into proper cultivation. Please, just accomplish these tasks and then you may return. Your home will be waiting for you.

> *From the hand of your uncle,*
> *Chanda Lal*

18 January 1917

Dear Ma,

I hope this letter finds you in good health. Probably Padma is reading it to you, and I am picturing the scene in my mind.

Perhaps Uncle has informed you, the money I sent has paid for the land that he and Ishwar bought in our Shahpur village. I am telling you so that you should not feel obliged to him. He should express to you clearly his gladness. But he has asked that I send more money for repair of the barn, and also for constructing a home on the new lands. I do not understand why so much money is needed. What sort of grand structures will these be? But I will do as Uncle says. It is my duty. My heart is sore with the thought of staying away from you and my wife and my son, who is still a stranger to me. I hope Padma is looking after you well.

Your son,
Ram

30 March 1917
My dear son, my world,

You cannot know how happy I was to get your letter. Now I am holding my head up high. At first, your uncle did not tell me about the money at all. But when I indicated that I knew that, with it, he had bought lands in Shahpur, he could no longer hide it from me. Now he has admitted that the money you are sending has made so much possible, also the rebuilding of the barn here and the new home in Shahpur.

I am proud of you, son, and you have given me more izzat in this household. For that, I am grateful. Your aunt has become quite arrogant after the wedding of her daughter with Gopal Singh's son. To have our family in relation to that one is beyond what she thought possible. But she is kinder to me than before, because it is through your hand that such wishes are granted. Oh, you are my treasure, you are a fragment of my own heart.

I am writing this letter through the son of the tailor in the neighboring village, who has been making a good business of this

*letter-writing. He is a good boy and from what I can tell, he
holds his secrets well.*

Your Ma

1 April 1917

My dear esteemed husband,

*Will you not come back to me? Today I have already written
a letter to you, but I must write more. You have abandoned me,
and left me without your protection. How can I go on living?
Have you not earned enough to keep this family fed for years to
come? Must the responsibility be only yours? You are not even a
son of this family, yet you are bearing all the burden.*

Forgive me for writing like this.

Theri,
Padma

PART THREE

I am a *rielera* and I've got my man
I have a pair of stallions
for the Revolution
one is called Canary
the other is Sparrow.

Farewell to the boys of Lerdo,
of Gómez and Torreón,
the cutthroats have said their *adios,*
and now they are long gone.

I have a pair of pistols
their aim is straight and true,
one for my rival
the other for my beau.

—based on the corrido La Rielera

18

APRIL 1917

THE UNITED STATES JOINED THE WORLD'S WAR. THIS FOLLOWED WEEKS of indecision, after Germany had sunk four more U.S. merchant ships, and American flags waved on every storefront on every street in the Valley from Calexico to Calipatria. War posters hung on the sides of movie theaters and post offices, beckoning to pedestrians as they strolled past. Every day, Amarjeet followed the news and reported to Ram what he learned: in its quest for Indian freedom, the Ghadar Party had allied itself with Germany, Britain's enemy, and now America's enemy too.

RamChandra Bharadwaj, Ghadar's leader, who had visited them three years earlier, recruiting Valley farmers and drawing Jivan's ire, was arrested with several others in San Francisco. A month later, he was indicted.

Now, at the dinner table, at the park on Sundays, any occasion when the Hindustanees met, Jivan warned: "Buy war bonds, and buy many of them. We must show our allegiance to the American government." He insisted that Kishen expand her vegetable garden, that she sign and mail a pledge card stating that her household would follow the practice of meatless Tuesdays, wheatless Wednesdays. He spoke about this with Clive Edgar and the banker Jasper Davis, with Stephen Eggenberger, with the sheriff, with the clerks at the general store, and made sure they knew. Amarjeet was aware why he was doing this: if they were ever suspected, even though they had done nothing wrong, all this would protect them.

Amarjeet did not like Jivan to pretend to be more loyal to the United States government than he truly felt. At one time, three years ago, he had wanted to fight for the Ghadar, but that was when Ghadar had aligned itself with the words of Thomas Jefferson and Patrick Henry, not gone against America. It was true that when the Singhs went into town, some Anglos would stare at them, but he did not like the way his uncle cowered. He would not hide behind the purchase of Liberty bonds. Not even when Ghadar's impending trial and RamChandra's face appeared on the front page of the *San Francisco Chronicle*.

AMARJEET TOLD RAM that he was required to register for the selective service. "We will go together," he said.

"Register for what?" Ram asked.

"The draft," Amarjeet clarified.

"Only the Americans are required, Jeetu," Ram said.

"Everyone," Amarjeet said. "Between the ages of twenty-one and thirty years. You and me."

"Everyone between those ages," Jivan agreed.

"What does it matter?" Ram said. "I am a foreigner. I will not have to fight."

"We must follow the law. We must be faultless," Jivan said. "If they ask us to register, we should register."

ON THE MORNING OF JUNE 1, Amarjeet woke early and hitched up the mare to head into town. For once, he was awake before Ram. He was excited to register.

"Don't take long," Jivan said, when they were ready and had climbed onto the buckboard.

"Chacha-ji, there is a full day of parades," Amarjeet said.

"Why must they have parades for such a thing? We do not have need of their parades. Finish the registration and come back."

Amarjeet said nothing, feeling reprimanded.

On the road into town, Ram said, "The problem is, Jeetu, you are bored."

"I am," he agreed.

"And you missed being a youth in Punjab."

"What do you mean?"

"A gang of friends. Mischief. You did not have what I had at fifteen, sixteen, seventeen."

Amarjeet was quiet. Ram was too close to the truth.

"When you are bored, the only thing you can do is visit Harry."

How did Ram know this so clearly? Sometimes Amarjeet thought the mile between their homes seemed too long, whether by foot or bicycle. "I like Harry. He's swell."

They began to hear the commotion from the brass band. The hum of people and the mayor's voice over the loudspeaker were carried by the dust-wind a quarter mile before they arrived.

"I know, Jeetu. I'm only telling you what I see."

They left the buckboard and horse on the outskirts and walked down to Main Street. The streets were filled with vendors of popcorn, candy, peanuts, and balloons. Many businesses had shut down for the day. A large tent was placed at the intersection of Main and Church Streets. Underneath it, the band played a happy tune that the orchestra had played at his high school.

"I always liked that song," Amarjeet said.

"What?" Ram asked.

Suddenly, Amarjeet was irritated. Of course Ram would not know the tune. "Look, the line is there," Amarjeet said, pointing to the post office.

Young men queued in front of the doors for the length of two blocks. Ram and Amarjeet joined them. At 8:59, church bells rang all over town. The post office doors swung open and the first young men stepped in.

"They will think badly of us, because of the Ghadar arrests," Amarjeet said.

"It doesn't matter," Ram said.

Amarjeet disagreed, but said nothing.

They stood for two more hours in the summer heat before the line advanced into the cool of the building. Five tables were set up as desks, operating simultaneously, each staffed by a Valley resident. Amarjeet and Ram stepped forward to the same table; Ram did not feel confident facing the interviewer alone. Nick Amsler, whose father ran the Swiss dairy down the road from their farm, stood at the table next to theirs. Amarjeet had gone to high school with Nick.

"Name?" the man asked. In front of him was a neat stack of blanks, a box to file them in, and two rows of fountain pens. He was near forty years old, his face bronzed from the spring harvest. Everybody was volunteering to contribute to the war effort.

"Amarjeet Singh Gill."

"Whoa, son," the man said. "You're gonna spell that for me nice and slow." Amarjeet did so, and the man noted the letters on a blank. He peered at them through his thick glasses. "That ain't so bad, when you look at it on paper. Date of birth?"

"April first, 1896."

"Birthplace?"

"Ludhiana District, Punjab, India," Amarjeet said, spelling that too.

Now the man took out another card from his file, placed it beside him, and read carefully. "Of what country are you a citizen or subject?" he said, as if seeing the words for the first time.

"India," said Amarjeet.

"Great Britain." The man peered at him.

"I mean it to be India," insisted Amarjeet.

"Amarjeet——" Ram said.

"I'll mark both," the man said, writing carefully. He did not seem to notice Amarjeet's irritation.

"By whom are you employed?"

"I work on my uncle's farm," Amarjeet said, then, after a pause, "What are you marking now?"

"You're not married, are you?"

"No."

"Okay. Another hard question here. What race do you boys call yourselves?"

"Caucasian," said Amarjeet.

"Oriental," said Ram.

"I'll mark both," said the man.

"We are not both," said Amarjeet. Suddenly he felt an arm on his shoulder, a man's face hovering beside his.

"How's it going here, Howard?" the sheriff said in a friendly drawl. "Good to see foreigners register—even when they don't have to fight—why, we want them to know how much we Americans appreciate that." His voice was friendly, but Amarjeet could see the message being conveyed to the clerk.

"No sir, sheriff. Everybody's getting along."

"Exactly what President Wilson's askin' of us."

"Don't I know it!" The clerk looked at Amarjeet again. "I'll put Hindu next to Oriental, so the men in Washington know what to do." He nodded at them. "Those men in Washington know everything."

Amarjeet and Ram exchanged a glance. In the next line, Nick Amsler had finished and stepped away.

"Oh. I forgot one up here," the man said, peering through his reading glasses. "These blanks are hard to read. Alien status?"

"Yes," answered Amarjeet.

The man marked it, then he read more off a booklet lying near him, then turned back to the blank: "But have you men"—he cleared his throat—"declared your intention to become a citizen?"

"No," Ram said.

Amarjeet paused. "Does it make a difference?"

The man shrugged. "I think so."

"No," Amarjeet said, finally.

"That's it," the man said, turning the card toward Amarjeet. "Make your mark or sign your name—right here."

Ram's turn was faster. He added that he was married. He added that he was father to a son. "It's a lot easier with the second one of you folks," the man said. Ram signed quickly. "The medical examinations are at the Masonic Hall. You all have a good day now."

"It does not matter if you were married or not," Amarjeet said as they stepped outside. The sunlight hurt his eyes. "You are exempt because you never declared."

"Never declared what?" asked Ram.

"You never filed any papers with the U.S. government to become a citizen. If you never do that, you don't have to go fight in the war."

"Ah," said Ram. "Good."

Amarjeet didn't answer.

"Did you file such papers, Amarjeet?" Ram asked.

"No," Amarjeet said. He did not add that, sometimes, he had wanted to.

THERE WAS A LINE at the Masonic Hall too; examinations occurred in the banquet hall and the lodge room upstairs. Ram and Amarjeet climbed these steps together, but at the top, they were taken to opposite sides of a cavernous room. Ram gave Amarjeet a look of impatience as they separated.

Curtains partitioned each exam stall. Ceiling fans spun overhead. Amarjeet's stall was positioned next to a window, and bright sunlight slanted across the space. He could see Mount Signal in the distance. Three men in white lab coats stood waiting for him. As soon as he entered, their eyes rested on his dastar. "I suppose you'll be claiming an exemption?" one of the men said.

Amarjeet broke out in a sweat. A wave of heat swept through him.

"I don't know," he managed to say.

"You don't know?" another one of them said, raising his eyebrows, a tall man with a beautiful face. Amarjeet felt the pull of him. He had broad shoulders, fine hands.

"I'm an alien," Amarjeet said.

"So—exemption claimed by reason of alien status," the beautiful man said patiently. He was about to make a notation on a clipboard.

The third man, older than the others, spoke up. "You aliens aren't really interested in serving, are you?" He laughed lightly. "All the benefit of living here without all the work. Well, our army needs brave men with spirit. We'll mark your exemption request."

"You don't need to," Amarjeet said. The moment was running away from him. "I'm volunteering."

The men exchanged glances. Their surprise satisfied him.

The beautiful man stepped toward him. They were almost the same height. In the small space, they could look each other in the eye. "You speak English very well, Singh."

"I have lived here since I was fourteen."

"You must take off your turban," said the man who appeared to be the senior doctor. Amarjeet unwound the dastar and lay the cloth neatly on the table. His hair fell to the middle of his back. He hoped they would not ridicule. He did not know what he would say in response. They asked him to read letters posted on a chart. They looked in his ears. They looked down his throat. They inspected his face, his nose and teeth and mouth. They examined his scalp with a magnifying glass.

"You won't need this hair in the army," the beautiful man said gently. He was about thirty. For a moment, Amarjeet forgot he was a physician.

They asked him to remove his clothes, and he did. The ceiling fan swept the air across his chest, his buttocks, between his thighs. He thought they could have killed him then—the three of them protected by their lab coats, while his hair hung loose—and no one would report it. They asked him to stand up straight with his arms out to the sides, and he did that too. The first doctor stepped forward and inspected every bit of Amarjeet's skin. They felt his abdomen, they squeezed his testicles, and, after asking him to bend forward and pull apart his buttock cheeks, they looked at his anus. They made notations on the pad. Amarjeet remained quiet. The senior doctor asked him to squat, flap his arms, and shake his legs, arms, and neck. Finally, they told him to put on his clothes.

More notations were made on the pad. More papers were added to his file. One doctor pulled out a tape and measured him and called out, "Five feet, eleven inches." The beautiful one marked it in the file. Another asked him to step on the scale. "One hundred seventy-three pounds," then "Black hair."

"Brown eyes."

"No birthmarks."

"What should we put for complexion?" someone said.

"Black Caucasian."

"There is no such thing."

"He is almost white."

"Medium," said the beautiful one.

The notes were made. Amarjeet signed a document.

The senior man spoke. "Welcome to the United States Army." He did not extend a hand.

Amarjeet picked up the cloth of his dastar. He gathered his hair, wound the fabric with nimble fingers, reclaimed his dignity. He made them wait until he was finished. "Please note it," he said. "I don't have to serve, but I am."

The senior doctor, twice his age, looked at him. Amarjeet looked straight back.

"Consider it noted," the beautiful one said.

THE STREETS WERE STILL CROWDED, although the band was silent. Amarjeet could barely believe what he had done. He felt elated. They watched the parade march down Main Street, drums beating time, tuba blaring. The Rifle Club came first on horseback, wearing chaps and Stetsons; the Imperial County Council of Defense, riding in a Model T, followed them. They had traveled that morning from Brawley to Niland to Fredonia, marching in each town's parade as they passed. Then came Fredonia's volunteers for the Red Cross, the Young Women's Christian Association, and the Women's County Food Conservation Committee. The brass band played on after the marching had stopped. Flags waved, ribbons were thrown, and still the men lined up to register, standing in a long snaking queue that began at the post office and ended at Charlie's Horse and Mule Rental.

They ran into Harry Moriyama, who had registered before them. He was cheerful, and to Amarjeet, always seemed unburdened. Together, they walked through the covered promenade. Flags hung from every storefront. The town's banks had set up tents and each had a young and pretty girl standing alongside the banker men, wooing the passersby for the sale of Liberty bonds. At the intersection of Main and Central, under the cover of a large ramada, a crowd gathered to eat ice cream and watch the square dancers, to hear the mayor speak about how Fredonia would contribute to the war effort: not only with fighting men, not only with war heroes, but also by planting castor beans for motor oil, growing hemp for airplane cloth, and bringing food, food, and more food for the region's cantonments. "Sign the Hoover pledge cards! Meatless Tuesdays! Wheatless Wednesdays! Porkless Saturdays!" The mayor's voice had grown harsh and dry. "Nobody will deny that the Imperial Valley did its share and more!"

"Will the local people really do that, Amarjeet?" Ram asked.

"Look at them, bhai-ji," Amarjeet said. "They will." A group of middle-aged women had huddled near the mayor and were listening intently. "We should too."

"My parents won't do it," Harry said. "I wish they would." Amarjeet felt vindicated. They walked around for a bit longer, then Harry left for home in his wagon. Without him, Amarjeet began to feel nervous. The weight of what he had done began to settle on him, heavy and stifling.

He and Ram walked behind the general store and untied the mare from the rail. "The medical exam was demeaning," Ram said, when they had started for home.

"They must check everything," said Amarjeet.

"Why must they check everything if we are exempt?"

"They must have a record of us all." The frame of the buckboard creaked underneath them. "Ram-ji?"

"Yes."

"I need your support."

"For what?"

"I have volunteered for the U.S. Army."

He saw Ram blink as the knowledge settled. "You volunteered."

"Yes." He thought Ram would be more surprised.

"I thought that you might, Jeetu."

"Why?"

"Sometimes when I see you, I think, what is there for you here?"

"There is the farm," Amarjeet said bitterly.

"Yes, there is the farm," Ram repeated, as if to say, *For some men, that is enough.*

"We will never be a part of them," Amarjeet said, "but maybe if I fight, they will accept us."

He saw confusion on Ram's face. Perhaps he did not know what Amarjeet meant.

"You must tell Karak Chacha first," Ram said. "Only after that, tell your uncle. Karak Chacha can speak for you as an intermediary." This was the proper way to do things. It was out of respect to the older man—the concession that the younger had been fearful of telling him.

"I am already part of the army now," Amarjeet said. Did Ram not understand? "Even if he insists that I remain, I cannot stay."

"I know," Ram said.

THEY RETURNED HOME after the heat of the afternoon. Jivan stepped out to the porch immediately, as if he had been watching for them. "You took long," he said.

Amarjeet felt a surge of resentment, but said nothing.

They found Karak alone in the barn, adjusting the plow. When Amarjeet told him, he laid his head against the steel of the implement and said darkly, "Are you mad? How will we manage?" He threw his hammer to the dirt. "How will your *uncle* manage?"

"What you say is true, Karak Chacha." Amarjeet's heart raced. He had always been intimidated by Karak. "I was not thinking of him."

Ram leaned against the wall, watching. Amarjeet had hoped for his help, but perhaps he felt it was not his place to say anything.

"My service will bring some income," Amarjeet said.

"Your damn service will bring your death!"

Amarjeet stepped back.

"Look—when your uncle and I went to war, it was because the money was needed. Here, the cotton and cantaloupe are doing well." Karak rubbed his forehead. "There is so much money to make, Amarjeet."

"I will come back soon, Chacha-ji, and—"

"Not if you are dead."

"Hear what—" Ram said.

"This is not your concern," Karak said sharply.

Amarjeet swallowed. "I will be back to help here again. In the meantime, the wages will come. Please, will you talk to him for me?"

As soon as he said it, Amarjeet knew it was a mistake.

"I won't."

Amarjeet felt a pit in his stomach.

"Are you more concerned with Amarjeet's death," Ram said, "or with his labor around the farm?"

"What do you know about it?" Karak snapped. "You never went to war."

RAM SAID HE WOULD SPEAK to Jivan for him. Amarjeet saw Ram approach his uncle while he was sitting at the table on the porch, looking at the accounts. Amarjeet had positioned himself inside the door to the animal shed. He could see them clearly. The mare nuzzled him and he reached out to pet her. He could not hear what was said. He thought that his uncle did not know he was there, but after they had been talking awhile, Jivan looked directly at him across the distance. Amarjeet felt as if he had been slapped.

Ram came to meet him. His face was serious, and Amarjeet could not tell if he was still sympathetic to him. "Jivan Singh wants to speak with you," Ram said.

When he approached his uncle, he did not look up, he did not know if his uncle was even looking at him.

"What have I heard from Ram? That you have gone and committed yourself to the U.S. Army?"

"Chacha-ji," he said in a small voice. He was twenty-one years old, a full adult, being treated like this. Amarjeet looked down at the crusted earth, the dust mixed with sand. He had never seen his uncle angry before. All through the Valley, Jivan Singh was known for his patience, for being a soft-spoken man.

"I brought you here so that you would not have to fight in another country's war. I wanted you to study. I promised your father."

Amarjeet stood with his hands clasped in front of him, looking at the ground.

"I forbid you to go, Amarjeet."

For a moment, he could not breathe. "Chacha-ji, they will send me to jail if I don't go." Easier to blame the U.S. government than to say the truth: Amarjeet did not want to stay.

"Go and ask them. Into town. Go now."

Amarjeet did not move.

"Go!"

"They will say no, Chacha-ji. And I will not ask. I gave my word. Just as you did. Just as my father did."

THAT EVENING, his aunt told him to come to the kitchen to eat his supper before the others arrived, so his uncle would not have to see him. From the tone of her voice, the gentle way that she spooned the food onto his plate, he knew her sympathy was with him.

For several days, he and Jivan did not speak. Even so, Amarjeet silently helped him cover the cantaloupe, cultivate the field of peas. He knew the work and there was little reason for any talk. At least in his labor, he could be blameless. While the others ate, he often went to the shed and sat with the mare and mules. He found the animals comforting.

One evening, a week after he had joined the army, his aunt came to find him there.

"Your uncle says you should come and join us at the table to eat," she said.

He followed her and sat with them, even though he had already eaten. The others were unusually animated, their faces flushed and smiling. Karak was there, although Rosa was not. Amarjeet did not meet anyone's eye.

He sat and Kishen served him as if he had not had dinner.

"Jeetu, your Karak Chacha will become a father soon," Jivan said lightly. "What do you think?"

So that was the reason. "Mubaraka," Amarjeet said, meaning it, finally meeting Karak's gaze.

Karak reached across the table and put a plate in front of him. "Ladoo, which I made myself. I'm sure it is awful." He glanced at Amarjeet with a strange, open smile, almost as if they were equals.

Amarjeet smiled back. He bit into the sweet.

"Bhabhi-ji, have one," Karak said to Kishen. "Your blessings are needed."

"May you be blessed with a son who shines like the moon," she said, taking another piece.

Jivan placed two rotis on Amarjeet's plate. "Eat, Jeetu," he said. That was how Amarjeet knew the standoff between them had ended.

THE FAMILY DID NOT TALK ABOUT THE WAR. It was not their war, even though Karak's younger brother was fighting in Egypt for the British king. How could it belong to them, when the Americans had sided with the British, and the British were committed to subjugating the Indians, and were fooling their countrymen at home into joining the British ranks? Into risking their lives to win spoils they would never enjoy?

In the Valley, there were melons and cantaloupes to plant. There was cotton to pick. Amarjeet helped his uncle purchase a second plow, a second cultivator. Meanwhile, Fredonia's public spaces were filled with signs for Red Cross dances, posters demanding they buy war bonds, sign pledge cards, plant kitchen gardens, knit scarves and socks for the boys to take to Europe. What did that have to do with them? The family cared about the Hindu-German Conspiracy trial, about the Indian soldiers who were fighting alongside the British in France and Mesopotamia.

Only Amarjeet volunteered to go into town whenever necessary. He would see former high school classmates at the war drive events. Sometimes they would greet him and sometimes they would not.

When the draft numbers were drawn in Washington, D.C., Amarjeet rode into town, purchased a paper, and sat on the bench at the general store to read in the afternoon glare. His eye immediately caught the numbers—his own, and Harry's too. He felt a wave of excitement.

ON THE LAST EVENING before Amarjeet was deployed to Camp Lewis near Seattle, Amarjeet and Ram were clearing silt in the canal when Jivan approached, carrying three small crates with him. They were often used as seats.

"I must see to some things in the house," Ram said, stepping onto the bank.

"Stay, Ram," Jivan said. "I prefer if you hear this. Come and sit," he said.

It was clear to Amarjeet that Ram did not want to stay. He wondered why his uncle needed an audience. Perhaps to prove something, perhaps to redeem himself. He could tell how much Jivan had grown to like Ram.

The three men looked out over the fields and were quiet. "Amarjeet," Jivan finally said, "we will manage without you. Your father may be angry with me—he wanted you to continue with your education, and I have failed him—but we will manage here."

Amarjeet wanted to interrupt, to defend Jivan's own actions to himself, but the words would not come.

"I want to tell you some things," Jivan said.

His uncle's eyes were hazel gray, and when he wore his green dastar, they took on the green hue. Looking at them, Amarjeet felt guilty again.

"I served with our own people, even though it was within the British army," Jivan said. "You will not have that advantage."

"Harry is coming too," Amarjeet said, thinking about how much bolder Harry was than himself. How much more comfortable.

"He is also different from the Anglos. He will have the same struggles. I am glad that he will be with you. Some men will treat you with respect and honesty. They exist even among the locals, see if you can recognize them. They will help you."

Amarjeet forced himself to nod. He did not have the patience needed for this conversation.

"Do you remember Pandit RamChandra? When he came to visit?"

"You did not like him," Amarjeet said, growing irate. "How can we even speak of him anymore? He conspired with Germans. . . . They will all go to jail."

"But about one thing he was right. There is a global color line, all the world knows it. Look around us. In their speeches, in their ideas, the Americans pretend it doesn't exist. Not only does it exist, Amarjeet, it is the basis of everything.

"I feel uneasy now not because you are going into war, but because you will not be in a unit with your own people. You and Harry will be two foreigners in your squad. You will be treated as expendable. That is my great fear. I know you will fight bravely. You are a Sikh, after all. But your commander must value your life too. Otherwise he will always choose you for the duty that is the worst, or the most dangerous, or the one in which you will gain no recognition."

Amarjeet could not believe this was true. The army had told him there would be no race prejudice in its ranks. President Wilson had said that too. But out of regard for his uncle, he stayed quiet.

"And there are cruel men, Jeetu. You will know them quickly. It is not easy to hide cruelty. Beware when you are alone with them and no one else is watching. Beware of them on the battlefield too. Their cruelty cannot be controlled there. It will extend to you and, without need, to the people that you are fighting."

Amarjeet had been tracing a line in the dirt with his shoe, but now he looked up. His uncle was staring at him. So was Ram.

"I know you are angry with me for telling you this," Jivan said. "You don't want to believe that anything I am saying is true."

Amarjeet was surprised. He thought he had hidden his real feelings well. "I am not angry, Chacha-ji."

"I do not believe in war anymore, Amarjeet. I don't know if I ever believed in it. But we are warriors. There is a reason that we wear the kirpan. We fight for justice. So be courageous. Act honorably. It is my duty to tell you not to fear death. To not hesitate to give up your life. So I am fulfilling that duty. When you come back you will be a changed man. Nothing will seem the same. But you are my brother's son." Jivan swallowed. "I want you to come back."

Amarjeet wanted to leave this conversation; that was all.

Jivan's eyes were wide and unblinking. Across the field, they could hear Kishen's voice calling them to dinner. Amarjeet made a move to rise, then he sat down again, and, out of deference, waited for Jivan to go first.

19

SEPTEMBER 1917

RAM DID NOT KNOW IF JIVAN WAS RIGHT, BUT HE FELT THE SAME SADness. On the afternoon the soldiers were ordered to gather in town, he drove Amarjeet and the family in the wagon. Before leaving, Amarjeet had read to him the letter that had come from the army with his orders. Beside him lay the small bag packed with the things that he had been instructed to bring. Already, he was holding it close to him. As they passed over the canal, Karak began to sing an old tune that they all knew, that even Amarjeet knew as a child, working in the fields. They rode without comment. Karak's voice was strong and floating, filling the empty desert air.

Near town, a Tin Lizzie pulled up behind them. Its top was down. "Tomoya!" Jivan called out.

The automobile rolled alongside the wagon. "You go to take Amarjeet," Tomoya said. "We go to take Haruki."

From the back seat, Hatsu Moriyama smiled and waved at Kishen. Harry was sitting in the driver's seat beside his father, and one of his sisters sat behind him. "Big day! Big day!" Tomoya said. To Ram, his cheerfulness seemed empty.

In town, they parked the wagon and the vehicle behind the general store. Thousands of people had already lined the streets. Flags waved, children cried, the band was too loud. They had arrived just before the parade. Harry and Amarjeet dropped their bags off at the army office, then rejoined the families, but did not stand too close. They were already separate in some unarticulated way.

The Fredonia High School band paraded before the Four Minute Men. The County Guard followed on horseback, then a long trail of Model T's and Model A's, with tooting horns and young women leaning out the windows, waving. Last came the winner of the year's desert road race, a garland draped around its grille. The mayor appeared. There was a great uproar from the crowd, and no one could hear his speech. Then a second band began to play a rollicking and cheerful song, and young people flooded the street and began to dance, faces gleaming, arms waving, legs kicking. Even their parents laughed.

Harry ran off as soon as the dancing started, but Amarjeet stayed with his uncle, taking in the scene with glistening eyes. He turned to Ram and said, "It is a good send-off, isn't it, Ram-ji?" His face was flushed. Sweat dripped from his temples. Ram could not disagree with him.

The evening brought fireworks, and afterward Harry came back grinning, his shirt damp and his hair mussed. Ram watched as he returned to his parents; Harry's father placed his hand on his son's shoulder. As the crowd thinned, the two young men set off to report to the Army Tent Grounds. They were slim-hipped and athletic and beautiful. In Punjab, where such things are allowed, they might have had arms around each other, in boyhood friendship and nothing more—two of them against the world. They turned and gave a last wave and Ram saw their faces, Japanese and Punjabi, in the midst of real Americans.

That night Ram could not sleep. The moon was full and luminous and at last he rose from his cot and walked to the edge of the cotton field and looked across to the Eggenberger house. Karak was barely visible, sitting on the bench by the front porch. A shadow among shadows.

Ram thought of joining him, but something prevented him. It was easier to remain two solitary figures together under a black sky. He thought of the expression on the Japanese boy's face when he turned to his father. He thought of the father's smile in return. A lifetime was conveyed in that glance. His own son was already three years old.

As the morning cast its very first shade of gray, he lay down again on his cot and closed his eyes. He remembered how he had felt about Mr. Moriyama long ago, when he had not acknowledged the man's favor of the Fresno scraper lent to level the cotton field. He felt a prick of remorse. Perhaps he had been wrong.

Sleep came quickly. Jivan woke him moments later. "It is time to go," he said.

BY DAWN, THEY HAD ARRIVED AT THE TRAIN DEPOT. The band was again playing, quietly, but still the sounds slashed the morning air. The soldier boys were in uniform now, and they no longer seemed like people of the Valley. Their families milled around the platform, subdued and quiet. The Singhs found Amarjeet standing in line, wearing the standard-issue green uniform and a dastar of dark green. When he saw them, he smiled, but it was without the openness of the previous night. They were not allowed to approach. The band stopped playing and the crowd was grateful. The train was waiting. Far behind them, in the last car, the Negro soldiers had already entrained. The line of other boys moved slowly, solemnly in the open air, and Amarjeet turned again and again to his family, but did not wave. There was an expression on his face that Ram could not discern, then an Anglo boy clapped him jovially on the back and Amarjeet grinned. A moment later, he turned, raised his arm above his head, and disappeared into the train. Leela kept waving. The Singhs did not speak.

The band began to play again, destroying the peace. The train sent up a wisp of smoke and inched forward. Several young women dabbed their eyes. Parents clutched at each other. A great hurrah went up from a group of youths clustered at the end of the platform.

Ram could see Amarjeet's face framed in the train window, Harry's profile beside him. The youths cheered as the train passed, their faces turned up to the soldiers in admiration; in their eyes Ram saw their awe, anxiety, jealousy. He knew that, seeing them, Amarjeet would not be sorry that he had enlisted.

THAT NIGHT, AFTER DINNER, they sat together on the porch behind the house. No one opened the whiskey bottle. Rosa joined them too, her legs propped up on a low stool. Leela sat near her, playing with a small wooden horse that Amarjeet had given her the previous day. She suddenly ran to Kishen and settled on her lap.

"When Jeetu Veer-ji comes back, Ma, I want him to take me to that fair." She still spoke in Punjabi at home; English had not yet overtaken her.

"That fair?" Kishen said. She smoothed the girl's hair and looked at Ram with an expression that revealed she did not know what Leela meant. "He will take you," she said, anyway.

"I want him to take me and buy for me everything that you did not buy for me, Ma. That's what I mean."

"He will, Leelu," Kishen said.

"Do you know which fair, Ma?" Leela whined. When her mother did not answer, she insisted, "Do you know which fair?"

"Leela," her father said.

She was quiet for a moment, then looked at Ram. She said more sweetly, "The fair that Ram Chacha also went to, a long time ago, before everybody got mad at each other. When Jeetu Veer-ji brought me that balloon."

"Ah," said Ram gently. "I will take you to that fair. Next time it comes, we will go."

The night sounds of the desert grew louder. "I must go and check the field," Jivan said. They had irrigated that afternoon, and there had been a breach in a farm ditch.

"I will go," Ram said. But no one moved.

"How old will I be when Jeetu Veer-ji comes home? Just a little older, right? Just a little older, Ma?" The girl had moved off her mother's lap and onto the thin arm of the chair.

"Oh, not so much older," said Karak lightly. "You will still have your teeth, they will not have fallen out."

"My teeth!" The girl made a face. Rosa laughed; she could understand enough Punjabi now, and the girl's expression was funny.

"You will still have your hair," Karak said.

Leela grabbed her hair. "I don't want to lose my hair!" she said.

"But probably your arm will have fallen off. Yes, certainly," said Karak, "now that I think of it, you will be so old by then, your arm will fall off. The right one first. You use it more."

Leela giggled and held her right arm. Kishen coaxed her off the chair and took her inside to sleep.

Jivan said, to no one, "I feel most for my brother."

"He made his decision, bhai-ji," Karak said.

"I feel I was responsible. I was with him that day," Ram said.

"But he had already made up his mind," Jivan said. "No, the fault lies with me. I wanted him to study, to go to university, but he refused." Jivan rubbed his face. "He is very intelligent. He came to this country and did not find enough to interest him. That is no one's fault but mine."

Karak yawned, rose, and announced that he was going to bed.

Jivan remained sitting in the glow of the kerosene lamps late into the night. Ram stayed with him. They sat in silence, and Ram noted that Jivan seemed a much older man.

THEY ALL FILLED IN for Amarjeet's absence. Ram took charge of feeding the mare, milking the cow, and helped Jivan bale the alfalfa.

Karak took up Amarjeet's errands in town. Ram helped Kishen with the cooking, hauling water for the laundry. On any morning, Leela might ask, "Isn't the war finished yet? I miss Jeetu Veer-ji." When her father told her no, it was not yet over, she would say, "Please don't forget to tell me when it's done. Okay, Abba? Please don't forget."

Sometimes Jivan would say, "If that silly boy were here, he could nurse the horse. I would not have to ask the veterinarian to come." When an extra man was hired for the harvest, Karak remarked, "That is one more man that we would not have had to pay." Or "When Amarjeet comes back, I will tell him what a shabby job he did with fixing these reins." But no one said anything when Amarjeet's wages came by mail. Jivan would silently open the envelope, look gravely at the amount on the check, and take it into the bedroom. Ram did not know if he cashed them or not.

One morning, Jivan was clearing silt from the area near the headgate. Ram joined him with another shovel. They worked quietly. The morning was still cool, and Kishen's breakfast had been heavy and delicious.

"It is good that you have come," Jivan said.

"The silt is too much today, perhaps we waited too long," Ram said.

"It is good that you have come to stay with us," Jivan said.

Ram hesitated. "More than three years have passed, bhai-ji."

"You have been a great help."

"If I must be in America, I am content to be here," Ram said.

Jivan did not look up from his work. He was struggling through a heavy section of silt. He seemed oddly lonely, even though surrounded by his family and all that he had built. Ram shifted position and stood near him. They pushed their shovels in and lifted, together.

20

Camp Lewis, Washington

1 October 1917

My esteemed Jivan Chacha-ji:

    We arrived at Camp Lewis a few days ago. First thing I did after arrival was to send off a detailed letter to Father telling him the situation. I told the truth, that you are furious with me for joining up with the U.S. Army, that you are completely against the decision. If I have overstepped my limits, please accept my pardon. I have done only as I thought correct in telling him the truth.

    After fulfilling that duty to Father, I am now writing this letter to you. There are boys here from all over the country, but especially from California and Oregon and Washington. We sleep in large cabins and eat all together. There are many boys from the Imperial Valley with me here, and as you know from my send-off, we have a good number from Fredonia. Of course, Harry is with me but there is also Everett Pike from

*El Centro, and Albert Nuñez and Sam Pinkerton, who were
at the Fredonia High School with me. Others seem familiar,
but I do not know their names. In this strange place they do
not know whether to talk with us as friends or not. During our
student days, if our eyes met by accident in the school building,
we would have looked away from each other. But here it is
different. We are surrounded by others we don't know, and it is
the Imperial Valley group with whom I have most in common.
Because of the Hindu-German trial, I feel some of them don't
trust me. Of course, I do not blame them at all.*

*And there is so much feeling of competition! We try to impress
the superiors through skill at running, or doing the obstacle
course, or speed in digging a trench. Some boys try to dominate
the rest of us, forgetting that we are on the same side.*

*I have been assigned to artillery for the 364th Regiment. They
need boys who are good with horses, and ones who will not be
afraid to be close to the action. I am proud to be in a mounted
unit. I am responsible for guns and caissons and cannons, which
we will cart in wagons.*

*Harry is by my side almost always and we sleep in the same
bunk. I stay near him at all times and some of the other Japanese
boys, and also, Chacha-ji, you will be happy—there are eighteen
other Punjabis here—many from Jullundur and some from
Ludhiana and Hoshiarpur. We met many of them in Stockton
at Vaisakhi celebrations. There are so few that I do not want to
think ill of any of them, but sometimes I wish they were not so
obliging or that they mixed more with the Anglos. Sometimes the
local boys mock our dastars, sometimes I feel that we are fighting
them instead of the Germans. But our superiors don't like that
behavior and now the Americans have left us alone. So you were
right, Chacha-ji. There is still race prejudice, but I don't think
it is of real consequence. The Negro boys stay by themselves in
another part of the camp, and we do not see them much. We are*

told they will fight separately from us, yet be just as fierce. We are told the army functions better that way. Perhaps that is the case.

Yours,
Jeetu

Camp Lewis, Washington

5 November 1917

My esteemed Jivan Chacha-ji:

My greetings to everyone. Please let Karak Chacha know, it is as he said to me before I left. I must watch my back here. Two days ago, in the line for mess a big Anglo fellow, a boy with a scar on his arm from an old knife fight—his name is Riker— shoved me to the side. "Get out of my way," he said, "and let a real man pass." I am not a small person, you know that. But this man is so large that he could look even you, Chacha-ji, straight in the eyes. Harry and my regular group had already eaten and left. Perhaps that is why this fellow thought that he could intimidate me. That is the sort of man he is—once I heard him mocking the Italians, who are small in stature and also sit together amongst themselves as we do. Another time I heard him speaking against the Jews, also the Irish.

He took hold of me by my shirt and shoved me aside, and not one of the bystanders came to help me. This affected me very much. I cannot lie to you. It reminded me of what you said by the cantaloupe field the night before I left. When he shoved me I felt so humiliated that I lay with my back on the floor, looking up at all of the other boys. When I stood up, they all turned back to their line, their lunches, their stupid talk. How can it be that not one of them would help me? I thought that I should do the proper thing and take the affair to my commanding officer. Then

I remembered something that you said, Chacha-ji: Never stand behind a horse or in front of an official. Both will kick you.

I went to that fellow, Riker, and challenged him to a wrestling match. We held the match outdoors in the marching grounds. Harry organized everything. Please tell Karak Chacha that all his years of wrestling instruction were not in vain. With everyone looking on, Hindustanees and Japanese and Italians and Americans too—I pinned that Riker using Karak Chacha's techniques. The others were cheering like mad! What a feeling that was!

It has been more than a week since this battle and that Riker has not bothered me again. And others look at me differently now. Some of the American boys even invited me to come with them to have some fun in town. I think I am the first Hindu boy they have asked.

There are twenty-six Hindustanees who are here now. I know them all like brothers and there is a great feeling of camaraderie between us.

Yours,
Jeetu

Camp Lewis, Washington

3 December 1917

Esteemed Jivan Chacha-ji:
Two more of our people have arrived today. Can you believe, almost thirty of us are here. We talk a great deal about why we have enlisted. I am sorry to fight the Germans when they wanted to help Ghadar, but they have to be stopped. As Sikhs we cannot allow them to kill civilians and take over Europe. Why Ghadar was so misguided in falling for their lies, I do not know. There is constant talk that the United States government will make

citizens of us. Whether true or not, the training they give us
is good, and it is not at all like fighting for the British king. I
know that was your worry. Here we are free of humiliating
restrictions and official race prejudice. You cannot say the same
of the English system. You will point out that for the Negroes,
it is the same here as it is for us with the English. You are right,
Chacha-ji. In that, you are right. But I cannot keep myself from
taking advantage of the opportunity that I have found here.

I am in the Ninety-First Division, and we have been given
a nickname of the Wild West Division, and for that we all
feel a lot of pride. Not only because there are so many cowboys
among us (we hail from Washington, Nevada, California,
Oregon, Utah, Montana, Wyoming), but also because we are
unlike boys from other parts of the country. We have tamed a
wilderness and most of us think nothing of desert heat. Who
else can say that?

Yours,
Jeetu

Camp Merritt, New Jersey

25 April 1918

Esteemed Jivan Chacha-ji,
Have you heard the news about Pandit RamChandra? On
the last day of the Hindu-German trial, he was shot dead. And
it was by none other than a fellow trusted Ghadarite! It does not
seem possible that he was the same man who spoke at our farm
that afternoon, who slept in the same bed that Karak Chacha
sleeps in. I am thankful you did not allow me to go with him. I
can freely admit that now, my pride is no longer preventing me
from admitting it. Around the camp, I can see the effect of this

news. *People again are looking at me with distrust. I hope it will
pass. It must* pass; *there is no other way.*

Yours,

Jeetu

Camp Merritt, New Jersey

22 June 1918

Dear esteemed Jivan Chacha-ji,

   *We will "ship out" in a few days. From Camp Merritt we
will march eight miles to the Hudson River, then take a ferry to
the docks at Hoboken, New Jersey, and then board a steamer to
the coast of Ireland, finally to arrive in Liverpool, England. It is
only now, when I am on the verge of leaving, that I understand
all that you were worried about.*

   *But, in the camp, something has happened, Chacha-ji. We all
came as separate people, and now we are leaving as something
united—all of us, although we may come from different
countries. You may say we are fighting a common enemy, and
sometimes that makes men falsely united. But it is more than
that. There are Germans who are here with me. Now they will
go and fight people of their same blood. How can that happen,
Chacha-ji? How can something man-made go against something
that was given to us by God, our own flesh and blood? And yet
to all these men it feels right, that we will all fight together for
this country. If you put me with one of those Imperial Valley
boys who was my schoolmate, you could not tell the difference.
I can talk like they do, eat like they do, laugh at their jokes and
they laugh at mine. You have always said they were good people.
Now it may be that I will die in their company. It may be that
one of them loses his life to save mine or that I lose my life to save*

his. *It is war, and we are fighting together on the same side, and we are American soldiers.*

I have done something, Chacha-ji. I hope you do not think badly of me. I have filed to become a citizen. In doing this, I have also cut my hair and shaved my beard. I know you will be furious with me. But, Chacha-ji, to be a U.S. citizen and a Sikh, simultaneously, does not seem possible. I pray that you will forgive me.

All of our people who are in the camp want one thing—to become citizens of the United States and to stop living in the shadows. From the beginning, the government has promised this to the recruits. Why else did President Wilson go with those immigrants in the parade that day to George Washington's home, showing them off to the entire country? Perhaps it is the government taking advantage of us, but we should take advantage of this chance.

With my army service, I can file for citizenship without a statement of intention and without need of proving that I have lived here for five years. It is true that in this enterprise I have disobeyed you from the start. But I feel that I did not act without reason. After the war is over I want to be part of this society, I want to vote. Is this country not founded on the same principles that we believe as Sikhs? Independence, honor, optimism, justice—do we not believe in those too?

My military service will change how the locals see us, I am sure of it. You have said yourself that we must buy many war bonds. You tell me that, because I am here, Clive and Jasper Davis come with pies and tarts that their wives have baked. Clive brought you a rented mule when ours was lame. Do not be too angry with me, Chacha-ji.

They have given us blue laundry bags into which we are to put all our things—the books that I brought with me, the photograph of Mother, the compass that you gifted me years ago.

I am to put everything inside that makes me Amarjeet Singh
Gill, son of Gurubhir Singh, Tarkpur, Ludhiana District. The
army says that it will keep this bag safe until I come back. I
come from a family of warriors, Chacha-ji. You told me once
that if I do my work well, Waheguru will steep my 5 fingers
in melted butter and my labors will be rewarded. I remember
every day these words. Please pray for my welfare.

In chardi kala,
Amarjeet

La Courtine, France

24 July 1918

Esteemed Chacha-ji,
   I am writing from an American artillery camp. We are
leaving tomorrow for a two-day train ride to the front. Some
men are filled with bravado, at least on the surface, for no one
wants to show their fear or any sign of weakness. But when they
smoke their cigarettes, sometimes their hands shake.
   Every step of the way we draw closer to where we will meet
our fate. But despite this, we are not unhappy. We are a group
of buddies, all of us one people. One fellow says something,
then another says a joke in response, it is an entertaining time-
pass.
   It is true that there are some disagreeable sorts. Harry says
that our sergeant, Sam Pinkerton from Fredonia, is a nasty
chap, and that may be so. Not one Japanese or Hindu or Italian
or Greek or Slovak or Jew ever liked Sam Pinkerton, because he
doesn't like us. But yesterday Everett Pike from El Centro said to
me, "You fellas aren't half-bad, ya know that?" He was talking
to me and Chola Singh and I thought, what a world this is—
that two boys from the same town could not talk to each other

at the schoolhouse, but across the earth they can talk and laugh while watering their horses at a mud hole.

Yours,

Amarjeet

War Zone, Western Front

29 September 1918

Dear esteemed Jivan Chacha-ji,

We are in territory that was won only three days ago at great cost to our men. Tomorrow, we will advance to the front. Our own company's soldiers will go over the top. I will be providing them with artillery cover, and I pray that I will do well for them.

Chacha-ji, I do not know what I am made of. I do not know if I will be able to kill a German, if needed, while looking him in the eye. I do not know if I will be one of those soldiers who must be threatened by his officer at gunpoint, in order to stand and fight. I do not bear any ill will toward those German farmer boys on the other side of the line. Once I kill one of them, will I want to keep killing many more? Will the appetite to kill overtake me?

Every day we feel as if we are at the edge of our lives, looking at what has gone past, at our childhoods, at our families. They are ordinary and beautiful at the same time. How can this be?

Yours,

Amarjeet

21

JANUARY 1918

ON SUNDAY MORNINGS, ESPERANZA WOULD VISIT HER PREGNANT YOUNGER sister, and Ram would see Alejandro drop her off in a wagon after they had attended mass. When Rosa was eight months pregnant and felt too uncomfortable to make the trip into town, Esperanza would bring a basket filled with freshly made tortillas wrapped in cloth, fully prepared so that Rosa need not work. Often Ram would be at the home, talking finances with Karak. He would hear Esperanza tell Rosa of news from the barrio, or of their madrina in Algodones, and the cousins who lived on both sides of the border. The family was close, Ram knew, and cultured too. Rosa had learned piano from her musician father. She read books.

One Sunday, while Ram and Karak sat on the porch reviewing accounts from the most recent sale of cotton, Esperanza arrived with another woman. She was slender, tall, and looked past Karak and Ram as if the men were not present.

"My cousin," Esperanza said, smiling, but this woman barely

glanced at them. Ram knew this would offend Karak, but Karak said
nothing as they entered the house. From their seats on the porch,
Ram could see Rosa sitting in her favorite chair. He saw her eyes
grow wide and brighten when she noticed this new woman on the
threshold.

"¿Prima, eres tú, Adela?" Rosa exclaimed.

"¿Quíen más?" the unfamiliar voice said.

"Eeeow!" A torrent of Spanish followed, but Ram could understand only some: they had not seen each other in six years, and to
the other woman—this Adela—Rosa was as pretty as she had been
as a young girl.

Ram and Karak looked up from their work. They could hear
Rosa show off the house: the Persian rug, the piano, the icebox—
which contained ice delivered every two days—the stove. Karak
cleared his throat; Ram knew he had minded the entire interaction.
He felt a tinge of disdain at how quickly Karak's life had been overtaken by these Mexican women. How he had not even been greeted
as this stranger entered his own home.

"Rosa is happy," Ram said, hoping to restore Karak's dignity.

Karak grunted. They continued with their calculations. From
the back door, the women emerged and walked to the other house.
Ram and Karak finished their work. Karak announced that he
would rest on one of the outside cots. After that, they could visit
Fredonia Park together.

Ram wandered to the animal shed, thinking that he would hitch
a mule up to the buckboard. The mare had come up lame two days
before and she had refused oats since yesterday morning. He heard a
soft footstep in the dirt and looked up to find the new woman at the
shed door. She nodded at him.

Ram entered the mare's stall to feed her again but she put her
ears back; he had never gotten on well with horses. In Lyallpur, the
work had been done by oxen who were calm and sturdy and slow to

excite, and that had suited Ram. The mare missed Amarjeet. Nothing could be done about that. Adela entered the stall too and spoke to Ram in quick Spanish and glanced at him, but he did not understand. Something in her manner discouraged him from asking her to repeat her words. What was the woman doing here?

She talked softly to the horse while touching her nose, running her hand along the injured leg. The horse would never have allowed him to do that. How could she take such liberties when she had just arrived as a guest, when the other women were chattering away at the Eggenberger house, as they were supposed to?

She reached down and picked up the horse's hooves, one by one. "The horse is hurt," he said slowly in Spanish.

She answered him, but, again, he could not understand. Her tone did not seem polite.

"Stop!" he said. "We called for the veterinarian."

The Mexican workers understood his Spanish, and Ram was very proud of that, but this woman did not stop what she was doing. She bent down to touch both of the front legs, one at a time, and shot him a piercing glance. She reached for the lead and attached it to the mare's harness.

"What do you think you are doing?" he said quickly in Punjabi, not caring if she did not understand him, only wanting to be more sure of himself. The alarm in his voice surprised him. He was glad she couldn't understand what he said. She spoke swiftly back at him. Was she angry too, now? Then she turned abruptly and led the horse outside. Ram would not dare put a hand on a strange woman, but he marched out of the shed to find Jivan near the pond, washing his hands and face.

"Do you know that new Mexican girl is inside the shed, taking away the mare?"

"Taking away the mare?" Jivan still had soap in his eyes, and he blinked rapidly.

"She has looked at the horse's feet and is talking to it and petting its face and now she is taking the rope and leading it away."

"No, no," said Jivan, sucking his teeth. "I asked her to examine the horse." He added gently, "A horse has hooves, Ram."

"What does she know about hooves or feet? She's a Mexican village girl."

"Rosa told me that she is very knowledgeable. Her father cared for the horses on a hacienda in Chihuahua. I thought she could help immediately instead of us waiting for two days for the veterinarian."

"But we must still have the veterinarian!"

Jivan looked at him with surprise.

"I insist on it," Ram declared.

"He will come," Jivan said mildly. "But let the girl look."

Ram did not go back, and he did not go into town to join the other men in Fredonia Park. He sat with Kishen on the porch, sifting lentils for dinner. He saw the woman and Jivan lead the mare in a circle, then stand in front to inspect the way that it stood. The woman showed Jivan something on the horse's leg, pointing to the area just above the hoof. When feeding the animals later that day, Ram saw a cloth had been tied there. A pungent smell rose from it. At dinner, Jivan told Ram and Karak the Mexican woman's instructions: the horse should be allowed to rest completely for five days.

ADELA'S MOTHER and Rosa's mother were sisters, Karak explained when Ram asked. They had an aunt who lived in Algodones, of whom they all, including Esperanza, were very fond. Ram wanted to know more. When Karak was out, Ram asked Rosa himself.

"She is my mother's older sister's daughter," Rosa said. "We are like sisters ourselves. When we were girls, we saw each other every day until my family came to El Norte. Her mother is my madrina."

"From Chihuahua?"

"Sí," she said, then added, "Adela went with Señor Villa's army when he was sweeping the villages in Chihuahua, gathering men to fight for him."

"She went with the army?"

"With her husband," Rosa said quickly, as if Ram had questioned Adela's honor.

"Ah."

"Her husband was killed, Ram." She paused, as if this fact were also evidence of her honor. "She left Villa and went to Algodones to stay with our aunt. Then she came here." If Rosa thought it was odd for Ram to ask these questions, she did not say.

"On her own?"

"¡Sí!" Rosa turned to him, smiling. "Adelita does many things on her own! Even as a child she helped her father with the horses and mules. She learned many things from the curandera in our village." There was pride in her voice.

Later, Ram wrote to Padma, *The Mexican women are strange. Some of our men say they have too much freedom. They are very forward, it is true. They look directly at any man, and are given liberty to choose their husbands. Some would say they are too loose. I wonder what you would think? Sometimes they offend me, then I realize, of what concern are they to me? Let them be as they are, a different people.*

It felt reassuring to write this.

ADELA CAME THE NEXT SUNDAY TOO, with Esperanza and her children, and stayed the day with Rosa. She checked on the horse once, spoke with Jivan, and went back inside Karak's house. Alejandro came to fetch them in the late afternoon, and Ram and Karak stood on the porch and watched the wagon, loaded with adults and children, turn toward town. The sky glowed red and orange. Rosa came out of the house. "Karak," she said softly. Something about her voice made both Ram and Karak turn around.

"What?"

"The water has come."

The men said nothing.

"Viene el bebé."

"Oye!" Karak said, stepping backward, his boot grazing the edge of the porch. "Ram! Ram! Go and tell Jivan Singh! Go!"

Instead, Ram ran to the roadway to tell Esperanza. What could Jivan Singh do if Rosa was about to give birth? He chased after the wagon, yelling, "Alejandro, stop! Stop! The baby is coming soon! You cannot go back!" Every person on the wagon turned to face him. Esperanza's eyes grew wide. "Take the children back to the barrio, Alejandro," she said. "Tell the partera—Señora Jiménez—to come."

Ram walked back to the Eggenberger house. Esperanza and Adela joined Rosa inside.

Ram sat next to Karak on the porch. "Do not worry," he said. "They have sent for the woman to help her."

Karak glared at him. "Are you mad? I live in America and my wife is to have her baby with a Mexican midwife? Go to Moriyama and use his phone. Call the doctor. The doctor himself must come!" It was lucky, Ram thought, that the door was closed. He hoped the women had not heard him.

Ram saddled the mare; she was doing better now. He did not like to ride, but it was the fastest way to get to the Moriyama farm. Did one need to rush when a pregnant woman's water had come? Should he have told Jivan Singh before leaving, or perhaps Kishen Kaur? He did not know the answer to all these questions.

He found Hatsu and Tomoya working in the vegetable garden. Tomoya showed him the phone that hung in their parlor, and Ram went through the dispatcher to the doctor's assistant. He repeated his request twice, but in the end, she understood. She would send the doctor as soon as he returned from another house call.

Outside, he found the Moriyamas seated in their Model T, waiting for him. Hatsu wanted to help Kishen with the other women. Tomoya would drop her there.

RAM ARRIVED ON THE HORSE after Tomoya had already left. Hatsu was in the Eggenberger house with Kishen and the other women.

Ram unsaddled the horse and put her in the shed. When he walked to Jivan's house, Karak and Jivan were sitting on the back porch. They looked up when he entered. Leela was sitting with them, drawing on a slate. "What are you doing?" Ram asked.

"We are waiting for you to make dinner," Karak said, gravely.

Ram made beans and cholé and rotis and had Leela take it, in a basket, to the women in the house. By the time the men slept at midnight, neither the midwife nor the doctor had come.

In the thick darkness before the sun rose, Ram woke to the sound of a woman's cry. "That is Rosa," Karak whispered. He had stayed at Jivan's home and slept on his old cot outside. They heard a female voice instructing her, calm and steady and knowing. The partera must have arrived during the night, Ram thought as he drifted in and out of sleep. But Rosa cried out again and again; the cries seemed desperate and Ram woke. He had heard labor cries before; he had been present when three of his cousins' children were born. But those did not sound like this. Karak was awake too. He ran to the house and banged on the door. "What is it? What is happening?" Karak said.

Kishen came to the door. "The baby is in an odd position. You must wait, Karak, and pray," she commanded. "Do Ardas." Ram and Karak sat on the Eggenberger front porch and waited for the dawn. As the sky grayed and brightened, Kishen emerged from the house. Strands of hair had escaped from her braid. Her chunni lay tangled around her neck. But her eyes were bright.

"Karak Singh, you are the father of a son!"

Ram had never before seen that expression on Karak's face: elation, relief, fear, humility.

"Let me see him," Karak said.

"Wait a few moments," Kishen said. "I'll bring you to him." They waited silently.

A wagon drawn by a single mule turned onto the path. A woman was driving it.

"What do you want?" Ram asked.

"Me mandó Alejandro Felix," the woman said.

"The baby is born," Ram said. "Already born!"

Suddenly Karak could wait no longer. In two long strides, he crossed the porch and burst through the front door.

Later, Kishen told them how it happened: the baby had been out of position, but Adela had moved his head down with her own hands so that he could be born—clear and healthy and crying—with Rosa unharmed.

THEY NAMED THE BABY Federico Singh Fernandez. He was large and pink and always hungry. He had inherited Rosa's white skin. He had a maroon birthmark on his tiny hip that darkened, then faded, then reappeared again. If Rosa was not holding him while he slept or ate, someone else was: Adela, Kishen, Ram, Karak, even Jivan. Ram held him often. He wondered if Santosh had had eyes as dark as this baby's, with that indecipherable color between black and violet. He wondered if his son had chirped in that same odd way in the first hours after birth. He wrote to Padma, *Describe to me what Santosh looked like in those days, how he smelled. Tell me everything.*

Esperanza returned to the barrio, but Adela stayed for almost a month, washing, feeding, and cleaning. She rose early in the morning while Rosa slept.

After Ram's hurried trip to the Moriyama house, the horse had again come up lame, and with this too she helped. If Jivan wanted to keep the mare, Adela could do something for her—but it would require that the horse rest for a full month afterward. Was that possible? Jivan said it was.

One afternoon, while Jivan held a towel over the mare's eyes and Ram pushed down her ears, Adela poured acid on the horse's leg. The horse groaned and tossed her head. Adela had prepared a poultice, and she placed this on a clean rag and wrapped it low around the pastern. The dressings would need to be changed every day, she instructed them, and the mare needed to be kept in the shed.

"That is impossible," Ram snapped. "She will not stay quiet for that."

"I will do the dressings, then," she said. "You need not bother."

This was not what Ram had meant to suggest. The next morning, she arrived when he was cleaning out the stalls. He felt a tide of resentment toward her. He was capable of doing anything on this farm. He had made a success of three cotton crops. He supported a family in Punjab. He wanted her to know these things.

They were silent around each other. Her expertise with the horse bothered him, as did her sincerity, her seriousness in everything she did. He wondered if she knew he was there. That bothered him too. She was in the animal shed the next morning, and the morning after that.

One time he arrived to find her sitting on the stool that was usually kept near the harnesses; she was unaware of him, bent over, holding her head in her hands. At first, he thought that she was only tired. He had heard the baby's cries at night and Karak had begun to sleep on the outdoor cot again—but when Ram came closer, he realized that she had been weeping.

He stepped away so that she would not know he had been there, and walked around the pond. By the time he returned, she had recovered. She looked at him but said nothing, and turned to the horse, and for a moment all he saw was her hair swept back in a bandana, the black curls spilling out underneath.

"I am sorry," he said in Spanish.

She did not turn around. "For what are you sorry?"

He hesitated. "Perhaps the horse is lame again because I rode the day that the baby came."

"It is not your fault." She had bent now to take off the bandage. "She had already had a week's rest. If not that day, she would have been hurt on the next day." She turned to look at him. She was older than him by a few years—not many—he could see that now.

He could not condemn her for crying, for he had done the same for weeks after leaving his country and his wife. He knew why she might sit and weep for no reason at all.

ADELA ROSE EVERY MORNING to change the horse's dressing, and Ram got used to seeing her when he came to take care of the other animals. They were comfortable with each other in the cool stillness. He liked the tremor of her voice as she comforted the mare. At night, his last thought before falling asleep was of seeing her again. She could have cared for the horse at any time, but every morning she was there.

When Alejandro and Esperanza came to fetch her, Adela gave instructions that the horse should be walked twice a day. Ram took up this job. Suddenly, there was an empty space, a longing, a secret that only he and the horse knew.

RAM WAS WATERING THE ANIMALS in the shed when he saw Alejandro's wagon come up the dirt path six weeks later, with Adela seated in the back. A chill went down his spine. When she entered the shed, the mare snorted softly, her ears twitching.

"She has missed you," Ram said in Spanish.

"The leg is healing well."

He felt a tinge of pride. "Did you see the baby?"

"He is so happy. Already he seems to smile, but I think it is only gas. Barriga llena, corazón contento." They laughed.

"Karak is very proud."

A car honked in the distance.

Adela bent over the horse's leg. "It will still take a few more days," she said.

"We have rented another horse for a month. Karak Singh went today to fetch him. To give time for the leg to heal." He wanted her to know that he cared for the horse too.

"Bueno," she said.

The honking grew louder. Ram leaned out of the door of the shed to see. A gleaming black touring machine rolled in front of Jivan's house. Karak sat in the driver's seat, grinning.

"You like it, Ram Singh?" Karak stepped out of the automobile.

"Where did you rent it?" asked Ram.

"I bought it, bhai! I thought, why waste the money on renting a horse? Or renting a car? I can buy it outright. So I did."

"But—the waiting list?" Ram said.

Jivan appeared. "What is this?"

"Our new horse."

Kishen appeared too, untying her apron. Behind her, Leela was jumping with excitement. "A Tin Lizzie! A Tin Lizzie!" Kishen reached out to touch the gleaming fender.

"Stop!" Karak said.

Kishen pulled back her hand, her eyes wide. Karak plucked a handkerchief from his pocket and gave it to her, waiting for her to wipe her fingers. "Now you can touch it," he said.

"How did you buy this, Karak?" Jivan asked.

"Shipment came yesterday on the express from Los Angeles. They had extras."

Jivan looked at him doubtfully. "The waiting list had more than twenty names."

"Fifty dollars can make that list shorter."

Jivan rubbed his hands together like a young man. "Let's go. Where will you take me? Let Kishen Kaur sit in the front."

Ram saw Adela leaning on the fence post, watching them. They had all been speaking in Punjabi.

Kishen pulled her chunni around her head and sat immediately in the passenger seat.

"Me too, me too!" Leela said, climbing into the back seat.

Jivan slid in next to her.

"Ram," Karak said, gesturing with his head that he should get in too.

Ram glanced again at Adela. He did not know if she would remain until he returned. "I'll come later. You go."

Karak's eyes darted from Ram's face to Adela's, then back.

Ram turned back toward the animal shed, suddenly ashamed.

HE DREAMED ABOUT ADELA the night that Karak bought the motorcar— her skin and her scent and her taste. He dreamed without his conscience interfering. When he woke, his shame felt like a boulder, massive and heavy. But he could not help himself. He turned on his side and faced Amarjeet's empty cot and released himself in the solitude. He went to the canal and bathed and when he returned, he took up a pen and paper and wrote to his wife. He wrote of manliness and virtue. Of tilling the land. Of the money that he had grown with each crop. He wrote of anything that would keep his mind on Padma, far away, and not with Adela, so near.

He wrote these lines at the end:

I must ask you something. Another man would not ask his wife but declare it only as an order. You know that is not my way. Never. Will you come and join me here, the way that Kishen Kaur joined Jivan Singh? I will make you comfortable. We will have our own house. We will have more children. After

some time, we can return home together and I will buy some
land and you will be the richest woman in the district. I do
not usually think these things, but now I feel it strongly. You
see, Kishen Kaur advised me. Sometimes a wife might not be
happy with her husband's family, and wants to live only with
her husband. Sometimes she may be miserable in her in-laws'
home. Will you come? If you say yes, I will fetch you and Santosh,
or if the new British laws will not allow it, I will arrange for
someone to accompany you. Do not worry about the money. All is
different now.

He read the last paragraph several times before sealing the envelope. He willed himself to believe that Padma's coming was the right
thing. That it was possible.

The letter lay on his trunk for one week, unsent. Every day, he
forgot to leave it for the mailman. Once he forgot to take it with him
into town. Ram did not know what to make of this failure.

THE FIRST SUNDAY that Karak and Ram rode to Fredonia Park in the
new car, Karak parked it on the road nearest the benches.

"Aren't you embarrassed, showing off to everyone? Don't you
have some humility?" Ram asked. "The motorcar is not a prize."
Ram thought he was talking not only of the car, but of every fine
thing that existed in Karak's home. Ram saved every penny to send
to his uncle. To him, Karak's spending was an offense.

"But it *is* a prize, Ram," Karak said, grinning. "Why not be
proud of it?" By the time Karak and Ram stepped out of the car, the
Khan brothers and Harnam Singh were leaning over the side of the
fence to get a better look. The top was down.

"Karak Singh, from whom did you steal this?" Harnam asked.

"They gave them away at the fair last week," Karak said.

More of the men were getting up to look.

Malik Khan said, "Model T Touring . . . other cars run smoother."

"I bought what I wanted to buy, Malik," Karak said. "What do you know about it?" The two men had never gotten along, all the Hindustanees knew that.

"Must have cost a lot, Karak Singh!" Sikander Khan said, shaking Karak's hand.

Three men climbed in the car. Karak cranked the engine, hopped in, and drove off, a tail of dust rising behind.

Ram was happy to see him go. He settled down on a bench under his favorite tree.

"Did very well with the cotton this year," said Ahmed, Sikander's brother.

"He must let everyone know," Harnam said.

"I would do the same," Ahmed said with a chuckle, lying down on another bench with his hands behind his head.

"Our mare became lame," Ram said. He wondered why he was making excuses for the car, while Karak shamelessly boasted about it.

"Nice to have a Touring rather than a Runabout," said Gugar.

"Too expensive, bhai," said Hukam, shaking his head. "A waste for our needs. I was looking at a Runabout. I put down my name for that. We'll get it in two months' time."

"What do you know of their needs, Hukam?" said Ahmed. "They have their needs. We have our needs. What do you know of them?" He fished a bidi out of his pocket and held it between his lips.

Ram was already tired of their jealousy. "We need the car because Karak Singh wants to treat Kishen Kaur very well," Ram said, "otherwise we will lose the only good cook in the valley."

The others laughed.

"She is a good cook," Harnam agreed. "Her makki-di-roti, sarson-da-saag." He kissed his fingertips. "Best saag-roti in California!"

"Have you ever had Jagdish Singh's wife's saag-roti? In Yuba City?" asked Gugar. "It is fantastic; it cannot be beaten."

"It is good," Ram agreed.

"I do not fancy saag-roti," Hukam said.

"When did you have it? Jagdish Singh's wife's saag-roti?" Gugar challenged Ram.

"In 1913, my work gang mate in Hambelton had an uncle there in Yuba City. We jumped on board the train to visit him," Ram said.

"So tell me, whose saag-roti was better?" Gugar asked. "Kishen Kaur's or"—he raised his eyebrows—"Jagdish Singh's wife—Ranjeet Kaur's?" He was smiling slyly. Ranjeet Kaur was known to be quite beautiful.

Ram laughed.

"Why are you shaking your head, Harnam? Did I offend you?" asked Gugar.

"No, no. No offense."

"Then tell, Ram, which saag-roti is better? Who is the saag-roti princess of California?"

"What is all this fighting and argument about?" Inder Singh asked. He was lying on another bench near them, his hat covering his face. "Saag-roti, of all things. Are you mad? Can't a workingman get some rest?"

"I don't mean anything disrespectful," Gugar said, still smiling.

"Fundamentally you are a dishonest man, Gugar," Inder called out, without removing the hat.

Ahmed and Ram laughed.

"I am asking a reasonable question of this young man who has tasted the food of both women," said Gugar.

"Your dirty mind puts us all to shame," Inder said.

"There is also Raghubinder Singh's wife, Priti Kaur in San Francisco," Ahmed said.

"That may be," Gugar said.

"She is very nice to look at," Ahmed said.

"That is not the criteria here," Gugar said. "I want to know from Ram who is the better cook."

"I cannot say such a thing in public," said Ram. "That is a private conversation."

"This is a private place, bhai," Gugar said. "Who is going to tell anything?" He looked at Ahmed and Hukam.

"I am!" Inder said from under his hat.

"What happens here in the park is private," Gugar insisted. "No one tells secrets. But let it go. You have a good situation. You have one of our own women cooking for you; now you have a car. I am having the next best thing, having one wife in India and one wife here. One Indian, one Mexican. We all do what we can to survive. There is no harm."

"You are comparing a car to having two wives?" Inder said, lifting the hat from his face. "I'll talk to you when all your children come looking for their inheritance. Better not to marry. After all, we're in America; these women give you all the privileges of marriage without marrying."

"What privileges have you had?" Ahmed asked.

"You are naive, my friend," Inder said.

"Yes, yes," Ahmed said, making a face at Ram, but responding to Inder, "and you are very worldly."

The men stopped talking when the group returned in the car. "Beautiful!" One of the men said, with gravity. Doors were opened and closed. The three men who had gone with Karak sat down in the park, but Karak said, "Come on, let's go." Ram, who had grown uncomfortable with the conversation, was glad to oblige.

A LETTER CAME FROM PADMA, written in her fine hand, answering the questions with which he had presented her twelve weeks before.

Father of Santosh! You tell me that Karak has been blessed with a child. You ask what our son smelled like the night he was

born. What a question, my life. I will never forget that night.
He smelled like God. O my husband—he smelled like God.

THE NEXT MORNING Ram hitched the mare to the buckboard, re-trieved the letter that he had written days before and made his way into town to post it. Later, when he told Jivan what he had done, the older man asked him only one question. "Does she know how to read, Ram?"

"Bhai-ji?"

"Does she know how to read?"

"Yes, and she writes her letters without the help of a scribe. She even writes poetry," Ram could not help adding.

"Good. With the new law, any immigrant must read. It may be in Punjabi. It need not be English. But you cannot go and fetch her, because the British will not allow you to return. That is how it is now." Jivan gave him the name of the lawyer he knew. Ram visited him the next day.

HE STILL FELT AFFECTION FOR HIS WIFE, after these five long years. He did. But there was something else. Ram waited a day before going to town to see the lawyer, telling himself he had work to do at the farm. He knew Adela's schedule in the seamstress shop. She was there on Tuesdays and Fridays and Saturdays, when she took work for the americanos, making dresses and evening gowns. The rest of the week she helped Esperanza with her sewing in the barrio, making baptism gowns and confirmation dresses. After word got out about Rosa's baby, she had sometimes been called to attend women during childbirth too. He knew all this because Adela had told him as they worked together on the farm with the animals. She spoke in Spanish, and he tried very hard to understand every word.

The lawyer told him, yes, Padma should be able to come join

him. She was his wife and that was reason enough, but also she was literate; she would have the entry fee when she arrived at the port. All of that would comply with the latest laws.

Ram was satisfied. He stopped at the Edgar Brothers store to buy a disc harrow that Karak had insisted on having, and told the salesman he would come later to pick it up. He went to Main Street, wandered in the commercial part of town where the Anglos and Orientals and Negroes and Mexicans mixed and, making a left here and a right there, arrived at Bessie Mae Belvidere's seamstress shop.

At the counter, a middle-aged woman looked up when he entered. "Can I help you?" she asked. She looked surprised.

Ram had not expected to see her, either. "No," he said at first. Then, "Yes, I am looking for Adela Rey Vasquez."

"She is in the back. Working," she said sternly. "Is it a matter of some clothing that we've completed for you?"

"No."

"She'll be free for her break at noon."

He told himself it was acceptable to wait for Adela. He had written to his wife to join him. He was still safe.

He left and wandered about town for an hour. Advertisements for Liberty bonds, recruitment, appeared everywhere. *Make the World Safe for Democracy. Wake Up America! Civilization Calls Every Man, Woman and Child! Our Boys Need Sox, Knit Your Bit. Food Will Win the War. Women! Help America's Sons Win the War!* He went to the bank and saw through the window Jasper Davis, who had lent them money for the first cotton crop. He was suddenly filled with a feeling of great goodwill, generosity. He went to the bank counter and, in a rush of exuberance, bought one war bond. He went to the children's clothing store and left a credit of three dollars there for Daisy Davis, Jasper's wife, to buy something for their daughter next time she was in town. At the general store he bought a box of chocolates, and left them for the girls at the telephone switchboard office. He had seen

Karak do all these things before. Somehow, this morning, he felt like doing them too.

"Awfully nice of you, Mr. Singh," the receptionist said, smiling. "Did Karak put you up to this?"

He shook his head. "Just on my behalf. For your help when baby was born."

"That's mighty sweet of you and your family."

He returned to the seamstress shop and there stood Adela, a cloth purse slung over her wrist, as if waiting for him. How solemn she was, wearing a simple green dress, her hair pinned away from her face. Her chin drew back in a delicate line to her jaw. Her face brightened when she saw him, but she composed it quickly.

"Hola, Ram. What brings you here?" She was smiling, but puzzled.

He stammered. "I rode in on the horse. Would you have a look at her?" His explanation sounded like a lie. He felt a churning in his belly. She was a Mexican. Wasn't she something unfamiliar, unclean? He could not answer that question. Was he contemplating the unthinkable? And *why* was it unthinkable?

"¿Almorzaste?" Adela asked.

"No," he said, surprised at her informality.

She suggested that they walk to the edge of the barrio, where an elderly woman sometimes sold tamales out of her kitchen. On the way, they passed the mare. She stooped to inspect its leg. "She has healed well," Adela said. "Very good!" she added, in English. Her smile was sincere, without reservation. She did not worry about what might be unthinkable.

He asked her about the store, about the seamstress for whom she worked. He gathered bits of information and knew that he would remember them later, turning them over and over in his mind: what she laughed at, despite her solemnity; how she spoke of Mrs. Belvidere, how she cooed to the dog that was crossing their path. He was losing himself. He could no longer assess what this look could mean, or that smile. He felt too much weight in every one of her actions. He was breathing in her air of sadness and longing and loneliness; it somehow matched his own. But it would not matter. Padma would soon be here with him. He was safe.

They crossed the railroad tracks and stopped at the tamal maker's home. They ate standing under a ramada. Beside the tracks, a stray dog was lying in the shade. Some boys kicked a ball down the dirt road. Two women with tubs and washboards sat in front of a tent house.

"You are a quiet man, Ram," she said, looking up at him.

He nodded but could not meet her gaze. She put her hand on his arm. The world stilled. They stood together alone, among the people, the mesquite, the crusted earth, the chickens. He felt the opening of possibility, perhaps an empty hut in the barrio, perhaps a bed that waited just for the two of them. What a comfort that would be, after all these years.

He moved his arm away. It was the slightest of movements, and yet he saw its full import on her face, how she pulled back into herself, how she once again became capable and serious. She was hurt; he knew. "Goodbye, Adela," he said.

On his way home, he remembered what Rosa had told him: that Adela had roamed with Villa's army. Had she wielded a gun? Had she ever killed a man? Rosa had said she had escaped when she could. Could Padma have done all that? He felt again the touch on his arm, the slow sensation traveling to his spine, to the hollow of his belly. Adela was aware of his marriage and son; Rosa would have spoken about them. Of course Adela knew everything.

She was a widow. Perhaps widows in the west did not know shame, and thought only how they missed the company of men and the pleasures of married life. Perhaps they did not think how they might dishonor their families.

As he turned onto the dirt path to the farm, he was filled with regret. Oh! He should have kissed her! He should have kissed her!

30 May 1918

My dear husband, Father of Santosh,

*When I read your letter my heart leaped at your desires—
that you would want me to join you, that you would take the
trouble, pay the cost to have me with you.*

*I confess I am scared, thinking about that voyage over the
water, and how I would be hindered by my bad leg. For several
days, I kept your letter with me. You can imagine that. I woke
early to milk the cows, to make meals in the kitchen, serving
food to Uncle and your cousins, all the while I had this secret
harbored in my breast. The paper burned next to my heart.
Every time I thought of the ocean voyage, my heart began to
race. But that evening I held Santosh. The thought came to me:
"We can go to your father! Soon we will be together!" Can you
imagine my feelings, husband? It was as if God were speaking
through the child. That is how I knew that God wished us to be
together.*

*Now I am courageous. To be with you, in my rightful place, I
could travel to a new home, I could live in a new country, learn
a new language. I will stay for as long as you want. I consider
what my life here has been and I know I could stay with you in
a foreign place for my whole life, if you asked that of me. I will
miss my parents, but my place is by your side, and Santosh's
place is there too.*

Theri,
Padma

10 June 1918

My wife,
*I have decided that you and Santosh must travel here
with your brother. I cannot come and fetch you because the*

British government is not allowing Hindustanees out of
India once they return on a visit. It is because of the dire
political situation that has developed through Ghadar Party
and the Germans. In April ending, there was a huge court
case here. Pandit RamChandra was killed in the courthouse
itself by one of our own countrymen. Perhaps the news has
traveled there, I do not know. It was a huge scandal, and the
white people trust us even less, but do not worry. I tell you
only so that you know the whole truth when you arrive and
you do not wonder why some Americans may treat you with
suspicion. But they are not bad people, Padma-ji. It will do
your brother Shankar much good to bring you, and perhaps
the misfortune in his poor wife's dying will be made better by
coming here.

Because of all these issues I consulted with a lawyer. He asked
me if you could read and write, and I assured him that you
could, but only in our Punjabi. I had to tell him that sometimes
you even wrote poetry, and that you used to do that when we
were children together. I almost showed him the poem you wrote
about the trees near the waterwheel. You know that I carry it
with me in my billfold and read it when I miss home. He asked
me also whether you suffered from any illness. I told him no.
He asked me if you were my lawfully wedded wife, and did I
have any way to prove that. I told him that in our country we
do not have certificates like they do in the U.S. to show that we
are married, or that we were born, that everyone in the village
knows these things, and that most of all you were bringing my
son, and if that was not proof of the marriage between us, what
could be? The lawyer seems like a man with a good mind, and
in the end he said that you should be able to enter, along with
Santosh. He was not as sure about brother Shankar, but after
I gave some information, he saw no reason why he would be
turned away, if you both had the money required. It is a matter

of $8 for each of you, which I will wire to Shankar so that you can give it to the authorities at the proper time.

I am telling more details than you need, for your brother will take care of everything. But you must be prepared for all that might happen. The journey is not easy, Padma, but you must come. I hope that you feel the same. I have written a letter simultaneously to Shankar with a full explanation. A steamship will leave from Calcutta at the beginning of October for Hong Kong, and there you will go to the gurdwara to wait for the steamer to San Francisco, where I will come and collect you. I know the granthi at the Hong Kong gurdwara and he is a holy and good man. That is where I met Karak Singh for the first time, before we voyaged together on the ship to Seattle.

It seems impossible that I should see you and Santosh before the year's end, but it can be so.

Your husband,
Ram Singh

21 June 1918

My son, fragment of my heart,

What is this I hear from your wife? That you are sending money so that she may join you and take my grandson away from me? These past two days I have thought of nothing else—can it be true what she tells me? Sometimes she lies to me out of spite. She says nasty things about your younger cousin. That he was looking at her inappropriately—such nonsense! As if Ishwar would do such a thing, with her limp! Why should she treat Ishwar in such a manner? I have kept this a secret from you because I did not want to hurt you when you are far away.

But I must tell you how she told me—that she is taking away my grandson . . . that silly girl that I have known since her birth! We were making rotis in the kitchen. Perhaps I spoke *a little too harshly when she burned a third one that morning. At that moment she said sharply, as if an ant bit her, "I don't have to work like this anymore!" I asked her why, what nonsense was she talking? Then an expression came over her face and she abruptly ran out of the kitchen. I had to cook all the rotis by myself that morning, because your Sita Didi was ill! None of your cousin's wives do any work at all!*

My son, all this time I have been thinking that Padma is a nice girl. I felt sorry for her because of her ugly leg. What a fool I have been. But do not be too concerned. Ishwar has been looking after me so she cannot do me any harm.

But you must tell me the truth, son. For if it is true, what shall I do without my grandson here? For all these years, I suffered without you, sacrificing for the good of the family. I know that Padma must have manipulated you to do this, for you would not have taken such a harsh decision on your own. Can you not change your mind?

Oye! It is my fate to have been made into a fool by my own son. If this is how you have meant for it to be, then, of course, I cannot stop you. You have contributed so much to the household that no one will go against you. What a pity that now that so many depend on you, you cannot think of me, your poor mother.

Your Ma

23 September 1918

Dear husband, Father of Santosh,

We are preparing to depart next week. How happy I am to go. I thought that I would miss the family here—miss these trees and this land and this home. But I will not.

I will have no difficulty adjusting to life in America. I am sure of this. The local people will speak a different language, that is true. But I will learn it. And what will I have to do with them? You will handle all where they are concerned. People are the same no matter what the country. All have sons and daughters—women everywhere love their husbands. I cannot wait to see your face again and to be in your presence.

I have made a mistake, my husband. Before your letter came telling her, long ago, I revealed to Mother-in-Law that I was coming to you. I do not know why I did this. Although she spoke sharply to me that morning I should have forgotten it— but I did not. In my pettiness, I let slip the information that I would not be here much longer. A strange expression came to her face, as if she already knew, as if she had triumphed over me because I had lost my temper and revealed myself. But how could she know? You had not told her, had you? When I realized what had happened, I ran from the house like a child. It was shameful. It has been months since that has happened, and still she has not forgiven me. I hope that you can. I want only to be with you, and for you to see your son, and to experience all that you experience.

In eight days' time Shankar will come to fetch me. We will leave for Patiala and catch the train to Calcutta.

Your loving wife,
Padma

2 October 1918

My esteemed husband, Father of Santosh,

I am writing from the Calcutta train depot and I will post this letter at the dock. It is a game I am playing . . . which will reach you first—the letter or me? Such a good game, with such a good prize.

The journey has begun, and it feels that I have been set free. For the first time, I can feel everything. I do not have to swallow my pride in my son, or my dissatisfaction or my wish to read a book or write a poem. Oh! That home stifles me! We all live in close proximity, yet no one knows anyone's heart! How much I missed you! How unkind the others were to me. But not my mother-in-law, dear husband. I do not mean her. She was always battling her own grief while missing you. She could not help it. She adores her grandson, and now all is being taken from her. Perhaps she too can come join us soon.

Shankar, as always since my birth, has been my protector and my guard. Santosh runs after him, copies his gestures, his voice, eats his bananas in just the same manner. If he mimics his uncle in this way, I can only dream how he will be with you! With what adoration he will follow you!

I must tell you, my husband, without worrying you with too much detail. In the village, they were not kind to me when I left. No one came to wish me well. It's true I am a woman and it would not have been proper to have too much hullabaloo. But I will say only this—I was happy to climb in the buggy after my goodbyes were complete.

It is too hot and wet here in Calcutta. Shankar tells me it will become more and more like that as we move along. I am looking out the window and thinking all the time that you saw all these same sights as you traveled across the country. I set eyes on the ocean for the first time yesterday. When I saw it, something happened to my heart, my mind—it is glorious and impossible. I cannot find words to describe it.

I cannot wait to sail upon it—what a marvel, to float on top of an ocean! More, I cannot wait to speak with you, so that you may tell me your thoughts on everything—the camels, the wet heat, the rude conductors, the motion of the train, the ocean, our son.

Your loving wife,
Padma

ON THE DAY OF PADMA'S ARRIVAL, Ram came to San Francisco alone, traveling north along the same railway that had brought him to Fredonia more than four years earlier. It seemed impossible that Padma would be with him on the way back. For these years, few things had assured him that she really existed: her letters, the photo he kept safe in his trunk, the sound of her voice that accompanied him everywhere since he first arrived, and never left him. To be with the body that belonged to that voice, to feel her warm whisper in his ear while standing on his cotton field, while eating his meals, to reach for the hand he had held as a child—impossible.

But the boy—his boy—he did not know at all. These were real and proper feelings, he believed. His thoughts of Adela receded into the background.

At the San Francisco train depot in late afternoon, with a December chill in the air, a ticket master directed him to the pier. He arrived there at dusk. He bought noodles from a Chinese vendor outside the terminal building and ate his dinner looking out over the wharf. The air hung wet and cold, so different from the dry wind of the Imperial Valley. Water splashed up against wooden pilings. Workers leaned against the warehouse buildings, smoking cigarettes. Gulls circled and called overhead. Several ships were in port and Anglo men, women, and children milled about the terminal building. In a corner, Negro porters gathered with their trolleys.

The waiting area inside was commanded by a large clock hanging above a schedule board. The cavernous room held benches, a booth where one could buy peanuts or popcorn, a long ticket counter attended by ten or twelve clerks. A policeman walked past, looked at him without interest, and moved on.

Ram walked to the schedule board and scanned the names of the ships coming into the pier.

An elderly man approached him. He wore a suit with a pocket watch, and carried a cane. But he had the air of a vagabond. "Who you looking for, son?" he asked.

Had Ram been squinting? Too obvious in his struggle to decipher the English? "My wife. On SS *Colombia*."

"Says it won't be in until early morning," the man said. There
was phlegm in his voice. Something unhealthy.

Ram was irritated. "I am seeing that," he said.

"Your wife isn't in first class, is she now? They bring them onto
the mainland direct if they're first class."

"Steerage," Ram answered, suddenly self-conscious of his own
appearance. He had worn his nicest pants and a dress shirt to greet
Padma. But he could only afford to purchase her tickets in steerage.

"They'll process her on the island, then. Might take hours. Tell
you, though, there's a place you might go early morning—a rock
jutting into the water. There's a small light there to warn the vessels
away. Stand next to it and you can see the ship on the way to Angel
Island. You'll like it. You might even see *her*." Ram asked him for directions to the rock. It was an hour's walk down the post road. There
would be a shack and a trail turning to the right, leading toward the
water.

Ram thanked him. He went to a secluded corner and stretched
out on a bench, hoping the policeman would not return. Seeing the
elderly man settle down on another bench close by, Ram tucked his
small bag safely under his head. He placed his hat on his face but
could not sleep. The excitement was too much. He would do as the
man suggested and go to the rock in the morning.

In the milky light of dawn, he followed the man's directions to
the outcropping. He was surprised by how accurate they were. Walking along the shoreline, he found the ocean unworldly. Fog drifted
above the water. Sunlight cut silently through the wet chill and the
ceaseless churn of the waves. When he noticed the shack, the air was
just beginning to warm. He heard the occasional, uneven clang of
a bell. The trail led into the cool darkness of a grove of trees, then
emerged in bright sunlight at the edge of the sea. He walked out
on the ragged surface of the rock, unprotected. The wind tugged at

his clothing. The light stood to his left, glaring white and weather-beaten. A bell was perched at the top, twelve feet high. That was the clanging that he heard. His legs felt unsteady. His boots could not find a grip. Although he was several feet from the edge, he walked forward gingerly. The sun warmed his back. He sat against the rail of the lighthouse, the wind against his face, humbled by the sight of the water meeting the land.

Ferries and tugboats chugged past, sails, a steamer bearing the wrong name and the flag of another country. Then he saw it, entering San Francisco bay like a dream—that was how Ram would remember it for years afterward. The fog parted and the ship appeared, the waves sweeping past the hull as if it were a sea beast, enormous. People were huddled on the deck, and—could it be?—a woman stood with a shawl gathered about her. She was next to a man, holding a black-haired child, but the child would not turn toward him. Perhaps she was too far away, but he thought he could see the shape of her shoulders, the curve of her face. It belonged to him; he was part of that curve, of that uneven way she stood.

"Padma!" he yelled. "Padma!" But the unceasing wind smothered his voice. The woman turned away. She could not have heard, not with the wind whipping against the ship, the water parting before it, the violent hum of the sea meeting the shore.

He watched as the ship churned past him, steam spouting from her funnels. She turned toward the land and sailed past an outcropping, beyond his view. He was suddenly filled with a great urgency. How long would it take for the officials to board the ship? For the doctors to examine passengers? How long for Padma and her brother to answer their foolish questions and prove they were literate, to pay that silly tax? Not long, or very long? Hours? Days? From his perch on the rock, he could see a ferry come to take the first-class passengers to shore. It did not matter how long it would take because, regardless, it would be too long. Was it possible for her foot to touch this shore? That she would be walking, alive, alongside him?

He returned to the pier in San Francisco, but she did not arrive that day. At nightfall he took a trolley to the old Ghadar headquarters. It was now called Yugantar Ashram, after the arrest and trial of the Indians and Germans and the murder of RamChandra Bharadwaj. Before Ram left for San Francisco, Karak had sent a telegram there on Ram's behalf. When Ram knocked, a Bengali man allowed him inside. A Tamilian prepared his dinner plate. There were others there: three Punjabis and two Marathi who were students at the university.

Ram slept on the floor, barely listening to their political talk. In the morning he went to the docks and waited again. The ferry carried some passengers from Angel Island. Four Hindustanees were among them, but she was not. The men were not dressed poorly, but they were tired and disheveled.

"Have you met my brother-in-law, Shankar?" he asked them. "He is traveling with his sister, my wife."

"There is a small boy with them?" a turbaned man said. He spoke like a rural man, a farmer.

"My son," Ram said.

"They came with us on the journey," one of the other men said, nodding his head.

"The boy is quite beautiful," another said, perhaps reading the anxiety in Ram's face. "Shankar-ji has not yet been processed. He is waiting still. I have not seen your wife since we arrived. They are keeping men and women separately."

"Don't worry, brother," the third man said.

Ram took them with him to the ashram. He ate and slept there again. They told him more: His wife had suffered from seasickness on the journey, but she traveled well despite her cane. She had written poems about the sea and, when they insisted, had read them aloud. The men had exchanged forwarding addresses with Ram's brother-in-law. They intended to be in touch. And the boy—at five years old, he was very mischievous, very smart. He would stare at the ocean with round eyes. So round, so dark—so curious! They had never seen eyes as black as his.

Ram said goodbye to them the following morning, before he went again to the pier.

That day, she still did not come. Other travelers walked from the ferry dock through the terminal doors: they had spent time on Angel Island too, coming from Tokyo, from Peru, Panama, Australia. He asked the young clerk who sat behind the immigration counter. Was there a list of people who had arrived on the SS *Colombia,* departing from Hong Kong?

"Immigration don't share the manifest list," the young man said, his face like stone, clean-shaven and unlined. Ram wondered if he knew that the lives of the people around him depended on who was on that ship, and who was not.

"My wife—she—" Ram said.

"No public list—"

"If I am giving to you her name, you can look for me?"

The clerk glared at him as if the request was unreasonable. But he unlocked the drawer on his desk and brought out the paper. Ram gave Padma's and Shankar's names, spelling them out.

"Nothing like that here," the clerk said, running his finger down the manifest as if looking at an accounting ledger. In one quick movement, he replaced the document inside the drawer and locked it again.

Ram felt a chill in his gut. There had been a mistake. The clerk had not looked carefully enough. The four Hindustanees had traveled with them on the voyage. Perhaps she was in quarantine. Perhaps she was ill. Perhaps she was wandering the streets of this same city, their son by her side, lost.

The next morning, taking the trolley through a rain-soaked gray city, he went again. A different clerk sat behind the counter. For a moment, their eyes met. Ram had seen him before, in another part of the building. The terminal was less busy that morning. There were no people milling about.

"Hey, you," Ram heard the clerk say. He gestured for Ram to approach him. "You still looking for passengers?"

"My wife—" Ram said.

"You been here for most of a week and I'm tired of looking at ya." He was balding. Wisps of gray hair floated about his head. "Here, you can see for yourself," he said, "I'm not so good at reading these strange names." He tossed the list across the desktop. Ram leaned over the paper. "Be quick about it."

"If her name is not there, what is the meaning?" Ram asked.

"That she wasn't on the boat, mate. Everybody on that boat is on that list."

Ram's stomach clenched in fear. "If the name isn't there, then the person didn't come?"

"That's how they do."

But he saw her name. It had always been there, he knew now, only misspelled: *Saker, male; Pudam, female, with one child.* His throat went dry.

"Why does an 'X' appear by their names?" he asked. "And this— 'SI'?"

"Means they were questioned." The clerk did not meet his eye.

"When will they be released?" Ram could hear the alarm in his voice. "Three days have passed. It is too long."

The man looked at him. He was not being unkind, Ram would think later. "Steamer left this morning, mate," the man said slowly. "Early, right at dawn. That means they were not allowed in."

The building swayed, as if the earth had moved beneath him. Later, he would not know why he ran. What did he think he could do? In a cold mist he arrived again at the outcropping where he had seen the ship pass on the way to the island. Of course, the ship was not there. The rain pelted his face, pooled at his collar, saturated his boots. He stood at the rock, leaning against the lighthouse rail for more than an hour.

In despair, he walked back to the city. He was a pragmatic man;

he found a telegram office. They would have to be told: his uncle in Punjab, Padma's parents. The third one he sent to Jivan: RETURNING P.M. TRAIN TOMORROW. He returned to Yugantar Ashram.

Years later, he would allow himself to forget his desperate return to the rock outcropping, looking for the steamer. If ever asked to tell the story, he would say, *I went to collect her, and she was not there, and that was that.*

IT WAS FAMILIAR TO HIM: The mesquite, the dunes, the ocotillo, the desert, the fierce sun, the boy waving at the gate. The crooked sign at the Fredonia depot, AMERICA'S DREAM. He watched without feeling as the scene flashed past the train window. Then with anger. So much anger.

They all came, as would have been proper and loving to welcome his wife to her new home, emerging from Karak's gleaming black car. Was it so obvious in the way that Ram walked, or stood, or looked at them through his tired eyes? They did not need to ask. He felt the weight of their collective gaze and wished he could escape it. His muscles were too heavy to move. He had lost all strength. Grief devours everything. Hadn't she died? Hadn't she?

17 December 1918

Meri pyari, my dearest,

Did you see me, my love? I stood on the hilltop as your ship approached the port. I saw you there, wrapped in a blanket, holding our son, standing next to your brother. I waved at you then. Did you see? Our boy—he is beautiful.

I have asked the lawyer. He says there is no hope. He says that you should have been allowed inside the country; you are married to a man who is a legal alien. But—now that you have been turned back once, they would not allow you in again. They perhaps would not even allow you to board the ship in Hong Kong.

It is cruelty, Padma. Is there another word for it? I cannot think of another.

Just hold on for two more years, so that I may finish the task that Uncle has asked of me. Hold on for two years and your husband will return.

Thera,
Ram

22

SEVERAL DAYS AFTER RAM'S RETURN, JIVAN TOLD HIM TO JOURNEY TO Stockton to visit the gurdwara, a day's ride on the Southern Pacific. Kishen was sitting with them after serving breakfast, after Leela had left for school. "There is comfort there for a hurt soul," Jivan said. "For a hurt man." They were looking at Ram with concern. He had risen late again, when the sun was already warm in the sky.

Ram chewed his food slowly; he had no appetite. "Bhai-ji," he said, not wanting to disagree. Several times, for holidays in January or April, he had been to the gurdwara: a modest temple raised by fieldworkers and students on sparsely populated land. Before it existed, the laborers sometimes carried the sacred book out into the fields with them, a version of Guru Granth Sahib so small it fit in the front pocket of their dungarees. They had raised money for the building through donations from the lumberjacks and the farmers, the intellectuals and railroad workers. All those who knew and needed what the building would be.

Now they came by rail or by wagon or by foot, they came if they were too tired or sick to work. They came from Oregon and Washington and Texas and Arizona and Michigan and Illinois. They came from New York. They came to discuss politics, to pray, to organize against employers and to organize against the British. They came if they needed a meal or a bed. They came when life was too difficult or if they needed money to repay a debt. The men ate home-cooked food in the langar, they performed chores around the grounds, their laundry was sent to the washers, they enjoyed one another's company in the evenings.

They came to worship too.

"Gurdwara is like mother," Jivan said.

"Go, Ram," Kishen said gently, pleading. Ram had never heard her voice an opinion about his affairs before. Something about the way she said it made him believe that the idea had first been hers. She had asked Jivan to speak with him.

But Ram did not want to go. He did not want to be comforted; his solace would be a betrayal of Padma's suffering. He finished his breakfast and rose to begin the day. The newly planted cotton field needed thinning. There would be a week of hard work ahead. He wanted to begin.

Jivan did not mention the gurdwara again until two weeks later. Ram was helping him clear out silt from the delivery ditch. The family would all go now, for the annual celebration of Guru Gobind Singh's birthday. All the Hindustanees would flock there, whether they were Sikh or Muslim or Hindu. "Everyone will come," Jivan said.

Ram thought that Jivan had selected this time to raise the issue so that they would not have to look at each other. The shoveling, the silt, the glare of the summer sun would provide a distraction. "But I will stay, bhai-ji," Ram said respectfully.

"Come, Ram. It will be good for you. Old friends will be there."

Ram forced himself to be cheerful. "You go, bhai-ji," he said. "Take everyone else."

"You must forget this sadness. Within two years you will once again be with your wife."

"You are right," Ram said vaguely, not wanting to argue. He was puzzled at his own inability to rouse himself from the sadness. Had he wanted to stay in California after all, without going back? Had he wanted Padma to live here permanently, like Kishen did? "It does not matter so much that Padma could not come," he lied. "Only two years. But I prefer to stay on the farm next week. And no one else need look after the farm and animals."

"Ram," Jivan said. He had stopped working and was leaning against the handle of his spade. The man did not like to be thwarted.

"Bhai-ji," Ram said, bending to clear the silt from his shovel. He could feel the weight of Jivan's gaze. But he knew that Jivan realized he would not be moved.

Ram drove the others to the train depot in Karak's car. It would be Rosa's first time at the gurdwara. Other men had married now, and would bring their wives and young children: Mexicans, Anglos, Negroes. Leela held Federico's small hand as he climbed aboard the train. Long after the adults had settled themselves in their seats, she leaned out the window and waved at Ram, her long hair pulled back in a braid, her eyes bright with excitement about the train ride. He felt a pang of regret. She had asked him, over and over, why he would not come.

THE NEXT MORNING, Ram heard the rattling of wooden wheels, and when he stepped around to the front of Jivan's home he saw Alejandro driving his wagon up the dirt path of the Eggenberger farm. Adela was sitting next to him with a basket on her lap. He watched her climb down, carrying the basket, and knock on the door. When there was no answer, she opened it and leaned her head inside. Ram was too far away to hear, but he saw Adela look back at Alejandro, heard her call out. He drove off without her. Adela went inside. It was not his house, Ram thought; it was not his concern.

Ram milked the cow, mucked out the animals' stalls; he fed the chickens at noon; at dusk he left oats for the horse and mules. Still

Alejandro did not come back. Adela remained in the Eggenberger house alone. He thought of her touch on his arm those many months ago. The thought of speaking to her again, after his failure in San Francisco, shamed him. But when he saw the dim lamp glowing in the window of the house, he finally walked across the field and knocked on the door.

"I saw the light," he said, when she answered the door. He was comfortable with simple Spanish now. He could speak well enough to give orders, to describe weather or soil, to tell a short tale, to fall in love. She seemed relieved to see him. "Have you eaten?" he asked.

"Where did they go?" she asked, ignoring his question. "Rosa asked me to come to measure for new curtains. I have been waiting all day."

"To the temple in Stockton."

"There is a holy day?"

"Yes," he said. He did not want to elaborate on it. Why would she need to know such things?

"They will be away three days. Have you eaten?" he asked again. After these many months he would have liked *her* company, in particular.

"They left no food. Alejandro said he would be back before dark. I don't know what has delayed him."

"Come and eat supper with me. We will see him when he arrives."

They ate by lamplight on the porch, which offered a clear view of the Eggenberger house. Ram had made chickpeas that Kishen Kaur had grown in her small plot at the back of the house. He put out spoons and forks for Adela's sake. He didn't know what she would think of seeing him eat a roti by hand. He was nervous as she tasted the food. He had always been proud of his cooking; Kishen had complimented it. The men in Hambelton used to be glad when it was his week in the rotation. But what did Adela know of Hindustani food?

She could not stop eating. "I did not have dinner," she explained, after he had finished his meal and was watching her eat more. He thought she would not be able to admit that she liked it, because of the unnamed thing between them, because of the touch that he had rejected near the barrio, because of something they both wanted.

But she surprised him. "It is delicious," she said simply.

He felt light-headed.

"Why did you not go with them?" she asked.

He could have said, *Who would have taken care of the farm?* But the words did not come. He merely shook his head. Let her make of that answer what she would.

The hum of cicadas swelled, then faded. An owl hooted in the distance.

"My husband would also cook," Adela said. This was not the response Ram expected. She had never spoken of him before. The air grew heavy.

"Why have you come here?" Ram asked. He confused himself. Did he mean to the farm that evening, or Fredonia? He had asked the question, but he did not know what he asked.

"The curtains," she said, surprised. "Why have you?" she stammered. "You mean to the Valley?" she asked. Ram thought of Hambelton and shook his head.

They laughed, but it sounded hollow. Perhaps they were both too hurt to say. There was a boundary between them, a border they could not cross, a line in the earth.

"I came because he died," she said.

"Who was he?" Ram asked, and realized this was the correct question. This was the answer he really wanted. Who had her husband been?

"He made shoes for the horses on the hacienda. My father was the caretaker and the trainer."

"Your husband did not farm?" Ram asked. He had assumed something else.

"Miguel was a blacksmith, working for the patrón. Papá found him that job. But Miguel was filled with hope for a new México, where he could hold his head high, a new future for the people. Villa and Carranza were fighting on the same side then. It seemed possible."

He did not dispute her. What did he know of war? She continued. "One afternoon Señor Villa and his army came to our village, and Miguel went to hear him speak. When he returned home, there was a strange look in his eyes. He collected his clothes and rolled them inside a blanket. I asked him, what was he doing? Did we not have our families here?" She shrugged her shoulders. "Did he not want to stay with me?

"But they had guns and horses and big dreams and so many followers. If you looked in their faces you could see they were the poor from the countryside, who did not eat enough, who worked their entire lives for nothing. President Díaz was snuffing the life out of them, one man, one woman at a time. He did not win his election fairly, he had done nothing but stolen the country from the people."

She was angry—he could see that in her eyes—but her expression was so stoic. She was speaking to Ram, but also she was not. He wondered why she was telling him these things.

"I did not have children. My younger sisters were married and living with their husbands. When I saw Miguel tie his blanket in a bundle, I added my mortar and pestle and cooking pot and told him that I was bound to him for life. He could not leave without me. He had to accept what I said.

"The men and horses traveled by train and fought whenever Villa told them. When there was room, the women traveled in the front cars. But usually we rode on top of the boxcars with the children. We fought Díaz's Federalists all over Sonora and Chihuahua, trying to control the railway.

"My husband marched in front with his rifle. I marched in back with the women, but he knew that I was there. I brought water when he needed. Some of us fought side by side with our husbands. At each day's end we washed the wounds and helped bury the dead. It seems silly now, but we were fighting for our dignity, for justice, for a voice in our country. For a time when we would always have food on our tables. When the rich and powerful would not cheat us.

"We fought that way for three months. Then everything changed. Miguel was shot down in the countryside. The bullet went straight to the heart. The blood spattered everywhere. The rocks, the railroad tracks. The men around him. I saw it happen. I ran to where he fell, picked up his gun, and started shooting too.

"We dug a hole for him by the side of the rails. Darkness was coming and it was not safe. Our fighters wanted to leave. But I searched for two sticks, tied them into a cross, and stuck them into the dirt, even though I knew the wind would blow them away before the morning."

She spoke without crying. Ram was frozen in his seat. How did she tell this story without a tear, without a whimper, as if it belonged to someone else?

"In that moment, God failed me. I do not tell this to mexicanos: sometimes I cannot believe in God. For how can such a thing happen if God were to exist? I kept Miguel's gun close to me. I fought against the Federalists, but when one of our men tried to put his hands on me, I pointed it at him too.

"'Señora, now I will be your man' he said. When I did not go with him, he threatened to kill me. No one would have gone against him." Adela's voice quivered. Finally, he saw feeling in her dark eyes. An unfiltered despair, the acceptance of the cruelty of life on earth. She looked directly at Ram, as if challenging him to ask her more. He was quiet. He did not want to know more.

"The next day we rode through another village. It had been almost four months since I had left home with Miguel. But that was at a different time; now Villa had gone mad, raiding village after village, putting innocents to death. We heard that in one town, he had rounded up the women and tied them together and set them on fire in the middle of the square. One of them had dared to question him about the death of her husband.

"I wanted to leave and return home, but I did not know how. One day as we marched onward, the soldiers riding before us set the buildings aflame. I realized where we were. It was my own place; it was the hacienda where my father used to work. I heard some of the men say that Villa was putting villagers to death, that he had taken two men who had refused to join their band and had them shot in the middle of the square. I did not wait to find out if such a story could be true. In my heart, I knew it was.

"Without telling any others I ran toward the burning hacienda and caught one of the escaping horses. I rode north to Los Algodones, where my madrina lives with her husband. She had told me to come to her if I was ever in trouble. She has always been my savior. I have always known the way to her home, even as a child: It is not far from the dunes that lay between El Norte and Baja, where the land is like one country. Abandon the train tracks before the border and walk west, past the dance hall to the grove of mesquite. There stands a tree with a double trunk, twenty meters high, the tree that everyone knows. My madrina's home is five hundred paces north. When I arrived, the horse was stumbling, foaming at the mouth.

"I stayed for many months while she nursed me back to health, listened to my stories, held me when I cried. One day a letter arrived from Esperanza. 'Come and stay with me, Adelita. Your own house is waiting for you here,' she wrote.

"My madrina encouraged me. 'Be with young people again,' she said. 'Perhaps find another husband. Go back among the living.'"

When Adela finished speaking, Ram did not know what to say.

"You do not believe me, Ram?" she said, after moments of silence.

"I believe you," he said. She had told him so much. He felt it was a gift.

The sun had set now, the evening had turned chill, and Alejandro still had not returned. They realized he was not coming. "Perhaps something has happened with the wagon," she said. "He does not like me much." She gathered the plates before Ram could say no. She helped him scrub the dishes in Kishen's tub. He sensed she wanted to work alongside him, that with the telling of her story, she felt unburdened.

"Buenas noches, Ram," she said, drying her hands on her skirt. "Thank you for the food. Gracias."

He could not meet her eye. "It is nothing."

He didn't watch as she walked back to the Eggenberger house. On his cot outside, in the darkness, he could not sleep. She loomed too close. He could not remove from his mind how she had told him of herself, reaching across a border, how she had become real, unpolluted, clean. What had he thought before? He could not remember. The moon was full, illuminating everything: the alkaline earth, the scrub, the growing cantaloupe, the Eggenberger house. In its glow, the distance between the two homes seemed like nothing. He remembered her crying in the shed by herself when she nursed the mare. He felt her tidal pull across the ancient ocean bed.

Now he rose from the cot and walked the distance between the houses. He did not know if he would knock, or just stand for a blessed moment and then return. When he drew close, the door opened. How long had she been watching him?

Had he ever hesitated about the touch of her foreign skin? He stepped forward and embraced her, burying his face in her hair. When he pulled away, she leaned forward and kissed him. Then he felt sure of himself.

He led her to the back room, and they lay on Karak and Rosa's bed. The smell of the desert earth came to him: the fields that he had tilled, the lands he cultivated as his own although they were not. The scent of her skin, the smoothness of her hair, her humanness, this overwhelmed him. To be touched, after five years, as if he were somebody, this overwhelmed him too.

It was only in the morning that he wondered: Had he gone to Karak's bed out of bitterness, as a way to be his equal?

23

THEY CONTINUED. IT WAS NOT ONLY THAT ONE WEEKEND, WHEN THEY embraced in the animal shed, aware of the horses' soft warm breath, or on his rickety cot outside, which he feared would fall underneath them, or back again in Karak's home. It went on and on, after the family came back from Stockton. He would see her on Sundays after he talked briefly with the men at Fredonia Park, while Karak and Jivan stayed with the others. He could sense Karak's eyes following him as he left.

They met in the back room of the dressmaking shop where Adela worked. Mrs. Belvidere had trusted Adela and given her a key. Adela attended the early morning mass on Sundays and joined Ram afterward. Ram did not know if she felt guilty about this. Weekly, when the Anglos were at church and there were few eyes to spy him coming and going, he and Adela would spread a blanket on the floor in the little-used storage room.

She did not ask about his life before California, although he knew that Rosa would have told her of it. She did not ask him why his first hours in the Valley had been in the doctor's shack. Although she might have known that too. He did not ask her about the man whom she had threatened at gunpoint, who had dared to approach her after her husband's death. She never told what she did to him.

They were surrounded by scraps of cloth, reams of material, spools of thread, the extra sewing machine. Mrs. Belvidere had been a child in Georgia during the Civil War. She did not discard things. They felt protected by her collections, by the trust that the imposing woman had placed in Adela.

They lay among the unmade clothes and the striped sunlight that shone through the blinds. The fabric was witness to their communion, a life outside society. It was witness to everything. His blood would quicken at the thought of that room; it would race if he walked past the street with Karak on a weekday errand.

Did Adela think of it in the same way? He did not know. She had purchased a sheath so that a baby would not come; he imagined that was her concession to his life in India. She neatly folded the blanket when they left. She locked the door so they would not be discovered and showed him the hidden exit from the back. How was it that she was not ashamed? It was the looser morals of western women, he concluded. In America, so much freedom and power was given to them.

He had always thought himself an honorable man. He had spent years condemning Karak's visits to the brothels, how free he was with women. The simplicity of his condemnation had been a luxury. He had never before felt temptation. Now pieces of himself were scattered everywhere, and he could not gather himself up and make himself whole.

The first time he realized that Karak knew, they were climbing back into the car to go home from the park. A moment before Jivan joined them, Karak looked at him with a raised eyebrow. "You have a new interest, is it?" Ram looked away, he could only look away, but Karak slapped Ram's knee affectionately, forgiving the transgression and dismissing it all at once, as if Ram's infidelity were nothing. Ram was filled with a hot shame, a knife in his gut as he thought of Padma, but he could not help going back to the Mexican—that was how he thought of her in those moments. The Mexican. He felt shame for that too.

He sensed Jivan growing more and more distant with him, but he was not certain. Did the man know about him? Was he disgusted? He had spoken with Jivan so often about Padma, about his son. Ram began to avoid Jivan, never spending any time alone with him. One day Jivan asked Ram to drive him into town. As they passed the barrio, Jivan said, "You know that area well, don't you?" Ram's muscles tensed.

Ram said only "Bhai-ji," and his heart hammered against his ribcage. Of course he did not know the barrio well; he did not go there openly, the Mexican men and Adela's family would never tolerate it. But he knew what Jivan meant. He did not wish to lie, to him of all people.

Jivan did not meet his eye. "I wish you did not know it well. But a young man has certain needs." Jivan sighed. "We must survive. We do not always have the luxury of keeping our values as if we lived among our people."

Ram did not know what to make of this comment. He felt a judgment in Jivan's words, but he felt better now that Jivan knew. Ram was, in a way, once more an honest man, as if he had stepped out of the shadows into a circle of light.

Perhaps Adela sensed it too; one afternoon, lying in the seamstress shop, their bodies half in sunlight, half in shade, she said, "Tell me about this—" She was pointing at the scar on his leg. It had been where the man in Hambelton had pounded on his shin, the oddly long wound that had kept him lying by the side of the road before he was able to stand and limp home.

"It is nothing," he said, "an injury from long ago."

She ran her tongue along the length of the scar, as if she knew it was not from long ago. As if she knew it was a wound that America had given him. The nerves skittered at her touch. The sensation ran up his leg and along his spine, sent a shiver into his skull. "I do not believe you," she said, teasing.

He sat up, suddenly enraged, and pulled on his clothes. "Stop. What you believe or not means nothing! I'll kill you!" She pulled up the sheets to cover herself, her eyes wide in fright.

He dressed quickly and walked out into the streets of Fredonia. He felt dizzy. Had he meant those words? He would kill her? At home he had whispered to Padma in their bed—"Die!" as a playful command against fate, as a way to ward off the tragic. No, he could not harm Adela, ever. He remembered the shock on her face, the quickening of her breath. After years, she had made him feel light again. He did not ever want her to die.

It was early yet; people were still emerging from church. The day of the attack in Hambelton had been a Sunday too. People had gone to church then, had prayed too. He and Pala had seen them.

Perhaps Adela knew that he had arrived in the Valley injured and desperate. Perhaps that information had been conveyed between Jivan and Karak, from Karak to Rosa to Adela. But he did not want her to know why.

He promised himself he wouldn't tell her. Surging clouds covered an angry sun. Silent lightning pierced the gray. He had seen this lightning before. It did not have to mean rain. Her bewildered face flashed in front of his eyes. He had walked more than a mile around the town's simple streets and returned to the dressmaker's shop. The Presbyterian church sat around the corner. He would not be noticed going back inside the shop. Could he tell without floundering? Could he say what happened?

She was sitting on the blanket where they had made love, dressed now, leaning against an old sewing machine, her hands playing with its foot pedal, which rested on her lap. When he entered, her face was searching, expectant, but tender.

The rain came. A torrent of water at first, then a gentle sprinkle. Was that why he told her, he wondered later? The rain drumming against the roof like a mother's song? The room felt different when it did not need to protect against dust and wind and sky.

Afterward there were crickets that covered the dirt paths and patios and wagons and motorcars, dark things that crawled out of the fertile earth. Then came the birds to devour them, dropping from the sky without warning. But before those unreal events had occurred, he had already told her, lying in the damp air of the fabric room.

After he spoke he felt fundamentally changed. Now she knew something about him that no one else knew, that his wife could not have understood. What did Padma know of the Anglos here? Of the lumber mill? Of who he had become? He had been someone before that day in Hambelton, and he had been someone different after: ashamed, humiliated. This was the man that Adela knew, and that Padma did not.

"You acted correctly," Adela said, after he told her.

"I did not save them," Ram said.

"You could not." She held him to her. "You could not."

THE DAY THE WHITE MEN in Hambelton had come for them, Ram and Pala Singh and Pala's cousin, Jodh Singh, had gone for a stroll; it was Sunday, a beautiful morning without work in early July. The previous day, the townfolk had celebrated Independence Day. The sunshine was brilliant but not too warm. The brine and tang of the ocean hung in the air. Although the streetcar was running, they walked their usual path into the town, past the canneries and the Chinese bunkhouses, past the other work-gang homes and the Japanese pool halls. The church bells rang as they entered the town; surreys and automobiles and a few teams were parked in front of the houses of worship.

In the leisure and beauty of that morning, they wandered to that portion of Hambelton to which they never traveled: where the houses on the cliff overlooked the strait, the islands hovering like a dream in the distance. The homes were large, the parlors and bedrooms shaped by the same wood that he and Pala and Jodh cut and sawed. A motorcar stood beyond the wrought iron gate of every home. So this is

where those ladies lived, they said to one another—although Jodh
was always so quiet and mild, so removed from the work-gang pack
that Ram often wondered whether he was listening. Here lived those
ladies with peculiar hats and beige dresses who could be seen strolling leisurely in town, sometimes with nannies in attendance, pushing frilled buggies before them. They were women of wealth, married
to the shippers and the mill owners. Their faces were too angular and
unnaturally pale, so unlike his Padma's skin, which knew the sun yet
was lovely to touch, soft and full around the cheeks and nose. Ram
sometimes doubted that they and Padma were the same creatures.
His stomach turned when he thought of touching them in the way
that he touched Padma. But he could not help thinking the thought.

But Pala disagreed. Theirs was the desired complexion, Pala
would say, that exotic paleness, as if one's skin would smudge if caressed by an unclean hand. It was a pity that these women could
never belong to them; he would so like to touch one, to see if they
felt like the women at home. Pala was unmarried, and if Ram had
been a little older, a little less obliged to be respectful, he would have
asked him, joking, how much he knew of touching in that way. In
those days, despite his marriage, despite the son he had not yet met,
Ram had been an innocent. He did not think unmarried men knew
the things that he knew. He glanced at Jodh, to see what he thought
of Pala's statement, but the man was gazing out to sea, his thin body
turned away from them, slightly stooped. Jodh Singh's eyes were always brimming with water, as if he had spent days inside a smoke-
filled hut in the Punjabi winter; one never knew if he was crying
or not.

Jodh's opinion did not matter anyway, for these ladies would
never acknowledge them; they would look at them and look away.
But they were not the only ones. Ram and Pala spoke about others
who did that too: the workers at the telegraph office, the vegetable
sellers at the market. Pala was bitter that people treated them in this
way. White people were all the same, he said. Just like the English,

the Americans used them for their own ends, treating them as they treated their horses, keeping them healthy enough to perform the needed labor, no more, no less.

Ram did not agree. Hadn't the English government provided the railroad that had carried him from Lyallpur to Calcutta? (Pala reminded him that Hindustani hands had built it.) Hadn't Government dug the canals that irrigated crops all over western Punjab? (No, it was the Punjabis themselves, who strove to make their own land habitable.) Hadn't Government forged the towns that settled around those canals? (No, Pala said. It was the villagers who courageously left ancestral homes and settled the wild barr. Didn't Ram understand his own family?) "That is true," Jodh said vaguely, and Ram did not know with whom Jodh was agreeing.

But Ram would not give up. He felt strange among the white people; he did not like them, really, but he could not understand Pala's anger. He reminded Pala that the clerk at the general store was always cordial, whether or not the store owner was present. The druggist had given them free bandages and castor oil more than once. Pala's face grew expressionless and Ram stopped speaking. The moment when Pala's anger would rise was always hard to recognize. Perhaps that was why Jodh was so often quiet.

The morning passed during this familiar debate. When they returned to town, the churches had emptied and the people of Hambelton were strolling through their streets and gardens. Pala wanted to return home. He was the cook for this week and the day was already half-spent. Ram liked that Pala did not feel himself superior to his men; he cooked on the weekly rotation even though he was the gang boss. So Jodh and Pala went home together and Ram decided to walk a little farther. Secretly, Ram wanted to see again the young woman who sold tickets in the kiosk at the cinema house. She was lovely in some way that his Padma was lovely, the shape of her face, the arch of her eyebrows, the fullness of her lips.

He would feel guilty whenever he sought out the girl, for he was a

married man, and she was of a different people, and he would not admit that she appealed to him. Sometimes, when he happened to see
her by chance, he would feel ashamed, humiliated, as if he had failed
at some huge endeavor. But as he saw the families gathered in the
churchyards, the young men talking on the street corner, a woman
picking up a toddling child, any small moment in an ordinary life,
he felt more and more alone. He walked past the cinema kiosk and
saw her there, just as he knew he would. He stood on a corner where
she could not see him.

Of course she was not one of those great ladies, with their stroll-
ers and fine clothes, the ones that Pala and he had talked about. She
was modest. Her father might work on the fishing boats, or perhaps
a sister served liquor in the Sporting District, and Ram fancied that
she had decided on some humble but more respectable work. For
this, he admired her even more. But she was still unapproachable, because Ram was a married man and from a different shore. He would
never permit himself to greet her and that boundary afforded him a
peculiar freedom. What would he say, anyway? His English then was
poor, and he did not waste his earnings on going to the cinema. On
his final pass before leaving, he thought she glanced at him and even
granted him a half smile. From this he gained some small satisfaction
and, in the late afternoon, turned toward K Street.

He was not far from home when he noticed the two men. He
approached the intersection with C Street, and they walked quickly
toward him from behind, wielding two-by-fours brazenly propped
over their shoulders. Later Ram would wonder if the wood had been
sawed in his own mill, so that he had helped create the weapons
used against him. He could not tell their intent until they were almost upon him, when he smelled the liquor on their clothes. His
guilty mind made peculiar connections: These men were brothers
of the cinema house girl. They knew he had spied on her from a
distance. One man raised his arm, holding the piece of wood, and
something (what was it?) told Ram to run, and he broke stride just

as the arm and the wood came down. Ram saw the man's face as he swung, cheeks bulging, teeth clenched, eyes large, a strange pleasure revealed—he was struck in the shoulder and he cried out, feeling his right arm go limp, and raised the other to shield his face. The second man hit Ram on the left side of his rib cage, unprotected and vulnerable. The pain from this blow overpowered the other, overpowered everything else, like the sun exploding behind closed eyes. He fell to the ground and was rolling and rolling and something struck the side of his head—was it the slab of wood? A stone on the road? One of the men cried out but Ram could understand only two words: *Cheap labor! Cheap labor! Cheeeeaaaaaap!* He knew they would hit him again. He wondered where the blow would land. Then he felt a shudder in the earth and heard the clatter of metal against metal. He raised his head as the trolley car rattled into the intersection.

Summoning all his strength, holding the side that had erupted in pain, he rose, swaying, then leaped for the trolley's step, his boot catching the hard edge. He threw his body forward into the car and landed on his right side, which hurt less than the other, but his foot still dangled over the pavement. One of the men grabbed it, running with the trolley, cursing. Ram kicked madly and the man fell back. The car was empty except for the conductor standing far in the rear.

Ram shoved himself against the steps where he entered at the front, leaning against the doorway, hoping the conductor would not approach. His chest heaved as he tried to catch his breath. *Cheap labor,* the man had yelled. There was also the girl. Why had he been attacked? Every movement hurt. A scarlet stain covered the front of Ram's shirt. He wanted to know where it came from, it was damp and heavy and alarming, but he was afraid to look. There was a gash on his shin, and he did not know how he got it, but he could see the white bone under the skin. He thought he would faint, but somehow he willed himself to stay conscious.

At the canneries, not far from K Street, the trolley slowed. Ram edged himself off the step and stumbled, falling by the side of the road. "Hey!" the conductor yelled as the car began to move again. "You there!" Ram half turned toward him, and he saw the conductor's eyes grow wide, his mouth hang open. The car sped up and moved on. Ram was relieved. He wanted to make it home to the other Hindustanees, that was all. The smell from the canneries clogged his head. After a few steps, the nausea overcame him and he retched at the side of the road. He sat in the dirt as nightfall came. He shivered, although it wasn't cold. His shin, his chest, erupted in pain whenever he tried to stand. No one passed. Finally he rose, vomited again, regained his balance and limped slowly toward K Street.

At the house, Ram stumbled to the back, where he knew Pala would be hunched over the outdoor stove. A pot was on the fire, its contents bubbling and steaming, the scent of ginger and garlic in the air, but the yard was deserted. Ram collapsed on the bench near the back steps, lying on the side that did not pain him. He heard faint voices from the house. It was dusk. Most of the men would be home or just returning from the wrestling match held at the neighboring field. Then Pala emerged, walking briskly, holding another pot, followed by Jodh and Satish Singh Dillon, the other work-gang boss who lived next door. Seeing him lying on the bench, Pala's expression changed from puzzlement to irritation to sudden realization. "Ram? Ram!" Pala put down the pot, contents splashing, and dropped to his knees at Ram's side.

"We were just walking with you, bhai," Jodh Singh said uselessly. "What happened?" But Ram could not answer; he had used all his strength to get home.

They brought him indoors, cradling him in a sheet with Jodh and Pala carrying him at his head and feet. Other men placed blankets on the floor of the pantry off the kitchen, and they settled him on top of them. The pantry was a closet without a door, near the back entrance, set in a corner of the house. During the day, light came in from the small window seven feet from the ground. It looked out over the side yard. The space was lined with shelves, mostly empty, but a few holding large tins of rice and lentils, and blankets that men did not use during the summer.

All the men had come downstairs now, and they crowded around the door of the small space to see what had happened, their voices loud from the whiskey they had been drinking since early afternoon. Satish Singh kept most of them away while Pala lifted Ram's shirt and asked for a bottle to wash the injuries. The whiskey stung his skin and made him cry out, and he wished that he could have been more courageous, but Pala spoke to him as a woman would and Ram felt comforted. Pala fetched one of his own shirts and held it to the wound on his chest. He asked Jodh to do the same for a gash on his arm, and the one on his shin. "Who was it?" Satish Singh asked, over and over, until Pala snapped, "Oye, bhai, can't you see he is in pain?"

Satish took in a breath and stopped talking, and Ram heard others call out from the kitchen.

"Crazy people!"

"Inform the police!"

"They won't do anything," someone else said lightly, with a half laugh.

"They will—"

Pala rose and turned on the men in the kitchen. "What will those bloody police do? Tell me, what will they do?" The others were suddenly quiet. Pala resumed cleansing Ram's wounds while Satish watched, expressionless.

After a moment Pala called out, "If anyone is to be told, tell the doctor. Go and fetch him."

"I will," said a young voice.

Ram suddenly roused himself. "No!" he said. "No doctor." If he wasted money that way, what would he send home to his family for this week? His eyes met Pala's.

"Hussein!" Pala called more gently to the boy—he was only fifteen, the youngest of their gang. "Go later—we can call the doctor after a day if needed. Let him rest for now."

Ram lay back, mollified. "I would like my bag," he told Pala. "Please."

Pala sent Hussein upstairs to fetch them. The carpetbag carried familiar things from a safe world, far away: Padma's photograph, a packet of her letters, the small amulet a Muslim friend had tied on his arm the day he departed, to ward off danger. He reached his hand inside and touched them and a whimper escaped his lips.

He closed his eyes. They had cried *cheap labor,* but the image of the girl at the cinema appeared to him, and the thought came again instantly—he had been beaten for watching her; in that moment he was sure of it, the guilt overpowering his rational mind. "Go and eat," Satish said to the men gathered at the door. "Dinner is ready and there's work tomorrow."

The men dispersed but Satish stayed, along with Pala and Jodh. Satish was holding a newspaper, a copy of the *Hambelton Times.* He had fought alongside the British cavalry; he was the only one of the men on K Street who could read and write in English.

"This is what they were writing in the newspaper last week," Satish said.

"What—that Ram would be attacked?" Pala said. All the men knew that he and Satish did not get along well.

Satish ignored his tone. "That some of the labor bosses did not want Hindus working here any longer. I don't know which ones. Maybe that Swedish man, and those Norwegians."

"Why?" Ram whispered.

"They say we are undercutting the pay for the locals."

"We are," Pala said.

"We're not!" Satish said. "We are merely willing to accept what the company will pay us. What is wrong with that?"

"We should be paid more."

"Then go and tell them," Satish said. He was angry. He took a long breath. "The paper reports that the owners felt threatened by labor leaders who said that if the Hindus were not removed by the end of the week, they would drive them out themselves."

"What does that mean, 'removed'?" Pala asked.

Lying on his back, gazing at the men standing above him, Ram saw Satish and Pala exchange a glance.

"Ram," Satish said, "what did those men look like?"

He felt a stab of fear. "I don't know," he said truthfully. He heard footsteps coming from the kitchen, then the scrape of wood against wood. Jodh was dragging a chair across the threshold of the back door, into the pantry. Ram was alarmed, but he was so tired. When the men left him, he was aware of his eyes closing.

When he opened them again sometime later, the sky had gone dark. Jodh was sitting quietly in the chair, his eyes half-closed, softly reciting Kirtan Sohila. Jodh's deep voice, the familiar chants invoking God's protection, all this comforted Ram. His mind traveled to an evening when he had fallen asleep on his mother's lap as she chanted the same prayers. His mother was not Sikh, and neither was he, but it did not matter. Everyone knew the prayers of the Guru. His aunt was giving birth in the next room. Yet, despite his mother's invocation, despite the visit from the village midwife and the town doctor, his aunt had not lived through the night, although the baby survived. He shifted position painfully. Moonlight streamed through the open back door and splayed across Jodh's shoulder.

Ram could hear Pala's voice outside near the stove, the clatter of metal pots being gathered up after their meal. He heard a beat begin on the dholki; that would be Hussein, the boy from Amritsar. A voice began to sing. Someone strummed the tumbi. The men would soon begin to dance. Some of them would be seated on the wooden benches in the side yard, some would sit on the chairs in the back. Their house had the largest yard and the men always gathered there. Almost one hundred of his countrymen lived on that street, a fifth of the total number of Hindustanees hired at the mills. He could hear their voices thick with whiskey, debating on and on: why they didn't call the police, why they were waiting to fetch the doctor . . . their voices were unguarded, and he knew they thought he couldn't hear. They did not know what Satish had said about the labor leaders' demand that the Hindustanees be fired. About the threat to remove the Hindus themselves, if they remained by week's end.

Ram heard one of the men advise Pala to report the attack to the police by Tuesday, otherwise their foreman would wonder why Ram was missing. The men jeered. Most agreed with Pala—why tell the police? They knew that the locals thought they were dirty, that they were a threat to family life, that their turbans were dirty and smelled foul. They knew most women in town stepped away if they encountered a Hindu on the street. What would the police do? And who would be told? That large deputy with the huge jowls who could not sit a horse properly? They laughed.

They cursed the mill boss who paid them $2.00 per day, while paying the Negros $2.10, while paying the Italians $2.75. They spoke in Punjabi and it did not matter who overheard them from the road. Most had fought in the British army. They were accustomed to living under a soft shadow of danger. They were used to making the un-familiar into the familiar. The whiskey was flowing. Pala's cooking was good. What mattered was the money; the well-worn route to the Western Union booth behind the post office, the dollars they wired to Patiala or Hoshiarpur or Lahore that would transform a mud hut into a brick cottage, or pay for a sister's wedding, or release a peasant father's mortgage from an urban moneylender. They measured their lives $2.00 at a time. Despite the letters that assured them that they were missed, loved even—these men with dreams and secrets and childhoods and wives and mothers for whom they yearned—they could not avoid that accounting, their value at home and abroad: $2.00 a day. They did not question it.

They sent Hussein inside to fetch another bottle from the kitchen. Ram heard the boy's footsteps approach, the sound of the open and shut cupboard. If Ram breathed lightly and lay on the side that did not pain him, folding an extra blanket between his legs, it did not hurt so much. Perhaps he might report at the mill in the morning. Jodh bent toward him to offer a tumbler of water, and Ram drank. He offered Ram roti and chicken and Ram refused. He was tired. Sleep came again quickly.

THEY ARRIVED AFTER MIDNIGHT. He woke to pounding on the front door, deep thuds that overwhelmed his ears and shuddered through his fragile chest, the screeches of torn wood. They must have used axes, or small logs retrieved from the river. He heard yells, shattered glass, the toppling of the shelf that stood by the stairs. Jodh's chair stood vacant, staring back at him like an omen. When he realized he was alone, panic overtook him. He knew that they could not see him from the front of the house. That he could escape out the back door if none of them were outside. Except that he could not move. His limbs were frozen.

He heard their boots on the stairs and he was thankful. But the shame came in a wave, overwhelming him. He should go up after them; he should help Pala. Gurbinder Singh used to keep a pistol near the mantel on the first floor, but he had left for San Francisco in June, taking the gun with him.

Something other than his injuries, other than his pain, did not allow him to go. He stayed in the pantry while they thundered on the stairs above him, walls shaking, footsteps bold and threatening on the thin wood floor. He breathed shallow breaths and wrapped his arms around himself, shivering, willing his breath to be silent. He closed his eyes, though it was dark. Glass crashed. The ceiling shook. Men spoke in a strange language. English words were barked out: *You dirty. You garbage. You raghead.* There were sounds he could not recognize. Were they throwing things? Bags, lamps? He heard the tremor of tumbi strings. *Take your blankets and get out of our mills.*

Voices shouted back in Punjabi. He heard the fierce beating of the dholki, then the crash of axe against wood and the drum was silent. A man yelped in pain. He heard Pala shouting, a bang against the wall. Twelve people lived upstairs; who was hurt? How many? Ram's heart hammered against his fragile ribs. He swallowed again and again, lying on his side, frozen.

Heavy boots clattered down the steps and it seemed all the men followed, some of them stumbling, sliding, trailing out the front door. There were more shouts outside. Other Hindustani houses must have been violated too. Men gathered in the yard where the Punjabis had just danced and talked. Above the fray, Ram heard a man shout, "That's the one from the movie house! Lookin' at my girl today!" Ram gasped. Had Ram brought this cruelty upon all of them? Which of the Punjabis had they mistaken for him? Perhaps Mohamed Khan, who also did not wear a dastar? The thought horrified him. Then he heard a club hit muscle and skin and something more. A man screamed an animal sound of pain. A voice full of rage, "What was—" Pala's yelling high-pitched, childlike, in Punjabi, pleading with someone, then a jump into loud broken English, pierced by sobs, "Don't hurt, don't hurt," as if he had forgotten the language in his shock. "Please!"

"I told you, not their legs. Fool!"

Ram's mind snapped into focus. He opened his eyes. Moonlight shone through the small window above him, illuminating the pantry. He uncurled his body slowly, coaxing himself to keep going. Pain shot through his left side. He continued anyway. He stepped onto the shelf and put his weight on the leg; his shin burned. But he clenched his teeth, leaned against the wall, and peered through the window. He was hidden in shadow and he could see out on the yard.

Forty or fifty men stood gathered in the moonlight. How could there be so many? A man wearing a dastar rolled on the ground, whimpering, holding his arm. Another lay near him, unmoving. Fear gripped Ram again, and he could not breathe. Who was that man? Was he dead? Behind him stood the other Hindustanees. The two groups stood facing each other. His countrymen were outnumbered almost four to one.

He heard a loud crack and an explosion, and heard it again. His mind made sense of it: a gun had been fired. A man yelled, "March! Walk!" Now he understood—they were driving the Hindustanees out of town. Ram's head began to swim. His legs gave way and he sank, slowly, to the floor.

IN THE MORNING, the house was empty. He woke to birdsong, sunlight. Had the events of the evening really happened? Looking out again through the window, then slowly opening the back door, he saw no sign of his companions or the locals. Benches and chairs had been toppled. Cooking dishes were strewn everywhere. Shards of glass lay over the dirt, glistening. There was a dark brown stain, still moist, on the dirt and grass where the fallen men had lain. He felt a chill in his gut. Later, in Jivan Singh's home, he would read in the Ghadar paper that the man on the ground had been Uday Singh. That he had died in a hospital in another town, ten miles south of Hambelton, two days after the attack. Ram had not known him well; he had arrived only a week before.

A smell of urine hung in the air, of men in terror.

So much had gone wrong for him: his father's death before he was born, his mother's lowly place in her brother's home, his own status in that house, among the children his uncle truly loved. Who would he have been if his father had lived, and had loved him in that way? If he had not been sent off to America? It was clear now: he was only meant to be the victim of men's malice, to suffer; his adventure abroad was always destined to end like this. An ocean separated him from all that he knew, and he was stranded here, among strangers who took pleasure in savagery.

He heard Pala's voice tell him to go north, cross the boundary into British Columbia, assert his rights as a fellow subject of the empire; the English king owed it to him. But no, Ram wanted to return to Punjab. He had twelve dollars in his pocket. It was not enough for passage home, but it was enough for a train ticket to the Imperial Valley. He had been ignoring Karak's letters, his invitations, but he knew the man would forgive him. Perhaps Karak would lend him money for the journey home. Perhaps Karak would look after him awhile . . . the way he had in Hong Kong, the way he had on the steamship during their passage west. He could go to Karak and take some time to plan his next step.

He heard Padma's voice: *Yes, my life, this is what you must do.*

He picked up his bag and his blanket. He would slowly make his way to the trolley, which would take him to the train, which would take him to Karak Singh. He would know what to do next.

15 December 1918

My husband, Father of Santosh,

By the time you receive this letter it will have been almost two months since I stepped on American soil. I am writing, ashamed, on the ship traveling back to India. Shankar's telegram will have given you the news that we were not allowed off the ship to join you. But now I will give you the complete explanation. If you no longer want to call me your wife, I do not blame you. But it is not my fault, Father of Santosh. I fear that I will never again see you.

I was so relieved when we docked in San Francisco, for while we were at sea in the belly of the ship, I was sick every day. In San Francisco, we were taken to a building on an island, where Shankar and I were asked to talk with the officers separately. It is a type of jail there, my husband. I took Santosh with me and followed a man to a room that was unkempt, and without sunlight.

He left me by myself there for a few minutes and another man, looking like an inspector, came and sat behind the desk. I was scared to be alone with that inspector. He looked so odd—his skin was so pale, I did not get a good feeling. He kept speaking with me in Bengali. Did he think that is my language? You know I have never been alone with a strange man, much less one that cannot speak my language. He kept looking at some papers and I sat in a chair in front of him.

I sat there for a long, long time. Poor Santosh was unhappy and wanted a toilet. I asked the man but he shook his head. I thought perhaps he did not understand our language, so I pointed to Santosh and with my gestures showed what our son

needed. He is five years old and he is a brave boy but I could see
how scared he was there. But still this strange man would not
show us the toilet. Has he never known a child?

Then poor Santosh, his face full of shame, relieved himself
right there. Now the man was quite upset and he started
scolding me. I cleaned as best as I could, but afterward there
was a slight smell. He made a face—but the fault was his own.

Finally, he called in one of our people. This man spoke to me
in Punjabi, but he had a strange way of pronouncing the words,
and some of the words were completely different altogether, so
the sum result was that I could only understand a portion of
what he was saying. He must have been from some other district.
Father of Santosh, you would have recognized his Punjabi
language, and you would have known these strange words,
because you have seen the world, you know how to do things
that I do not know.

The white man would say something, looking straight at me,
even though he knew that I would not understand, and our
countryman would speak to me in his strange Punjabi, of which
I understood only a part. He asked me if I knew how to read
and write. I said that I do. I said that my father believed that
even a woman should know these things. I said that not only
myself but my husband knows how to read and write and he is a
very prosperous farmer and making lots of money.

He asked me to prove our marriage. I showed him the paper,
the one issued by the village panchayat, but he didn't believe me.
He asked why it did not have the king's seal. I answered that in
the village, we do not use it, although in Lyallpur proper it is
used. He said that without the correct marriage paper I would
have to prove that I could read, in English would be preferable,
but Punjabi would suffice.

He gave me some book and asked me to read it. It was in
formal Punjabi language and the words all were strange to me

but I pronounced them slowly. The white man looked skeptical and he directed the Punjabi man to take the book from me and he did so. I sensed that they were both against me—perhaps our countryman was even more against me than the white man. I grew frightened again. Santosh must have sensed my uneasiness for he started to cry. Our countryman told me that the book was the Christian Bible. Then he said that he didn't think I could read at all, even in Punjabi.

I protested. I asked them if I could read a book that I brought. You know that I always keep the Gita with me, that small one. So I opened my bag and showed it to him and told him that I could read it. He shook his head.

But I read it, my husband. You would have been proud of me. There were portions that I knew well, because my father and I used to read them together. When I was finished, the Punjabi man said it seemed I did not know how to read, that I had merely memorized some lines. I told him that he could point at any part of the text and I would read it. But he said no. We were arguing like this as Santosh wandered to the other side of the room and suddenly pulled a few papers from the shelves, and some books fell. I felt so bad I immediately got up to check him.

That is when everything stopped. As I walked to Santosh, that white man saw me, and asked something which the Punjabi man stated to me—he asked why do I have a limp? I told him that I had a disease as a child. He told me then that it would not be a matter of whether I could read or not, the U.S. would not allow persons such as me into the country.

I felt that he had plunged a knife in my heart. I told him that I was your wife, that your son was there with me in that same room. But he would not listen, my husband, he would not listen. All humanity was gone from him. It was only after they made me leave the room and could not see me anymore that I allowed the tears to come. I kept thinking that they would call me back in, that they would recognize their mistake and realize that I was your wife and that I should be with you, but no one came. By the end of the day, all life had gone out of me.

Five days I stayed there on American soil, in the filth of that jail. I don't know how I withstood the sadness of boarding the ship again. I think I did only because Santosh was with me, and because I was always under my brother's watchful eye. It is still not clear why he was not allowed in. Perhaps he was, but he refused to enter because I would be all alone. I have not asked him, and he has not told me. It is not clear, my husband. Did you not say that I would be allowed to enter because I am your wife? I should be able to join you whether I could read or no? Whether I walk with a limp or no? Two days after we left, a Chinaman jumped off the ship into the water. Do you know a secret, my husband? Despite Santosh, despite you, I wanted to jump too. I am ashamed to say it. And probably Shankar felt the same, although he did not confide it to me.

I will not tell Uncle when I return. I can no longer tolerate that house. I will go straight to my parents' home. Please forgive me. Santosh will miss his cousins but how would they treat me in Lyallpur now? Everything has been spoiled and I do not know how to fix it. I can only ask, as a supplicant, can you inquire if anything can be done? I feel this has the finality of death, and that your inquiry will be in vain.

> Your hapless wife,
> Padma

PART FOUR

With tears in my eyes
I turn back to my homeland
taking one last look.

—Author unknown, from *The Japanese
American Family Album*

When all the Japanese are forced out of the country, the cantaloupes may thrive as they do today, and a lettuce ranch may be as green as today and the American nation will prosper with great power, but the American history will not be so glorious as it is today with the words of Liberty.

—M. Shigematsu,
Secretary, Japanese Farmers
Association of Imperial Valley, 1920

24

NOVEMBER 1918

A T FIVE O'CLOCK ONE MORNING IN NOVEMBER, THE FREDONIA POWER Company blew its emergency whistle and the fire department rang its bell in the cool dawn. People knew what that meant. They had been eagerly awaiting the end of the war; the United Press had made a false announcement four days earlier. By sunrise, paperboys had situated themselves on street corners around town, holding bundles of the *Fredonia News,* shouting its headline: PEACE! and in smaller letters underneath: KAISER IS OUT! GERMANY SURRENDERS! GREATEST WAR OF ALL TIME OVER!

When they heard the bells sound, Jivan and Karak and Ram drove into town. Kishen had no wish to come with them. "What do I have to do with that war?" she asked. "I only want Amarjeet to come home." The men could not disagree. But they went anyway, parking on the outskirts of town and walking to city hall.

The Fredonia Band was playing at the steps of the courthouse. Offices and schools and businesses remained closed. From the homes in the surrounding farmland, people streamed into town despite the

Spanish flu that had laid so many low. Every day there had been another death in the Valley. The streets were overrun with farmers and
cowboys and housewives and yelling children, dogs, horses, wagons,
chickens, a few goats, almost all of the town's one thousand automobiles. Even those who lived on the east side—in the barrio and Japantown and the Negro neighborhood—crossed the railroad tracks to
hear what the mayor would say. A parade had lined up, but the fire
department could not squeeze its trucks and horses past the crowd
on Third Street. On the hour, every hour, the band played "The Star-
Spangled Banner" and the unruly crowd grew calm, some whispering the lyrics, some belting them out, others standing silently. Even
young children stopped to listen. Fathers removed their hats. Several
mothers were crying.

Cars cruised up and down Main Street, horns blaring, contrap-
tions and noisemakers tied to rear bumpers: iron tubs containing
metal scraps that rattled, exploded in the ears. Passengers leaned out
of the car windows, whistling and chanting and singing.

Karak stepped into the crowd, clasping the hands of the banker
Jasper Davis and Terrence Mark, who managed the farm implement
store, but Jivan and Ram hung back, feeling joyful but not connected to that wider joy. Perhaps it was Jivan's dastar, perhaps it was
their mood, but they stood separated from the crowd. A car drove
past, dragging a shattered wooden box labeled KAISER. They thought
this was silly.

Karak rejoined them, bringing Clive Edgar with him. The land
agent shook Jivan's hand. "Your son will be home soon, John," he
said warmly.

"Very soon, I hope, very soon," Jivan said, and no one bothered
to correct him; they had known each other too long. Clive left them,
and they ran into Malik Khan and Gugar Singh, then other Hindus
who gathered weekly in Fredonia Park. Their mood was light, happy.
Everyone knew a village-mate back home who had died serving in
the British army in France or Mesopotamia, and most had a brother

or cousin or uncle who had left home to fight. They stood clustered far from the tent that sheltered the band and the mayor. As the group expanded, they grew more and more conspicuous.

A car passed them and the driver leaned out to shout, "See what has happened to your damned German alliance now!" His words fell on them like shrapnel, meant to wound. The men blinked and looked at each other.

"Who is that?" someone asked.

"Silas Treet," Jivan answered. "Proprietor of the *Fredonia News*. He doesn't know we fought on the side of the British and Americans."

THEY RECEIVED LETTERS from Amarjeet telling of being billeted in a French home and marching and drilling with his platoon. The army bought them tickets to shows, organized ball games, taught them auto repair and accounting. Grateful French drank with them in the taverns and cafés and brothels and introduced them to daughters of marriageable age. *They think,* Amarjeet wrote, *we have saved the world for democracy.* At home, the families waited for their return.

Finally, in February, the Singhs and Moriyamas received letters from Washington officials, stating that their young men would soon return. They would board a ship in Le Havre. They would disembark in New Jersey thirteen days later.

The afternoon the letter arrived, the Moriyamas had just finished hauling the last of the strawberry harvest to the shippers. When Tomoya read the letter to his wife, their exhaustion disappeared. Hatsu sat on her bed and wept, her hands covering her face, her body convulsing. Her husband sat by her, his own eyes brimming with tears. Their older daughter had married and moved away years ago. The younger had done the same after Harry left; it had been only the two of them for years.

After they recovered, they telephoned several other Japanese families in the Valley to tell of the good news. The Singhs had just purchased a telephone, and Tomoya called Jivan too. Had they received the same letter regarding Amarjeet? Was he coming home on the same ship as their son? Yes, Jivan replied to both questions. The men laughed, euphoric, relieved. The feeling carried like static over the phone line. Harry had mentioned Amarjeet in every letter. The boys had been true companions throughout. While the boys served together, the friendship between families had grown stronger too.

By late afternoon, Tomoya and Hatsu arrived at Jivan Singh's home. Hatsu stumbled as she stepped up to the porch, and Kishen laughed with her, and although they had never done it before, the women embraced, as if they had always lived in the west. They entered the house and Tomoya stayed on the back porch with the men.

Karak poured Tomoya a whiskey. The men talked of what the military had done since the fighting had ended, how the American Expeditionary Forces had been flung all over the world. How Harry was being awarded a medal for his courage in battle.

Tomoya was flush with excitement, with a sense of vindication. Harry had been required to register for the draft—he had been born in the U.S., so there was no getting around that—but he had not been required to save people, he had not been required to risk his own life doing so. Despite his good manners, Tomoya could not hold back, his pride in his son was evident. A Japanese boy had done what so many Americans did not do. Why should the Moriyama family not be considered as "good" as any local one, he thought with anger. With his son's actions, Tomoya achieved victory in a battle few knew that he fought.

He could not help himself; he told the story again even though the Singhs knew it. Perhaps he would not have boasted this way in the company of other Japanese. But the Singhs listened to him patiently, sincerely.

Amarjeet had written the Singhs a letter telling of what Harry had done: During the Argonne Forest advance, the regiment had

almost finished digging in for the night when the Boche began to
"let the Doughboys have a few shells." One exploded close to their
artillery unit. A piece of shrapnel lodged itself in Amarjeet's leg. He
did not feel it at first, but then the pain became a red-hot thing that
burst inside him. He could not think. He could not move. He knew
only that he was safe inside the trench.

But other men were hurt too. Harry went over the top of the
trench and pulled a man to safety, dragging him to the rim. Amarjeet collected himself, hobbled forward, helped pull the man inside.
Another shell fell, lighting up the night. Harry left again to find another man farther out—Sergeant Sam Pinkerton, from Fredonia—
and together they pulled him in the same way.

Amarjeet and Sam and the first man were taken to the field hospital in the rear. The shrapnel was removed from Amarjeet's leg and
the wound was stitched up. Later, an officer visited and Amarjeet
vouched for Harry's bravery.

Now Tomoya was filled with pride; his son was safe, the peace
had been signed. Men and women wore poppies in memory of their
dead, but his son was coming home a hero, having saved those he did
not need to save.

They sat on the back porch until after the sun set and the stars
appeared and a whisper of dust rose with the breeze. The air caressed
them. From the front of the house they heard hoofbeats and a horse's
snort. Later, Tomoya would wonder: Why a horse and not a motorcar? Didn't Western Union have money for machines? Which of his
hired men had told the boy to look for him at Jivan's farm? Later he
would wonder: Why did an officer wait so many days before paying
a visit?

By the time Ram rose to greet the visitor, the Western Union boy
had already made his way to the back and inquired, mangling the
name, "Is a Mr. Moriy— Moriyami— Morayama here?"

"I am," Tomoya said, standing.

The lad handed him the telegram, jumped back on his horse, and cantered off. Later Tomoya would wonder: Why wasn't that boy in uniform, overseas?

He tore open the envelope and read. He grabbed the back of a chair for strength. Then his legs crumpled beneath him and he fell to the ground as Jivan lunged forward, trying to catch him.

25

JUNE 1919

HARRY HAD DIED OF SPANISH INFLUENZA IN THE FIELD HOSPITAL, ONLY A week before he would have boarded the ship to come home. This was the fact that Amarjeet had been trying to understand for three months, as he journeyed back from war. Now, as the train approached the depot, he looked up to see the crooked sign proclaiming FREDONIA: AMERICA'S DREAM. The full impact of Harry's absence hit him. How would he face Mr. and Mrs. Moriyama on the platform?

But, of course, the Moriyamas were not there. Why would they be? Through the window of the rail car, Amarjeet spotted his own family in the midst of others, milling around the depot. He gasped the moment he saw them. In their faces was an eager expectation, a worry, expressions of relief and disbelief mixed together.

As he stepped off the train, the sixteen boys he had traveled with said goodbye. He had not known any of them before the war, except by sight. Sam Pinkerton had been one of them—the sergeant whom Harry had hated, but pulled into the trench and saved. Now Sam clapped Amarjeet on the back. "Feels good to be home, don't

it, Jeet?" he asked. "Feels real good," another soldier responded for
him, and Amarjeet's gaze took in all of them, every one, including
the three Negroes who had emerged from the rear car into the bright
sun; he had joked with them on the platforms during the stops in
San Francisco and Los Angeles.

"Take good care of yourself now," said Sam quietly. Already the
Anglo boys were standing together, eyeing their waiting families. If
Amarjeet had wanted their recognition before the war, he had it now.
All the soldiers were grinning, every one wearing the uniform of
the American Expeditionary Forces for this last brief moment before
joining society again: African faces and European, Hindustani and
Chinese and Mexican.

Amarjeet approached Jivan, managing to smile. Karak slapped
him on the back, Jivan and Ram and Kishen embraced him. His
uncle did not comment on his lack of a dastar, his clean-shaven face.
Amarjeet grinned at the gleaming motorcar. Rosa was holding Federico and he touched the toddler's cheek. She announced that she
was pregnant again, speaking with so much enthusiasm that they all
laughed. He gave Leela the French doll he had brought for her. But
he could not keep up the display of happiness. When he was eating
Kishen's food on the back porch, the tears came, the first he had
cried since Harry's death. The conversation fell quiet. He rose from
the table and went to the olla, splashed water on his face. When
he returned they were still silent. He expected the sympathy in his
aunt's face, perhaps in Ram's. But he had not expected the kindness
he saw in his uncle's eyes, the deference in Karak's manner. Then he
was reminded: they had been soldiers too.

AMARJEET HAD RETURNED FROM FRANCE, but he could not leave it behind.
On the train to the French coast, journeying through a blood-soaked,
pockmarked, desolate land, shredded churches, schools, courthouses
speeding past the window, he thought only of the gloom in the church

hospital, of the way that Harry had looked at the end. The nurse had allowed him to see the body. Harry seemed asleep, a burden lifted. Distant. They would never again be together. Death is the boundary that cannot be crossed, even by love or adoration.

When Amarjeet boarded the ship for the two-week journey home, it was Harry's voice that he kept hearing: how the fella in the neighboring bunk was crackers, how the ship had shuddered during the storm, how he loved the desert much more than the stomach-lurching rhythm of the sea. There were other Imperial Valley boys on that boat and Amarjeet ate with them and talked with them while they smoked on deck. One had been a high school classmate and had known Harry too. The morning they sailed past the Statue of Liberty, the entire ship surrendered to a sacred stillness.

They entrained in Hoboken and sped west across the continent, seeing their own country transformed but unravaged by war: billboards proclaiming MAKE THE WORLD SAFE FOR DEMOCRACY. FREE DOUGHNUTS FOR DOUGHBOYS IN UNIFORM. Everywhere appeared murals of French orphans, widows in rags, arms raised in defiance. He did not immediately understand that the billboards and posters were of a place that he had just been. He had come home to an unfamiliar land, one he had once known, an immigrant now from army lines. But he had a job to do for Harry. And he knew now what he had not known when Harry was alive, that the emotion he had felt was love. His heartbeat had quickened whenever Harry was near. He could not deny that now.

The morning after his return, Karak gave him a ride to the Moriyamas' house in the Model T, arranging to pick him up in an hour. After he drove off, Amarjeet stood quietly in the front yard. His courage seemed to have deserted him. Nothing had changed since he had left. This was the same dirt road. Along the path to the barn were the same sakura trees that Harry's sisters had planted years ago. In the corner stood the bamboo garden, taller and more regal. But a heavy silence hung about the home.

At the door, he felt the heaviness of his guilt. How could the Mori-yamas forgive him for coming home without their son? Mr. Moriyama appeared at the screen door and peered at him. His face was a stone.

Mr. Moriyama called out a commanding stream of Japanese and Harry's sisters came rushing to the front step. Amarjeet was surprised to see them. He bowed and greeted them by name—Masa, Yuki. As girls they had been shy, though they were older than Harry. Both of them had been born in Japan, years before the family had arrived in California. Their father had not wanted them to mix too much with the non-Japanese boys, and as a show of respect, Amarjeet had kept his distance. Years ago they had both married truck farmers and moved away, one to Bakersfield, another to Texas.

Masa stepped forward, returning his bow. "Welcome, Amarjeet-san."

"Okay," her father said, after a moment, backing away from the door and allowing him room to pass.

Amarjeet entered and took off his shoes. He was startled to find Mrs. Moriyama standing just inside, wearing a gray housecoat over her petite frame, as ephemeral as a shadow.

She was broken now. Fragile. Grief changes the body, he thought; bones shrink, muscles are rearranged.

"I have come to give you something," Amarjeet said. The older sister interpreted for him, even though Mrs. Moriyama had under-stood, was already nodding. He hesitated. "Something from Haruo."

Mr. Moriyama's eyes darted from Amarjeet's face to the ground and back again. "Come." He nodded. "Sit down."

The room was swept and neat, immaculate as it always was. Books on shelves guarded by glass panes. Porcelain teacups on a decorative tray. Harry and he had done homework together in this room. He felt that he had misspoken, that he was ill-mannered. He should not have come only to give them something. He should have come to share their grief, to offer condolences, to do something. To do whatever is done.

The younger sister brought lemonade, strawberries. Mr. Moriyama sat across from him and Mrs. Moriyama placed herself in a wooden chair in the corner, the most uncomfortable chair in the room. She was staring at Amarjeet, as if he could change what had happened, as if he owed her something. Her stare was unwavering, her eyes deep and beyond despair. Amarjeet's heartbeat quickened. Had he been wrong to come? But how could he have stayed away? He had promised Harry, and he knew he would have come even if he had promised him nothing at all, if he did not even have the letters.

"How you are, son?" Mr. Moriyama asked. Amarjeet's eyes welled up. The question was asked so gently. It was asked with true concern, as if *he* were the one who had lost Harry. He had never before heard Mr. Moriyama call anyone "son," not even Harry. It was too American.

Amarjeet took a deep breath to control himself, aware of Mrs. Moriyama in the dark corner. He stared at the hands on his lap. His hands.

"You come home quickly," Mr. Moriyama said. "That is good. Some boys still there. And you are safe. That is very good too." He nodded, a small trace of a bow, for emphasis.

"The trip was long," Amarjeet said. "The ship was not comfortable. The food was terrible, but they tried to treat us well." He was starting to blather. "The French loved us." He gave a little laugh. Harry's parents were staring at the ground. Yuki sat at her mother's feet. Masa stood at the edge of the room.

"That boy Haruo save. He come back?" Mr. Moriyama asked.

Amarjeet grew quiet. Mrs. Moriyama locked her gaze on him again. He felt more composed now. "Sam Pinkerton, from the Valley. Our sergeant. That's who Haruo saved. I was on the train with him," he said. "Also Jedediah Smith from Bakersfield," Amarjeet volunteered.

Mr. Moriyama gave a curt nod, then his face was stone again. "He die alone?"

The direct question startled him. Amarjeet pursed his lips to keep the tears at bay. He thought of the field hospital set up in the village church. Cots were lined up in a section of the sanctuary that had not been shelled. Military doctors and nurses and volunteers from the countryside treated the fallen soldiers. Harry was surrounded by stricken boys; some lay silent, some moaned deliriously. Some had lost a leg or an arm or their genitals or the ability to breathe freely. Whenever Amarjeet visited, it stank of blood, vomit, and urine; he could smell that smell even now.

"I sat with him as often as I could. Whenever I did not have to drill or care for the horses." Was that guilt he heard in his voice? The other boys visited the taverns or played basketball in the warming spring air. Other boys fraternized with the daughters of the families with whom they were billeted.

Amarjeet reached inside his pocket. "I brought you these letters. Harry was writing them to you. So many of them, every day in the hospital. He didn't want you to get them with the other things." They had argued when Harry said he thought he wouldn't make it back. Amarjeet's voice cracked. "He wanted me to carry them to you myself."

He held the letters out like an offering. His hands were shaking. When Mr. Moriyama took them, Amarjeet felt hollow, devoid of substance. "And there is this. He wanted me to give you this too." Mr. Moriyama took the small box and opened it slowly. Inside was Harry's gold chain. His face flushed pink. Mrs. Moriyama made a small noise, like a chirping bird, a squeaking mouse. She rose quickly and left the room. Amarjeet saw Karak's motorcar turn from the roadway and he groped for his handkerchief and suddenly he could not contain his tears. "I am sorry Mr. Moriyama I could not bring him back with me I am sorry I am sorry I am—"

Masa closed her eyes.

Mr. Moriyama was waving his hand. "No no, Amarjeet. No no no no no."

THE NEXT AFTERNOON, Masa arrived at the Eggenberger farm, driving the Moriyamas' team and wagon. Amarjeet was in the barn, mucking out the mare's stall.

"Mother wants to see you," Masa said. "If you will accept to visit." She spoke in clipped, clear English.

He followed her on horseback. When they got to the house, he saw that Mrs. Moriyama had been waiting. "Come, come," she said, indicating the formal dining table. She spoke in Japanese, looking steadily at Masa and glancing at Amarjeet. Amarjeet wondered why. Several years ago, her husband had arranged for an English tutor to visit this home as part of the county Americanization classes, and she and Kishen had sat with that woman, in this same room, every week for six months.

"Please sit and speak with her," Masa said. "She has questions that she wishes you will answer. She would be grateful if you would do this service."

Mrs. Moriyama had tea ready, and she poured it into the porcelain cups. Mr. Moriyama did not appear to be home. She moved quickly, as if she wanted to complete the conversation before her husband would interrupt. She sat across the table from Amarjeet, facing him, and Masa placed herself at the head, between them. Mother and daughter spoke to each other in rapid Japanese while Amarjeet looked from one to the other, palms on his knees, patient.

"Mother says—"

But Mrs. Moriyama waved her daughter aside. She leaned forward in her chair, hands clasped in her lap, and spoke herself.

"First I come here. I work fields," she said, her eyes fixed on the table's edge, her hand indicating the outdoors.

Amarjeet nodded.

"When husband come to Japan. Marry. Father not poor. But I come here, I work in fields. We must live?" She paused, making sure he understood. He nodded back.

"Her family in Kagoshima Prefecture was not poor. She never

had to labor in the fields," Masa said. "My father told her he owned a home here and had much money, but after they arrived she saw it was not so. They picked fruit in the Central Valley orchards for three years."

"My hand bleed." Mrs. Moriyama held up her palm, as if to show him. "Husband say we come to Imperial Valley. Make our own farm."

"My father was always ambitious," Masa said. Mrs. Moriyama flashed her a look that Amarjeet did not know how to read. There was another exchange in Japanese. "She says that together they planted strawberries, peas. My sister and I were small. We were put to work too. But my father always gets the credit."

Amarjeet kept his face expressionless.

"I never want come here," Mrs. Moriyama said, suddenly fierce. Her daughter interrupted, but Mrs. Moriyama again waved her away.

"I come here. I wear western clothing. I want women know I smart. I come here. I go Christian church on Sunday and wear a hat. *Hat.*" Her hand knocked the teacup, but the tea didn't spill. "Christian church, but I no understand English. Because—we must live? Other women must know I smart. For Masa. For Yuki." Her eyes were glistening now, bright. "But, when I need peace, I go to Buddhist temple." She pulled a handkerchief from her pocket and smothered her eyes. "Cannot change. Cannot change the truth. But, we must live?"

Masa's and Amarjeet's eyes met. Mrs. Moriyama did not seem to notice. When she spoke again, she had collected herself.

"Haruo was smart boy. That was why other mothers accept me." She seemed to gather herself together, sit taller. "Tell me truth, Amarjeet-san," she said quietly. "Did he have girl in town?"

Amarjeet glanced again at Masa. Her eyes darted away. "Don't answer," she said sharply. "My mother won't accept—"

"Yes," he said. Even after all Harry's hiding, all the ways he had protected his parents, he would have wanted his mother to know.

He heard Masa release a breath.

"Who was she?" Mrs. Moriyama asked.

He hesitated for only a moment. "Anna Halliday. The daughter of the school superintendent. We were in school together."

The silence was heavy.

The expression on Mrs. Moriyama's face shifted. She would know too that Anna's father had run for mayor the year before. "Tell me, Anna-san care for Haruo?"

"He wrote to her, Mrs. Moriyama," Amarjeet said gently. "She wrote back. Her letters came every week. Sometimes two or three. He was frantic for them. After the war, they wanted to marry and move to Los Angeles." Amarjeet looked at Mrs. Moriyama. "He gave me letters for her too."

Masa stared intently at her mother, as if she was worried.

"White girl," Mrs. Moriyama said. "And pretty girl." She wiped her eyes. "He always have good taste."

Amarjeet said nothing.

"You see Anna-san, yes? When you give letter?"

"Yes. Don't worry. Her father won't know."

She handed him a box, neatly wrapped in a swatch of cream silk patterned with green leaves. Amarjeet untied it carefully. It was the same necklace that Amarjeet had handed to Mr. Moriyama the day before. Harry's necklace. "Please give Anna-san this. You tell Anna-san it from Haruo family. You tell Anna-san. We know Haruo want it." She wiped her eyes. "Please remember Haruo. You tell Anna-san."

"I will, Mrs. Moriyama," Amarjeet said. "I will."

26

AMARJEET TOOK UP HIS OLD CHORES AT THE FARM. HE WORKED QUIETLY. Other than his moods, he was dependable; he did not say much and he was not too curious about what had happened while he was away. He enjoyed the children the most: Leela, who was now eight; Federico, who was a year and a half. Sometimes he would put Federico in the baby carriage and wheel him around the farm. Rosa gave birth to twins, Grace and José, and Amarjeet loved them too. He found comfort in the children's openness, in their sadness and anger and happiness, which they showed without cover or restraint.

Once he overheard his aunt and uncle talking about him—Kishen pointing out to Jivan that his nephew had grown moody. That she found him staring out into the fields, seeing something that wasn't there. That he had grown angry with her when she had asked if he would be home for dinner. "Be patient, Kishen-ji," his uncle had said. "The boy has just returned from battle."

Ram wanted to spend time with him now, in a way he had not wanted before.

"What was it like over there?" Ram asked him once, and Amarjeet did not know what to say.

"What shall I tell you?"

"How did Harry win his medal?"

Amarjeet told him. Then he spoke about the weather.

Amarjeet thought he might, eventually, perhaps when he had rested enough, go back to India and bring back a bride. Ram had failed in bringing Padma, but there was a difference. Ram was not a citizen, and Amarjeet was. He would do this just as soon as he recovered a bit from the war, when he stopped hearing that pounding in his ears, when he could sleep again. He noticed sometimes that Karak and Rosa would argue; he could hear their voices across the expanse between the houses. He met Adela; he noticed Ram and she would share an occasional glance when they thought others weren't looking. It did not bother him.

What interested him was France and the war. He realized that people at home knew more about it than he had known over there: strategy and battle plans, General Pershing's refusal to split American forces under British or French command. How that meant more Americans might die than the alternative. How the U.S. Army planned full frontal assault: simply throwing more young bodies at the battle line until Germany ran out of young men to counter them. Was this patriotism? Had it made the world safe for democracy?

Between harvesting and planting he went to the library in El Centro to learn more. The general had issued the order for expedited citizenship just before the first all-American offensive at Saint-Mihiel. So that all the immigrant soldiers would not desert. When Amarjeet read this, his throat went dry. He thought the ploys of strategy were used only against the enemy.

He read about the German in Brawley who had been tarred and feathered for refusing to buy Liberty bonds. He read about the German who had been lynched in Illinois. This too made him sick. He had not hated the Germans during the war. Harry had not hated them either. The Germans, the French, the British, the Americans—

they had been a bunch of farm boys, wishing for their mothers, dreaming of their sweethearts, shooting at each other across a no-man's-land. The morning the armistice was announced, some men on the line had run forward to embrace the German soldiers they had shot at just hours earlier. The farm boys had not wanted the war. They had never wanted the war. If he—Amarjeet Singh of Tark-pur village, Ludhiana district, son of Gurinder Singh—had shot and killed people, he did not want to think about that now.

To him, the war had been about carrying supplies to the front line on his cart and coming back to the rear with that same cart loaded down with bodies. There had been so many, many, bodies. There had been no difference between them, save the tint of skin or hair: Irish and Chinese, Sicilian and Jew, Mexican and Arab and Japanese. If he had served alongside Negroes, he knew there would have been no difference there either.

He told himself he had made a good decision; he had his citizen-ship. Why, he was capable of anything! When he walked among the locals in town—how many had seen what he had seen? How many could have done what he had done? To witness carnage, to come close to the essence of life because one had been close to death, to see humanity's depravation—it was not the same as wisdom, but it was close. He knew why the army did not want Negroes on the front lines. It was not because other soldiers would not accept them, or that was not the only reason. It was not because they could not exercise valor—of course they could. It was because the U.S. gov-ernment did not want them to be admired, lionized, when they returned.

IN JULY, Amarjeet passed Everett Pike, one of the boys from the war, on Main Street in front of the post office. Everett waved first.

"Hey, Jeet! Where ya been all this while?" he said, his smile big, his voice bigger. "What're you up to?"

Amarjeet was glad to see him too. "Farming again." He felt a whiff of embarrassment.

"Me too. You know, my old man'll never let me off that damn farm." They laughed.

Shortly after they had returned, Everett had organized a ball game in the field outside of town for the boys from the military. He had been a great batsman in high school. Sam was there, so was Herb, a few others Amarjeet did not know as well. After the game, they had stayed in the park, drinking hooch under starlight, talking about men they had known in the war. It had been good to do that.

"Big things in the works for the veterans," Everett said now, kicking the dirt road with the toe of his shoe. "They're callin' a meeting. No one who's been over there should miss it."

"Oh?"

"Hotel Barbara Worth." Everett raised his eyebrows and dropped them. "Classy."

"When?" Amarjeet asked.

At that ball game, the other vets had mentioned other times they had met, times that Amarjeet had not known about. Once at Everett's parents' home. Once at Mount Signal, for a picnic with some girls from their old high school. Once at the Hotel Dunlack for a dinner hosted by Sam Pinkerton's father. Sam was civil to Amarjeet now, even warm, ever since recovering from his injuries and coming home. It was good to know that saving his life may have changed his views. Somehow, wherever he was, Amarjeet felt Harry knew that. It had been Harry who had gone over the top of the trench to get Sam out of the line of fire, but Amarjeet had pulled him down inside, to the deep safety of the dugout. But still, Amarjeet had not been invited to the dinner.

"You didn't get an invite?"

"Naw—" Amarjeet said.

"Here." Everett plucked a card from his pocket and shoved it into Amarjeet's hand.

If you are a veteran, honorably discharged, soldier or sailor,
regardless of rank or political convictions, regardless of whether
you served overseas or on the home front, please add your
number to our group, at 2:00 P.M. at the Hotel Barbara Worth.

"See? You're a Doughboy, ain't ya? Tomorrow, all right?"

Perhaps it was too much to ask that he be invited to the west side of El Centro, whether to a home or hotel. But ball games that the vets organized themselves, picnics with no women present—these he was asked to attend, along with Mohamid Nawaz, along with Ho Look, Wong Yan, William Anjai and Py Okaymoto, Manuel Pedro, and Haygash Pampeyan. It did not matter that he was not invited, Amarjeet told himself. How could the families of these boys understand the bond their sons shared over there? He could not expect their women to feel safe with people not their kind.

"Sounds swell," Amarjeet said. He would be there.

THE NEXT MORNING, he dressed in his good shirt and dress slacks and asked to borrow Karak's car.

"Meeting up with a girl, are you?" Karak said, looking him up and down.

If he had told Karak that he was going to the Hotel Barbara Worth, Karak would not have believed it. "A veterans' meeting." Amarjeet could not keep the pride out of his voice, but Karak did not seem to care.

Amarjeet parked on Main Street. Some of the boys were out front, gathered around Sam Pinkerton. He was telling the others a joke and they were leaning in to hear. As Amarjeet approached, the men erupted in laughter.

"Hey, Jeet," Sam Pinkerton called, "long time no see!" Amarjeet recognized other boys in the gathering, all of them dressed well, shaved and trimmed with crisp shirts and gleaming shoes. They clapped him warmly on the back, struck his arm, fellas he hadn't seen in four months, since leaving Camp Lewis. He knew he carried some of the aura of Harry's heroism, just because they had been so close. They moved inside as a group—ten or twelve young men of the Valley.

The lobby opened up like a cavern before them. The air inside was unbelievably cool, fresh, and inviting; he had heard about the indoor plumbing that kept it so, pipes through which cold water flowed and chilled the air. In the corner, a string quartet played and the sound floated toward them across the space and emptiness. Their shoes tip-tapped on the marble floor. He wanted to loll on the orange velvet sofas, straight-backed and majestic.

They were being directed into a dining room by two hosts, middle-aged men dressed in suits and vests despite the weather. The boys formed a short line behind others who had come before. The hosts were jovial, bantering with the young men. It was clear that they knew some well and did not know others. Through the doorway Amarjeet could see tables set with white cloth, paneled walls, and regal chandeliers hanging from a distant ceiling. A group of Anglo men mingled and talked, hands in pockets, backs straight, at ease and confident. A cloth sign hung near the entrance: VETERANS! WEL-COME TO THE AMERICAN LEGION: IMPERIAL VALLEY POST NO. 16.

Before Amarjeet reached the head of the line, one of the hosts called to Sam, and he left his place to speak with him. The host glanced at Amarjeet and talked in a low voice. Sam turned in Amarjeet's direction for a second, a mercurial instant, but did not meet his eye.

Something was rising in Amarjeet, something that had been born in boot camp and grown in the artillery line, strengthened in that moment he had sworn an oath to a new country in Camp Lewis. Sam did not come back to join them, but stayed, hovering, beside the host. When Amarjeet reached the head of the line, he questioned the host directly: "Is there a problem, sir?" He felt the weight of Sam's gaze.

The man leaned toward him. A bit too close, smiling. "It's just that—I've got to make sure that everyone who's at the meeting appears on this list." He had heavy cheeks, jowls that twitched when he moved.

"Come on, Mr. Sanders," Sam said. "He's a buddy."

"I'm sure your friend understands my difficulty, Sam. I can't help it. House rules are house rules. You can only appear at the meeting if you're on the list." His tone was exasperated, as if Sam were the unreasonable one.

"Mr. Sanders—"

The man shrugged. Shook his head.

Sam Pinkerton looked at Amarjeet then. The look held knowledge of all that had happened. The fact of the trench. The fact of Harry, going over the top to save him. The fact of gunfire. The fact of the blood. The fact of Sam's tears as he was pulled into the safety of the dugout, Amarjeet waiting in the trench, holding the weight of Sam's legs, both the broken and the good one.

Behind them, the young vets were unknowing. Their laughter rose to the ceiling as they listened to another joke. Amarjeet remembered the words of President Wilson, captured in a newspaper article he had read: the American Legion would see no distinction in race or class or status.

"I reckon I'm not on that list," Amarjeet said, "no matter what my name is."

"Mr. Sanders—" Sam said again to the host.

But Amarjeet had already turned to go.

Sam grabbed his arm. "We'll meet you. We'll meet you after"— Sam seemed to struggle to remember the words—"at the Palm of the Hand of God." His face brightened at finding the name. It was the only decent restaurant close to the railroad tracks, on the east side, where the whites hardly went. Shame enveloped Amarjeet.

"Sure, Sam. I'll meet you fellas right after the meeting at the Palm. Maybe we can have dinner." Amarjeet got back into Karak's car. He wondered if Sam had considered, for even a moment, turning his back on that host and coming with him now.

ONCE, IN THE FIELD HOSPITAL IN FRANCE, Harry had said to Amarjeet, "Can't believe I survived that shell but this damn flu's got me laid up in here." Harry almost never talked about the shell; from that topic, it was a small step to thinking about the buddies they'd lost. Harry's voice was raspy and low. Amarjeet could tell it hurt him to talk. "I still think about your mare, Jeet. She was a good horse, weren't she? A damn good horse."

Amarjeet's eyes began to well up, unexpectedly. He did not blink the tears away. The mare's last act had been to save his life by taking the blow of the impact. "Am I crazy, Harry, to cry for that horse when all those fellas were dying around us?" Amarjeet asked. He was whispering, so that the flu-sick around them would not hear.

"Naw . . . you weren't crazy, Jeet. You weren't the one who was crazy."

"You saved those boys and I'm still cryin' for my horse."

"Come on, Jeet."

"What made you?"

"Made me?"

"Save that jackass Jed Smith?"

"Well, there's nothin' wrong with Jed. He's just a fella like us. Why wouldn't I pull him in?"

"What about Pinkerton, then?" Everyone knew what Pinkerton thought about Japs.

"Oh, that's easy!" Harry said.

"To show him what a Jap could do?" Amarjeet had grinned.

"Hell no. I saved him 'cause I hate him. I had to save him. Weren't no other way about it." They laughed then, because Harry would always have something to hold over Sam Pinkerton, and there was no getting around that for their whole lives. But Amarjeet felt that something more had happened. There was a bond between Sam and Harry, even though one of them was dead. They had crossed a boundary together, a line, to a place beyond love and hate.

THE NEXT TIME he was at the Moriyamas' home, helping to mend the fence that ran along the western border, Amarjeet told Harry's father what had happened at the American Legion meeting. They were nailing together wooden boards, hoisting fence posts into ditches they had dug the day before. He could not talk about it at home, where his uncle might, with a glance or a word, remind him that he had warned Amarjeet this would happen.

Mr. Moriyama was kneeling in the dirt, pushing hard against the wood, making the slats fit into the fence post. Sweat dropped from his forehead into his eyes. He was pushing harder than he had to but remained quiet during Amarjeet's telling. Amarjeet thought he had not heard him. Suddenly Mr. Moriyama sat back on his haunches. "You did right thing and leave," he said. "Keep your self-respect. You did right thing not go to restaurant and wait."

Amarjeet felt the comment like a slap on the face, though Mr. Moriyama had meant to be kind. "Yes," he said without conviction. Because he hadn't told Mr. Moriyama what happened after. He *had* gone to the restaurant. He had to know, for this once and for all time, whether he could trust those fellas or not.

Sam and the others never came. Amarjeet sat by himself for an hour, watching the door, like a dog waiting for his master. That's what humiliated him most.

AMARJEET BEGAN TO VISIT the Moriyamas regularly, helping them with chores that Harry would have done. Harry's sisters returned to their husbands, believing their parents to be settled in their grief, and the Moriyamas were glad to have Amarjeet's company. He helped build an addition to the barn. He helped Mr. Moriyama frame Harry's Distinguished Service Cross and hang it in the parlor. Mrs. Moriyama fed him Harry's favorite food. Perhaps they knew how much he had loved their son. It was a relief to be in this bubble, protected from the world by the density of their conjoined grief.

He no longer wanted to leave the farm as he once had. When the Valley gathered for the Armistice Parade, he did not march, he did not even watch from the sidelines. That part of him was in the past. The future rose up before him as a whiteness, as a blankness through which he could not see. What Amarjeet wanted he could not name. He thought he desired to belong to something bigger than himself, to have good work that was not farming, to have children, to love someone again, to not always protect himself from something he could not name.

IT WAS MR. MORIYAMA who told Amarjeet what he should be scared of, when Amarjeet visited him on a Sunday in April 1920. Mr. Moriyama had heard that Assemblyman Jones had taken the podium at city hall to declare that almost three thousand Orientals had cultivated farmland in the Valley. "Take heed!" the assemblyman warned. "Take heed those numbers don't increase!"

In May, the Fredonia newspaper ran an editorial titled "The Hegemony of the White Race." The California Oriental Exclusion League moved into an office off Main Street and began lobbying to restrict access to farmland. They hosted dinners, convincing the county supervisors to write a letter to the governor. The old 1913 law excluding the Japanese from farmland had been ineffectual, they argued. Now the state legislature introduced a new bill. Behind fancy legal jargon, behind its show of fairness, it closed the old loopholes. All that was needed was for real Californians to vote in the November election to approve it.

A few days later, the paper ran a headline that read: "Tri Color

Map Shows Asiatics." A red, white, and blue map segmented the Valley with blade-sharp lines, showing the land that the Japanese and Hindus farmed. Red depicted Moriyama's farm, blue for Jivan Singh's next door. Lands cultivated by Anglos appeared in white. The colors splashed like an indictment beyond the boundaries of Fredonia to Brawley and El Centro, Calexico and Calipatria.

The red and blue sections cover more than 75,000 acres, the article under the map stated. *It is known that a large portion of the Oriental Holdings have escaped observation.* Amarjeet first saw the map at the feed store, but soon he would see it everywhere: behind the counter in the General Store, in a pamphlet for Senator Phelan's reelection campaign, on the windows of the barbershops and the Chamber of Commerce and the Western Union office.

"Time to fight," Amarjeet said, sitting at the Moriyama's kitchen table, reading the article for the third time.

"For what is there to fight?" asked Mr. Moriyama.

Wasn't it obvious? "Time to fight for your place in the Valley," Amarjeet said. "Your home."

Mr. Moriyama said nothing, merely looked at him. Amarjeet knew what he was thinking. If Harry were alive, they wouldn't have been in this situation. Harry had been a citizen. He would have been immune to an Alien Land Law. He would have protected them.

LATER, EVERYONE WOULD REMEMBER IT as the year that changed everything. They would say it was because the war had ended and the markets were devastated; cotton prices plummeted from thirty-five to sixteen cents a pound. The cotton farmers had been patriots, people said, heeding the country's call; they provided fibers for the fighter planes, for the uniforms, for so much more. They did not deserve this fate when peace returned, even if they had made a fortune. But what could be done now? Europe was slowly recovering, fighting had stopped even among the colonies and protectorates and dominions around the planet, and American cotton was not needed as before.

It was not only cotton. The entire country had fallen into bad times and everyone felt it. Banks refused to loan money. Shops fired employees. Workers went on strike. Women in the fields and factories were pushed back to their homes, relinquishing their dignity so the menfolk could reclaim theirs. Race riots erupted in cities across the country.

Crime increased across the Valley. Entrepreneurs smuggled whiskey from wet Calexico to dry El Centro, where Karak would go to shop; Anglos spirited Japanese and Chinese across the border. Butter and milk and eggs were often stolen from boxcars at the train depot. The sheriff told Jivan that his deputies ran more hoboes and drifters out of the Valley every week. They were found everywhere now, in town and in residential districts, begging for money, food, clothing, shelter. Many claimed to be ex-servicemen. The Valley jails began to fill. The American Legion issued a warning: Beware these fake beggars! They had not truly served in the military! Neither Fredonia nor any other community owed them a living.

Karak and Ram looked for other crops to grow instead of cotton: alfalfa through which to rotate, perhaps barley. They learned from Clive that Southwest Cotton Company had contracted to take $2 million worth of Pima cotton at sixty cents a pound. It was a special price for a special commodity, not mere regular cotton. They visited their ginner, Jake Smiley. Could he include them in that deal? They had twenty-five acres in Pima, it would help offset the loss they would take on the other fifty-five. He told them he would buy only five acres' worth. Every cotton grower in the Valley was coming to him. "I feel for you boys," Smiley added, as they left. "I know how it is. It ain't easy." Karak began to drink more, visit Mexicali often, to argue, or yell, if Ram questioned him on anything.

27

JUNE 1920

ON A WINDY MORNING, RAM WATCHED AS A LARGE WAGON PULLED BY A team of four mules stopped at the Eggenberger house. Two men knocked on the door; four more waited near the wagon. He had seen Karak leave the house after breakfast and knew Rosa was inside with the children. He walked toward it, feeling protective. As the men stood at the door, she opened it a crack and peeked out. Ram watched as the men entered. Surely she would not have let them in willingly.

"Hello! Hello!" Ram yelled, running toward the house. By the time he had reached the walk, the men had lumbered back outside, two of them hoisting between them the refrigerator, four others rolling the piano along.

"What are you doing here?" Ram asked.

The men barely looked up as he approached. "You Karak Singh?" the largest of them asked. He spat a stream of tobacco into the dirt.

"No." Ram hesitated. Perhaps he should have said yes.

"Don't know why it's your business."

Ram sped through the open door and found Rosa collapsed in a chair. "What happened?" he asked.

Tears streamed silently down her face. She held a handkerchief in both hands, wringing it, pulling it apart with trembling fingers.

"¿Qué pasó?" he asked more gently, kneeling so he could face her. From the bedroom doorway, Federico stared at them with unblinking eyes. In the back, one of the twins was wailing.

"Karak couldn't pay back the loan."

"What loan? He bought from Sears with cash," he said.

"I do not know! I do not know!" she said in Spanish. "There is something he could not pay back. I don't know!"

The statement was a jolt, a jumble of information. Then Karak's recent behavior suddenly fell into place. He had sold farm implements back to Hanson's. He had wanted to hire a family of workers that included eight adults and seven children, but Ram had refused. They may have had children working for them in Punjab, Ram said, but he would not do it here. And what if the sheriff discovered them?

"What if?! What if?!" Karak had yelled, his eyes bulging. "You are talking what-if and we are facing disaster!" He had sped off in his car, leaving Ram to negotiate with the workers alone.

Ram looked now at Rosa, holding her son tightly against her. "Where is Karak?" he asked in Spanish. Federico had started to cry too, and Rosa let his tears fall; the handkerchief remained wrapped around her hand.

She shook her head, her features contorted. "He left early this morning. He never tells me where he is going."

Might he be at the bank, Ram wondered, asking Jasper Davis for help? But he could be anywhere . . . at the ginners, at the Consolidated Fruit offices . . . even Mexicali. His marriage had not stopped him from going there. Had he known these men were coming today? Had he told Rosa?

He heard the men calling to one another outside. Through the window, he saw they had rolled the piano up a ramp onto the wagon and tied it down, along with the new Victrola. The mules pulled forward under the weight. Karak had bought the piano through the Sears catalog when the store on Main Street would not sell to him. Rosa had played it every evening after the day's work was done. Ram would hear the notes drifting through the space between the two houses, changing the air, making the farm—its people, animals, plantings—part of something grand and rich.

"Come and stay with us today, Rosita," Ram said. "You can help Kishen in the kitchen. The children can play together."

He helped her carry the twins to the Singhs' home. Federico followed behind. Rosa had never needed an invitation and came to visit the Singhs almost every day. But he could see the gratitude in her eyes.

Karak arrived in the car that evening, after Rosa had returned home. Ram stayed away; one must spare a man humiliation whenever possible. After dark, he heard Karak's yelling across the clear distance between the houses. Rosa shouted back. Their sounds were like animal noises. Ram sat up on his cot. Yellow light leaked from the windows of the Eggenberger house. On his own cot, Amarjeet was already asleep a few feet away. Karak and Rosa were shouting words—Spanish, Punjabi, English—but Ram could not make out a single one.

There was no moon and the stars were alarming, like needles piercing velvet sky. The mountains loomed. Through the dark he heard the crash of breaking glass. Ram leaped up, slipped on his shoes, and ran toward the house. Inside, he heard screaming and the distressed shrieks of children. He banged his palm against the door. "Karak! Karak!"

The sounds fell silent. The door opened slowly. Karak's eyes locked on Ram's, round and savage. His shirt was open at the collar and his chest heaved.

Blood thundered inside Ram's head. Rosa was slumped on the floor, leaning against the chair in which she had sat that morning, miserable, holding her head in her hands. Pieces of glass lay near her.

"Bhai, I want to see the books," Ram whispered in Punjabi, his gaze unwavering. "May I look at them?" Karak stepped away from the door, glaring at him for the lie. When he went to fetch the ledgers, Rosa began to sweep up the glass with her apron, her head bent. She did not look at Ram. Karak shoved the books into Ram's hands and grabbed his jacket in one swift motion. The door slammed behind him. Ram bent to help Rosa. They heard the motorcar's engine spark at full throttle, and the fading sound as it sped off.

Karak still had not returned when Esperanza came to visit the next day. From Jivan's porch, Ram saw Rosa and the children climb into Alejandro's wagon. Rosa did not return for three days.

When Karak came back the morning after she left, Ram asked him where he had been. "At the lawyer's office," Karak said, refusing to acknowledge how long he had been away. Ram stared at him, but said nothing. After dinner that evening, Karak asked Jivan to buy his automobile. "For any amount—five dollars, ten dollars, one hundred dollars," he said, ignoring Ram, who sat by silently, listening.

"I'm giving five," Jivan said. "I am merely keeping the car safe for you, nothing else." Jivan handed him the money without meeting Karak's gaze. The men did not look at each other; their feeling was too great. Karak signed over the title and handed it to Jivan, along with a receipt. He drove the car behind Jivan's house and tucked it away from view. It was important that the authorities not find the document or the automobile on the property that *he* leased, in *his* home. Everything must be kept with Jivan on Jivan's property. That was how the automobile would be saved, though the refrigerator, the Victrola, and the piano were not.

The following morning, Karak met the lawyer at the courthouse and filed for bankruptcy.

STEPHEN EGGENBERGER BOARDED A TRAIN in Los Angeles to come visit them. Jivan, Karak, Ram, and Amarjeet sat on Eggenberger's porch and the Swiss man broke his news: Times were very bad for everyone, and that was true even for him in the city. His business needed cash, his wife's health was poor, and he greatly regretted it, but he needed to sell his land. He said the words so quickly that the other men seated around the table almost did not understand. "Consolidated Fruit Company is interested in it for purchase," Eggenberger said. "The same company for which Clive has been working."

"Clive is working now in Consolidated Fruit?" Jivan asked.

"For two months now. He added them as a large client."

Jivan exchanged a glance with Karak, with Ram. "We did not know."

"I have not yet an agreement with them, but they tell me that you would be kept on the long-term lease. Just like sharecropping: one-third to two-thirds. You will not have to go. You may stay in your homes. I wished that you know. For all these years the cost and the profits from this land we shared. You and Moriyama and Roubillard. I would like that you know first."

"When you will be selling?" Karak asked.

But before Eggenberger could answer, Jivan said, "Sell to me eighty acres, Stephen."

Eggenberger blinked in surprise. Both men knew that Jivan had put more work into creating this farm than anyone else. Jivan had helped build a wing of the house. He had leveled the eastern field. He had helped harvest every crop and had raised the second shed for the animals.

"I had not thought that you have the money," Eggenberger said.

"I have money," Jivan said. Ram's eyes traveled from one man to the other. Karak clenched his jaw.

"You are—" Eggenberger hesitated. "You are Hindu. I thought it was not allowed." He said the words with no malice.

"I will buy and hold the land in Leela's name. She was born here. Or I will place it in Amarjeet's name. Right now, one hundred percent legal, it is legal. What happens after election, no one is knowing, but if you sell now, no question will be asked."

Eggenberger nodded. "Ja. I will sell to you, my friend." His eyebrows flashed up in admiration. "Naturally, I will sell to you." He hesitated again. Eighty acres was a lot of land. "I am in need of mon—"

"I will not haggle with you, Stephen." Jivan cut him off. "Not after all that has happened between us. Whatever Consolidated Fruit is paying, I am able to pay the same."

28

OCTOBER 1920

IN SIX WEEKS, JIVAN HAD SIGNED THE NECESSARY DOCUMENTS AND OWNED 80 acres of land that he had been farming for thirteen years. The other 80 acres, on which the Eggenberger house sat, were transferred to Consolidated Fruit. Moriyama's land was sold to the company also. Two miles away, the 160 acres on which Karak and Ram had grown cotton were also transferred, as was the adjacent land on which Roubillard competed with them. The company kept all the leases. Overnight, reality had changed, the stability of the earth seemed lost.

"I wish you had purchased this land too, like my uncle did," Amarjeet said to Mr. Moriyama. He had been helping with repairs around the farm. They were eating Mrs. Moriyama's rice balls for lunch, seated on the bench near the water's headgate.

"Attorney general already say. Japanese cannot be citizen."

"You could still have bought the land."

"No matter, Amarjeet," Mr. Moriyama said.

Amarjeet could not tolerate his passivity. He got up abruptly, to control his tongue. "Ain't you going to the Japanese Association meeting? They put up signs everywhere. They want to speak to the Valley residents. Convince them to vote no on the law."

"I aware of meeting."

"At my old high school." He did not need to add, *Harry's old high school too.* "I'll come to fetch you. We'll go together." He did not know why he cared so much. Was it because of Harry? Was it because he smelled the danger to the Hindus too? Was it because of the injustice of it all?

There were categories among the Orientals; everyone knew that. The Japanese could not be citizens. The Hindus could.

ON TUESDAY, one week before the election, Amarjeet picked up Mr. Moriyama early. They would help to set up the school gymnasium for the meeting that night. They did not know how many people to expect.

The Japanese Association wanted to appeal to the people directly, to tell them that if the Asian farmers left, the Valley would decline, that Anglos would not farm the land they owned, and they would not replace their Japanese sharecroppers with Anglo tenants because the Anglos did not want to do such work; it was too demanding, too hot, too menial. The grower-shipper corporations would buy the land and hire cheap labor. If the Japanese left, what would happen to the family farm, to the dream of the Imperial Valley?

Mr. B. R. Katoh was organizing the meeting. Amarjeet and Mr. Moriyama joined him and four other men who were unfolding chairs in the gymnasium, arranging them in long rows. They had a podium in place. Two women had just arrived, bringing bags of Japanese pastries and bottles of lemonade, when School Superintendent Robert Halliday entered. Behind him were four other Anglo men and Deputy Elijah Hollins.

"Mayor said this meeting's canceled," the superintendent said. "Threat to public safety." He was Anna Halliday's father.

Mr. Moriyama looked at Amarjeet, as if to confirm that he had known this would happen all along.

"We want only talk with people," Mr. Katoh said. "Tell them our story."

"Mayor's orders," Deputy Hollins said, stepping forward. He was chewing tobacco. He thrust out his chest, thumbs tucked into his belt. A pistol hung by his hip.

Amarjeet felt rage build up inside him, like a rock, unyielding. He watched as the Japanese men stacked the chairs together and began to put them away.

AMARJEET ROSE ON ELECTION DAY and went to the high school, *his* high school, to cast his vote. Out front, men held signs for Harding, for Cox.

At the door to the schoolhouse, he was stopped by Deputy Hollins, the same officer who had shut down the Japanese Association meeting before it had even begun.

"Voting day today, Singh. You have to be a citizen."

Amarjeet was prepared. He took out his documents. The certificate of naturalization. His honorable discharge from the army. He showed them to Hollins without speaking.

"I didn't know they were handing those out to Hindus," Hollins said. His finger poked at the certificate. Amarjeet was surprised that Hollins knew who he was. He no longer wore a turban, and he had been away from the Valley for a year and a half.

"Now you do, I guess." He spoke quietly.

When he reached the clerk's desk, he did not wait to be asked again. He merely showed the papers. The clerk glanced at the deputy, who stood by the doorway, his thumbs hooked on his belt.

In the booth, Amarjeet drew the curtain, held the pen with

shaking fingers. He filled in the ballot for Cox. Harding's platform called for a "return to normalcy." Amarjeet did not believe that was possible. He voted NO for the Alien Land Law. When he left the voting booth, he avoided meeting anyone's eye.

It was clear to him now. Everyone was struggling, but to the real Americans, it did not seem right that aliens could struggle alongside them. That some might actually be succeeding when the Americans came up short. Orientals were to be fieldworkers and packers because such laborers were desperately needed and could not be too uppity; workers and packers always knew their place. It was only the *best* Oriental entrepreneurs who should be made to leave: those who discovered ways to protect unripe cantaloupe, invented hybrid lettuce, grew peas where others had failed, earned themselves nicknames like the "potato king" and the "strawberry baron." The successful ones who had settled and raised families and made homes here, the Japanese—especially the Japanese—must go.

Four days later, Amarjeet brought the newspaper from town and laid it on the table on the porch. The Alien Land Law had passed, by a vote of 3,962 to 1,743 in Imperial County. Such a large majority. Mr. Moriyama had been right all along.

Now if Harry's family wanted to farm in Fredonia, they would have to depend on the kindness of the Consolidated Fruit Company, on its willingness to break the law. The Moriyamas could not purchase land in the Valley as Jivan had, or even lease it. They had no citizen to rely on; Harry was dead.

AMARJEET AND HIS UNCLE were standing with Mr. Moriyama on his porch. They could see the western border with the Singhs' land. "What will you do?" his uncle asked.

"Lease finished January one," Tomoya said.

"I know," Jivan said.

"Consolidated tell me they no renew. They tell me—it breaking law." He smiled a bitter smile. "They offer me foreman job same land."

Amarjeet and Jivan were quiet. How could one respond to that humiliation? Amarjeet saw his uncle kick the dirt with his boot.

"They offer pay. Take order. Same land I farming." Tomoya snorted. "I say no."

For a moment, Amarjeet felt a gulf open between them. His uncle and Mr. Moriyama were not equals anymore. He felt uncomfortable, distressed.

"Clive knows you all developed the way to cover cantaloupe and protect from the sun," Jivan said. "Now entire valley is following your way. He is knowing you shipped those peas last month. Right after that bloody election. Two months earlier than anyone else."

Tomoya looked at him gratefully. "He is not law."

"He gains from the law, Mr. Moriyama," Amarjeet said.

"You can form syndicate," Jivan said. "So many have done that. Jasper Davis from the bank would support you. Definitely Jasper can collect one-two other Anglos to form it. Bypass the law."

Amarjeet knew his uncle was grasping. He did not want Tomoya to leave.

Tomoya was making an imprint of his shoe in the soft sand, absently. "Long ago I decide I make home in this place and raise family. Not travel like other men. Every three years, every year, they pack everything and go new farm. No way." His face was stoic. "Moriyama Tomoya not live like that.

"I go join older daughter, her husband in Brownsville. No law in Texas. Or I go Bakersfield, live with younger daughter."

Amarjeet and Jivan did not respond.

"Listen what I tell you," Tomoya said. "You farm this land too." His gaze took in both of them. "You and family. You take it." He indicated the fields around them. "For twelve years I here. It better than land in Japan, better than land in Hawaii. If Consolidated offer, you take."

Tomoya held Jivan's gaze. The election had changed what did not need to be changed. Jivan looked pained. Amarjeet could see: his uncle felt guilty for buying his portion of Eggenberger's land. "I will tell Karak and Ram," Jivan said.

Tomoya's face betrayed no emotion. "What country take only son and not let you to stay?" he asked.

JAPANESE QUESTION WAS SOLVED IN TEXAS
(by Associated Press)

BROWNSVILLE, Texas., Dec. 20 – Tension in the lower Rio Grande valley over the arrival of prospective Japanese colonists appears to have been eased off as a result of the promise made by two Japanese families at Harlington to return to California.

WHITE BABIES ARE INCREASING

FREDONIA, California., Dec. 22 – According to the registrar, the number of white children born in the last few months exceeded the number of Japanese and Mexican births in the township, while heretofore the Japanese and Mexican births have always far outnumbered the white births. In November's records, sixteen white births and only five Japanese and six Mexican births are registered.

HINDUS PROVED GOOD SPRINTERS
CHRISTMAS

FREDONIA, California., Dec. 26 – All the Hindus in town were chased out Christmas afternoon, following an altercation between a Hindu and an American in front of a Main street barber shop. Bystanders took up the argument and the turban wearers found the streets uncomfortable. By dark not one was to be found in the city. No regular fights were staged, most of the scrimmages being foot races with no serious damage resulting.

ANOTHER JAPANESE COLONIST
WARNED TO LEAVE TEXAS

BROWNSVILLE, Texas., Jan. 7 – T. Moriyama, a Japanese Colonist, was met at the train by a committee from the American Legion, the Chamber of Commerce and the retail merchants and farmers organizations and told to leave in 48 hours. He promised to obey. He was informed that public sentiment made it impossible for the Japanese to colonize here and trouble was probable if they persisted.

NIGHT CLASS IN AMERICANIZATION

FREDONIA, California., January 12 – Plans for a night school class in Americanization are under way, John N. Beattie, in charge of night school classes at the high school, announced today. "We would like to have in the class those people who need to be taught the requirements of American citizenship, Japanese, Mexican, Spanish and Hindu people," says Mr. Beattie. "In the class, we will teach reading, writing and civics, so they will understand the language, laws and ideals of the United States."

Mr. Bhagat Singh Thind
Gurdwara House of Worship
1930 South Grant Street
Stockton, CA

January 13, 1921

Esteemed Bhai Bhagat Singh Thind-ji,

Greetings. Perhaps you recall our meeting in Camp Lewis about 18 months ago? At the time, I had just returned from France and was awaiting discharge from the army. We were sworn in together as new citizens in the large hall. While the rest of us were clapping to the band's music, tossing hats in the air, you sat quiet and somber in your army uniform, wearing the dastar with such dignity. You said something curious to me at the end of that ceremony—that we should be on guard for losing the citizenship that we had just gained, that sometimes all is not as it appears on the surface. At that time, I did not know what you meant. But clearly through your age and experience you knew better than I.

This week, a Japanese family who have long been our neighbors moved away because of the new California land law. It is a tragedy. Their only son, my closest friend, died in France just after the peace. He had saved the lives of two fellow soldiers during the war. He was a citizen of this country by reason of his birth. If he had survived, they could have kept their farm and livelihood through him. Now they are without either. In the high school I attended, Americanization classes are now being offered to teach the ideals of this country. I read of this with so *much bitterness. Of which American ideals do they speak? There are two Americas. I know this now.*

You had asked me to write to you if ever I was unhappy with my life after the war. What had you meant by that—"unhappy with my life"? In these dark times, what is to be done? For those of us who risked life and limb to save the world for democracy, what can we do now?

You spoke so strangely to me at that moment after we took our oath. When others were celebrating, you seemed to see the future.

Sincerely yours,

Amarjeet Singh

January 17, 1921
Mr. Amarjeet Singh
Rural Route 9
Fredonia, CA

My dear Amarjeet,

I am surprised and delighted to receive your letter of 13th instant. If you are inclined to combat the darkness of these times, won't you come and join me in the battle? I have been traveling around the state, and also to Washington and Oregon, lecturing and teaching Americans about this injustice to us recent immigrants, when they are only immigrants themselves! I reveal to them how the British have influenced American politics to undermine Indians, so that we may never win back our own country. You see, I have always believed that we should be citizens of America, so that we may have a secure base from which to fight to remove the British.

I ask you now—come and join me. You will act as my clerk, handle correspondence, make translations, and help build the movement. Despite our past failures with the Germans, there is still hope for us here. Your high school years in America will be a great asset to us. We are being funded by Ghadar money and by donations to the gurdwara.

Here is the crux—Bureau of Naturalization has appealed the grant of my citizenship. The appeal has gone all the way to the Ninth Circuit Court level. At first I was discouraged, but my lawyer is very capable. We will fight this to the Supreme Court, my young friend. You are in the same boat as me, whether you recognize it or not. What will happen if our U.S. citizenship is rescinded while we have already renounced our British citizenship? We will be stateless, and for those of us who are married to American women, they will share our fate.

But of one matter there is no doubt: it is better to be a man without a country than a citizen of an enslaved country. Come and join me.

In chardi kala,
B. S. Thind

February 10, 1921

Bhai Bhagat Singh Thind-ji,

Your offer is quite flattering to me. I am not deserving of such a role in the movement. Surely you are mistaken? It cannot be me that you have in mind?

Yet, my anger grows every day. Yesterday while walking in town, a man knocked the turban from my friend Gugar Singh's head. I stopped Gugar Singh from saying anything to the man, despicable though he was. There is no safety here. There is no telling what would have ensued. We picked up the dastar from the filthy ground and we left the place.

Last week my uncle organized a meeting with the businessmen in the local Chamber of Commerce. Theme of the meeting was: How can Hindus fit in and be better residents and stay away from lawlessness? I was humiliated to attend such a

*meeting. Yet I understand my uncle's action. I understand why
we have need for such a thing.*

Sincerely yours,
Amarjeet Singh

February 16, 1921

My dear Amarjeet,
   *I have made no mistake. I am desperately in need of an
assistant and you must fill that role. I will send money for your
travel and you will stay in the gurdwara with me. Gurdwara
is like our mother—whether you cross the desert on hands and
knees, or swim across the ocean, or come with broken heart,
gurdwara brings comfort. Always we Sikhs take care of our own
and anyone else who seeks solace. We do not let others suffer,
whether they be of our faith or not. How, then, can I abandon
you to your anger?*
   *Name of the train depot here is Santa Fe Union Station.
Train comes twice a day. Telegraph the details after your
arrangements are made. If you do not come, I'll be greatly
disappointed.*

Fateh,
B. S. Thind

March 1, 1921

Bhai Bhagat Singh Thind-ji,
   *Situation has become unbearable here. Is this the country for
which I joined the war? Where are those ideals of the United
States that I fought for? Democracy? Tolerance?*
   *I have asked my uncle for permission to join you. I am ashamed
to say I have gone against him in the past, but in this, I needed his
permission. He has given it and more. He gave me his blessing.*

You should know that I have begun to wear a dastar again, proudly, as you do. You have inspired me, bhai-ji. That one can be an American, and wear a dastar, and work for Indian independence—all can be counted in the same man.

Please look for my telegram. I will come.

In chardi kala,
Amarjeet Singh

PART FIVE

I want to say—I cannot say too often—any man who carries a hyphen about with him carries a dagger that he is ready to plunge into the vitals of this Republic whenever he gets ready.

—President Woodrow Wilson, speech in Pueblo, Colorado, September 25, 1919

29

SPRING 1921

AMARJEET LEFT BEFORE THE SPRING HARVEST, ON A WINDY AFTERNOON when sand swept over the hood of the Model T as the family drove to drop him off. There was no parade and no band as they stood with him on the platform, near a trunk filled with clothes and books. Only an Anglo businessman waited with them, and farther toward the front, a Negro woman with her teenage son. The train whistled its approach, the four passengers boarded, and suddenly Amarjeet had left them, again.

The storm held off until they returned that night, then sent sand blasting against the side of Jivan's house, through crevices around the windows and roof. The next morning, they spent hours clearing both homes. At Moriyama's deserted house, sand collected against the eastern wall. Two date trees had fallen across the path. Scorpions sheltered in the sitting room where Amarjeet and Hatsu had talked about Anna Halliday. No one cleared them out. The fertile land sat untilled and abandoned.

To Ram, it seemed everyone had reconciled themselves to Amarjeet's absence, especially Jivan Singh. Without complaint, Jivan hired a man to help with Amarjeet's chores. The family's routine seemed unchanged, but everything had been altered. Jivan would say that he did not care about being a U.S. citizen himself, but he would never forgive what happened to Tomoya. "It is the principle that matters and for which Thind and Amarjeet are fighting! What shall happen to us all if we lose the right to citizenship too?"

Ram felt immune from the effects of this possibility. After all, he was going home, wasn't he? He could return whenever he wanted to, just as soon as he could extricate himself from the allure of the western money, from the prestige it purchased at home, from his involvement with Adela. That most of all. Still, Ram felt that the creature that had hunted the Japanese was coming for the Hindustanees too. He felt it when he saw the scar on his leg from the beating in Hambelton. He felt it when he thought of the San Francisco shoreline and remembered the vision of Padma holding Santosh, far away on the ship's deck.

With the failure of the cotton market, Karak began to speak about trying a new crop. In mid-March, Clive drove out to the farm and asked if Karak and Ram would like to farm Moriyama's former acres. They were sitting together near Jivan's back porch, like the old days. Karak had opened a bottle of whiskey. Nearby, Kishen Kaur sat cleaning the chimneys of the kerosene lamps. Leela was inside with her school books. Jivan was quiet, listening to their talk.

"Yes," Karak said, without hesitation. He had told Ram of the same idea weeks before, and Ram had not liked it then.

Ram was indignant. "Too much land for two men," he said in English.

"We can hire the workers to do all we cannot do," Karak said.

"Consolidated will help you boys any way we can," Clive said. "Get you pickers, planters, wagons, anything."

Ram did not understand how the decision could be made so quickly. Clive was looking at him with a strange expression.

Ram turned to Karak and spoke in Punjabi. "It is wrong to farm that land after Consolidated threw Moriyama out."

"Tomoya told to me," Jivan said in English. "It is good if you and Karak take his land."

"It's Consolidated's land," Clive said.

Jivan looked at him calmly, one landowner speaking to another. "That is not how we think of it," he said.

BY ANY MEASURE, lettuce was not like cotton. The cotton plant was coarse and hardy and could be picked several times over eight or nine months. After harvest, the cotton could be stored until it was time to sell, used long after it was grown.

Lettuce had a growing season of only 120 days. It was delicate, required harvest during a peak window, needed ice for shipment within hours of picking. In urban markets in the east and west, up-standing citizens paid top dollar for it in posh restaurants, reputable groceries. If a Valley farmer had the right amount of acreage, if he picked at just the right time, he could make tens of thousands of dollars off a field of lettuce.

Ram and Karak prepared the fields over the summer and fall and planted during Thanksgiving. Weekly, Clive came to check the crop, sometimes alone, sometimes with Jonathan Hitchcock, the vice president of Consolidated Fruit. One day in early December, the four men sat on the back porch and Clive and Hitchcock asked to look at the books; they asked about how Ram and Karak had ne-gotiated prices for seed and workers. Ram thought this was strange. He went inside to fetch the ledger. He returned with the book to find the three men talking lightly about the weather, but his eyes met Karak's and Ram read his irritation. Karak shared his sense of insult. In the old days the accounts were theirs. When Clive worked for Eggenberger, all that he had wanted to see was the slip of official paper with the broker's quoted price, the amount of produce shipped.

The men looked at the records carefully. Clive pulled the ledger close and pointed out entries to Hitchcock without addressing Ram and Karak. Hitchcock took out his own notebook and a silver fountain pen, and copied numbers in a neat script. He noted dates and names of suppliers. His fingers were too slender, his nails too clean; Ram knew he had never farmed. Karak and Ram glanced at each other again. Karak licked his lips, clenched his jaw. Ram noted the redness framing his tired eyes.

"We will be using our own harvesters," Karak stated.

"That is how we do things," Ram added.

"If your Mexicans can put aside their mañana persuasion, they might get the lettuce out while still fresh," Clive said. They all laughed at the joke, except for Hitchcock, who smiled patiently, folding his pen away in a leather case. His eyes were so blue, Ram thought, so pale. They talked about Clive's children's expectations for the Christmas holiday. He had promised his daughter a pony. Later she hoped to take it to the midwinter fair. The conversation lapsed. Their goodbyes were cordial.

Karak and Ram stood at the jackrabbit stone and waved as Hitchcock and Clive Edgar drove off in Hitchcock's cream Packard.

"Why do they need to see the books in that detail?" Ram said.

"They are a corporation, bhai, a big conglomerate; this is the way they do things." Ram wondered at Karak's support of them.

"They spoke between themselves, without addressing us," Ram said.

Karak hesitated. "As long as they give us our money, I don't care how they talk."

Something in his tone made Ram turn to face him.

"Tell me—what has happened?" Ram said.

Karak hesitated again. "Rosa—" he said.

"Yes?"

"Yesterday. She moved out of the house with the children and left me alone." He took a deep breath and rubbed his face. "What should I do now? She says I have not been a good husband to her. After I bought her all those things." His expression was bitter, shocked. "She is crazy," Karak said. But Ram did not agree.

THEY WERE BECOMING TRUCK FARMERS, like the Japanese. The lettuce crop was beautiful, if ever truck could be beautiful—lime green, fragile as a flower, traveling east in refrigerated carloads to early markets in Boston and New York and Philadelphia. The price was high. When Clive came to see them, he could not hide his pleasure. "You boys still bringin' it in. Bringin' it in!"

The day the money was wired to them, Karak came home late. He told Ram that he had gone to the Chinese store on the east side and purchased a gold ring. He visited Rosa that night at Alejandro and Esperanza's home. He came back without her, but he was smiling.

RAM THOUGHT OFTEN of the old distinction that he had heard since childhood: there is a land of one's birth, and there is a land of one's work and action. Janma bhoomi and karma bhoomi. Separate places. The distinction was meant to explain the pain of being broken in two. As if using words to describe the separation made it natural. But it was not. He knew that now. He existed in two places at once. America, Punjab, Adela, Padma. These worlds would never merge. It was impossible. His son was almost nine years old now, and Ram did not know what he looked like. Ram's uncle knew him better than he. The boy's teachers, the neighbors, the vegetable vendor in the village market knew him better too.

That February, for the first time, he kept most of the profit from the harvest for himself. He did not know why. He could not hide from himself a resentment, a sense of disappointment . . . in what? In Padma? Because she had returned to her parents' home? Because he now sent money to that home as well? Yet all the failure had been his; he could not decide to return. Or perhaps it was his fate, written on his forehead. He had been in the States for a third of his life. To divide the world into janma bhoomi and karma bhoomi explained nothing. He would be forever suspended between two lands, never whole.

30

A RIDER CAME BEARING A TELEGRAM FROM AMARJEET, IN THE MORNING, when Kishen Kaur was wrapping their lunches for the field. Amarjeet sent telegrams so rarely that Karak tore it open and read: "Supreme Court decision Bhai B. S. Thind-ji's citizenship rescinded because of his race. Hindus are not white."

They had been about to go out in the field, to prepare the ground for planting. But now they sat back down at the table. Finally, Jivan spoke. "They think they are telling us who we are," Jivan said. "Instead, they have told the world who *they* are."

At work in the fields, Karak spoke to no one. Later, Ram drove into town and brought back the evening's newspapers. For a few hours, the papers sat abandoned on the table on the porch. Jivan and Karak returned from the fields. They bathed. They ate. The lamps were lit and Jivan played the phonograph.

"Father of Leela," Kishen finally said, looking at Jivan, "we must read it." Jivan did not meet her eye. Kishen nudged her daughter forward.

The girl picked up the paper and held it under the circle of lamp-light. Her voice was low. Her accent was American. "Supreme Court rules that high caste Hindus are not free white persons within the meaning of the naturalization law." Leela cleared her throat. "There-fore, under a recent decision of the court excluding the Japanese, they are not entitled to citizenship. Hindus will now come under the Alien Land Laws and are subject to all the restrictions that apply to an Alien race." She put down the paper. For a moment she looked merely puzzled, then tears welled in her eyes. "I am sorry, Pita-ji," she mumbled.

"For what are you sorry, Leelu?" Jivan asked.

"I— I don't know."

"It is not your fault."

The cicadas droned in the night. "We are in the same position as the Japanese now," Jivan finally said. But Ram could see the guilt conveyed in his eyes. Jivan was not in the same position as Ram and Karak or Tomoya. His acres had been bought before the land law was passed and were held in Leela's name. Leela had been born in Fredonia; she was a citizen by birth. Leela could not be stripped of citizenship. The law would not affect Jivan at all.

WITHIN WEEKS, many Hindustani men took their blankets and left for Texas, for Arizona, where the land laws had not yet been passed. Some returned to the lumber mills in Washington and Oregon. Others found work laying track for the Southern Pacific in the few places where track had not yet been laid. A few, like Jivan and Karak and Ram, stayed on. Now, on Sundays, the park was sparsely popu-lated. The grower-shipper corporations bought up the land that the Hindustanees had leased from their absent landlords. The companies hired Filipinos and Japanese to supervise and Mexicans to harvest. The Hindustanees with Mexican wives remained, the ones with chil-dren and dreams of children, the ones who had wished for a home as soon as they left their old unsatisfactory one. When they met each other in the streets, they recognized in each other's eyes the challenge that they had accepted. They were to be "strange" so that the Anglos could be normal, they were to be dirty so that the Anglos could be clean, they were to know their place so that the Anglos could be sure of theirs. If their sons and daughters sat in the same classrooms as the Anglo children, they were to consider themselves fortunate, so that the Anglos could feel generous.

They used to drink with their white land agents and neighbors, they used to gift credit at the clothing store for the wives of their bankers and lawyers, they used to buy candy for these men's children, but now the Hindus stayed on the east side, shopping in Japantown and hiring farmhands from the Negro settlement. Times had changed.

IN THE FABRIC ROOM, Adela looked at him intently, as if she knew that something was wrong. She kissed him softly and he immediately loathed himself. What was he doing in this town, among strangers, with a woman who was not his own, so far from everything that he knew and loved? Suddenly he could not stand the textiles, the scent, the dust motes floating in the sunlight.

"Shall we walk?" he asked.

He could see she was puzzled. It was not often that they stepped into the open together. But truly, who would care? Perhaps the men in the barrio, but they did not matter to him. The Hindustanees in the park? Their gossip did not matter either.

Just walking with her in the open air made him feel a stranger. She belonged here; she was of this desert land and he was not. They were both of no consequence, but now, with the new laws, he was less than she. Everywhere they went, he sensed it. He was no one; he did not exist, coming to California had meant his death.

He stopped walking to face her. "I will go now, Adela," he said, not knowing clearly his own meaning.

She looked confused. "What is it?" she said.

How could he tell her? How could she understand?

He remembered something that Karak often said: western women had too much power.

CLIVE EDGAR VISITED RAM AND KARAK the next week, and they sat near the back porch, just like the old days, except that Hitchcock was with them. They had just finished another lettuce harvest; it had done well. The Anglos were jovial, easy.

"Mr. Hitchcock and I were considering what to do now." Sitting next to the vice president, Clive had become something that he had not been before. "You boys are fine farmers and all. We don't want to lose you." He stretched his arms behind him, cradling his head in his hands. Ram saw the revolver that Clive's father-in-law had given him years before, lodged in a holster by his left arm. Clive had shown it to them on the day he announced his engagement. Pearl inlays in the grip, his initials engraved on the barrel. For years, Clive had not carried it, saying that it was too fancy.

Ram and Karak were quiet. Hitchcock was observing them. He was a handsome man. Tall, slim-hipped, a straight nose, long and delicate fingers. A smattering of gray on his temples. Light blue eyes. He walked with a limp from an unknown injury. He used a cane with a silver duck's head handle. The limp, the cane, the handle, all added to his dignity. Everyone at the table knew that the Punjabis' lease would run out in three months. The time to make decisions was now.

"How about we just keep the terms of our contract?" Clive said.

"Without a paper lease?" Karak asked. They had never had a paper lease with Eggenberger, but they had signed one with Consolidated on the very first day.

"We'll just run our operation like we've always run it," Hitchcock said. His voice was smooth, cultured. "County won't know. Attorney general won't know. Lettuce market is so high now."

No one asked the obvious question. What if the contract wasn't honored? The entire enterprise would be against the law.

"We've trusted each other for years, haven't we?" Clive offered. "Done business on a handshake?"

"We think. We think on it, Clive," Ram said, before Karak could say yes.

Hitchcock and Clive climbed back into Hitchcock's car and Clive tilted his head out the window. Clive and Karak exchanged a glance. Ram felt them united against him.

Later, Ram found Karak out in the field, repairing a leak in the main irrigation ditch. He had flooded the small canal and was lifting soil from the trench to fortify its wall. He did not turn, even though Ram called his name as he approached. "I don't trust Clive," Ram said sharply. He had brought along a shovel but did not stoop to help.

"Clive is an honest man," Karak said. His shoulders and back were wet with perspiration. He worked the shovel with a soldier's bearing. "Hitchcock is right. The market is so high now. If we make a success this season, it will save me from ruin. You cannot do this little thing for your friend, after all the money I have helped you make?"

It was true, Karak had helped him make a lot of money. But he had helped Karak too.

"Three hundred twenty acres in lettuce, bhai," Karak said. "Both fields. A fortune. Rosa will come back if the crop goes well, if I pay every debt. The children will be back." He paused. Something caught in his throat. "Don't you miss them, Ram? The way they used to run and laugh here."

So that was Karak's hope.

"I barely know the twins and already they are three years old. At least Federico remembers a little."

Yes, Ram had missed the children. Without them, the farm seemed a place of misfortune.

"We need more protection," Ram said. "We can keep a written lease in someone else's name." He knew he was stepping on unsteady ground.

Karak snorted. "Whose?"

"Rosa's," Ram said.

"Are you mad?" Karak said.

"She doesn't come under the Land Law," Ram said. "The lease can't be taken from her." But that was not the only thing. "She's white," he added, knowing the statement would enrage Karak.

"*We* are white," Karak snapped, spinning to face him.

"They don't think so," Ram said.

"What is white? What is white!" Karak's eyes had grown wide.

"What?" Ram said, not understanding.

"It is not only the color of skin!"

Ram was exasperated. "The children, then," he said. "Put the lease in Federico's name."

"She would have full control still," Karak said. "Women have too much freedom in this country."

"You want her to return to you, but you will not allow her to hold the lease?" Ram asked. Four years ago, before Adela, this would not have seemed absurd to him. But now it did.

"I will not," Karak said.

"Then Jasper Davis at the bank! Or the lawyer! Damn it! Someone who will protect us. Do you think we will survive just going on as before?"

"I won't go to another man and beg him to protect me."

"How do you think some Japanese have stayed?" He did not mention the Moriyamas.

"I am not so desperate. You think the sheriff would kick me out? Do you think Clive would betray me? For all these nine years he's made a living only because of me. I grow the crops from which he profits."

"It is not about the sheriff. It is not about Clive," Ram said. But he could not name to Karak what it was. It was how Clive acted differently when he sat next to Jonathan Hitchcock or Roubillard. The man who could be easily swayed, the man who was not himself unjust, but easily joined in another's injustice, that was a man not to be trusted.

"You have always supported Rosa," Karak said.

"What?"

"Your sympathy is with her. Do you think she will come be with you?"

"What?" Ram said again, then he understood Karak's meaning. Had the man lost his senses? Ram had never wanted Rosa. "I want to go back home, Karak."

"But in the meantime you can enjoy—"

"Now. I want to go back now." Ram had not known this truth. It had slipped from his mouth without warning. To return to a place where everyone spoke his language, where he need not explain history or food, or be trapped in the cage built of people's stares. He had held his breath for a decade. Could he finally exhale?

Karak paused, but only for a moment. "What about Adela?"

Ram's muscles tensed. He had never discussed Adela with Karak. "What concern is that of yours?"

Karak's eyes met his. Ram glared at him, daring him to continue.

Karak took a breath and his expression shifted. "Think of one last crop," he said. "All of Moriyama's land and ours together. It would fetch enough money to reestablish me. It would win back my wife and children. And you will go back like a warrior dragging a treasure chest."

Ram said nothing.

"It is only one more season. You don't mind living here," Karak insisted. "You never have. That's why you tried to bring Padma."

"That is also none of your concern," Ram said. He threw the shovel, unused, on the ground and walked to the house. The days went by and Ram did not pack his things or buy passage or close his bank account.

He had a feeling he could not name. That things could never be the same. That when he went back home, there would be another leave-taking, another death, a hole of ten years in his life's fabric.

Clive returned three days later. It was Ram who met him first, near the roadway. "We will need seed for the entire field," Ram said loudly, as Karak approached. He did not meet Karak's eye.

31

JULY 1923

H E WOULD STAY FOR A LAST LETTUCE CROP, THAT IS WHAT HE TOLD himself. Eight more months, maybe nine. Everything could remain the same until then. He need not even tell Jivan until later.

The next Sunday Ram went to the dressmaking shop at lunchtime, as usual. The street was deserted. He knocked softly and Adela opened the back door.

There must have been guilt on his face—or something else. She pulled away from him. "What is it?" she asked. Her eyes expressed his own worry. He was surprised at how well she knew him. The decision was an intangible thing, but he could feel the truth of it come between them, as if it had shape and form.

"After the harvest next spring, I will go home," he blurted out. It was a relief to say it out loud.

"Oh!" she exclaimed, then the knowledge settled. Her face flushed, slowly. "You never cared for me, did you?" she said.

This way of speaking about care was strange to him, as if care were an active thing, not prescribed by the situation. Who were they to each other, after all? Neither Punjabi nor Mexican society recognized them; how could they define themselves? They stood in a borderland, belonging to no one, to neither side, undefined. He wished he had said nothing.

"I do not get your meaning, Adela," he said. A torrent of water was rising around him. He was about to drown. "We can continue until I leave." He hoped she would be satisfied, perhaps smile just as she had when she had greeted him at the door.

"Continue what?"

"Continue—like this." His glance took in the fabric room, the clouded window and shabby curtain, the sewing machine wedged in the corner. He felt a surge of shame, then of fear.

"There is nothing to continue," she said.

"What is the matter?" he said. But she had already thrown her shawl around her shoulders, opened the door, and left him alone in that cluttered room.

He did not allow himself to go after her. There were people on the street now, and the future had just opened in an uncertain direction. He did not have the courage of the weekend before, when they had walked together outside. He waited until the people were gone, and by that time, she had disappeared.

In the days that followed, he thought about what had happened but could not understand it. For the four years they had visited that sewing room, she had known that he was married. By accepting him, she had accepted this fact. It was a simple issue—Mexican women were peculiar. Why had she run off like that?

The next Sunday he went back to the seamstress shop. Standing on the dry earth, he tapped his knuckles against the wooden door, but no one answered. He did the same the following Sunday. Then a great emptiness overtook him, and for a half hour he wandered about the town, not knowing where he walked, not caring if he was on the west side of the railroad tracks or the east. He hated her for not understanding his duty, for not understanding that he was not free.

He asked himself, over and over: In a few months he would return to his real life in Punjab, as if he had never existed in this place, so what did it matter? And yet, he could not escape the feeling—there was something of real life here too.

HE AND KARAK PLANTED BOTH FIELDS in orderly rows of lettuce seed, fertilized with chicken manure, irrigated with care. They hired Alejandro's team to weed, to thin the seedlings so the roots could go deep, but whenever the crew came, Adela was not with them.

Clive and Hitchcock came to visit as the plants turned bright green and glistened in the sunlight, as the crucial days approached for the lettuce to be harvested and packed into crates and loaded onto iced boxcars. Standing on Jivan's farmland, gazing out at Moriyama's field, Ram felt at peace. It was his last work in California and it was beautiful. Ram knew Karak thought so too. A week before the harvest, he woke to find Karak sitting on the jackrabbit stone with an expression Ram had never seen before—something between hope and fear. If all went well, the field could be worth tens of thousands of dollars. After giving Hitchcock and Clive their share, after paying back loans, they would once again have money to spare, money to buy things, money to win back a wife and family, money to say enough was enough, money to go home, dragging a treasure chest.

32

APRIL 1924

A S AN OLD MAN, RAM WOULD BELIEVE THAT IF DIFFERENT WORKERS HAD harvested that season's lettuce, on that day marking Karak's official birthday, Ram's life would have been different. For his journey was no different than any other; one small choice led to another and another, until the large thing was decided, the one that could not be avoided, a moment that determines a life.

The lettuce from Moriyama's field grew ripe first. Alejandro's crew of twelve workers arrived on Tuesday evening. A woman was with them. When Ram saw Adela, he felt a hand clutch his heart. She did not look at him. Perhaps she would cook for them, perhaps she would pick lettuce too. He promised himself that he would not approach her.

They woke the next morning before the sun rose. Hot gusts blew in from the west. The workers spread out in the first rows as sunlight leaked over the horizon. Adela was among them.

Across the acres of flat land, the view to the roadway was unbroken. Ram saw a cloud of dust rise behind a motorized vehicle. His gaze followed the truck as it moved past the packing shed, and the tool shed that stood near it, then turned off the roadway onto their land, doubling back to the structures on the farm's dirt road.

"Who is that?" Karak said.

A group of men jumped from the bed of the truck like an invading army. Ram counted about twenty of them, but could not tell who they were.

"I will go see," Karak said. Ram caught up with him and they climbed into the Model T together. By the time they arrived, the men had taken over the yard outside the packing shed, stacking crates that Ram and Karak had assembled the week before. Others moved wooden boards off the truck, taking axes to the wood to assemble more crates.

Now they could see a group of pickers that Ram did not recognize on the western edge of the field, heading down the rows with their bags. They must have accessed the field from the back path, a little-used turnoff from the roadway.

Clive stood in the packing shed with his back to them, although he must have heard them approach. He was inspecting the crates that Karak and Ram had assembled the day before.

"Clive," Karak said. The man spun around to face them.

"Who are these people?" Karak asked.

"Who do you think they are?" Clive asked lightly.

"We are using our own pickers. You know—"

"Not this time. We gotta get it outta the ground fast."

"Already my workers are here," Karak said. "Tell these people to leave."

"That ain't how we're doin' it now." Clive's face had begun to darken, a shadow under his sunburned skin traveling from neck to cheek. There was pleading in his voice, as if he wanted Karak to agree with him, to see it his way and make things easy.

Suddenly Ram knew. "Clive, you are stealing this crop from us?" he said. Outside the packing shed, they heard an axe crash through wood.

Clive's eyes darted between them. A large blond-haired man carried in a stack of board and knocked against Ram, and Ram stepped forward to regain his balance. "Stealin'," Clive said, looking relieved, as if it were easier to be indignant rather than sorry. His tone grew defiant. "You callin' me a thief?" The blond man stooped to lay the planks against the wall. When he rose, he walked past without acknowledging them. Ram felt a surge of anger. "It ain't stealing when Consolidated Fruit owns the land," Clive said.

"Two-thirds of crop is ours," Karak said.

"Two-thirds!" Clive snorted.

"What trick you are pulling here, Clive?" Karak said. They were alone again; the three of them. For a moment, after Karak asked the question, Ram saw a glimmer of the man they knew. Then he went back to unstacking the crates again, and the expression vanished.

"Best tell your pickers to leave," Clive said, "so you don't have to pay 'em too."

Ram and Karak looked at each other. Clive slammed down a crate extra hard. Karak stepped toward him but Ram held his arm. "Let's go," he said in Punjabi. "There is another way." Karak shook his arm free.

Ram took the driver's seat now, and on the eastern edge of the field he called to Alejandro. "Clive has brought over some men on his own," he said in Spanish. "Don't pay them attention. Just do your work." He was surprised to hear the command in his voice. "Don't let them take our crates, even if you have to guard them." Alejandro's confusion showed on his face.

"Force them off if you have to," Karak added.

Alejandro raised his eyebrows. He nodded. "Sí."

Ram turned the car away. "Get to the sheriff!" Karak said.

"We cannot go to the sheriff," Ram said.

"But how else—"

"What can the sheriff do, bhai? It is not legal for us to own that crop."

Karak was quiet. Breathing hard. Ram stopped at Jivan's house and Jivan stepped outside immediately.

"What is happening? I saw the truck—"

"They are seizing the crop, bhai-ji."

Jivan's expression grew hard. "Clive?"

They did not answer.

"I knew he would do something like this—" Jivan said.

"Should we go to the lawyer, to the sheriff, who?" Karak asked.

"Go to Hitchcock himself," Jivan said. "He is giving the order. Tell him that if he does such things, no one will work for him in the future."

"He doesn't care," Karak spat out. "He wants this crop, now. What does he care about who works for him in the future?"

"What else can we do, Karak?" Ram said.

Karak took a deep breath, as if to push away his panic.

THEY PARKED ON THE ROAD in front of the Consolidated Fruit offices. Karak was out of the car first, striding through the door. They found Hitchcock standing at an open file cabinet.

A clerk sat at the counter in front of him.

"How can I help you boys?" Hitchcock said, before the clerk could speak. He was wearing reading glasses, and he tipped his head forward so he could peer at Karak and Ram over the frames. Pale blue eyes assessed them. Ram felt numb.

"Hitchcock, what is the meaning of your workers in my field?" Karak said.

The clerk looked at Karak, then at Ram.

Hitchcock raised his eyebrows. He walked toward the counter. "*Your* field? Last I knew, the Consolidated Fruit Company owned that farm." His lips curled into a faint smile.

"You know our agreement," Karak said, his voice straining.

"You plant and irrigate, and you get paid for that," Hitchcock said.

Karak's words failed him.

"We get two-thirds of the crop. For months we have been working."

"And you brought in a good field too," Hitchcock said. "We'll handle it from here. Harvest and shipping are more complicated matters."

Karak lunged forward and put his hands on the counter. The clerk stood and stumbled backward. A paper floated to the floor. Karak's face was two feet from Hitchcock's. The vice president's foot edged backward.

"You are lying," Karak hissed. "From beginning, you have been lying only."

He glared at Hitchcock, and Hitchcock gazed back. They stood, frozen, for a long time, Karak's face contorted in rage. He spun on his heel and threw open the door. It slammed against the wall as he left.

"You act this way," Ram said. "Very bad."

But Hitchcock had already lost interest in them, turning quietly to his work.

"Very bad." Ram repeated. He beat his fist on the counter. Hitchcock and the clerk flinched at the sound. He had a vision of jumping across the countertop, smashing Hitchcock against the file cabinet. But he took a deep breath and followed Karak to the car. He had not known he was capable of so much anger.

RAM DROVE THEM BACK. Karak sat beside him, staring at the road, unseeing. "Clive has been drinking my whiskey, sitting at my table, laughing at me for years."

"Hitchcock is the boss," Ram said. "He made this decision. Not Clive."

"Is that so?" Karak said, in a tone that made it clear that he did not agree.

Clive was not at the farm, but his people were out in the field, in the packing shed, working at a furious pace. Acres had been cleared while they were away. Before the vehicle had come to a stop, Karak jumped out and ran toward the workers. "Get out!" he screamed, his face flushed, his voice desperate. "Get out! Get off my land!"

Ram turned off the engine and ran after him. In the field, two or three workers straightened up and began to back away. Ram caught up with Karak and grabbed his arm, led him back to the car. "That is not the way, bhai," he said.

"Even if you run one off, there are twenty others. What can we do?"

Karak's breathing slowed, but he didn't seem to be listening.

On the east side of the field, Alejandro's crew had filled a wagon full of crates with the morning's harvest. It was parked far from the packing shed, behind their camp, and the workers were gathered around, as if protecting it. Ram felt a surge of gratitude. "Look," Ram said. "We have that load and we will have at least another before all is done." Karak sat on the car's running board, gazed out into the field, and did not move.

The packing shed was still full of Clive's crew. When Ram approached, four Filipino men stood inside, staring at him suspiciously. It was his shed, Ram thought. "I need water," he said in Spanish. They said nothing. It was his olla, his water. He poured it into a tin cup and drank. An axe leaned against the wall. A saw, hammers, boxes of nails sat on a table. The men had been busy. More crates had been made, stacked all the way to the ceiling. "Where is Señor Clive?" Ram asked in Spanish.

"He left a few minutes ago," one of the men said. "He said he would return soon." Ram felt a slight alarm but did not know why. The four men lingered, staring at him silently, although their crewmates had already stopped work to eat.

When Ram returned to Karak he saw Jivan approaching too. Together, they coaxed Karak up, and the three of them walked toward Jivan's house.

"Kishen Kaur says that we will not solve this problem on an empty stomach," Jivan said. "I agree with her." He smiled faintly, but his voice was sad.

As they walked, they passed Alejandro's camp. Adela was crouched near the kerosene stove by a tent, making tortillas, and the men sat eating nearby. Ram felt a pang of jealousy. At Jivan's home he turned back to see her, to see the land. There was an unbroken view to Consolidated's motorized truck, parked with authority near their packing shed. In the other direction, mules stood hitched to the Singhs' wagons, their heads slung low. The midday sun beat down on them.

THEY SAT AT THE TABLE on Jivan's porch and ate without speaking. Kishen brought out plates of fresh rotis and dal. The truth hung heavy in the air around them: they were being robbed, slowly and painfully, while they watched, knowing there could be no retribution. Karak did not look up from his meal. He ate vigorously, his jaw working, but his expression was vacant. He rose to leave before Kishen had sat down to eat.

"Where are you going?" Jivan asked. "To rest?"

"I will go for a drive. How can I sleep today?"

"That Hitchcock is one mean fellow," Jivan said. "Everyone knows it. Our people and the Anglos too. Clive could not have worked for a worse person."

Ram knew the words were meant in sympathy, but Karak did not answer, and neither did he.

"Where are you going to drive?"

"To hell," Karak mumbled. Then, as he turned away, "It does not matter; I'll be back."

Ram watched as Karak climbed into the car. The food sat uncomfortably in his stomach. He wished he had not eaten at all.

"Bad business," Jivan said. He sucked his teeth. Suddenly, a wave of weariness overtook Ram. He said goodbye to Jivan and Kishen and walked to his cot to lie down. He was grateful to close his eyes, to escape, for just a moment.

HE SLEPT MORE DEEPLY THAN HE MEANT TO. He regained consciousness slowly, lying on his side in the heat. Ram's throat was dry. His shirt clung to his stomach, his back. The air about him did not move. The ramada's shadow lay sharply outlined against the dirt. The cow lowed from her stall. Then a shriek shattered the stillness. An animal sound, high and desperate, like a flash of light in darkness. He leaped up in a sweat. He could not breathe.

Shouts and screams were coming from the packing shed. Ram ran toward them. A man dashed out of the shed door, face contorted, grotesque, wielding something high above his head. It was Karak. A form moved on the ground nearby. Clothing and hair and dirt splashed red. A deep moan emanated from it, loud and mournful. Farther away, a man limped, desperate, pitiful, toward a familiar cream car. Karak ran for him, uttering sounds that were not words. Ram did not understand. A scarlet puddle grew around the form near the shed, then legs and arms flailed and the torso was still.

"Oye! Karak!" Ram yelled, racing to him as the packers scattered, as the workers in the field straightened up to see. He heard his own voice rise, loud and commanding. "Oye! Oye!" Later, he would wonder how he was aware of all this: Adela's skirt fluttering past, Jivan and Kishen approaching from a distance; Alejandro's men retreating to their camp.

Ram reached Karak and leaped at him, grasping for his shoulder, his leg, his torso, any way to pull him to the ground. In their combined fall, the axe was flung away. Ram had not considered its blade, and then he was on top of Karak, forcing him down. But he could not keep hold of him; his body slid on Karak's slick back. The scent of guts and blood clogged his nostrils. Ram's hands could not grasp him. He hit Karak and Karak hit him back, and in the confusion, Ram did not see that the limping man had reached the cream motorcar, that he was stooping at the front, cranking the rod. The engine spit and turned over, loud and assuring. Ram looked up to see Hitchcock scrambling into the driver's seat. His contorted face flashed in the windshield as the vehicle lurched off, erratic, its engine firing furiously.

Suddenly Karak stopped. His body went limp. Ram's fist slammed hard against his face. Blood covered them both, arms and legs and clothing. It coated Karak's hair and cheeks. Ram thought it was Karak's own, then realized there was too much—it belonged to that form that lay writhing on the ground near the shed. The tang of the blood suffocated him. Ram convulsed. The bile came up like an explosion and he vomited over the sand.

Karak was bawling, then whimpering, then bawling again, his face covered with tears and dirt and the redness. Ram sprang back in revulsion. He tasted his vomit, wiped his mouth on his sleeve.

"He called me a goddamn Hindu," Karak spat out. "Said I was worth one boxcar of lettuce. Why did you stop me? Why did you stop me?" He glared at Ram. "He told me to take my blanket and go home."

Ram forced himself to look, to turn his head although the terror had pinned him, seized control of legs and arms and mind. The body was still, laying in blood and soil. What was he seeing? The whiteness of bone? A gash near the heart? A mangled neck? A torn shoulder? With a jolt, he recognized the face.

It was Clive.

33

SHERIFF FRANK FIELDING ARRIVED IN HIS MODEL T, A CLOUD OF SMOKE and dust coming up behind him, Deputy Elijah Hollins seated by his side. Jivan had instructed Ram and Karak to sit on crates and wait near the turnoff from the roadway.

"It's our good luck that Fielding has come," Karak said, with apparent satisfaction. But Ram did not feel relieved at all. Karak began to yell as the men emerged from the motorcar. "Don't bother with me, Sheriff! Clive is out in my field. By the packing shed. Go and see him!"

The sheriff ran to the packing shed, his large form moving quickly, and then he stood for a long time, staring over the pool of blood at Clive's body.

Deputy Hollins stayed with Karak and Ram, towering over them, standing guard. Clive had been dead for an hour. Jivan had not allowed Karak to approach the body or to wash the blood from his face. He had sent Kishen back to the house.

The sheriff's face was pale as he approached them. He swallowed. "Get up," he whispered. "What did you boys do here?"

Ram rose. His legs were shaking. He felt the earth shift under him. But Karak Singh stayed on the crate, hunched over, clasping his folded legs, gazing at the dirt in front of him. "He pointed a gun at me, Sheriff. He drank my liquor and ate my food and then he pointed a gun at me. I had to do it, Sheriff—"

"Shut your mouth," Jivan said in Punjabi.

"You ask! I was mad, damn mad."

"Saliya, shut your mouth!" Ram yelled.

"You would have done the same. He was robbing from me. Robbing!"

The sheriff pulled Karak off the crate. "You're under arrest," he said roughly, placing him in handcuffs, walking him to the car.

"I know, Sheriff, I know. But go see to Clive! See to him!"

Ram waited. He thought Sheriff Fielding would come for him too, but he did not. Another police car with two officers inside turned onto the dirt road. The sheriff shouted instructions for them to stay with Hollins and climbed into his Model T. Jivan was standing near the sheriff's motorcar. Ram stumbled toward him.

The vehicle's window was open. Jivan placed his hand on the door. "Where will you hold him, Sheriff? Not Fredonia?" Jivan said. "You won't hold him in Fredonia!"

"I can't take him to El Centro until the morning," the sheriff said, leaning out the window, one hand on the steering wheel. He sounded so weary. "They had a jailbreak there." Lines had appeared on his forehead, around his eyes, but he gazed at Jivan evenly.

"Frank," Jivan said, hanging on the car window, his eyes wide with alarm, "everyone is respecting you in this town. I know." His voice was high pitched, desperate. His hand trembled as he grasped the handle of the door. "But at the jailhouse? Please! Please—"

Karak leaned forward, staring at Ram from the back seat, strangely calm, as if the men were speaking of someone else.

"I'll watch 'm," the sheriff said. "You have my word. I know about those boys from the lodge—"

Jivan gave a miniscule shake of his head. The automobile inched forward before his hand released the window, then the car stopped again.

"John," the sheriff said quietly, and Jivan stepped toward him once more. "Damn Karak for being a hothead," the sheriff said. "Get yourself a good lawyer. Try Clarence Simms. You didn't hear that from me."

34

AFTER RAM HAD WASHED CLIVE'S BLOOD FROM HIS OWN BODY, AFTER Deputy Hollins's notes were taken and the grounds searched and Clive's body removed, the farm was deserted. A ghost farm. There was no sign of Adela. Even Alejandro was gone. All the workers had run from the field after the killing. The police had set out into the desert, trying to find witnesses to question.

Ram did not know if they found anyone. And even if someone were found, he didn't know if the worker would talk to the police.

Lettuce littered the field, half-harvested. Consolidated's abandoned truck stood near the packing shed. In Alejandro's camp, tin plates lay scattered about. Adela's stove had been knocked on its side. The Singhs' wagon was still hitched to the mules. They hung their heads in the heat but balked when Ram approached. Ram unhitched the animals patiently, took them to their shed, and watered and fed them.

He left the lettuce uncovered in the wagon bed. The crop did not matter now.

Walking back to Jivan's home, he noticed movement in one of the tents. A shadow cast against the canvas. The flap of the tent opened and shut with the breeze. Perhaps one of Alejandro's workers was still here after all.

Ram bent down to peer inside. It was the prayer tent; the Virgin stood dignified in her blue robe, her hands in prayer, her face solemn. A man knelt before her, but he was not praying. He was tying a bundle together, frantic. Ram held back the tent's entrance flap and the man spun around, the dirt crunching under his heel.

"¡Señor!"

Ram could see the fear in his face, in his eyes. He was just a lad. "Where has everyone gone?" Ram asked in Spanish. The boy flinched when he heard Ram's voice. He was related to one of the older pickers—a nephew or a godson. Ram had talked to him and Alejandro the previous day about wages.

"Se han ido, señor." He did not meet Ram's eye. Ram felt a surge of pity. The boy had not asked for this.

"Let me give you something for your labor. I will give the rest to Alejandro to pay the—"

"I do not want it. None of us workers will take your payment, señor. This place has an evil spirit. Something bad has happened here. Very bad." The boy glanced at the statue of the Virgin. He made the sign of the cross.

"Did you see?" Ram asked. "Did you talk with the police?"

"I didn't see anything," the boy said, in a way that made Ram believe the opposite.

"Did anyone else?" Ram wondered if it was better or worse for Karak if someone admitted they had.

"Nobody saw anything," the boy insisted, struggling with his bundle. He glared at Ram, challenging him to disagree. He would push Ram out of the way if he had to.

Ram released the canvas flap and left him inside. He counted out two one-dollar bills for the day's wages. He left them secured under a hand spade, where the boy could see.

IN THE HOUSE, Jivan, Kishen, and Leela were at the table. A plate of food sat before Leela, untouched. The girl had been at school all day, but her mother had spoken with her, and now she was staring at Ram with liquid eyes, her lips quivering.

"What will happen to Karak Chacha?" she asked. Beside her, Kishen's face looked drawn, gray.

"He will be all right," Ram said. "He's in the jailhouse now, Leela." He stopped before he said too much. A fear was gnawing at him, something he did not want to name.

Jivan was staring into the distance, as if in a trance. Ram suddenly missed Amarjeet. His decisiveness. His ability to think quickly.

"Could we have stopped this?" Jivan asked under his breath.

"Maybe he didn't do it, bhai-ji," Ram said. "Maybe it was one of the Mexicans." He didn't know why he said this. Ram knew Karak had killed Clive. He knew that Jivan knew that too.

After a long moment, Jivan spoke. "When I was stationed in the Northern China provinces with the British, there was a camp master who was very cruel to us. One day, for some small reason, one of our young soldiers—he was from Amritsar, well-educated, but with a terrible temper—he chased down the camp master and killed him. It was a very dishonorable killing. No one should die in that way." Jivan turned toward him. His eyes were misty, clouded. "The next day, some British enlisted men found the Punjabi and shot him."

Ram swallowed. "I know," he said. "I know." He leaned forward in the chair and held his head. His temples throbbed, his eyes were burning. There had been a lynching of a Negro man in Riverside County the previous month. He knew Jivan was thinking of that too. Ram imagined the town's menfolk clamoring at the door of the jailhouse, forcing the sheriff to give up Karak. The fear sat like ice in his belly. He stood up abruptly. "We must go," he said. They looked up at him.

"Where?" Leela asked.

"Bhai-ji—" Ram said. There was an edge to his voice.

Jivan rose slowly, strode to the door, and put on his boots. He turned to look at Kishen and Leela. He suddenly seemed a much older man.

"We must go help Karak Chacha now," Ram said. "We'll return late. You eat your dinner and sleep." Leela stared at him. "Take care of your mother, Leela," Ram said.

Kishen moved toward her daughter and put her arm around her shoulders. "You go," she said. "Don't worry about us."

In the bedroom, in the large trunk, Ram found Jivan's shotgun and some ammunition hidden among the folded bedsheets. He paused at the threshold.

"Lock the doors," he said. "Don't let anyone in."

"No," Kishen agreed, as they left. Ram heard the door latch behind him.

They climbed into the car and started down the farm road. Across Jivan's cantaloupe field, inside Karak's home, Ram saw a flicker, a glow. He felt a chill.

"Did you see that, bhai-ji?"

"What?" Jivan asked. He was not himself, Ram thought. Jivan seemed fragile now.

He kept his eyes on the window in the distance and saw the glow again, as if someone had moved a lamp near the glass, then covered it.

Ram scrambled from the car and ran to the door of Karak's home. The light was gone again. His knuckles rapped against the wood. There was no answer.

"Open up! Whoever is there! Open up!"

Stillness, silence.

Ram pushed on the door with his full might. It groaned. He stepped back and slammed his shoulder against it, and the latch gave way all at once.

Moonlight filtered through the window. A form was crouched on the cot in the sitting room. Even in the gloom, he recognized

Adela instantly. She had pulled a blanket around herself and was huddled against the wall, eyes wide, hair unkempt. The lamp sat near her on the ground, unlit now. "Adela!" he said. He heard her whimper. "Adela!" He crossed the distance between them in two large steps and clasped her to him. She began to shudder, gulping in air.

"Why are you here? Why did you not come to the house?" His fingers scrambled for the matches, for the lamp, almost knocking it over.

She looked at him with hollow eyes. But she was relieved to see him. That was clear. Her expression told him she had witnessed everything. He was sure of it.

"I ran here," she whispered. "I ran here—afterwards."

"Where is Alejandro?"

"People were scared. They wanted to go. They took our burros."

He held her.

She wriggled in his grasp. "I know how to take care of myself," she said. She covered her face with her hands. "Alejandro's coming back right now, I'm sure. In the morning, maybe."

Ram felt a surge of anger against Alejandro. Behind him, he sensed Jivan's presence and turned. The older man stood in the doorway, watching them.

Adela did not notice. "It is all right. When Father died, it was all okay within a day. That is how these things are."

"You saw it happen," Ram said. It was not a question.

She looked at her lap. Her vacant eyes alarmed him.

"Ram," Jivan said.

They had to protect Karak. He could not stay here.

"Come," Ram said. "I will take you home."

She did not move.

He got up and gathered the blanket around her. Then she refused his help, walked to the car on her own, and climbed into the back seat. She was shivering, although the night held the April warmth.

Jivan followed them out. "Karak has a pistol," he said, reminding Ram.

"Yes," Ram said.

He found it in the place where Karak usually kept it, on the top shelf of a cupboard in the kitchen. Ram did not like the weight of it inside his pocket.

They rode in silence, Ram driving, Jivan staring at the glow of headlights on black roadway. Adela sat almost invisible in the darkness in back. The moon shone on the skin of the sand dunes. Adela said calmly, "The Lord knows Karak is not a good man. But if that other had not pointed his gun at Karak, he would not have attacked him." Ram and Jivan exchanged a glance.

"Which man?" Ram asked.

"The one who . . . the man who . . . What is it you call him? Clive."

"He took out his gun?"

"The other man was watching this," Adela said.

"Other?"

"Jefe. The cripple with a handsome face. Karak became too angry. You know how he does. Clive told him to take his blanket and go home. Take it and go." Her voice was monotone.

"Clive pointed a gun at Karak?" Ram blurted out.

"How can someone say, 'Take your blanket and go'? As if that man were nothing? How can he say, 'A Hindu is worth only a boxcar of lettuce'? When he has grown the crop himself? How—" The words caught in her throat. "Karak is not a nice—"

"Which man had the gun, Ad—"

"Ram—" Jivan interjected.

Adela fell quiet. Ram silently berated himself for his impatience. He heard a muffled sob and realized that she was crying.

"Peace, daughter," Jivan said. Dark fields sped past their windows. The car sputtered under them.

After a few moments, Adela spoke again. "Karak held an axe.

Clive has a gun. Did you know? Clive has a gun? The handsome man, the cripple . . . There was blood on his leg. It was not his blood!" She said the words lightly, as if memorizing them, as if making sense of them to herself. "He was scared after Karak . . . after Karak . . ."

Ram shuddered. What had happened after the moment Clive was holding the gun? What had Karak done?

"You must tell them, Adela," Jivan said.

"What?" Her eyes grew wide with alarm.

"You must tell them."

"Tell what?"

"Tell the sheriff about the gun. It will help Karak."

"After what he has done to Rosa?" she spat out. "Everyone knows—"

"They will hang him—" Jivan said forcefully.

"Bhai-ji—" Ram said.

"Already everyone despises me," Adela whispered, as if defeated. "If I tell, our neighbors will run me out of town. They threaten me—"

"Why?" Ram asked. He half-turned in his seat and glanced back at her.

"You don't know?" Moonlight streamed inside the car. Her eyes looked into his. Her face was filled with disdain. The car swerved to the right then recovered.

He turned back to the road and shook his head slightly.

"Because of you. Because . . . everyone knows . . ."

He was quiet. He had not been aware of this. He felt Jivan's gaze on him.

"So answer me—" she said.

"Because it is the truth," Jivan said.

She did not speak for the remainder of the ride. At the barrio, Ram walked with her to Alejandro and Esperanza's front door.

Alejandro answered his knock, Esperanza stood behind him. She had been crying, and when she saw Adela, she made the sign of the cross. "Gloria a dios," she said. Her voice held a tremor. She

helped Adela to the chair in the front room. In those moments before
Alejandro and Esperanza could acknowledge him, before Rosa appeared, Ram slipped back outside.

AFTER THEY DROVE across the railroad tracks into town, Jivan said,
"First thing is we need a lawyer. I do not want some fellow who the
court will assign. I want Clarence Simms." Simms had represented
Harnam Singh recently, in a case where he had been accused of as-
saulting his cousin. Harnam had spoken well of him.

"We will get him," Ram said.

"We cannot afford him."

"We can. We will," Ram said.

At the Western Union office, they sent a telegram to Amarjeet.
They needed money and Amarjeet was making a steady income.

"I am ashamed to send such a message to my nephew," Jivan said,
when they were seated again in the car.

Ram grew irate. It was not a moment for such reflection or for
shame, or for respectability. "It doesn't matter," he said. "Night is almost here. Let's eat and go to the jailhouse." When Jivan grew quiet,
he regretted his tone.

They went to the Chinese settlement, and in a small, empty
café, they saw Malik Khan seated at a table, alone. He was in street
clothes, perhaps finishing errands in town. He hailed them, smiling.
They bought their bowls of steaming noodles and sat with him.

As soon as they were seated, Jivan blurted out, "Karak attacked
Clive Edgar." Ram knew there could be no secrets now, but he felt a
flash of embarrassment for Karak. All the Hindustanees knew that
Malik and Karak had never liked each other. Karak would have
minded Jivan's outburst.

Malik grinned. At one time, Clive had worked as the Khan
brothers' land agent too. "Karak can never control his temper. And
Clive has changed in recent months. Perhaps he deserved it."

"Clive is dead," Ram said.

Malik's smile faded. His eyes grew wide as the news settled, as he realized what it meant.

"Consolidated was seizing our lettuce crop," Ram said. "They meant to sell it as their own."

Malik snorted. There was anger in his eyes. Ram did not have to spell out more. Malik knew they would have no recourse after Consolidated's theft. It was the Hindustanees who were breaking the law.

"They're holding him in the Fredonia jailhouse," Ram said. "The sheriff is keeping watch—"

"But who else will be there?" Malik asked.

Ram knew he was thinking of the lynching in Riverside. The man had been hung from a mesquite on the main roadway.

"Hollins?" Malik said. "He's no good, that Hollins. He will not hold back a crowd." His expression grew hard. "He will not want to."

"Sheriff said they'll move him to El Centro tomorrow," Ram said.

"But tonight," Jivan added. "That is the worry."

Surely the men from the lodge already knew. From the legion too. Those organizations were large; it would be hard to hold back all those men. By tomorrow morning, the entire town would know.

"Does he have a lawyer?" Malik asked.

"We want Clarence Simms," Jivan said. "He is expensive."

It had been only a few hours since the killing, and Ram was starting to glimpse the future: Karak would go to trial. He might hang. What would happen for Ram's plan to leave for India?

"Don't worry, bhai-ji," Malik said to Jivan. "God will provide for us."

They finished their meal without speaking. Malik rose first. "I always thought something could happen like this, with Karak's temper," he said. "Don't worry," he said again, opening his billfold with stubby, rough fingers. Dirt was lodged under each nail.

"Take this." He grasped Ram's hand and pressed a bundle of

notes into his palm. "For the lawyer. Nobody has had a prosperous year."

"No, no," Jivan said before Ram could respond. "A Sikh does not take help from anybody." He shook his head, walking away.

"Bhai-ji," Malik said sharply, his eyebrows knit. "Now is not the time to be proud. Not after all the help you have given everyone here. That Clive, he is—was—turning into a bad man. Ever since he's worked for Hitchcock. There is something British about him." Then, as if he had just thought of it, "There is something British about them both."

Ram folded the bills tightly and stuffed them in his pocket.

IN THE DARKNESS, Ram and Jivan stopped the car at the Edgar Bros. general store. The jailhouse was a quarter mile down the street on the left. The slope of Superstition Mountain rose nearby.

They were quiet. Cicadas droned from the scrub.

"It was stupid to come," Jivan said.

"No," Ram said. He placed the guns in the back of the automobile, where they couldn't be seen. They would be only a few steps away. "We will not need to use these," he said. But he wasn't sure.

"The sheriff will be able to protect him," Jivan insisted.

"Bhai-ji," Ram said, out of respect, but he puzzled at Jivan's change of heart. The night air carried dust and chalk. After an hour, a warm wind picked up from the west. Ram smelled a strange odor sweeping through, like the rotted pungence of the Hambelton canneries.

At nine thirty, when the moon had risen and dimmed the stars, they saw a wagon in the distance, traveling toward them. Five men rode inside. Ram could not see who they were. The hair on his neck bristled. He suddenly felt helpless, small. How could he and Jivan hold off a group of Anglos who wanted Karak?

But as the wagon drew near, he noticed the dastars. Closer still, and he recognized the men: Harnam Singh, Hukam Singh, Ganga

Singh, riding in the back of a wagon driven by Malik Khan, sitting next to Sikander. Relief swept through Ram. His muscles went limp. He saw the glint of moonlight on a rifle.

Jivan said only "They have come?" as if he had known they would.

The men exchanged nods. They situated the horses behind the power generator and deposited their guns in the back of the wagon. Seated on the mound of dirt near the facility, they had an unbroken view down the street to the jailhouse. The sheriff had left the electric light on inside the jail. His motorcar, and that of Deputy Hollins, stood nearby.

A while later, another automobile trundled down the road. It was Inder and Husain and Ganesh, all the way from Calipatria. Jivan stood up. One by one, he held their hands in his own. A half hour afterward, eight more countrymen came from Holtville; then eleven from Brawley, seven from El Centro, three from Westmoreland. They came from Calexico, Imperial, Niland. By the time the moon was high, fifty-five men had gathered.

The Punjabis sat in the darkness and watched. Hidden by the generator, they would not be noticed from the street. They might be mistaken for the shadows of tumbleweed, creosote, greasewood. Ram placed himself next to Jivan, facing the roadway, his back to the others. He imagined Karak a few hundred feet away, huddled inside a dirt-floored cell, chasing out desert mice and scorpions. Would he suspect they were watching over him? Would he care? Ram felt Jivan's hand on his arm. Weariness made itself known in his sunken cheeks, his lined brow, the loose jowls. Ram wondered, how had Jivan aged so fast?

THE WHITE MEN CAME IN THE DEAD OF NIGHT, when the moon neared the outline of Superstition Mountain. In its silver glow, carrying guns, walking in a loose pack past the Punjabi men, they did not look real.

Ram counted thirty-one. They had been drinking. Ram sensed the bootleg in their uneven gaits, in the not-so-hushed whispers. As they approached the jailhouse, one man yelled out, "Deputy Elijah Hollins! We know you're in there." His voice traveled like an arrow to where the Punjabis hunkered, listening. "Let us in now! We just want to have a word with your new guest." There was no answer. "You know the one we're talking about! That one got Clive Edgar. We want that towelhead got Clive." Angry laughter. The Punjabis were as quiet as death, frozen, listening.

A man in the back fired a gun into the air. The sound vibrated through Ram's breast. He felt the men around him flinch.

The door of the jailhouse opened slowly. The sheriff's silhouette emerged as the electric light shone around him. "Last I checked, it's against the law in this county to be firin' a weapon for no reason." His gruff voice rose high in the night air. He stepped outside, shutting the jailhouse door, placing himself in front of it. He stood on the boardwalk, a foot taller than the rest of the men.

"Sheriff—fancy you bein' here," a voice said.

"I'm askin' you gentlemen to calm yourselves or I'll arrest you for disturbin' the peace." His words pierced the night air, echoing like a coyote's howl.

"You go on an' arrest us, Sheriff. We'll be glad to spend some time with that Hindu you got in there now." More laughter.

"Come to think—why *don't* you arrest us? Arrest the whole damn lot of us."

Ram saw the sheriff standing in front of the door, his hands on his belt, making himself as big as possible. "You fellas quiet down now," he said. "I know you were talkin' over at the lodge tonight. You all are good men, you got wives and children to go home to. They don't want to wake up tomorrow morning and hear their menfolk got themselves into trouble."

"Why don't you send Deputy Hollins out here to talk with us, Sheriff?"

"Deputy Hollins ain't available right now. I'm available. And I'm tellin' you: go home."

"Don't think we can do that," someone said from the back. There was a challenge in that voice. The dark pantry in Hambelton flashed before Ram's eyes. A cluster of men, the weight of fear. The still form that had lain on the ground that night. He shook his head, forcing himself back to the present. The men around him shifted. A cricket chirped in the shrub. Bats emerged from the mesquite, their wings darker than the night, and swept over the jailhouse gathering. The sheriff stood alone between the Anglo men and the door.

A lamp hung on a hook next to him, and the sheriff fished a match out of his pocket and lit it. A circle of gold surrounded him, separate from the glow of the single bulb that shone through the jailhouse window. "I can see all of you now," he said. "I can see right back to Harlan there."

A man in the front said, "I tell you what, Sheriff, how 'bout you let us in there and let us take what we want, and we won't tell anyone you done that."

"Always knew you were the smart one, Cyril," another voice said, slurring the words.

Ram looked at his countrymen around him. He could not see their expressions, but he could feel their anger, as if it were a living thing. Gugar leaned toward him. "Let's go," he whispered. Ram was sure he meant to fetch his gun.

"No!" he hissed. "Stay here!" He looked at Jivan. The older man had closed his eyes, merely listening. Ram felt a moment of alarm. Suddenly he knew everything depended only on him.

Gugar gestured toward the wagons and cars, his jaw set in defiance, his eyes wide, as if he wouldn't comply with Ram's wishes any longer. Ram was being called upon to act and he knew he would fail; what he should say or do would grow clear only days or months or years from now, when it would be too late. Just as it had in Hambelton.

Suddenly, Ram sprang out in front of the cluster of Punjabi men and ran toward the jailhouse. He could not feel his legs move. The sand muffled his footfall. "Good evening, Sheriff Fielding," he called. He was out of breath, but it was not from running.

All heads turned, startled.

The sheriff squinted into the night toward him. "Ram Singh? What are you doing here?" An expression crossed his face. Relief? Surprise?

"Sheriff. Just I come to visit my friend," Ram said. His voice quivered. He spoke louder to cover it up. "I didn't know—so many people here." He made himself look at the faces of the drunken men. In the lantern's light, their skin looked gray, unnatural, cloaked in shadow. Most were without hats and their hair lay tousled, their clothes uneven. The odor of dried sweat hung about them. Karak would have known who they were. He would have recognized several of the voices, the faces, been aware of who was friends with whom. Some of the Hindustanees standing behind Ram would know such things too.

It came as a revelation: these were not the town's powerful and wealthy. In their shabby clothes and scuffed boots, he saw men who labored in the soil, small-time farmers, soldiers who had returned from war and not found their place. He counted only four rifles among them.

"Your friend also in jailhouse?" he said. The light was shining full on him, and he knew they saw every expression, although he could only see their faces dimly, in half shadow. He forced himself to smile. "Oye! These jailhouse friends!" He forced himself to shake his head, as if in good-natured disbelief. *What shall we do with our jailhouse friends?*

The sheriff watched him with his mouth open, as if about to speak. The door creaked and swung out and Deputy Hollins emerged from the building and stood in the lantern's glow. For a moment his eyes locked with Ram's.

"Sheriff, visiting hours is now?" Ram continued. "Because I have many people, many many people who come also to visit my friend. I told to them, wait until daytime." Ram looked skyward. "You know—sun is coming out." He signaled for the other Punjabis to join him, a small wave of his right hand near his right hip. *Come into the light,* the hand said. *Come without your guns. Just your presence is enough.*

He heard their boots padding against the soft sand. The Anglos tilted their heads, looking at something behind him. Ram made a show of turning to see. Malik Khan stood nearest the light, Gugar Singh a bit behind. Their hands were empty.

He felt a surge of courage and turned back to the sheriff. "I told them, wait. But, see, they come anyway!" Again, his eyes scanned the Anglos clustered around the jailhouse. Was it possible? Something had changed now; there was less menace in their stances. Less defiance in their faces. Is that all it had taken? That they saw real people on the other side?

A sense of pity swept through him. Had these farmers not suffered under men like Jonathan Hitchcock too? Hadn't the shipping companies cheated them, allowed their picked fruit to rot on the roadside so they could maintain market price, sent harvesters to their fields only when it was too late?

"You people really smart, very smart," Ram said. "You bring guns. In case coyotes and gophers or some danger come—like this." He snapped his fingers. "Suddenly!"

How many, in their darkest moments, had dreamed of doing what Karak did?

"Us Hindus don't know so good the ways here. We keep guns nearby. We think—we get them *if* coyotes come. If." He spoke softly. "We don't want to use."

The Punjabis shuffled in the sand and dirt behind him. He heard the sound of a cleared throat. A sniffle. *Ram Singh,* he imagined them saying. *Very good, Ram Singh.* A cough smothered the chirp of the crickets. *Well spoken.* He turned again. They stood together, some with arms folded across chests, some with turbans, wide stances, direct stares. They looked like order, he thought. They looked like civilization.

Despite his unsteady legs, despite the sweat running down his back, Ram saw the truth: the Hindustanees outnumbered the Anglos by almost two to one.

"Oh God! I told—wait until daytime. They come anyway. Sorry, Sheriff. Sorry."

"Eugene. Harlan." Deputy Hollins's voice rang out through the darkness. "Why don't y'all take the others and go home. Your families'll be looking for you."

The men didn't move.

From the edge of the pack, a man lunged at Ram. "That no-good goddamn—" He swung at Ram's face, but Ram lurched backward and the man's fist caught air.

"Towel-headed nigger killed a man in cold blood—"

"Oye!" Gugar Singh shouted behind him. Anger swept through Ram, an emotion he should have felt years before.

"I'll kill—" the Anglo said, but others were holding him back.

"You won't!" Ram said.

"I'll *kill* you—"

A shot rang out. Heads turned. Deputy Hollins was pointing his pistol into the air. The sour scent of gunpowder wafted through the night.

"Get out of here, Cyril," Hollins said, "before I have to bring you in." He jerked his head to the right. The gesture said, *There will be another time.* The gesture said, *The sheriff is watching.*

Ram could see its effect sweep through the crowd. The men looked at each other. "Go on now," Deputy Hollins said. "This ain't the proper time nor place." Their feet shuffled. Some of them began to move.

"This ain't the last of this, Sheriff," the man named Cyril called out. "Hollins, I expected different from you—I thought you were one of us."

"Whether he's one of you or not don't make no difference, Cyril," the sheriff said, "he's a man of the law." Ram saw the sheriff look at his deputy, but Hollins looked away.

"You too, Ram Singh," the sheriff said. "You and your people get on along. I don't need any trouble on your end. All you men stay away from each other. If I hear one thing happening between any of the men in this county tonight, I'll drag you in and slam you all into the jailhouse together and ship you off to L.A. in the morning. You won't have no judge or jury or nothin'."

"Sure, Sheriff," one of the Anglos said. Some had already started up the road.

Sheriff Fielding opened the door and gestured for Hollins to go back in. The sheriff remained outside a few moments, making sure the men dispersed.

The Punjabis began to walk back toward their vehicles. Ram turned to follow them.

"Ram," the sheriff called out again. "Over here." He stayed on the boardwalk and waited for Ram to draw near.

"You know something I don't about Clive Edgar? He have a gun?"

"No." Ram swallowed, surprised at the quick lie. "I don't know, sir."

The sheriff stared at him, as if sizing him up. "We found three Spics near the property and questioned them. They told me they hadn't seen a thing. Couldn't find any more."

Ram made himself look into the sheriff's face.

"Two days from now, Karak's going to be charged with murder. He keeps saying Clive had a gun, but we didn't find a gun there." The sheriff looked him in the eye. "Could be the difference between him hanging or not hanging."

Ram felt his mouth go dry. His heart beat loudly in his ears.

"That means either he's lying, or there's a gun around that got taken or lost. You want to save your friend's life, you might see if someone knows something about that."

"Sheriff," Ram said. He had to close his eyes. When he opened them, the sheriff was still staring at him, assessing.

"You and your friends make yourself scarce. I don't want to hear no more from you tonight."

But the Punjabis did not leave. They sat on their roost near the generator long after the sheriff went inside the jailhouse. Surely the sheriff knew they were out there and let them stay.

35

THE MEXICAN BOY HAD BEEN RIGHT. THE LETTUCE FIELD HAD AN EVIL spirit. Ram sat in view of the Moriyama house on a crate under a mesquite. The spot had always been a place of rest. Clive had died on the other corner of the field, far away. He had not ventured there— since. Perhaps he never would.

The Mexicans' camp had been cleared. He wondered when they had come. The field was half-harvested and plants were beginning to wilt. Already he could smell the acrid scent of lettuce spoiled in the heat.

The future was a blank wall beyond which he could not see. The money that he had dreamed about would not arrive. He wanted to go back to Punjab, to the wife and son waiting for him, to return to the life he should have had. He had saved Karak's life at the jail-house, though he had not been able to save the men in Hambelton. He could not help Karak any more now.

Across the unbroken view of the field, he saw Jivan walking to-ward him. Ram watched his progress, crossing the furrows in the broken earth. When he reached Ram, he pulled up another crate and sat down.

"What did the sheriff ask you yesterday?" Jivan asked.

"When?"

"When the Anglos had left. When he spoke to you privately." Ram was surprised that Jivan remembered. For the first time, he did not want Jivan's opinion. But he could not lie.

"He asked why Karak says that Clive had a gun."

"What did you say?"

"I told him I don't know."

Jivan looked at him. Ram felt his own weakness. It was Karak's life they were talking about.

"She must tell, Ram."

"She is just a village girl. No one will believe her." But he knew Jivan sensed the real reason. He could not hurt her. He thought of how she had fought off the man who approached her after her husband died. He remembered her despair when she told that story.

"They will hang him," Jivan said.

"They will be cruel to her." He did not know whether he meant the Anglos in the courtroom, or the Mexicans in the barrio.

"Why should they be cruel to her? You cannot allow yourself to be misguided. His life is worth more than that."

Ram felt a stab of anger. Jivan, of all people, knew best the unwritten rules of the Valley. Karak and Jivan and Ram were aliens, and they would never be equal to the Anglo men. But Adela was a Mexican, and just a woman. She counted for nothing at all.

"He killed a man, bhai-ji."

"It was not without reason. For that, he deserves to die? Have you no loyalty?" Jivan's voice was hard.

That is not what Ram meant. "He has ruined me," Ram said. But that was not what he meant either.

36

KARAK'S ARRAIGNMENT WAS IN THE SAME COURTHOUSE WHERE THE Singhs had come for Karak and Rosa's wedding years ago. In the intervening years they had come to file for Karak's bankruptcy, for Jivan's purchase of land. But in Ram's mind it was full of ill will, the place where Karak had been classified as brown and Rosa as white, where they couldn't marry.

With Malik Khan's money, they had retained the attorney, Clarence Simms. Karak's case was written up in the newspapers, gossiped about at dinner tables and social clubs all over the Valley, and Simms was eager to represent Karak Singh. But funds were short. They had visited Jasper Davis at the bank, and he had used the Model T as collateral and lent them some more. In these two days, they had not heard from Amarjeet.

As Jivan and Ram reached the top of the courthouse steps, Ram saw four Anglo men loitering outside. "Goin' in there to get the hangman's noose, boys?" one of them said, in a voice that slithered. "You gonna need it."

Jivan was walking ahead of him and Ram turned to look at the man, but said nothing. He felt a presence from behind, the heat of a body against his back.

"What's the matter, towelhead?" another voice said. "If the law don't get your friend, you know we will. Get him tonight, as a matter of fact." Ram swiveled to find the source of the voice. A broad-brimmed hat, a sunburned face, familiar from town streets. The man smirked and winked. The first Anglo wedged his body between Jivan and the door and would not let Jivan pass. A young man harassing an old one. Ram stepped forward, past Jivan, and pushed the young man out of the way.

Perhaps Jivan was off balance already; when Ram spun around, Jivan lay on the ground, the second Anglo looking down at him, laughing. Jivan had landed on his back and side. He pushed himself up on his elbow. Onlookers yelled from the street. A policeman was approaching. Ram did not want a scene. He stooped to help Jivan up and they rushed inside.

A crowd was milling at the door of the courtroom in which Karak would be formally charged. When Jivan and Ram pushed themselves to the front, the crowd jeered. The bailiff asked, "You are family?" Ram nodded. He let them pass.

Inside the courtroom, it was calmer. Faces turned to greet them: Gugar Singh, Malik Khan, Harnam Singh. Ram's throat constricted with emotion. Farther away from the aisle sat another man, wearing a neatly wrapped blue dastar. He rose to greet them. Only then did Ram recognize Amarjeet. Jivan clasped his nephew's hands in both his own, tears welling in his eyes. "Chacha-ji!" Amarjeet whispered. His face had grown thin, even gaunt. He was young but not youthful.

Amarjeet sat between them. Reaching inside his suit jacket, Amarjeet brought out a small cloth bag, held it between slender fingers. He unwound a thick roll of bills. Jivan's eyes grew wide. "Where did this come from?" he whispered.

"The granthi at the gurdwara telegrammed requests for support of Karak Singh. So many of our countrymen gave. Even from Vancouver and New York and Philadelphia."

Ram stared at the money. Were there Hindustanees that far away who felt for Karak? Did they think Karak had done nothing wrong? He remembered Jivan's accusation by the lettuce field. Perhaps Jivan was right; he *was* disloyal.

Clarence Simms entered the room and nodded at Jivan and Ram. His eyes swept over the other Hindustani men seated there. He was a slight man who rarely smiled. Ram did not understand why he was so respected. When they had visited him the previous day at his office, he would not look them in the eye. His voice was too soft. Ram wanted him to state an opinion about the murder, the weather, anything, but the man would not.

Simms settled himself at the table in front, next to the table where the district attorney sat.

The courtroom was full now: reporters from the Valley papers, men who led the American Legion, the Chamber of Commerce. The air was filled with their respectful murmur. In the far corner sat Clive's wife and his in-laws. Kate Edgar was wearing a black dress, a black hat with a veil. She sat with her eyes lowered, meeting no one's gaze.

It hit Ram fully, then. Clive Edgar was dead. There was a woman without a husband. There were children without a father—just as Ram had grown up, just as his son was growing up, far away. Karak Singh was responsible. How had he befriended a man who could do such an act? How could Ram hope for his release? Yet he did. He *was* loyal to Karak. The feeling came as a revelation.

The door to the side of the judge's dais opened and Karak appeared, wearing handcuffs and led by the bailiff. The air grew charged. Bodies shifted and people craned their necks to see. Karak searched the crowd. His eyes locked on Ram. He had shaved and was wearing the pants and dress shirt that Ram had fetched for him, but his skin was gray, his eyes sunken and dark. In the two days since Ram had seen him, deep lines had appeared around his eyes and mouth. What had the man experienced in those two days?

The bailiff removed his handcuffs, and Karak sat down at the table next to Simms, his back to Ram and Jivan and Amarjeet, facing the judge's empty chair. They all rose when the judge entered. The courtroom was still as he settled himself in his chair, as he straightened his robes. His face conveyed no expression. As the charges were read, he addressed no one other than Clarence Simms and the district attorney.

Karak's shoulders slumped, his head bent before the judge. He stood almost a head taller than his lawyer, but seemed the meeker man.

"How do you plead?" the judge asked, finally looking at Karak.

Ram heard Karak clear his throat. A familiar sound.

Clarence Simms cut in. His voice was stern and magnetic; not the same voice that Ram had heard in his office. It was a voice to which people listened, that knew command. "Not guilty, your honor. By reason of insanity." A murmur rose from the audience.

"But I was not crazy, your honor," Karak said. "I had a reason, I was damn mad—"

"Keep a civil tongue, Mr. Singh," the judge said dryly.

Karak turned around to look at them, and Ram wished he had not. He saw despair in Karak's face, humiliation. He was already a changed man. For a moment, Karak's eyes rested on Amarjeet, as if only now recognizing him, realizing he was there.

"I'm setting the trial for June eighteenth," the judge said. "Nine weeks."

THEY KEPT HIM IN A CELL at the back of the courthouse, and the sheriff allowed him visitors, but only one at a time. In the waiting room, Jivan said that Ram should be the first.

Ram hesitated to go. He feared being alone with Karak now; the man's misfortune was too great. But he followed the bailiff through a short, dark hallway, where three cells lined one side. Karak was in the middle. The other two were empty. He had changed back into the striped prison uniform. He was wearing shackles on his legs. They had finally vanquished him, Ram thought. Made him do the thing for which he could be legitimately punished. But Ram could not name who "they" were.

Ram brushed up against the bars of the cage. A small window near the ceiling allowed a ray of sunlight. Karak turned toward him and the chains on his legs rattled. Ram could feel their weight on his own ankles. How could Karak come forward when he was wearing those chains, even if they were long enough?

They stared at each other. Up close, Ram could see what he did not in the courtroom: the gray hollows under Karak's eyes, the sagging muscles in his cheeks, the grief.

"I did it for both of us, you know that," Karak said.

Ram was surprised by his bravado, the attempt at justification.

"Our treasure chest," Karak said.

Despite himself, Ram said, "Yes, I know."

"I was mad. Damn mad."

Ram was silent. He did not want to hear those words again.

"They won't quarrel with us Hindus anymore. Now they know we won't tolerate it. Even if I hang."

"They won't dare quarrel with us, Karak," Ram said, to mollify him. He stared at his own boots, at the line where the iron bars met the floor. From this narrow vantage, it was unclear which one of them was imprisoned.

They did not speak for a while. Karak sat on the bench, holding his head between his hands. Ram remained standing near the bars. It was comforting to be there, to stand silently with Karak in the sadness. Ram had not expected this.

Finally he said, "Jivan Singh. Amarjeet Singh. Kishen Kaur. Everyone seeks the best for you. Everyone is fighting."

Karak nodded, but he did not come closer.

Ram could think of nothing more to say. Then his mother's voice came to him, intoning a sacred phrase. "In the remembrance of the Divine, there is no fear of death. In the remembrance of the Divine, all hopes are fulfilled."

Karak closed his eyes.

Night was falling. Ram turned to go.

"Please," Karak said, "ask Rosa to come see me. I will spend the night here. She can come in the morning. They'll take me back to El Centro afterward."

"I'll do that, Karak," he said.

37

KARAK HAD NOT BEEN INSIDE A JAILHOUSE SINCE HIS DAYS IN HONG Kong, when he had brawled with a white British soldier. They had called it the "brig." In the afternoons, they had been let out for exercise and every meal consisted only of rice with a dried paste. He shared the cell with a family of mice. But when Karak's lieutenant learned that Karak was there, he managed to free him in just two days. That lieutenant had liked Karak. He had watched out for him. Sometimes they drank together, although afterward, the lieutenant would visit the Filipino brothel where the white officers went, where Karak was not allowed.

Now, it was different. He had killed a man. There had been a moment of rage when he had not known what he was doing. Even now, he did not know, exactly, what happened. Only that Clive had arrived and stood in the shed near the door. That Hitchcock was with them. That Karak had been breaking up wood to make more crates, because Consolidated's workers had taken the ones that he and Ram had made.

If they were by themselves, Clive and Karak would be civil, decent, understand that they were both men. But with Hitchcock present, Clive could pull that gun out of his holster and point it at Karak.

That same gun that he had shown off to Karak years before, when he had announced his engagement to his wife, drinking Karak's whiskey in Jivan's yard. Karak had held that gun then—pearl inlay in the grip, Clive's initials engraved on the barrel—he had felt the weight of it in his hand. With Hitchcock there, Clive could laugh at Karak. He could tell Karak to take his blanket and go home.

A glimmer of sunlight had caught the revolver's barrel, bounced off the perfect circle of its muzzle.

They say rage blinds one, but it is not true. Rage takes away more than sight. It robs hearing and taste, feeling and reason, leaving only the ancient scent of fear and anger and the need to destroy. Karak had wrapped his hands around the axe's wooden handle. The wood had felt solid, heavy, satisfying. And when he lifted it to swing—that had felt good too. The man collapsed, his life bled out on the land Karak knew so well, where the dirt turned to sand, where the shadow of the packing shed appeared in late afternoon. Where, when the wind blew from the northwest, he could smell Kishen Kaur's cooking across the unbroken distance.

Karak had not been crazy when he had killed Clive. He would not absolve the Anglos of their guilt by accepting that. He had been enraged because they threatened his life, his existence. There was a difference.

Now, strangely, he felt closer to Clive than ever. He felt the man inside him, like someone he had loved. As if he would step through the doorway soon, to visit. *What's that hellfire got into you out there?* Clive would say, laughing his raspy laugh. *Why you acting different when Hitchcock is near?* Karak would ask, handing him a glass of whiskey. Was he dead? Had he killed him? He could not clear his head.

At the end of the hallway, Karak heard the sound of the wooden door scraping against the floor. He heard Sheriff Fielding's voice, then Ram's, and a woman's muffled answer. The door closed again.

He stood as Rosa approached the cell. He knew how much he

had changed from the way she looked at him. His chains shifted and rattled, but something humiliated him even more—he had led Rosa to this place, where prostitutes and thieves came, where lowly drifters stayed the night before they were run out of town. They had lived together in a house, owned a car, a piano. Now the sheriff, Hollins, Jasper Davis, all of them would know that his wife had stepped into this place because of him. He had last seen her several weeks before, when the lettuce was being thinned. When that lettuce field would have set everything right again.

"Entonces, ¿es verdad?" she finally asked. Her voice sounded deeper than usual, bouncing off the hard brick walls, filling the empty space of the cell.

"It is not true in the way they say it happened," he said in Spanish.

She frowned, tilted her head. "What do you mean?" The words caught in her throat.

Karak drew closer. She was looking at him with anger, eyebrows knit, but also distance, as if she did not recognize him. He could not tell if she had been crying. She had lost her youth, but still, he felt drawn to her. She had worn her best dress. The dress protected her against the dirtiness he had brought to her, protected her against him and what he had done.

He felt a familiar resentment stir again. After all, he had done it for her, hadn't he? Because that lettuce would have earned the money that would have brought her back, he was sure of it.

"I am not crazy, Rosa, as that lawyer said." His hands gripped the bars. "I was mad. A farmer has a right to be mad when his crop is stolen from him." He was tired of explaining this to everyone.

She seemed frightened by his fervor. Her silence left him flailing. Where did she stand? With him, or with them? He would not allow her to question his dignity.

"That is what I told the district attorney." He saw the surprise on her face. "That's right! He visited me in El Centro. He came to the cell."

"He came to your cell? In person?"

So she did not believe him. Did she respect him more because the D.A. had come to visit?

"Did you tell him anything?" she asked.

"I told him everything." He saw her expression change. She spoke slowly, as if talking to a child, as if talking to their children.

"He came to trap you. Don't you see?" She said it without feeling, as if he did not matter anymore. "You Hindus always trust the Anglos too much."

He felt the flash of clarity in her meaning. The D.A.'s jovial conversation. How he had brought a stool and shared soda pop and had wanted to know about Karak's past in Hong Kong, in Shanghai, in the Philippines. About his childhood. He had been made a fool when he agreed to grow that lettuce. Now Rosa knew he had been made a fool again.

"No," he said.

The intensity of her gaze was too much, the round luminous eyes, the full lips. Suddenly the tears came and her face contorted.

"No," he said again, in his most authoritative voice, and turned his back to her. Why did she question his knowledge, his dignity in everything?

They stood like that for a long time. Why did she not have the sense to leave?

He could hear her sniffling, wiping her nose. "The children ask about you."

He stiffened, readying to defend himself again.

"They miss you," she said.

How good it was to hear—just that little bit.

"Federico always thinks of life on the farm," she said.

He turned to her. She was looking at him, but it was not with love; what he saw in her eyes was pity. He stepped toward her but she did not reach for him. He put his hands over hers as they grasped the bars. They stayed like that—her hands clenching the bars, his placed upon hers. She did not take her hands away. On the day of their wedding, those hands had cut his hair, had remade him. She had determined so much of his life. But now she stood looking past him, her eyes focused on something beyond his shoulder.

"I am scared for the children in school," she said. "I have kept them home for these days."

He released her hands. He had not thought of what would happen to them. "You cannot keep them from school," he said.

"They will go to the one near the barrio."

"The Mexican school?" There were so many consequences. He had been angry at Clive, he had been humiliated, he had defended himself, and now the consequences grew and grew like roots in the soil.

"What will you do?" she asked. The question itself made them separate people. And it was without meaning; there was nothing for him to do but wait.

"Jivan Singh will know what to do. Ask him. And Ram." He knew that she would not ask.

Rosa stepped away. "I am going back," she said. He felt a pang.

"Will you—visit again?" he asked. He would be taken back to El Centro, and the distance would be difficult for her to travel, but that was not why he asked.

She didn't answer immediately. Her lip was quivering. "Por supuesto." But she didn't look back as she stepped toward the door.

38

CLIVE'S MURDER WAS SPOKEN ABOUT IN THE VALLEY'S BUSINESS OFFICES and dining rooms, in the gambling halls in Mexicali, in the sun-scorched fields. It was written about in editorials in the newspapers. Slowly, pieces of the story were fleshed out. People learned that the shippers were stealing a field of early lettuce from farmers who had worked hard to bring it up. That lettuce prices that April had been high, so very high. Slowly, alongside their condemnation of the crazed Hindu, another opinion took root and spread its leaves to the sun. Hadn't this man bought candy for their children, left gift credits at boutiques for the wives of his business associates? Hadn't he brought chocolates for the girls at the telephone exchange? He was clean-shaven and handsome and a skillful farmer. And hadn't they, themselves, suffered at the hands of swindling shippers?

Perhaps Clive Edgar had not deserved death—but it felt good that someone had finally stood up to those damn shippers. Always, always, the little man fought the big man, and always the big man won.

The trial was looming, Amarjeet stayed with them, and Ram's plans for returning to Punjab receded into the future. The lettuce field remained unpicked and rotting and the flies and vermin came. Finally, Amarjeet hitched up the plow and turned it over. He did the work on his own. Somehow, Ram could not bring himself to help and Amarjeet did not ask him.

Clarence Simms wrote a letter that Amarjeet read to them before dinner one night: Had Jivan or Ram seen what had happened moments before Clive screamed? Before the fatal blow was struck? Had Clive disliked Karak? If they could find someone who had seen something, that could help. He would visit them soon, to discuss these matters and others.

"Have you spoken yet with Adela?" Jivan asked.

"No, bhai-ji."

"Adela knows something?" Amarjeet asked.

"Maybe," Ram said quickly.

"Then she should speak with us," Kishen said, as if it were obvious. "She must."

Jivan and Ram exchanged a glance.

"Kishen Kaur is correct," Jivan said.

A WEEK BEFORE THE TRIAL WAS SCHEDULED, Clarence Simms pulled up to the farm in his yellow Packard. They gathered around him on the porch. Even Kishen stayed near, leaning against the door, listening and trying to understand.

They offered him the most comfortable chair. He pulled out papers and files and placed them on the table, but he did not open them. He looked at Ram and Jivan without smiling. He was not a friendly man, but he had a good reputation. They had to trust that.

"Unless we present evidence that shows that Karak acted insanely, or that he had some justification for what he did, he will hang," Simms said.

Justification, Ram thought. He knew the justification, but that was not what Simms meant.

"They steal the crop. Right in front of him, they steal," Jivan said. "It means nothing?"

"I will be blunt, Mr. Singh," Simms said, addressing Jivan. "Karak is Hindu. The crop doesn't belong to him." The lawyer looked at Ram. "It doesn't matter how hard he worked that land with you. It doesn't matter that people have called this section Singh Farm for more than a decade. Under the new laws, that was not Karak's crop. It was not your crop. I'm sorry."

No, he was not a friendly man, but somehow Ram believed in his sympathy. "People call it Singh Farm?" Ram asked.

"Many do."

"What do you need?" Amarjeet asked.

"Karak keeps talking about a gun. He says that Clive waved a gun at him, then Karak lost his temper. Others have told me that Clive started carrying a gun regularly a couple of years ago. But when we found the body, there was no gun in the holster. Can we find someone who will state that he saw Clive with a gun that afternoon?"

"Why must we do this?" Ram said, agitated. "It is not enough to say he was crazy? He *was* crazy. You did not see body, Mr. Simms." Ram's voice broke. "I saw."

"People generally do not believe claims of insanity. I am invoking it as a defense because—" he hesitated. "We don't have much else." Simms's expression was stoic, professional. "But if there was a gun, Karak can claim he acted in self-defense. It is a much stronger case."

The silence was heavy. Ram felt it was directed at him.

"If we are finding someone to say they saw gun, Karak will be free?" Ram asked.

A wave of expressions crossed Simms's face. Ram thought that he had said something unknowing.

"No. He will go to jail for a long time. But if he was threatened with a gun, and we can prove it, he might not hang." Simms looked Ram in the eye.

After the lawyer left, when Jivan and Ram were alone, Jivan said, "We will go together to ask her."

"Bhai-ji," Ram said, wanting to disagree. But there was no choice now.

THEY DROVE TO THE BARRIO IN LATE AFTERNOON, after the sun had lost some heat. They parked off the main roadway and walked the remaining two blocks. Women and children stared from open doorways, following their progress. A cluster of men watched them from a front porch. "Why do they come here?" one said loudly, so Jivan and Ram could hear. But the Punjabis ignored them.

At Alejandro's and Esperanza's home, Jivan stood back and Ram knocked on the door. It opened a few inches and Adela's face appeared in the crack. She must have seen them coming.

"We have something to ask you, Adela," Ram said in Spanish. "May we enter?"

"We do not want to talk in public," Jivan added.

Her face grew pale and she hesitated. But she opened the door wider and allowed them in. She was alone. Ram looked around, wanting to see everything; he had never spent time inside her home. But she would not meet his gaze.

"What do you want, Señor Singh?" she asked in Spanish, addressing only Jivan.

Jivan glanced at Ram. They had agreed that Ram should be the one to speak, but now he began talking. "Karak Singh's trial will begin in a week. You must come to the court and tell them what you saw."

Her face showed surprise, then indignation. She clasped her arms in front of her waist.

"If you do not," Jivan continued, "Karak Singh will be sentenced to death and then he will hang. If you do, perhaps the jury will have pity. Perhaps he will live."

Ram clenched his jaw. Jivan spoke as if she were responsible, as if the entire trial rested on her shoulders.

Her eyes grew round. She began to breathe quickly, then she gained control of herself.

"I do not understand. What do you want me to tell them? I saw nothing." She would not look at Ram.

The realization came to Ram slowly, tinged with contempt. She meant to deny everything. His eyes met Jivan's.

Adela grit her teeth. Her expression turned to stone. Surely she had killed the man who had approached her after her husband's death; surely she was that hard?

"You come and ask this, but every day people threaten us now," Adela said. "Alejandro's workers have left. People say Rosa should not have married Karak. That only bad things can come of such mixing. Do you know what the men in the barrio say about her, about Esperanza? About me?"

"I know! You already told us," Ram said, impatiently, his anger rising.

Adela still would not look at him.

"Rosa's children will not have a father," Jivan said.

"He beat her!" Adela cried.

"He does not deserve death!" Ram said.

"Have you not hurt us enough! In the barrio, we think your farm is a haunted place, evil!"

Through the window, Ram could see two men standing nearby, watching the house, smoking. They had been among the cluster of men who had stood on the porch. Far away, a dog barked.

"The lawyer's name is Clarence Simms," Jivan said, turning to go.

Ram followed him. He could not look at her again.

She closed the door behind them, quietly.

39

JUNE 1924

ON THE MORNING OF THE TRIAL, PEOPLE FILLED THE COURTROOM BENCHES early, long before it was to start. Jivan, Ram, Amarjeet, and Kishen seated themselves in the second row. They breathed in the summer heat, felt its weight on their arms and legs and minds. Other Punjabis were scattered throughout the room. At the door, the bailiff began turning people away. Ram would not look at the back corner where Jivan said Clive's wife and her parents sat. If he saw them, he knew regret would overwhelm him.

Voices rose from the street and floated through the open windows. A horn blared. Ram and Amarjeet rose and stepped toward the open window. The courtroom was on the second floor. A crowd was forming around an automobile that had just arrived. Some women were among them, workers from town, domestic help. Some men sat on other men's shoulders to see. In seconds, Karak emerged from the car and was led by a deputy to the building.

From the building's front steps, Sheriff Fielding and a deputy yelled at the crowd to back away, but people were milling about, ignoring them. Men climbed the trees growing near the courthouse wall, situated themselves on creaking branches. Faces appeared in the courtroom windows. A man brought a ladder and sat astride the top rung. Finally, the attorneys filed in. Clarence Simms turned to acknowledge Jivan and Ram. The clerk took his seat before the judge's dais.

From the side door, the bailiff led Karak into the courtroom. He was dressed in a three-piece suit, clean-shaven, dignified. A hush fell over the crowded room. Karak looked directly at Ram, and Ram knew: Karak was not scared. The bailiff led him to his place next to Simms. From where Ram sat, at an angle, he could the side of Karak's face. When the jury filed in, Karak did not turn his head.

Seeing the jury, Ram felt a moment of despair. These were sun-burned, hardened men, struggling to survive. How would they find compassion for an alien farmer who had been a success? But they were alert, he noted; they carried themselves as if tasked with some-thing important. "Look at them, Jeetu," Ram said, leaning toward Amarjeet. "How will they understand Karak Singh's life?"

"They do not need to, bhai-ji," Amarjeet said. "They need only decide that he was insane, or that he was protecting himself."

"How will they do that without understanding him?" They were all thinking of Adela, but no one said her name.

The judge was a large man with thick, graying hair. People said he was stern, that he did not think like the common man, that he had come from Pennsylvania and his father had been an abolitionist. Amarjeet had told Ram that he saw hope in that.

Now the judge looked at the faces in the windows and narrowed his eyes. "Clear those spectators," he said to the bailiff, loud enough so the entire courtroom could hear.

"I've tried, Your Honor. There are too many of them."

"Tell them again," he snapped.

Occasionally, Ram had seen the judge about town. He was a farmer too, and owned land on the north side. The newspaper had printed an

editorial insisting that he should recuse himself because a few years earlier, he had leased a quarter section to a Hindu—Mohan Singh, whom
Ram knew. But the judge had refused to step away from the case.

The district attorney stood up and approached the jury. He was a
short man but carried himself with importance. He smiled broadly,
looking polished in a gray suit. A gold watch dangled from an exqui-
site chain, pearl cuff links cinched his starched shirtsleeves. He was
jovial, folksy, many in that courtroom thought he would one day
represent the county in Washington, D.C. When he spoke, they felt
he was one of them, and as he told the men on the jury that Karak
Singh had attacked Clive Edgar with the intent to kill him, Ram
could see that the jury believed him. How comfortably the information seeped into their consciousness.

"The defense will try to tell y'all that it was an act of insanity.
That the defendant did not know what he was doin' when he swung
that axe. But we'll discover that Mr. Singh knew exactly what he was
doing, and that if he hadn't been stopped, he would have harmed
others. Mr. Jonathan Hitchcock, an esteemed, upstanding, and inte-
gral member of this community, a farmin' man like us, will state that
Singh meant to kill him too."

Ram could see Karak keeping his head down, clenching his jaw,
staring at the wooden table before him. Simms placed his hand on
the back of Karak's chair, as if protecting him. That was kind, Ram
thought. Perhaps there was more to the man than he knew.

Simms stood briskly and buttoned his jacket, allowing silence
to fill the room before he approached the jury. Ram could see: His
manner made those men uncomfortable. They did not trust him.
"The defense will not challenge that Karak Singh killed Clive Edgar,"
Simms said. "It is obvious that he did." Ram saw Karak flinch. The
jury shifted in their seats, some stole a glance at Karak. Ram wished
that the lawyer were not so stiff. Simms did not draw out his vowels
like other men. Ram had never heard him claim to be a farmer. If
he did those things, perhaps the jury would believe him. "What the

defense will show is that Mr. Singh was insane, irrational, when the killing happened. The very nature of the killing shows insanity."

JONATHAN HITCHCOCK WAS THE FIRST WITNESS. The courtroom was quiet as he made his way to the stand, the knock of his cane on the floor resonated through the room. He walked slowly. Outside, the cicadas buzzed. The windows were propped open, men were still perched in trees, but everyone was quiet.

Hitchcock placed his hand on the Bible to take the oath, standing tall and erect, like a man who had never known fear. He settled himself calmly in the witness chair, adjusting his suit, gazing first at the men on the jury, then at the district attorney. He did not look at Karak at all.

The district attorney picked up a file of papers on his desk and strode toward the witness stand, situated himself at an angle to the jury, and began his questioning. Hitchcock gave his name, his age, his education, his position with Consolidated Fruit. "I have loved the Valley since moving here two years ago from Atlanta," he said. "It is a place for real men, for those not scared to work hard."

Ram saw several jurors nod their heads. He felt a chill in his gut. Could it be so easy for Hitchcock to win them over?

"Can you tell us what happened that day, Mr. Hitchcock?" the district attorney asked.

Hitchcock licked his lips. "Clive Edgar and I were working together to get the lettuce to market soon. We had to get it picked, packed up, and shipped out. Singh knew we'd be coming to take charge of the harvest that day. He knew we had hired pickers and packers, and that we would be providing crates for the job. But he was in the packing shed when we arrived, chopping wood to assemble crates for the lettuce." Hitchcock spoke calmly, both his hands resting on the handle of his cane. "He began to abuse us as soon as we entered the packing shed."

"You say he began to abuse you as soon as you entered. Did you or Mr. Edgar do anything to provoke him, Mr. Hitchcock?"

"Absolutely nothing."

"You are sure?"

"Absolutely sure."

"Were there any other people in the packing shed with you and Mr. Edgar and the defendant during this conversation?"

"No. I did not see any others," Hitchcock said. "We were alone."

"So as far as you know, there were no other witnesses to what happened in the shed before the killing."

"None."

The district attorney paused, as if to make sure the jury understood this point. He walked to the table, put down his file, picked up another, and began to question Hitchcock again.

"Was Mr. Edgar carrying a gun that day, Mr. Hitchcock?"

"I don't know. I don't think so."

Ram saw Karak straighten in his chair.

"But you don't know?"

"If he had been carrying a gun, he would have used to it to save his life. He would have used it to stop Singh when he started waving that axe."

"But he didn't?"

"Upon entering the packing shed, and hearing Singh's abuse, we were immediately put off," Hitchcock continued. "Yet Mr. Edgar and I had a job to get done, and we entered the packing shed to do it. Singh brandished that axe to try to make us leave. But we wouldn't be deterred. Although he was threatening us, I didn't believe he'd be so determined as to take action. But it was clear now that had been his intent all along."

"Mr. Hitchcock, how would you explain that Mr. Edgar's body was found with a holster? How would you explain that the holster was empty?"

"It was a busy day, sir," Hitchcock said. "Have you never been absent-minded on a busy day? Left your home in the morning without something you should have taken with you?"

The courtroom was quiet. Ram imagined every person was reminded of the time they had done that very thing.

"Would you say, Mr. Hitchcock, that you or Mr. Edgar did anything at all to provoke the defendant?"

"We did nothing. We only wanted to do our work peaceably."

"What did the defendant do next?"

"He yelled at us to 'Get out of my shed! Get off of my farm!' Then, before I knew what he was doing. He swung at Mr. Edgar with the axe and wounded him."

The jury was listening intently, bodies bent forward, focused on Hitchcock's elegant face.

"The axe hit him somewhere in the upper arm or shoulder," Hitchcock continued. "I was very fearful and stumbled back, but I thought the best escape for us both was if I could start my car and we could leave the farm to safety. I believed that Mr. Edgar's injuries would not prevent him from running. But somehow they did."

Now Hitchcock looked at Ram. Cold blue eyes that alarmed him, focused directly on his face. "It's only because of that Hindu that I didn't die too."

"Which Hindu?" the district attorney asked.

"That one." Hitchcock pointed at Ram. All eyes in the courtroom turned to him. Ram froze.

"He wrestled the defendant to the ground," Hitchcock continued. His voice was hollow, his face without expression, because now he was telling the truth. "That gave me enough time to crank the engine of my car, allowing me to escape."

BY NOON, Ram felt that Karak's case was already lost, for how could anyone counter the version of events narrated by that elegant man with the cold blue eyes? Ram had seen how the jury had reacted to his confidence, his authority. Even if Adela told them what she had seen and heard, why would those men believe her? When the judge dismissed them all for a break, Ram and the others did not talk about this.

While the courtroom emptied, Ram, Jivan, Amarjeet, and Kishen decided to stay, for fear they would not be allowed back inside. Jivan and Amarjeet talked quietly in the corner. Kishen Kaur walked slowly in the aisle. Ram rose to ease the ache in his back. The scent of stale perspiration was stifling and he edged closer to the open windows. He heard yelling, heckling, on the sidewalk below. "¡Puta!" A male voice rose above the rest. "Whore! You go in there, you'll be sorry!" the man shouted in Spanish.

Ram leaned out the window. Opposite the courthouse, a group of Mexican men stood in the shade of the promenade near the drugstore. On the road in front of them, in the merciless sun, Adela was walking by herself toward the courthouse steps. His relief and pride rose together, one emotion.

Several of the men taunted her, jeering. Ram felt their menace himself. Then, one of them leaned forward, positioned himself, and spat. The spot of liquid landed on the hem of her skirt. She did not flinch. His stomach lurched in anger. "Oye!" he yelled out the window and pedestrians turned to look.

She glanced up at the building and Ram thought she saw him. She brushed the hair from her face—a familiar gesture—and walked up the courthouse stairs, out of his line of sight. He felt tears sting his eyes.

ADELA TOOK THE WITNESS STAND THAT AFTERNOON, after Simms and the district attorney had consulted with the judge in his chambers. She seemed prim, rigid, wearing a white blouse with a high collar. She clutched her handbag to her belly. She raised her hand and took the oath in Spanish.

"I beg the court for its patience," Simms said. "I would like to ask my questions to Mrs. Rey in English, without a Spanish interpreter. But I ask that her Spanish answers be translated into English for the benefit of the jury."

"Proceed," the judge said.

"Do you speak English, Mrs. Rey?" Simms asked.

She responded in rapid Spanish, glancing at the young man who stood next to her, below the witness dais. His hair was neatly combed. He wore a jacket and tie. "I cannot speak so well," he translated for her, "but I understand."

"So you understand everything I'm saying to you?" Simms asked.

"I understand," the young man translated. She was holding a handkerchief, and Ram could see her working it, kneading it with her fingers.

"Do you know anything about Clive Edgar's death?" Simms asked.

"I saw the killing with my own eyes." A murmur went through the courtroom.

"Where were you when you saw this?" Simms said.

"I was in the packing shed, getting water from the olla that always hangs there, hidden in the corner."

"What is your feeling toward Karak Singh?" Simms asked.

"I hate him," she said grimly. "My cousin is his wife. He beat her. They no longer live together."

"Do you gain anything by coming here today?"

"Yes," she said, and swallowed. "The hatred of my neighbors. They threaten to hurt me. Today a man spat at me. Another pushed me in front of this building."

"Then why did you come?" Adela glanced at Ram. For a microscopic moment their eyes met, her expression softened. Ram held his breath.

"Porque . . ." she said, hesitating.

"Because . . ." the translator said.

She stuttered, looked at her hands, the handkerchief, the bag. For a moment, her features strained for composure.

"As God is my witness," the young man translated, "one must tell the truth."

Clarence Simms allowed the silence to linger for a moment.

"Mrs. Rey, please tell us what you saw happen between Mr. Singh and Mr. Edgar," Simms asked.

"Karak and Clive were arguing in the packing shed. When Karak would not stop building the crates, Jonathan Hitchcock entered the shed." She paused. Her cheeks flushed. "Then Clive took out his gun and pointed it at Karak. He said, 'A Hindu is worth only one boxcar of lettuce. Take your blanket and go!'"

Murmurs swept through the courtroom. Jivan and Ram exchanged a glance. The judge banged his gavel against his desk. As the courtroom grew quiet again, Simms resumed his questioning.

"So Mr. Edgar pointed his gun at Mr. Singh and told him that he was worth merely a 'boxcar of lettuce' and that he should 'take his blanket and go'?"

"Yes."

Ram looked at Karak. He was staring at his folded hands on the table, his head bent. Something about him seemed calm, resigned.

"What was Mr. Singh's response?"

"Karak's face grew red. I have never before seen him like that." Adela held the handkerchief to her eyes. "Before Mr. Hitchcock came into the shed, they had only been arguing . . . just words. But when Señor Hitchcock entered, Clive pointed the gun. Karak was so angry." She breathed deeply. Her chest shuddered, and Ram could feel the breath, the shudder, within his own body. "He ran toward Clive, shouting, screaming. Clive could have shot him at any time, but he didn't. He just kept pointing the gun. Then Karak swung the axe and hit Clive in the shoulder, and Clive gave such a yell . . . he dropped the gun . . . Then Clive started to run, but Karak chased him. He swung the axe again, and Mr. Hitchcock was running too . . . and . . ." Adela covered her mouth with the handkerchief. Simms waited until she composed herself.

"What happened to that gun, Mrs. Rey?" Simms asked.

Her face flushed. "After Clive dropped it, I picked it up."

"Why?"

"I thought Karak might try to use it."

"And where is the gun now?"

"It is here." She reached inside her bag.

She held up a .45 Colt, a grip inlaid with pearl, a monogram engraved on the barrel.

For the first time that day, Ram felt a surge of hope.

40

TWO AFTERNOONS LATER, AFTER THE LAST OF THE WITNESSES HAD SPO-ken, after Clarence Simms had delivered an argument in Karak's defense, Ram entered the barrio and knocked on Esperanza and Alejandro's door. It was Rosa who answered. There was despair in her eyes. It seemed as if she had not spoken for days. She turned away, leaving the door open.

"What is it?" Esperanza said, coming to the threshold. "Oh!" she said, after seeing Ram.

"Esperanza?" Alejandro's voice boomed in the background.

"It is Ram Singh," Esperanza said.

Alejandro came to the door. "What do you want?" he said. His tone was not kind.

"I am looking for Adela," Ram said in Spanish.

"She is not here."

"Where is she?"

"We do not know," Esperanza said. "She left without telling us."

Ram thought it was a lie. "Just . . . I want to talk with her."

"We told you," Alejandro said, "she is not here."

A knot was forming in Ram's stomach. "Where has she gone?"

"We are telling the truth," Esperanza said, without anger.

For a moment Ram wanted to force the door open, to see if Adela was standing there, just listening on the other side. "I don't want to hurt her—I just want to thank her. She did something brave. She—"

"She has no need of your thanks," Esperanza said, suddenly irritated. "She did it for Rosa's children. Now she is in danger and men threaten to kill her."

Ram wondered how much Esperanza knew about the two of them. He put his hand on the doorframe. "Please, tell me where she's gone."

Esperanza stepped backward. "I'm telling you, we don't know," she said.

Alejandro wedged his body between them. "If we did, we wouldn't tell you." The men locked eyes. "Adiós, Ram," Alejandro said calmly. For a long time, he had been the worker, and Ram had been the boss. There was no pretense now. "Please go without a fuss."

The door shut. Ram turned around slowly. The truth hovered like the desert heat, ever-present, suffocating, immutable. He believed them.

He drove to the seamstress shop. The bell chimed as he opened the door. Sitting behind a sewing machine, a gray-haired woman gazed at him without blinking. Mrs. Belvidere did not recognize him; she had met him only once before, a dark-skinned man who spoke strangely, who came from a place that she did not know. He needed to be charming, mild. Certainly she would have known about the trial and Adela's role in it.

Ram clasped his hands behind his back. "I am looking for a woman who works here, Señora Adela Rey Vasquez."

"Does she know you?" Her voice was tremulous. "What do you want with her?"

"I have an urgent message to give her. She knows me well. My name is Ram. I am related by marriage to her cousin Rosa." The woman did not seem impressed by this information.

"Adela no longer works here. I begged her to stay. But she told me that she had to go away for a while."

He should not hold out any hope. "Did she say when she would come back? Did she say where she was going?"

She looked at him with suspicion. "I asked her the same thing, Mr. . . . Singh."

She had guessed the name without him giving it. He had underestimated her. Nothing in this town could be secret. "She is a nice girl," Mrs. Belvidere said finally. "How did she become mixed up in a mess?"

"Yes, madam," Ram said, hands still clasped behind his back. He did not want to answer her question. If he could just seem good enough, compliant enough, would he get more information? "I hope she is safe," he said.

"Yesterday morning, some fellas from town were asking for her. I won't say who they were. They said they had some business with her. I asked what kind of business would two grown men have with a Mexican girl like her? They just laughed." Mrs. Belvidere's voice might have a tremor, but she spoke clearly. "It didn't sound none too nice. Well. She was a good girl, and I asked her to stay, but she said she didn't think she'd be back."

Her words beat upon him. He could not accept their finality. He turned to go.

"If you find her, tell her that I will miss her. She was a fine worker. Don't know who I'll replace her with," the woman said.

"I will, madam," he said.

DID PADMA STILL WAIT FOR HIM? After eleven years, he supposed she did. Waited for him as a wife waits for a husband. Because they were defined by each other, and there was truth in the definition. There was truth in the child that connected them. There was truth in the longing that he had felt as a young man. But there is the land of one's birth, and the land of one's work and action, and for some, they are not the same. He remembered the longing, but he did not feel it anymore. He knew, from her occasional letters, that she did not feel it either.

He could not go back now. How could he return when Adela was gone, when he sat in the debris of Karak's ruined life after Clive's destruction? But he knew: He *could* go back. He did not *want* to.

Sitting on Jivan's porch, gazing beyond his cantaloupes to the turned-up lettuce field, Ram recognized what he had lost—a child, a wife, a home, a country. For her help in a desperate moment, for her courage in a world gone mad, Adela deserved his thanks, but it was more than that. He owed her something, yes, but it was more than that too.

As the realization came to him, he shrank away from the field, from Jivan's home, from the letters and newspapers and dust and sand. He knew where she would be. Long ago, sitting together on the back porch of Jivan's home, she had told him herself. The place that was her haven. For the first time, he knew what he wanted. He knew where he belonged.

He slept and rose early. There were few things he needed. He carried them in one bag, rolled inside his blanket, just as he had when he rode the train into the Valley. He said goodbye to Jivan Singh and Kishen Kaur. He blessed Leela. She was crying, even though he had not said that he was crossing the boundary, had not explained that, after reaching the other side, he might not be able to cross back. She was fourteen now and felt deeply things that adults had long ago lost the capacity to feel.

Amarjeet drove him east on the road to Yuma and beyond. They stopped at Andrade; he would cross at the checkpoint at Los Algodones. The younger man embraced him, and Ram took his bag and blanket and walked. The officer at the border patrol shed waved him through. The earth was crusted with alkaline. A hot breeze blew from the west, carrying dust from the dunes. He turned to look at

Amarjeet, who raised his arm to hail him, a small figure across the expanse of the boundary.

He began to walk. The sun beat down. It was exactly the way that she had described: The sand dunes. The dance hall. The lonely street that led directly west to the grove of mesquite, and the tree with a double trunk, twenty meters high, the tree that everyone knew. Walk five hundred paces north. There was the friendly shack. The garden that her aunt tended, housing chickens and peppers. And yes, there she was, near the fence, her hair swept back, hanging laundry in the breeze.

He had not known what he felt for her, this person bred from different soil. He had not known home could also be a second place, far from the land of one's birth. A long time ago, he had thought it was not possible.

When Adela saw him, her face showed only surprise. Then there was something else, ancient and deep and of the earth. He recognized it inside himself. And he knew, finally, how to name it.

APRIL 1974

TWO THIRTY A.M. ON HIS NIGHTSTAND ALARM CLOCK. THE NEIGHBOR'S white light shone through his window, but his mind was still filled with the images of his not-dream. He had sweated through his nightclothes. He rose to use the bathroom, shuffling stiffly past Anika's room, past his son and daughter-in-law's door, making himself remember other images that were not not-dreams, things that he had seen on the television just that night: Cronkite reporting the South Vietnamese air strikes. The Hearst girl's voice on the audiotape. An American Indian with a single tear in his eye, seated on a paint. For some reason, when he needed other memories in the middle of the night, when he needed to ward off the not-dream, the television pictures came to him most easily.

In his bedroom, he put on fresh pajamas and lay down again, the bedsheet tucked under his chin, closing his eyes. The not-dream had left him for years, but Karak was dead now, and perhaps his mind needed to remember. In the not-dream, he and Karak are young men again, working in their old packing shed, building crates from wooden boards. In it, Ram is chasing Karak in the late afternoon sun, Karak is enraged, running with the axe. Ram is running to catch him, to stop him. The red pool forms and grows, reaching the shed wall, then the empty lettuce crates, finally the edge of the harvested field. Ram slips in the dark liquid. The slickness. The smell of wounded flesh. Is that how it happened? Hard to know now, through memory, dream, not-dream. He had not fallen in the blood. Had he? He hears Clive's big, jovial voice from a full decade earlier, hoarse, as if he is suffering from a cold: "Nothing better than Mexicali whiskey and Mexicali women." His laugh and Karak's ring out together. In Ram's not-dream he falls asleep and wakes, sleeps and wakes, sleeps, and hears Clive's animal scream, the harbinger of death. Hitchcock, limping, pathetically trying for the motorcar, turning and turning the crank.

Ram woke with a start. He was crying. That surprised him. In recent years, he would meet Karak for lunch if he were asked, or Karak would come to Ram's home for dinner, uninvited. Karak bore the burden of keeping the friendship, of needing it more. But now the thought loomed up before him. Ram had loved him too.

ON THE TELEVISION, a baseball game was running its course. The camera panned the stands, again and again, thousands of people with paint on their faces, smiling in the sunlight. Los Angeles newscasters were speaking on national television. His grandson, the one who did not know a zucchini from a cucumber, said a game like this had never before been played. Ram's son, Dave, had turned up the volume. A record was about to be broken. Ram watched his family as his family watched the game: even little Anika, even the dog.

"I don't see why make such a fuss if a Negro man hits a ball," Ram said.

"Black, Bapu-ji," cucumber grandson said. "We don't say Negro anymore."

"Why?" Ram asked.

His grandson ignored him.

Ram could not deny it, he enjoyed annoying the boy. "In my day, they called Hindus Hindus. They called Sikhs Hindus too."

Dave gave him a look.

"Nobody minded what you called them," Ram said.

Leave the boy alone, Dave's look said.

"Oh yeah?" said the grandson. "Maybe if you Hindus played baseball, people would have cared."

"Robert!" Dave said. "Mind yourself."

Ram made himself look at the television screen. He deserved the boy's comment. He should not be provoking a child—his grandson, most of all. What was the matter with him? The truth was, long ago, some of those Sikhs had not liked being called Hindus at all. He sat like that, quietly, while the boys, Anika, the parents, the dog, the broadcaster's comments filled the room. The Negro man hit the ball. Ram's family erupted in cheers. Anika jumped on the sofa; his grandsons pummeled the air. Two white teenagers ran the bases with the black athlete, the reporters hooting, the fans' static hum in the background. The television camera went in close. The black man had confidence, and a smile, and something else—humility.

"Dignified," Ram said, meaning it. He felt the others look at him.

He rose slowly and made his way to the telephone. It was situated on a table in the corner, away from the noise. He had memorized the phone number. When Karak's daughter answered, he told her simply, "Yes, I will do it."

"Mr. Singh?" Grace said.

"Yes, yes. This is Ram Singh. I will speak about Karak. I called to tell you."

There was a pause, then a small sound. He did not know if she was crying, or merely quiet, or if she had heard him at all. "Thank you. Thank you, Mr. Singh, very much."

Her English words unsettled him. For years now, Karak had

been the only person with whom he spoke Punjabi. The language was harsh, loving, the bearer of truth. Spanish was warm, comfortable. But English was cold, the language of strangers. Karak's daughter spoke with him in English, because she did not know everything that had happened. That because of Adela, Karak's life was spared, and he spent only ten years in San Quentin. That it was Ram's threshold that her father crossed first, after that decade was done. That when she was a small girl, before her childhood memory lapsed, Grace Singh had called Ram "Uncle."

EPILOGUE

SHE WAITED FOR HIM. A YEAR AT FIRST. THEN TWO, THEN FIVE, THEN more. In those years she waited for him with every breath she took, while she walked the outskirts of Lyallpur on that childhood path, the one she had walked with him. When the rain came, she waited for him, watching it fall, smelling life in the soil, sitting just under the roof's edge, because he loved the rain. She waited for him while she washed clothes by the river, or gathered with the women at the waterwheel, or tasted the first mango of the season. She waited for him when she removed the rag, red with blood because another moon had passed, another chance lost to bear him another child.

There was one other who waited too. He had grown in her belly, waiting. When he was born, he was waiting. He spent his childhood waiting, his face taking the form of the man-boy for whom he waited, as if Nature were compensating him for his fatherlessness.

The letters came, and they were written by him. But as the years went by, they were only an odd reflection of a boy she had once known, a lad she had once loved. There were four people now: the boy and girl who had shared a moment upon this earth, and the man and woman who had lived on to write about them. The letters spoke of memories that had glowed orange and red but then turned matte and gray. What did it matter ten, twenty years later, that they both admired that grove of figs where they had first lain together? That they both loved Masiji when they were children? That Ram would say Padma's kajal, rimming her eyelashes, was so dark it turned his day into night? That she still wore her wedding bangles?

She became angry and did not know it. Her son would not have a sister, and she could not show she cared. Slowly the truth grew apparent, even to her. In the waning years of her beauty, when the full course of her life had been revealed, she took up with an older man, a good soul, an ex-soldier. For a few years, he was the companion she had not had. She realized such kindnesses could be allowed: pretended ignorance, averted eyes, doors left unlatched at the appropriate hour. Her aged aunt, at the moment of her discovery, said only that she too had spent a lifetime without a husband.

After thirty-five years, her Ram returned home. He arrived with no announcement, only a small suitcase that stood beside him on the doorstep. She thought it unfair that he would have known about his arrival a full month before she would, traveling toward her by ship and train and bus and rickshaw while she performed her daily routine—cooking, washing, helping their son's wife care for a young boy and girl. Miracles were possible: the white men could depart, the nation could be cleaved in two, Ram could cross the threshold of the house that he had built but never seen.

When he entered, their son rose from his seat. Then, after Ram accounced his name, after Santosh realized who he was, he stooped and took the dust of his father's feet; he was a Hindu child, after all. They embraced for the first time: her husband and her son. Ram gazed into Santosh's eyes.

But Ram barely looked at her. His gaze rested on her face for only a moment longer than it did on the others'. She was glad for this. She feared that if he looked for long at her face, he would see the anger, or perhaps it was hatred.

She could not deny that he glowed—resplendent, luminous, come from another world.

The news spread that he had arrived. His son and uncle and cousins took him to see the lands that he had purchased, the school that he had built, the households made prosperous with the dowry he had provided. A lamb was slaughtered. A servant was sent to market to buy eggplant and fish. With the other women, she cut and cooked and bent over the heat of the stove, preparing the feast. In the evening, the men talked of the infant government in Delhi, the new laws that had allowed Ram's visit. She heard it all, sitting by herself in the kitchen, long after the meal was finished. He spoke of returning home, and she thought he meant returning home to her, but then she realized: he was returning home to that other place. There is, after all, a land of one's birth, and a land of one's work and action. Which should one call home? Perhaps if she were a different woman, another kind of wife, it would not have mattered. But it mattered to her. Who was there with him, in that other place?

Her granddaughter came and brought her to bed, but did not stay with her as she usually did. For the first time in years, Padma lay there alone.

Hours later, she heard him outside the bedroom. His hand swept aside the curtain. He stood silhouetted in the doorway. She lit a lamp and allowed herself to look him in the face, the way she could not in the outer rooms. She thought he would read her hatred, know her hardness of heart, but in the glow of the lamplight, she knew that was not what he saw. She recognized in him the beginning of an old man—the shadow of the boy she had known. That fold around his lips, that length in his cheek—yet, still, the youth in those eyes that had seen her grow from a girl to a maiden. Yes, he was radiant. Had he not died and come back?

She could not know how he grieved for his childhood, for the man-boy waiting at the San Francisco dock, for the father he had not been.

He stepped forward and clasped her. Together, they wept.

ACKNOWLEDGMENTS

I am grateful for the support, encouragement, and resources provided by the following individuals and institutions: the South Asian American Digital Archive (www.SAADA.org); the Imperial County Historical Society/Pioneers' Museum, especially Lynn Housouer CEO, Tim Asamen, Donna Brownell Grizzle, Dianna Newton, Norman Wuytens, and the members of the Agricultural Gallery; the University of California Desert Research and Extension Center, especially Khaled M. Bali; the Stockton Gurdwara Sahib, especially Bhajan Singh Bhinder and Tejpaul Singh Bainiwal; the Angel Island State Park, especially Casey Dexter; the Whatcom Museum in Bellingham, especially archivist Jeff Jewell; the Clatsop County Historical Society, especially archivist Liisa Penner; the California State Library; the Oregon Historical Quarterly; and the staff of Anza-Borrego Desert State Park. Many thanks also to the MacDowell Colony, Alice d'Entrement, and Natalie Tarbet for providing me—at crucial times—with a much-needed room of my own.

I deeply appreciate and am indebted to the members of the Pioneers' Museum's East India Gallery and their families: Robert and Karmen Chell; Dr. Gurbax Singh Chahal; Norma Saikhon and Richard Fragale, who both left us too soon (Norma—how I wish I could place this book in your hands); Emma Singh Jimenez; Lilia Singh Santillan; Virginia Gutierrez; Richard and Shirley Dillon; and the late Anna Singh Sandhu. With warmth and courtesy, you invited me into your homes and hearts, sharing stories told over your dinner tables and passed on to your children. I hope I have not disappointed.

For opening the portal to far-away places and next-door neighbors, I say shukriya, gracias, arigatamaya, and Danke vielmals to Zyanya Ávila Louis, Louis Cid, Amrit Deol, Kaori Hattori de Panepinto, Harjot K. "Sonia" Gill, Adam L. Kern, Judd Liebman, Sophie Liebman, Luis F. López González, Angela E. Radan, Katherine Seidl, Bunty Singh, Harpreet Singh, and Mako Yoshikawa. Thanks, too, to Deborah J. Bennett for her translation of the corrido, *La Rielera*.

For sharing with me their knowledge, time, and expertise, my thanks to Paul A. Davis, Paul Rudof, and Pamela Talbot.

My affection, admiration, and appreciation to my longtime friends in the Cambridge Writers' Group—I'm lucky to have had your unwavering insight and counsel for many, many years: Richard "Pic" Harrison; Betsy Hatfield; Betsy Morris; and Jeanie Stahl; and to those who still sit with us in that gracious circle, William R. Crout, Joan Powell, and Mary Ellen Preusser.

I am grateful for my tribe, who lift me up and feed me and always have my back, who have read and re-read countless times, and who know what it is to face the blank whiteness: Deborah J. Bennett, Eve Bridberg, Daphne Kalotay, Thomas H. McNeely, Julie Rold, and Mandeliene Smith.

For assisting in so many ways, I thank: my friends at MassDEP's Office of General Counsel—you know who are—for picking up the slack when the line hung loose; Carolle R. Morini, Lisa Starzyk, and Mary Warmement, librarians extraordinaire; Megan Lynch, Helen Atsma, Sonya Cheuse, Sara Birmingham, Laura Cherkas, and the team at Ecco; Maria Massie, for her grace and calm, for always pointing me toward true north; and Lee Boudreaux, who took the leap and had faith—your words have stayed with me a dozen years.

I am indebted to the following writers whose works of nonfiction helped me understand the created world of Fredonia and beyond: Benny J. Andres Jr.'s *Power and Control in the Imperial Valley;* Tara Singh Bains and Hugh Johnston's *The Four Quarters of the Night;* Rajani Kanta Das's *Hindustani Workers on the Pacific Coast;* F. C. Farr's edited *History of the Imperial County, CA;* Harold Gould's *Sikhs, Swamis, Students, and Spies;* Jayasri "Joyce" Hart's documentary film *Roots in the Sand;* Yuji Ichioka's *Issei;* Joan M. Jensen's *Passage from India;* David Laskin's *The Long Way Home,* which conveys many moving accounts of real soldiers' adventures in the Great War; Karen Leonard's *Making Ethnic Choices;* Patricia Preciado Martin's *Songs My Mother Sang to Me;* Johanna Ogden's article "Ghadar, Historical Silences, and Notions of Belonging"; David Omissi's edited *Indian Voices of the Great War;* Elena Poniatowska's *Las Soldaderas;* the writings of Dalip Singh Saund; Eric Michael Schantz's article "All Night at the Owl"; Nayan Shah's *Stranger Intimacy;* Baba Gurdit Singh's *Voyage of Komagata Maru;* Khushwant Singh's authoritative *History of the Sikhs;* Seema Sohi's *Echoes of Mutiny;* Ronald Takaki's *Strangers from a Different Shore;* the writings of Bhagat Singh Thind; Dorothy and Thomas Hoobler's *The Japanese American Family Album;* and Otis B. Tout's compilation *Imperial Valley, The First Thirty Years,* which perhaps reveals more (by its exclusion of certain residents' stories) than he intended.

I am grateful to Bharthi Reddi, Mamatha Reddy, N.S., Alexi Lownie, Kathy Seidl, Lisa Youngling Howard, and Angus, who every day, through living and being, made possible the writing of this novel.

And finally, my abiding love, respect, and gratitude to Raghunath and Rekha P. Reddi, who came to believe, truly and deeply, in the way only parents can.